BOURBON STREET

THE DREAMS OF AENEAS IN DIXIE

A NOVEL AND PIXILATED, PICARESQUE EPIC

DAVID B. LENTZ

WORDSWORTH
GREENWICH
PRESS

ALSO BY DAVID B. LENTZ

NOVELS

America, Inc.
Bloomsday: The Bostoniad
Bourbon Street
The Day Trader
The Silver King

STAGE PLAYS

America, Inc.
Bloomsday: A Tragicomedy

POETRY

Old Greenwich Odes
Sonnets from New England: Love Songs
Sonnets on the Common Man

COLLECTED LITERARY WORK

Essential Lentz

NON-FICTION

Novel Criticism

WHAT PEOPLE ARE SAYING

"Told through the vehicle of the tale, it is like a street-car rattling past the bars and drunks and jazz and creeping vegetation, the lonely souls, the nectar-draw of sex, the steaks and bourbons, that combine to make *Bourbon Street* a wonderful book and cement the place of Lentz as a writer of formidable scope and ability." – **Bruce McLaren, Author of** *The Plain of Dead Cities*

"A journey: if you know what it means to miss New Orleans, then you really should read this book." – **Yvonne LaFleur**

"Hot as a New Orleans' summer." – **John A. Taylor, Jr., CLU**

"His plots are richly woven tapestries. They twist and turn, dip and rise and, finally, resolve. They are engaging and enthralling." – **Chuck Hudson, Amazon**

"He writes on a higher plane for a higher purpose." – **Wilton Bulletin**

"Lentz's approach to writing is soul driven." – **Weston Forum**

"Lentz especially likes to explore how creative people survive and contribute in a large and often impersonal environment. What is the role of a talented individual, an artist for example, in a complex, vast society?" – **New Canaan Advertiser**

"*Bloomsday: The Bostoniad*, an American *Ulysses*, is a literary feast, a gem of a novel."
– **Leonard Seet**, Author of *The Spiritual Life*

"*Bloomdsay: The Bostoniad* is an astonishing book. Lentz has accomplished this feat not only with prodigious erudition, but also with a delicate whimsy and an exquisitely chiseled poetic language. For this is a poetic prose of the first order. But here's the crux of the matter: this is a major work by a major writer and sophisticated readers will relish it. A masterpiece."
– **Terry Richard Bazes,** Author of *Goldsmith's Return*

"*Bloomsday* is a wow with a humorous, shrewd, heightened language, like Oscar Wilde on crack. At times the novel reminded me of the best of JP Donleavy. I am a little in awe of what Lentz attempted here—and accomplished! This is a grand achievement."– **Corey Mesler,** Author of *Memphis Movie: A Novel*

"I'm sitting in my kitchen transfixed! It is hilarious. It (*Bloomsday*) is so good, I hate to have it end. Totally delicious." – **Agnes Potter**

"*Bloomsday* was a delight and I didn't want it to end. *Ulysses* is a masterpiece, but I enjoyed reading this book much more than *Ulysses*… I grew to like the characters, to care about them and it was their plain humanity that I loved… A literary masterpiece… Laugh out loud comic moments, moments of touching tenderness and the language is a delight. You must read it."
– **Paul Raymond Smith**, **Goodreads, United Kingdom**

"If *Ulysses* is the grandparent, *Bloomsday: A Tragicomedy* is a legitimate grandchild. Just as the play is not an inferior distillation of the novel (*Bloomsday: The Bostoniad*), it is not a dilution of the creativity of Joyce. It's a courageous act to stand up and ask to be measured against Joyce or *Ulysses*. *Bloomsday* is a work rich with wit, punning, wordplay and wisdom. *Bloomsday* is so rich with allusion, it's difficult to track its inspiration. The more you look, the more you find."
– **Ian Graye**, *Goodreads #4 Best Reviewer*, **Brisbane**

"Loved it *(For the Beauty of the Earth)*." – **Emma Stephens**, Author of *For a Dancer*

"So there's corruption in this book. Lots of it. But even the outrageous greed of the Keynesians here is just a small part of the complete landscape of megalomania Lentz describes."
– **Brian Schnell**, *#1 Reviewer*, **Goodreads**

"This novel *(For the Beauty of the Earth)* is about what happens when you lose everything."
– **Ridgefield Press**

"As in most of his stories, there is more than one tale to tell in this novel *(For the Beauty of the Earth)*… The protagonist is a kind of Adam before the Fall with a great Achilles heel."
– **Darien Times**

"***For the Beauty of the Earth*** offers a timely and cautionary tale about the seductive power and potential for abuse among those who manage billions of dollars in stock equity."
– **LeAnn Neal Reilly**, Author of *San Sebastian's Head: A Novel*

"*Sonnets from New England* is a world of lovers pulsing, breathing, absorbing, secreting so passionately even angels are envious." – **John H. Sibley**, Author of *Being and Homelessness*

"The language in *Sonnets* is by turns playful and profound, and the reader is continually impressed with both." – **Chuck Crabbe, Author of** *As a Thief in the Night: A Novel*

"Few arrive on this earth with such gifts. David Lentz' passion for life and love for all of creation is evident throughout the *Sonnets*. Timeless." – **Roxana Bowgen**, Author of *Agapanthus Rising*

"*Sonnets from New England* tacitly acknowledges the enigma and evanescence of life. One hears in these sonnets the sensibility of a contemporary avatar of Wallace Stevens. It is when Lentz describes nature that his lines relax the most, and these tautly structured sonnets expand, as if imbibing the pristine air of the pastoral New England environs the poet describes. "Poetry has its itinerary. The personal is the surest route to the universal; we explore another soul, and discover our own. By recreating pivotal moments in his life and articulating values that sustain him, David Lentz helps us find true north in ourselves. This is the most important connection art can make." – **Eric Sonnenschein**, Novelist, Author of *Ad Nomad*

"The satire that infuses *AmericA, Inc.* is barbed with witticisms worthy of the greats—luminaries in the field of political shaming. Luminaries like Voltaire and Sterne." – **Gary W. Anderson**, Author of *Best of All Possible Worlds: A Novel*

"Lentz will go down in history as a great writer whose work will transcend time and assuredly reshape public discourse. From the first to last line this brutally funny stage play -- *AmericA, Inc.* -- is a classic example of exceptional writing with a biting sense of wit, and a clear and cogent understanding of political satire. Lentz is an exceptionally talented wordsmith. Through his august body of work he constantly strives to reshape dialogue on what constitutes great literature while hammering his own work, like the artist he is, forever pounding at the forge of public opinion with the fierce heat of his incredibly rich mind." – **Goodreads**

"We need to read books like *The Day Trader* in the hope that there are a few writers clever enough to see beyond the chaos, as they have a profound idea of what made things come to such a pass. The people intimidated and thwarted by big business interests will certainly appreciate and possibly find solace in this book."– **Krishna Bhatt,** Author of *The Royal Enigma*

"Lentz has a talent for blending a compelling story line with pathos and humor, a measure of literary and historical allusion, and vivid imagery. The result is the literary equivalent of high definition -- the reader is bombarded with rich text that infuses the senses." – **Greenwich Post**

"Lentz especially likes to explore how creative people survive and contribute in a large and often impersonal environment. What is the role of a talented individual, an artist for example, in a complex, vast society?" – **New Canaan Advertiser**

WHERE TO FIND THE BOOKS OF DAVID B. LENTZ
A Partial Listing
Available at fine bookstores worldwide and
Internet booksellers based in 29 nations:

www.abebooks.com	USA
www.amazon.com	USA
www.amazon.ca	Canada
www.amazon.co.uk	UK
www.amazon.fr	France
www.amazon.de	Germany
www.amazon.jp	Japan
www.bn.com	USA
www.boganmeldelse.com	Denmark
www.bokklubben.no	Norway
www.bokrecension.se	Sweden
www.bookya.de	Germany
www.booky.fi	Finland
www.buch.de	Germany
www.buchfritze.de	Germany
www.buscape.com.br	Brazil
www.ecampus.com	USA
www.eurobuch.com	Germany
www.flipkart.com	India
www.foyles.co.uk	UK
www.goodreads.com	USA
www.infibeam.com	India
www.jump.co.za	South Africa
www.loot.co.za	South Africa
www.nbcindia.com	India
www.nokaut.pl	Poland
www.powellsbooks.com	USA
www.reviewscout.co.uk	UK

www.stylefeeder.com	USA
www.studentbooks.ch	Switzerland
www.bookfinder.com	USA
www.cdwow.com	USA
www.lovereading.com	UK
www.word-power.co.uk	UK
www.biggerbooks.com	USA
www.whsmith.co.uk	UK
www.eruditor.com	UK
www.holisticpage.com	Australia
www.readireland.com	Ireland
www.kirja-arvostelut.com	Finland
www.okian.ro	Romania
www.ellipse.ch	Switzerland
www.bookfayre.cz	Czech Republic
www.lalibrarie.es	Spain
www.store.bg	Bulgaria
www.eason.ie	Ireland
www.brl.com	The Netherlands
www.sax.com/dk	Denmark
www.bokkilden.no	Norway
www.webster.it	Italy
www.billigast.se	Sweden
www.wook.pt	Portugal
www.goethe-universitat.de	Germany
www.indiaplaza.in	India
www.bookshop.blackwell.co.uk	UK
www.cdon.no	Norway
www.buscalibros.cl	Chile
simania.co.il	Israel

Copyright ©2010, 2015 by David B. Lentz
Bourbon Street: The Dreams of Aeneas in Dixie

All rights reserved by David B. Lentz.

Without limiting the rights reserved above, no part of this publication may be reproduced, stored in or introduced into a retrieval system, or transmitted, in any form, or by any means (electronic, mechanical, photocopying, recording or otherwise), without the prior written permission of the copyright owner of this book.

This is a work of fiction. Names, characters, places and incidents either are the product of the author's imagination or are used fictionally, and any resemblance to any actual persons, living or dead, events, or locales is entirely coincidental.

Author's Photo: "At Old Greenwich Harbor" by **Virginia A. Lentz**

This book was printed in the United States of America.

For more information, please e-mail: Wrdzwrth@aol.com.

To the First True Muse,
Miss Virginia

Contents

PROLOGUE: INVOCATION OF THE MUSE 15
MRS. SIP, PIXIE OF DIXIE 16

CHIMERA I: STORM AND BANQUET 20
APPARITIONS IN A FLASH FLOOD 22
THE DIVINE DEBUTANTE..26
SYMPHONY FANTASTIQUE..35

CHIMERA II: THE SACK OF TROY 41
HIGH COTTON 42
ALLIGATOR SOUP 52
ELYSIAN FIELDS 56

CHIMERA III: THE WANDERINGS 63
FISHERMAN'S PARADISE 64
FOOL'S PARADISE 75

CHIMERA IV: DIDO 81
THE ADMONITION OF AMBITION 82
NAPOLEON AT CAMP 89

CHIMERA V: FUNERAL GAMES 102
CRESCENT CITY STEAKS 103
UPTOWN IN AN ELDORADO 108

CHIMERA VI: THE UNDERWORLD 115
DEMON BOURBON 116
FIRES OF JOY 125

CHIMERA VII: WAR IN LATHIUM 130
NO INSTANT GRITS 131
PRIVATE BATTLES 137

CHIMERA VIII: AENEAS IN ROME 142
PICTURES OF HAPPINESS 143
PROTEUS AND THE JESTER...149

CHIMERA IX: NISUS AND EURYALUS 156
BEIGNETS AND *CAFÉ AU LAIT* 157
THE BED IS THE BATTLEFIELD..162

CHIMERA X: PALLAS AND MEZENTIUS 167
THE *BON VIVANT* 168
HALCYON HALLUCINATIONS 174

CHIMERA XI: DRANCES AND CAMILLA 182
THE PASSING PARADE 183
AWAKENING IN THE AMERICAN DREAM 187
LOTUS LAND...192
SIR KNIGHT OF THE TOOTERS 196
THE PLEASURE 201

CHIMERA XII: TRUCE AND DUEL 206
MILLIONAIRES ROW...207
AENEAS IN DIXIE...215

EPILOGUE:
THE PARADE OF FUTURE ROMANS
IN THE UNDERWORLD 230
INTIMATIONS OF IMMORTALITY 231

THE SHIELD OF AENEAS 237
THE FLIGHT OF FANTASY 238

Dedication

TO VIRGINIA, EMILY, JASON,
MOM AND DAD

Acknowledgements

The author wishes gratefully to acknowledge the contributions to this work offered by Virginia Lentz, Phyllis O'Leary, David Joel Lentz, Jason and Emily Lentz, Douglas and Jeffrey Lentz, Enid and Edward T. Rice, CLU, John A. Taylor, Jr., CLU, Michael and Warren Newton, Joseph E. Connolly, Michael Weinberg, James Stevens, Evan Roskos, James Ackerman, Brian Moss, Chuck Hudson, Joan Russell, Kate Garn and Yvonne LaFleur.

He wishes also to commend the new prose translation of Virgil's *Aeneid* by David West, published by Penguin Classics.

BOURBON STREET | 14

NEW ORLEANS

1984

PROLOGUE:

Invocation of the Muse

"I sing of arms and of the man, fated to be an exile . . ."
— *The Aeneid, Book I* by Publius Vergilius Maro

Mrs. Sip, Pixie of Dixie

Bourbon Street reclined before him, beckoning like a French Quarter courtesan in the perfumed mucksweat of the evening in the City That Care Forgot.

Aeneas John Jam wandered on foot into the *Vieux Carre*. A solitary saxophonist regaled him with the yearning, blues ballad, *You Go to My Head,* immortalized by Billie Holiday. The jazz reverberated off French style, three-storied buildings framed with wrought-iron balconies and festooned with striped awnings.

He navigated through the crowd past fast blues trumpet fingers of gas lamps and Dixieland cabarets blasting a piquant jazz jambalaya of *Sugar Blues, Cornet Chop Suey, Potato Head Blues* and *Tiger Rag.* Talented, young tap-dancers performed their art robustly. Driving silver taps onto Bourbon Street outside the cabarets for spare change.

The omnipresent line of chic Uptown New Orleanians and wellheeled tourists queued politely outside Galatoires. Exchanging pleasantries in the unseasonably warm evening. Aeneas envied these patrons as he had only a few dollars in his wallet. Inside the restaurant, waiters attired in white coats worked below the whirling, brass, Hunter ceiling fans.

Aeneas strolled by Jean LaFitte's Old Absinthe House, Arnaud's and the Desire Oyster Bar. Discarded oyster shells filled the air with their fecundity.

"Shoeshine, Captain? Shine 'em up," asked a hardworking, old man outside the Royal Sonesta.

But Aeneas could not afford a shine. His poverty seethed bitterly within him. Because even the bootblack on Bourbon Street carried more cash. Than the gifted, young artist.

He was a creative practitioner devoted to his art of photography. For whom no monk's vow of poverty could impose more sacrifice.
Willingly consumed by his art, the creative talent of Aeneas was his only sanctuary. He possessed little else of worldly value. Lacking basic necessities, his lifestyle was, at best, Spartan.

"It's show time, ladies and gentlemen. It's what you came to see," shouted a barker with a classically harsh and gravelly voice. He opened and closed the front door of a beer joint to provide passersby with a glimpse of a topless dancer working with a feather boa among drunken tourists.

A city garbage truck stopped to load a mountain of empties at Pat O'Brien's.
At a tailor shop a sign read:
New Crotch
Only $5.
Aeneas thought:

If I had five bucks, I'd order one.

A long queue for admission to crusty, ramshackle Preservation Hall, where feisty old men — who had played jazz since its inception — improvised again on *Basin Street*.

A trumpet player sang through callous lips:

"Come down ta New Oh-leens. Da land o' dreamy dreams."

An oil tanker on the Mississippi bellowed a series of powerful, deep, intimidating blasts to punctuate the fetid perfume of the night air with the voice of the River.

From Royal Street a lofty pillared pantheon was barely visible. Gray drapes of haze enshrouded the Hibernia Bank Building on distant Carondelet Street. Aglow in quiet dignity above the tumultuous din of the French Quarter.

Aeneas walked by the Gumbo Shop onto Chartres Street. Pausing to peer into a bridal shop's display window, he stared at the mannequin dressed in a pristine wedding gown with veil and train.

Visions of his estranged wife haunted him. Vivid and real. He could not escape the pictures flashing in his imagination. The pixels were crystal clear. Both his salvation and damnation. Cruel and true and almost unbearable in their photographic clarity.

My dreams drive me mad. If I weren't meant to attain my dreams, why was I born to see them? God's idea of a joke, perhaps. They are such a bitter refuge. The root of freedom. My only hope. And who can live without hope?

I'm alone now. The loneliest man God ever made. On this Black Saturday. Since Adam before Eve.

St. Louis Cathedral was completely quiet and aloof. Its edifice beautifully lit with gray spires spearing into the sullen, sodden, Louisiana sky.

The aroma of steak wafted over to him from the Chart House and the juices in his mouth involuntarily teemed.

What I wouldn't give for a steak. Or an oyster Po' Boy at Maspero's. I'm starved.

A window in the Pontalba apartments shuddered open. To admit the night breeze sweeping off the Mississippi.

Steering toward the River, Aeneas arrived at his destination — the *Café du Monde*. He closed his eyes and deeply inhaled the warm, homey aroma of freshly baked *beignets* and chicory coffee. He bought three French donuts and a cup of *café au lait*. Dining at a sidewalk table upon his only meal of the day. Casually savoring the rich, sweet, fresh fingers of bread and powder sugar. Chased by the bitter, muddy, chicory coffee concoction. Aeneas Jam's banquet upon the *banquette*. His communion by the River.

He thought much about home – New England. Since he had left Boston, images of the landscape endured within him.

What, in the name of God, am I dong here? So far from home. Seven long months. Third wedding anniversary on June 16th. In this bewildering land of dreams. Soon engulfed in a tempest. As clouds gather. From a storm brewing.

He finished his humble sustenance and climbed the Moon Walk from which Jackson Square, the statue of Andrew Jackson and the St. Louis Cathedral in the background conspired to present a stunning portrait of old New Orleans.

The Riverboat Natchez rested stately in its berth. Its bow crumpled by a collision in the fog. Against an oil tanker in the fleet that perpetually steamed upriver from the Gulf of Mexico.

The River laps against the levee. Like a tranquil lake on a midsummer night. Upon a pristine New England shore. The rigs of the flagpoles clang in the breeze. Ah, I remember. The clattering masts of an armada of yachts in Marblehead Harbor. In the cool, fresh, salty, Atlantic, sea breezes. Unlike this infinite Dixie steam bath.

Ships signaled back and forth along the River. Horns communicating in the darkness. An oil tanker sailed cleanly beneath the Mississippi River Bridge. The wharves of the port well lit. Loading sugarcane, crude oil, Brazilian coffee and pecans bound for northern destinations.

In the distance the wooing of a train. Heading into the yards from Memphis, Houston or Atlanta.

Aeneas perched upon a bench on the Moon Walk staring at the River.

He recalled the overview, through the window of the Delta Airlines flight from Boston, of the River's course. It twisted torturously up from the Gulf of Mexico bearing tankers, freighters, tugs and barges upon its serpentine back. The River glistened in the sun's glare like a cottonmouth in a vast marsh.

She's gone. Gone.

In swirling eddies and churning whirlpools, he saw the meandering, turbulent reality of the condition of his own existence.

What's the point, after all?

He leapt onto the railing, balancing tenuously over the abysmal pernicious drift of the Mississippi.

The moonlight delineated the wrinkled ancient eyes of the current.

Vortexes spinning and sucking and spiraling. In the crude oil murkiness of the River.

Shall I throw myself into the River? And drink your draft, Mrs. Sip? Until I fill the unquenchable longing.

Swept off my feet. Taken as your lover. Clutched to your dusky bosom. Our meandering souls will wed.

Blissful in our alluvial connubial bed. I shall bridge and breach you, Mrs. Sip. Until I slake my mortal thirst.

Aeneas fought off the futility. And cast himself back onto the Moon Walk.

You're my kindred spirit. Both Fate and Fortune. The love of my life. Sweet Dixie Liffey. Will you have me, good widow? Redeem me, mighty Mrs. Sip.

He dislodged his golden wedding band.

I, Aeneas John Jam, am your devoted loverbuoy. Mrs. Sip, to you I pledge my troth. Forsaking all others. Buoyant in the comfort of Southern undercurrents. Adrift amid silken skirts of silt. Soothed by warm, tender sediments. Jealous of your torrid rushing lust. To commingle with the august Gulf.

Let us marry. Even if it mars us. We're no strangers to conflict. Confederate Amazon. Ever our twain shall meet. Deep River. The Great American Nile. What a lustrous couple we shall make. Antony, your Cleopatra beckons.

He pitched the wedding band into the liquid, languid, lurid River.

I am mad for you, Mrs. Sip. Simply mad, my Muse. I am your humble vessel. Interpreter of your speechless, soulful, mutable splendor. The indigent artist who'll plumb your fishy depths. You may bank upon it. And capture your murky, mucky immortality. I stand in awe of your urgent, turbulent, big-hearted burble. What say you then? My reticent belle, your babel is not lost on me. I now pronounce us. Missed her and Missus Sip . . . I rib her. I Yank the Muse from my frame. Mrs. Sip, my Dixie Pixie.

As his view from the Moon Walk of the moon was obscured by storm clouds, Aeneas resolved to leave the *levee*.
He crossed the railroad tracks and bypassed playing fountains, an old Civil War cannon and the Jax Brewery. A pair of honeymooners gleefully boarded a horse-drawn carriage for a tour of the Quarter.

He disembarked the embankment to roam through the black iron gates of Jackson Square and then down Chartres toward Canal Street.
On a whim he ducked into Napoleon House, alighting upon a barstool.

The image fresh in his mind from the *levee* of the logo of Ajax. Painted on the brick pixels of the brewery. Aeneas ordered a Jax Beer. By no means to be had. He preferred a Pimm's Cup. But surrendered to Dixie on tap. To foster beautiful dreams. Held in abeyance by the *café au lait*.
Desperate for shut-eye. He counted small denominations of spare change for the bartab.

Sparring with a trace of hay fever from spring blooms with sniffs. He blasted into a ragged ivory handkerchief that fluttered like a poor flag of surrender.

When his Dixie on draft arrived, he turned toward the River and lifted the glass with a nod in veneration of Mrs. Sip.

A sip of Dixie in your honor, Mrs. Sip. You stunning piece of creation. May the pixels always do justice to the pixie in you.

He tossed half the vessel of beer down the hatch.

Inadvertently, flinging his smiling nod in the direction of a most engaging, trim, young lady sitting alone at a table. Who approached and posed her most commanding presence on a barstool beside him.

"Mah name's Didi. How are y'awl doin' tonight?" she asked, beaming a nice, friendly, Southern smile.

"I've seen betteh days," he replied with a brave grin. "Come heyuh ovid?"
Sniffsniff.

"All the time. Hey, are *you all* from New Or-le-ans?" she asked.

"You don't sound like it none."

"I grew up in Boston. Pahts of me are still growing."

"Massatusitts?"

"By way of Troy, New Yohk. My parents lived there. My fatheh was Associate Professoh of Classics at Russell Sage. A long time ago.
When I was a little kid, we moved to Boston. He became a Professoh of the ahts of the Antiquities at Hahvid."

"You here on business? Or pleasure?" she inquired.

"Pleashuh," he muttered. "You?"

"Yeah, me, too. You came to the right place, dawlin'," she said with a seductive smile. "We got plentya sweet dreams down here, babe."

"Is pleashuh your business, madam?"

"Mah business is to experience every excess of life."

"Aeneas John Jam. At your sehvice."

"Aeneas? That's a new one on me."

"I cehtainly hope so."

"It surely is a classy name. I don't believe that I ever met an Aeneas before."

"It's from Greek legend. You ever read any Vihgil?"

"Virgil who?"

"Publius Vehgilius Maro."

"In my entire life I have never heard of that Virgil. Although New Orleans is chock full of Virgils. You got a nickname? One I could actually spell, if I had to."

"Call me Jack. Everyone else does. Jack Jam."

"I like your looks, Jack Jam."

"You're none too shabby yourself."

"Seems like you could use a little lift, Moon Pie."

"I guess I got the blues."

"Why don't you all come along with me? Tonight, I happen to be staying at the Royal Orleans. I just split with my significant other."

"Me, too."

"It must be Fate, Jack Jam. That of all people, we should find each other here. Wouldn't yawl say so?"

"It's true: the Fates are fickle mistresses."

"So here we are together. Just off Bourbon Street . . ."

"In the entihe civilized wohld, every vihtue and every vice known to man can be found on Bourbon Street. In the 14 blocks from Canal Street to Esplanade. Eveh think about that?"

"Matter of fact, Jack, I'm thinking 'bout it right now."

"Bourbon Street is a monument to human folly."

"Just thinking out loud, Jack — we might find ourselves a tiny bit more comfortable at the Royal Orleans. At my suite. What do you all say, sweetie?"

"The Royal O?"

"Yep. I got a nice little weekend special. On a double room there. It comes with champagne at breakfast."

"I am a man of . . . ratheh modest means. At the moment."

"It don't matter none to me, Sugar. It ain't your jack I'm interested in, Jack. Believe you me. Shall we go?"

Aeneas hastily consumed his Dixie Draft. Exiting Napoleon House with Didi. Uncertain who conquered whom. Envisioning rich spoils.

Together, the pair of exiled paramours paraded arm in arm in the French Quarter. Wandering erratically and erotically. Flotsam and jetsam amid the drift of the crowd flowing toward Bourbon Street and the entry to the Royal O.

In the City
That Care Forgot
Jack Jam
had a night
to remember.
* * *

CHIMERA I:
Storm and Banquet

"A squall came howling from the north, catching his sail full on and raising the waves to the stars. The oars broke, the prow was wrenched round, and as they lay beam on to the sea, there came towering over them a sheer mountain of water . . . Here and there men could be seen swimming in the vast ocean, and with them in the waves their armour, spars of wood and the treasures of Troy."
— The Aeneid, Book I

Apparitions in a Flash Flood

Ominously, the first immense storm of the monsoon season moored in New Orleans as a spirited prelude to hurricane season. Generous to excess, Mother Nature lashed the city with its most opulent commodity – water. Kindly withholding cyclone winds at the moment. *Bayous* swelled and the River strained its banks. Easily breaching its *levee*. Besotting streets of the Big Easy with cataclysmic floods.

In Aeneas Jam's apartment in the Garden District, the ballad, *Louisiana 1927*, played upon his FM radio. Cheering rather than disillusioning, this *bayou* folksong rendered a romantic dimension to the present downpour.

"What has happened down here
Is the winds have changed.
Clouds roll in from de North
And it starts to rain.
Rained real hard
And it rained for a real long time.
Six feet o' water
In the streets of Evangeline."

The third day of unrelenting deluge in merciless monsoon fashion in a part of the earth below sea level composed as much of water as land posed monumental drawbacks for civilized humans living here.

"River rose all day.
River rose all night.
Some people got lost in the flood.
Some people got away all right.
The River has busted through
Clear down to Plaquemine.
Six feet o' water
In the streets of Evangeline."

The singer's voice honest, straightforward and unpretentious. The simple, earthy quality in his song implied that Louisianians had not cornered the Market in answers. This quality spoke of their ability to weather hurricanes, tornadoes and floods. To survive. Endure. And rebuild, when necessary.

Thus, to say that the catastrophic elements of a harsh universe did not have the last word. But rather they, as Louisianians, did. Because of their will and the spirit of their human nature.

Aeneas identified with this earthy, silent stubbornness in times of hardship. He learned it from his grandfather who, like the Acadians, came from Canada, where he was a fisherman. Always strong when it mattered most, he had taught Aeneas that it was not what one was compelled to suffer that counted. But how one emerged from it.

"Louisiana, Louisiana.
They're trying to wash us away.
They're trying to wash us away."

Four inches of rain had fallen in the last *hour* with no sign of the torrent's diminishing. The phone rang.

"Jack? It's Andre Boudreau. From UPI."

"Hello, Andre."

"How are you all doin'?"

"All of me is barely treading wateh. I'm up to my ass in alligatohs. You?"

"I'm in a jam, Jack."

"Then you've called the right man."

"Listen, I'd like you to get some pictures of this here flood."

"I'll be glad to. If I don't perish fihst in this godfohsaken parish."

"Weather repoht now says maybe 17 inches before it's over. Maybe more."

"It's rain. Not nucleah holocaust."

"The *levee* broke over at Robert E. Lee Boulevard. They're sandbagging."

"It could always be worse. At least, it's wahm. Be glad it's not snow."

"Those damn rusty, old pumps ain't doin' a bit o' good. The politicians blew all the money the voters approved for modern ones. We oughta hang 'em by the balls."

"I'll get you some good shots. As soon as it cleahs."

"I know we gonna have people lookin' foh 'em. Give us the same quality you've been sending us now. Hear?"

"I promise."

"I need 'em yesterday."

"I undehstand, Andre."

"Bah."

Aeneas hung up the phone and checked the depth of flood. The calamitous water had risen to the curb forming a brown torrent. Little Muddy. All byways now *bayous*.

A little ditty scampered into his mind:
Hope for the best.
Prepare for the worst.
Life is a play.
And we're all unrehearsed.

He calmly set inherited colonial antiques atop dozens of Snow's New England Clam Chowder cans. To add four more inches between safety and calamity. As he did so, Aeneas felt somewhat helpless and entrapped in a natural disaster with the worse yet to come. Caught in malevolent forces many times larger than he.

Nature with her awesome sound and Fury. Summoning the wits and wills of men. To save themselves in the absence of divine intervention through invention.

He turned the radio dial hoping to find a weather report on this Sunday morning. Much Christian revival music and many religious services with grotesque preachers growling in accents of the Deep South.

One preacher barked, "If you believe in the Lord Jesus Almighty, our Heavenly Father, put your hand on the radio. And feel the power of His Glo-ry."

Aeneas imagined thousands touching their hands to old RCAs and feeling in their fingers a warm hum that was the glory of God.

On another station a Baptist minister preached, as a gospel group sang exuberantly in the background, "We goin' ta get you all steamed up for them Sunday Soivices."

Gospel singers broke into *Amazing Grace*, a baroque selection in light of the cataclysm.

He remembered another ditty written on the men's room wall at Napoleon House:
"At times, we may sincerely doubt,
Dear God, that you exist.
As if you ramble here about,
Why let so much grief persist?"
Aeneas changed the dial.

"The SS President will become a floating ballroom when Lionel Hampton comes aboard for the Jazz and Heritage Festival."

A DJ, forced by the flood to work overtime from the late shift, announced: "A funnel cloud touched down across Lake Pontchartrain this morning. Parts of New Orleans had golf ball size hail. In the past four hours, we've had 4.5 inches of rain. This could turn worse than the Great Flood of 1978, which dropped 12 inches of rain in 24 hours."

Aeneas peered outside onto the streets, where floodwaters climbed rapidly to levels in places over the hubcaps of abandoned cars.

Must be God's punishment. For the collective vices of the good people of New Orleans. For too much smoking, drinking and chasing women.

On the FM station a talk show of callers:

"Let's tawk to da parish president faw all dis human displeasure. Dose pumpin' stations doane woik. Dis is woise dan Betsy. And dats pretty bad."
If the public you'd appease,
The rules are simply choice.
When you speak in your best voice,
Watch your dems, dose and dese.
"Ah guess ah woane be able to make it ta choich dis mohnin'. Ain't no way ah can make it," a young girl observed. "Uh-uh."

"Cheer up, dawlin'. God understands. It's all part of His plan," the DJ said.

A high-and-dry Uptown man quipped, "This is a ploy to bring the Grand Isle Tarpon Rodeo to New Orleans. We have tarpon feeding up here on St. Charles Avenue."

A young woman with a tinge of hysteria in her voice: "Ah woke up dis mohnin' and they was a wotah moccasin swimmin' in ma be'room. Ah saw dat snake an' ah stood up on mah bed an' started screamin'. Mah daddy woke up. He took a broom. An' he swep' dat snake raht out da doh."

It's a watery hell here in the Land of Dreams. Floods. Possible plagues, if the sewers back up. Clouds of cockroaches. Tornadoes. Hail the size of beignets. *It'll start raining toads next. Or better yet, water moccasins.*

On television a backwoods dweller along the Pearl River north of the Lake perched upon his rooftop jutting from the floodwater. After the fourth year in a row of bad flooding, he wore a stoic calm on his face as he was interviewed by a rainwear garbed newsman. The country gentleman had no flood insurance:

"My wife and I were born beside this river in that house over there."

The camera panned to an island of roof amid raging floodwater.

"I was born back here. I hunt and fish here. I love the river. It's my home. I'll never leave it. We'll just build it up again ourselves. And soon it will be good as new."

The TV anchorman said that more than 14 inches of rain had fallen in 36 hours. The floodwater rose to within an inch of the doorjamb.

Then the rain abruptly abated.

Aeneas slid into knee boots and pulled on a Black Diamond rain hat. Gathering camera equipment and film, he emerged into the flooded city like a grotesque Southern parody of Gloucester's *Captains Courageous*. Currently, Captain Uptown. Leaving antiques perched atop calamity chowder cans, he ventured into this Cajun version of Venice. To make what he could of the Chaos of the Great Flood. And capture its wonder on film for United Press International.

He waded past the front of the columnar, ivory, antebellum home in which he lived in a small apartment. He waded vigorously to St. Charles Avenue, where he found no tarpon. Vigilant of snakes.

A vision of a woman he did find. Poling a pirogue down the Avenue through the steamy mists like every man's phantasm.

She stood stately and well balanced in the pirogue. And piloted silently and effortlessly through the liquid shimmering streets. Floating upon a mirror of oak trees.

Dressed like a *bayou* goddess gondolier in a column of snowy silk and chiffon. The soft cloth, wet from the rain, fell with grace from her shoulders to hug her body. Showing off a statuesque figure. The rain undermined the opacity of her attire.

With her head held erect and slick auburn hair, she poled with determination past mansions stately in the background.

A high water mark of a vision emerged from the grim floodwaters.

Aeneas seized this image and photographed the woman in the pirogue on St. Charles Avenue for UPI as she poled out of earshot.

Within several hours the streets of the Garden District were nearly dry. The spring steam bath resumed. The sun shone intensely bright.

As if nothing at all had happened. Except a Louisiana rain shower.

> Thus, the great flood
> inspired visions
> greater than itself
> giving the flower garden
> of his imagination
> a good drink.

* * *

The Divine Debutante

Under a black light in the pan of developing fluids, the amorphous form of an elderly jazz trumpet player clarified into view on the soggy Kodak paper.

A thin, affable man with smiling eyes, short gray hair and adamantine lips. Glasses with a thick broken frame mended with electrical tape. Wearing a white cotton, short-sleeve shirt and loose, cuffed, dark, polyester trousers. His archaic brass horn stood upright on its flared bell upon a hardwood floor between his black wingtips adorned with white socks. The jazzman perched upon a rickety, dusty and scarred wooden chair.

Aeneas had shot the image lying prostrate upon the floor of the cabaret. Composing the photo of only the jazzman's wingtips, white socks, baggy pants and horn. As the trumpeter awaited his turn to improvise upon a sweet, old, musical ode to Dixieland.

The phone rang.

"Aeneas Studios."

"Mr. Aeneas Jam, please."

"This is he."

"Diner's Club calling. You are now more than 120 days overdue on your last payment. When may we expect to receive it?"

"I have no ethly idea, sih. Money's ratheh tight at the moment."

"I'm afraid I am going to cancel your credit card privileges, Mr. Jam. Please cut your credit card in two and return it to us with your final payment. Do not make any further purchases. Good day."

When he hung up, the phone pealed, again. He imagined desperately needed new business. Perhaps, another assignment from UPI. Or a prospective art buyer.

"Is this an asylum for the mentally handicapped?" the caller inquired.

"It is."

"How many residents do you currently have?"

"One."

"I'm looking for something a little larger."

"Sih, you have dialed incorrectly."

Another call.

What next?

"Aeneas Studios."

"Aeneas Jam, please."

"Speaking."

"This is Acadia National Bank calling. Your payment on your automobile loan is overdue. On your 1977 Mercury Grand Marquis. We must have immediate payment. Or arrange for repossession."

"It has been repossessed. *Already.*"

"Not by us."

"No, actually by the New Ohleans Pahking Authority. I had a few stinking unpaid pahking tickets. You know how pahking is here in the Quahteh. So they slapped a Denveh boot on that old Grand Mahquis. And towed it away. Can you believe it?"

"When do you intend to recover it, Mr. Jam?"

"Just as soon as I sell a few pieces of aht."

"Our records here at Acadia National show a substantial balance due. Very long overdue — 150 days."

"I'll send it along shohtly."

"How soon, please?"

"Next week, sometime."

"By the fifteenth, please."

"I have an idea. Why don't *you* just pay the pahking tickets? And you can *have* the cah. It's a pissah cah. It's only got about 165,000 miles on it. Mostly country miles."

"No, thanks. We'll look for your check on the fifteenth. Have a lovely day, sir."

"I cehtainly will."

Such is the lot of the aesthete in America. In hot pursuit of the American Dream. Poor as a leper from the Black Hole of Calcutta. More profitable to collect trash for the city. Christ, I need some new business. And soon. But remember, Aeneas John Jam, you are an artist. Someday, you'll look back on this. And laugh.

Throughout the morning other calls summoned him. From American Express. Offering to ship his check overnight to them for free. New Orleans Power & Light. With its charming, omniscient power to delight. And South Central Bell. One of hell's Bells. Not saving him from the day's knockout punch. The threat of a property lien by the IRS. All wanting money immediately. Of which he had none to spare. Lacking further lines of credit. All maximized to their respective limits. And collecting usurious rates of interest.

Jazz and classical music played during business hours. On his modest stereo the refrains of Billie Holiday sang *Easy Living.* To coax the greenbacks out of the wallets of thrifty Midwestern tourists on a tight budget in the Big Easy. Attending a big basketball tournament at the Superdome. The repertoire of the blues soothed his tortured soul.

As no photography or developing remained to be done, he currently read Shakespeare's *Midsummer Night's Dream.* Awaiting customers, he jammed remnant pinches of a pouch of Captain Black Gold Tobacco blended with vanilla into a Peterson pipe. Bought from a tobacconist next to Antoine's, when he could afford it. Sometimes venturing to buy a new pipe that was a "second" to celebrate a rare sale.

Smoke wafted through his gallery with the scent of chocolate chip cookies baking in the oven.

The walls of his small studio and large window in his shop front displayed his portfolio of work. Waiting hopefully for a passerby to admire his art in the display window. And turn purposefully from Decatur Street through his door to make a major acquisition, indeed, perhaps of a collection of his work. Providing cold cash to keep his landlady from banging the door down for the rent. Cash that he could fork over to the bank. And Parking Authority. Not to mention a deserving Diner's Club and American Express. To reward their patience with minimum payments. As balances skyrocketed in favor of his worthy creditors through the simple miracle of compound interest.

He peered over his book as one of the most striking young women that he had ever laid eyes upon entered his gallery. And in New Orleans stunning women were deliciously common.

She carried with her the rich, sweet aroma, which hung heavy in the fetid air, of the praline shop next door. A magnificent figure. Chestnut brown hair. Possessing sufficient beauty to shake him where he lived. An epiphany of femininity. A feast for the eyes.

Aeneas recognized her instantly as the woman in the pirogue whom he had photographed Uptown during the great flood. He wondered if she had seen her photo in the Sunday *Times-Picayune*. He waited patiently as she browsed throughout the gallery studying his photography.

The ancient stereo played Modest Mussorgsky's tender, regal and elegant *Pictures at an Exhibition*.

She lingered at the series of black-and-white photos that Aeneas had taken of gentle, wizened jazzmen playing cool riffs in the clubs on Bourbon Street. Of a middle-age Creole woman in a leotard, tutu and toe shoes at the bar of a ballet studio. Of a spheroid baker, dressed in white, baking *croissants* at Café Madeleine. Of two puerile women with faces painted like pixies indulging at Mardi Gras in fresh oysters at Felix's. Of a seasoned, bow-tie attired, bartender mixing a Pimm's Cup amid a surfeit of bottles at the Old Absinthe House. Of a call girl in a smoky haze listening attentively to jazz at the piano bar of *Lucky Pierre's*.

They were only a few of the denizens of Bourbon Street. The subjects of his artistry. A complex tapestry in progress. Nearly infinite in its idiosyncrasy.

His visitor studied curiously his photographic treatments. Aeneas sensed that she knew photography simply by the way she viewed his work. He perceived a thoughtful aspect, respect possibly, in her incredible brown eyes speckled with hints of jade.

When she articulated her praise of his work, she spoke without a drawl. Definitely not the slow, drawn-out Mississippi or Alabama dialect.
Her speech was genteel and non-regional. Like the conscious, non-accent adopted by Uptown New Orleanians.

She was well-dressed. Simple yet elegant. Silk and denim. High heels and lipstick. Touches of gold upon the wrist and diamond ear rings.
Her chestnut hair hung loose and smelled of exotic spices and roses when she shook her head. From a family with money, she seemed disarmingly accessible, at first. In her mid-twenties, she wore no wedding band. Both intimidating and inviting in her appearance. Her body language and her posture told him that she approved of his work and was ready to buy.

"Let me show you something which may be of special interest to you," Aeneas offered as he extended a hand directing her to the back of the gallery. "This is one of my most memorable photos. I took it a few weeks ago. The woman in the pirogue proved to be a most exceptional model. Unfohtunately, I didn't know her. The floodwatehs were too deep. And she poled away from me. Like a gondolieh. Right down St. Chahles Avenue."

"*You're* the photographer?" she asked pulling a crumpled newspaper clipping from the pocket of her jeans. "You took the UPI photo?"

Aeneas read incredulity in her voice. Astonishment. Radiant praise. Almost critical reverence.

"Why, yes," Aeneas said, calmly beaming. "My name is Aeneas Jam. My friends all call me Jack. Occasionally, I am invited to submit my wohk to United Press International here in New Ohleans."

"Aeneas, I'm Lavinia Palmer. And my daddy intends to sue you."

"I'm sorry, I didn't quite catch that."

"For every red cent you've got."

"Beg your pahdon?"

"I got stranded Uptown. At the house of this friend of Percy. He's my boyfriend. They fish and hunt ducks together near Lake Charles," Lavinia said. "Daddy was having a big party for me. Percy doesn't much go for that debutante stuff. Neither do I really. But it makes daddy real happy. So I just commandeered this pirogue of Percy's friend. Next thing I know, this gawd-awful picture of me is in the *Times-Picayune*. Relatives saw it in Baton Rouge and Mobile. Daddy was appalled. Out of his head crazy mad. Cause I was all wet. Like a drowned nutria. And all."

"It's one of the best photos I've eveh taken in my . . . entyre life," Aeneas managed to blurt out. "You were a vision. The spirit of nature in all her abundance. Amid the floodwatehs you were an island of beauty. A nymph . . ."

"Watch who you're calling a nymph, buster."

"I mean, you were a picture of grace and loveliness. I nohmally secure a release. But because of the flood, as I have said, I simply couldn't this time."

"Then you ought notta published the picture," she said. "Have you any idea how much money my daddy spent to present me to society?"

"I have not the first clue."

"A small Fortune."

"Then you don't need my much smaller, indeed, miniscule – perhaps, even negative — Fohtune. My amiss Fohtune."

"It's not just the money. It's all the years of classes in etiquette, dance, piano and voice. To learn the social graces," she explained. "The parties. The clothes. Mardi Gras Balls. Years of private school. All down the drain in one picture. Surely, you have some sort of insurance liability coverage for this sort of thing."

"Are you kidding?" he said pitifully. "I have very little money. Just now. I live on the brink of bankruptcy. And I'm not eageh to be pushed into it."

"It may not seem like much to you all. But it means a lot to my daddy. With mamma gone and all," she said.

"My creditohs are descending upon me like the eagle of Prometheus. Stealing the liveh of my ahtistic soul," he raved grandly. "Just because I missed the last fo-uh or five monthly installments."

"Daddy gave an earful to some folks at UPI. He has some clout in this town," she said. "He told them never to give you another piece of work. Or he'd sue them, too."

"Perhaps, we can wohk something out. Through some photos that interest you here in the gallery. Choose a few that you like. And consideh them a gift. A penance," he offered.

"I just don't know. Daddy was just as mad as he could be. It isn't the money. Hear? We're well enough off."

"Most deb daddies are."

"He may be up for Rex this year."

"Listen, I'm a stahving ahtist. Literally. They just cancelled my Dineh's Club cahd."

"Well, I can see that you have real talent. It's evident in *all* of your work," she said.

"Why, thank you. I vihtually always secure a release. But I just couldn't get to you. And the picture, I thought, was really quite remahkable. Memorable," he said. "I am truly sorry. From the bottom of my heart, Miss Pahmeh. Please don't ruin me."

"I would hate to see daddy sue a talented, up-and-coming photographer.

He eats up young men like you for a light snack. It just wouldn't seem right," she said softening.

"No, it wouldn't be right. But I am prepahed to offeh selections of my wohk as recompense for your trouble. It's the best I can do right now. In good faith."

"You are very sweet," she said looking him up and down. "And rather handsome, too. If I may say so."

"I'm in your hands, Miss Pahmeh."

"I have an idea. That might appease daddy."

"Apaht from samples of my best wohk? I'm all eahs."

"If you might just happen to have some type of job here in the studio. I just love photography myself. I dabbled in it at Sacred Heart. And studied it at Sophie Newcomb. I have been thinking about photography as a career path."

"You must love it. To suhvive. Aht is an insatiably cruel taskmasteh. You have to be a masochist to be an aesthete in America."

"I *do* love the art of photography. And the creativity it entails. It's different every time you trip the shutter. People consider me artistically inclined. So I've been told."

"Told by whom? Pehcy? Or your fatheh?"

"By them, too."

"I can't affohd an assistant right now. I can bahely make ends meet alone."

"I could sure use a mentor. And you would perhaps value a business partner . . ."

"A *business pahtneh*?"

"Someone with resources you seem to lack. Like capital. And a line of credit."

"I don't know . . ."

"I'm pretty sure daddy might go along with it. He has the final say. Since we'd be using his money. He knows lots of people who need to have their pictures taken. He has many business and social connections."

"I don't think it would wohk out."

"Fine. I'll just tell daddy that you and I couldn't come to terms. And let you deal with his attorneys. Perhaps, you've heard of Styffe, Crucke, Poltroon & Shister."

"Styffe Crucke? They're my wife's divohce lawyehs. They're a pack of wild dogs."

"SCP&S does have a tough reputation. Are you prepared to deal with them?"

"No."

"Then deal with me."

"Listen, I won't have some Uptown novice come in here thinking she can just take oveh. I'd ratheh take my chances against your fatheh in court. And staht oveh if he cleans me out. Hell, I'm almost bankrupt as it is. So what difference would it make to lose to him in court?"

When she did not respond, he continued.

"I mean this studio isn't much right now. But I'm young and the best goddam photographeh in New Ohleans. Bar *none*. No one else is even *close*. I have ambitions. I expect to do well downstream. Profit from my talent. And make a name for myself."

"I'm absolutely certain that your destiny is to become an important photographer. Or I wouldn't still be here. Besides, I like a man with drive."

Lavinia opened up her purse and removed her checkbook.

"Money talks. So I'm willing to buy that picture of me in the flood with the negatives. How much do you want for it?" she asked, arching lovely thin eyebrows.

"$1,000. In American money."

"$500. American Express."

"$700 cash."

Lavinia reached into her purse and counted seven $100 bills for Aeneas.

"I'll just wrap up the prints and film foh you," he offered.

"Don't bother."

He passed her the enlarged print and negatives of *The Divine Debutante*.

Lavinia asked to borrow his faux-gold pipe lighter and promptly torched the negatives. Tossing the burning film into his scratched, archaic, metal trashcan.

Then she tore the print into tiny little pieces. And sprinkled them over the little conflagration fueled by his art. Like a burnt offering to gods of the antiquities.

"Well. So much foh aht," Aeneas mused.

"I'm sorry, darlin'. The photo *was* a tiny bit indiscreet."

"Do you have a portfolio?"

"Why, yes. As a matter of fact, I do. It's right outside in my Cadillac. Let me go fetch it," she offered.

She's beautiful. Bright. Uptown. Spirited. Street smart. And sexy. She can sell. And she's rich. Dear God, if it's not too much, I pray. Please let her millionaire father own a brewery, distillery or chain of liquor stores. And allow this deal to happen. She wears the mask of my soul's mate. Please spring young, humble Jack from yet another unholy jam.

Lavinia left in a rush and returned briskly. She spread open the portfolio upon his haggard and chipped desk. With its overlapping Olympian rings of chicory coffee stains. He turned the pages of black-andwhite images slowly. Intent in his silence, he studied closely her book of photography.

"I shoot scenes from the Quarter. Like you all," she commented. "I developed the film myself, of course."

Aeneas remained reticent.

"That photo of St. Louis Cathedral in the fog is one of my favorites," she said. "I used f-11 at 1/30th with a 105 lens."

He did not speak.

"And that shot of Sweet Emma at Preservation Hall won an award," she claimed. "First prize."

He thumbed through her portfolio again stopping occasionally.

"Who are the photographers that you admire?" he asked.

"Ansel Adams. Richard Avedon. David Hockney. And Annie Leibovitz."

He nodded assent.

"Well, what do you think?" she asked.

"Have you eveh considehed modeling?" he returned. "You'd be wicked pissah."

She seemed genuinely saddened by his remark. It implied that she was not adept in her photographic forays and should seek an alternative line of work. She did not wish to sell her appearance, which was constantly praised by men. And deemed an omniscient threat by women. She sought his respect for her creative talent.

Aeneas observed her involuntarily pained expression. He remembered how difficult the words of early critics were to him as a neophyte.
But no artist can grow without perceptive, intelligent criticism.
He knew that an artist can only hope for a blend of inspired insight and humanity.

She seemed transformed in her vulnerability. The Uptown bravado fled. Obviously accustomed to getting her own way, now she seemed more sensitive underneath the artifice of the debutante exterior. The veneer of Uptown's upper crust. She was irresistible to him in this new light.

"The pohtfolio is a deal-busteh," he said. "I think that your wohk with me might seriously compromise the quality of the gallery. I simply can't risk that. My intellectual capital is more precious to me than a monetary capitoline. I'm sorry. I'll take my chances with your fatheh. Here's the name of my attohney," he said, scrawling down the name of a law firm that just opened a few doors down. "That's Newton Associates."

"I sure do love a challenge. And I learn real fast," she proffered.

"I appreciate your offehs. They're most generous. Really," he replied.

"I'm sorry. Your wohk is promising. In spite of obvious technical flaws."

In truth, her work was far better than he let on. Working with her could prove engaging, almost redemptive in its spiritual upside.

For better or worse, what is not tolerated among ordinary people tends to be forgiven among the most ravishing of the species. No doubt, she had received frequent second chances on that account. He admired her business sense. And her entrepreneurial spirit. She certainly seemed a worthy daughter of Rex, the reigning King of Mardi Gras.

"What can I do to close this business proposition?" she asked earnestly.

"Model foh the studio. In addition to the otheh deal points."

"Listen, Jack. I expect to get engaged to Percy soon. We talk about it often. We're making plans to be together. He's very . . . controlling. He won't go for it. My daddy neither. Not one bit."

"This would be on the up-and-up," he promised. "Uncompromising of your integrity. Or anyone else's. In any way. Strictly business."

"It would save the extra expense of a model's fee. Which the studio could capture on any commercial shoots. So what do you say?"

"Here's my offeh. I'm willing to consideh letting you wohk with me. As a minority pahtneh with 10% ownehship."

"Make it 30%. What's 30% of nothing?"

"I'll make it 20%. But you need to come up with $20,000 cash to buy-in. Up front."

"Make it $10,000."

"Make it $15,000."

"Let's split the difference at $12,500."

"Done. But you would staht off on the business side. Is that cleah? And move into photography when I see that you're ready."

"To start, you take the photos. And I'll manage the business end of things. But I expect you to be a mentor to me. In the art of photography."

"Let's give it a try," he advised. "Staht as business manageh. You can sell. Model on occasion. I'll teach you photography, in good faith, as we go along. When you're ready, in my judgment, we'll display your aht in the studio. And split the profits 80-20%."

"That'd be just fine. I can have daddy's attorneys draw up a partnership agreement. For your review. At no cost to you. Since they're on retainer with him."

"Agreed."

"There's one little tiny *caveat*, Jack."

"What's that?"

"My daddy needs to sign onto this deal. Since it would be partly his capital."

"I undehstand. *No problemo*."

"When can I start?"

"Staht tomorrow. If you like."

They shook hands on the deal. And she wrote him a check drawn to the Whitney Bank for the first of six monthly installments of the partnership fee.

Aeneas was suddenly flush with cash. A business partner with the most beautiful woman in New Orleans. Whose father was up for Rex. And rich as Midas. He could hardly comprehend the fickle turn of Fortune for the better.

No more beignets for a while. The Bass Weejuns could stand a shine. Perhaps, buy a new pipe. Not among the seconds for a change. And a full pouch of a custom blend of tobacco.

"Tell me something straight-up. Now that we're pahtnehs. And as a man of my wohd, your anseh won't change anything that has transpihed between us," he said.

"Okay. Shoot."

"Was your fatheh really planning to sue me?"

"Well, he *was* pretty upset about the publicity."

"Yes or no?"

"No."

"I see."

A brief silence ensued.

"Now, partner, you tell me something," she requested.

"What?"

"Is my work really all that flawed?"
He paused to reflect.
"No," he replied. "It's not."
"*Ciao*," she said, smiling as she walked toward the door of the studio of which she was now a minority shareowner.

> Her
> daddy
> didn't
> raise
> no
> fool.

* * *

Symphony Fantastique

Right from the outset Lavinia seemed clearly unattainable. Aeneas responded to her nearly perfect features. He imagined that her impact upon him was indicative of her broader sensual appeal and that men reacted like him involuntarily to the power of her physical presence.

He learned that she was a direct descendant of a line of French knights who had fought with honor in the Middle Ages in wars against Belgium. Despite some initial manifestations of manipulative inclinations, she proved to be responsible, hardworking and eager to learn.

Aeneas noticed in the course of their daily contact that she turned other men into swine without intending to do so. She was so striking that she inhibited men from productive action. Unwillingly, she generated a frequent disintegration of men who saw her and responded with egotistical or idiotic manifestations of incompetence.

Bright, articulate, handsome, prosperous, young men would stumble upon her in Jackson Square and feel compelled to approach her. Inevitably, they hurtled themselves into a painful, stuttering, trembling, catatonic disintegration. He witnessed this phenomenon repeat itself with uncommon frequency, a constant intrusion upon her.

A mere frown from her proved sufficient to induce a panic of humiliation and to bring about the sad, fatal tumbling of the ego. And men concocted the most banal and mad mumbo jumbo to try to endear them to her. Often they complimented her with such committed zeal that she found them impossibly unrealistic, which caused her great embarrassment. They idolized her. Posed her upon a towering pedestal. And lost her.

The most fortunate aspect concerning timing, a critical piece of most worthy ambitions, is that it changes, if given a chance. His father once sagely advised him never to rush a woman.

Lavinia came to work uncharacteristically somber and announced that she and Percy had broken off their relationship permanently. Aeneas advised her not to be upset and that any man who would let her walk away was a *complete cretin* and unworthy of her. Clearly, the remark served him well.

Some men, especially artists, cannot endure without the existence of a perfect dream to drive them. Without such phantoms of the imagination, the grim realities of the world seem insufferably overpowering and consuming. The problem with such a notion is obviously its dangerous fallacy, lack of substance and blindness to weakness. The logical consequence of such a perspective is disillusionment. But then there were always more dreams. An endless stream of them, in fact. Hidden deep within the soul. Like the primeval wellspring of Mrs. Sip.

Aeneas could not help finding in Lavinia the humanization of a dream. She was his ideal woman – the epitome of sensuality. A portrait of femininity. Flawless. Real. And intimately close.

His recent suffering had heightened his consciousness of his own undeniable vulnerability at her hands. Accordingly, he acted with marked, prudent restraint. Aeneas idealized her in silence and masked his affection for her. It emerged most visibly whenever he served as mentor and taught her about his art. Despite his ingrained New England caution, he found himself falling in love with her. And he could not do otherwise.

His abundant affection for her was out of his hands. It existed. He could only attempt to control it so that it could not hurt him anymore deeply than he had already suffered.

Lavinia reacted well to his wit. His sense of humor protected him and yet held him in good stead with her. She seemed genuinely and naturally drawn to him. After all, he was a fit and intelligent young artist with ambition and talent. She seemed to give him credit for his personal strengths but also was hurt by her breakup with Percy. And so the two wounded souls found grace and sought sanctuary in each other's company more and more.

After patiently waiting a fortnight, Aeneas realized that in not taking any chances to be hurt by his affection for her, he diminished the odds of his being crushed. And while he may not suffer the ramifications of rejection by this beauty, neither would he come to know her more intimately.

He did not wish to impose upon her. Nor misread her interest, which could have been simply platonic or business or friendly in the way that Southern women can be. Gracious and flirting but noncommittal. Touching one lightly on the lapels of a jacket or straightening one's tie. A fleeting brush of the hand upon the wrist. Quick repartees and playful laughter. Thoughtful gestures and pleasant courtesies. In the end it all could have meant nothing more than the common respect shown between colleagues in close quarters.

Since he could not read her sentiments clearly and wanted to avoid a gaffe, he waited patiently for genuine, sincere signals of interest on her part. The dilemma engendered a perverse kind of conspiracy upon his ego. For a man's ego is far more fragile than a common hen's egg. And once the shell fractures, it's twice as messy.

Ironically, without such bloated self-aggrandizement most men could accomplish nothing worthwhile. And wise women have known this great flaw of the male of the species. He thinks more of himself than he deserves. Yet sympathetic women give some men more credit than they are due. This game of deception gives both genders certain false powers for better or worse.

Thus, men become slaves to their own egos and in rising to the heightened image they perceive of themselves, some become better men. Others suffer ignoble falls from grace from which even more ludicrous dreams become a prop.

Aeneas sensed acutely that Lavinia was photogenic. He made a carefully constructed series of advances, which they had agreed from the outset, about her modeling for him. He told her that she was stuck on the wrong end of the camera. To reposition would be profitable downstream. And help her empathize with her subjects when she controlled the shutter. He proposed that she build a compelling portfolio of her work to demonstrate mastery of a range of photographic techniques and creative talents.

He was surprised to find in her an almost inexplicable shyness originating not from insecurity, which she had never known in great abundance. Instead, she seemed merely not to think of herself as extraordinary. Either relatively more or less attractive from day to day. And impatient with any point of view that differed from her harsh and highly critical assessment of her image. She was skeptical of all flattery unless it was connected to her work or intellectual powers. And to these she seemed genuinely receptive and sometimes quietly hurt by unintended and often unspoken, but incorrectly implied, criticism.

Despite the Uptown veneer, she was a sensitive soul at heart. Strong when the whole world seemed bursting at the seams. And tearful unexpectedly over matters that to him seemed mere trivialities of life.

Together, they made a well-balanced team both during and after business hours. Her art in more practical and everyday business dealings proved a boon to the studio. Her proficiency at selling his photography of Bourbon Street brought him much needed immediate new business.

Single businessmen or tourists in particular were unable or unwilling to resist her appealing, respectful presentations about the background or techniques or subtle natural and architectural idiosyncrasies that art buyers love to hear. Many sales concluded with dinner invitations to fine French Quarter restaurants, which she inevitably declined with a grace that can come only from practice.

Lavinia cheerfully and with a warm smile regaled each visitor exiting without a purchase in the great Southern retail tradition: "You all come back, now. Hear?"

Many of them did return and bought photography and became regular customers. Unafraid to work long hours, including evenings and weekends, she demonstrated true entrepreneurial spirit and imagination. Because she owned a piece of this business, which was not given to her, like nearly everything else.

She drafted a marketing plan, which proposed advertising, publicity and social events to promote the studio. New signage was ordered.

Quotes were underway for freshly re-painting the studio's exterior according to the strict color code self-imposed by residents and shop owners in the Quarter. The display window was rearranged to become more inviting. They installed a toll-free telephone number.

Her pride showed in her work. And her social contacts and her father's business connections began to pay handsome dividends, too. As people in high places began to pop into the shop to peruse the work of Aeneas Jam. Gradually, he raised his prices and was compelled to spend more time shooting and developing film leaving the business management of the studio in her capable hands.

She opened new lines of credit through her contacts at the Whitney Bank and refinanced his business debt at significantly lower interest rates saving the studio much unnecessary financial overhead. Urgent calls from impolite and impatient creditors became less frequent and then disappeared altogether.

A new ability to focus upon his own photography and the spiritual lift that she brought when they worked together in the studio enabled him to produce his best creative work. Her arrival heralded a creative renaissance in the photographer. He began to experiment with new lighting and lenses that were unaffordable previously.

"When will our contract come back from the attorneys?" he asked.

"It's on daddy's desk. He is reviewing it. And wants to talk it over with you. Man to man," she replied.

"When? The whole legal review process seems to be taking foheveh."

"In just a day or two."

"Fine. I just don't want to walk too fah down the primrose path on a vehbal agreement. And get in too deep without a written document."

"I understand, Jack. I'll set-up an appointment with Ida for you and daddy in his office. Ida keeps his appointment book."

"Don't schedule it foh tomorrow mohning. We have the Storyville Old Style Beeh photo shoot."

"I know. I already blocked it off."

Storyville Old Style Draft Beer was the first paying photo shoot to emerge from an advertising agency that worked for Lavinia's father.

Storyville Beer was one of the agency's new clients. They wanted sepia shots of a nineteenth century beauty, dressed tastefully but somewhat provocatively, in the style of E.J. Bellocq. For new beer bottle labels and a new regional advertising campaign. To send six-packs and cases leaping off grocers' shelves into shopping carts throughout the South.

The partners agreed with the agency to handle the photography project in trade for creative ads that featured his work in print medea predominantly targeted for tourists and affluent residents of Uptown New Orleans.

They stayed to set-up lighting and props late the evening before the photo shoot that would follow in the morning attended by the agency creative directors and the client. All sides consented to Lavinia posing as the model after reviewing some black-and-white head shots that Aeneas had produced. They agreed to set-up meticulously as prescribed by the graphic designer's thumbnail layouts so that the client and agency people would not be kept waiting.

In fact, it was Lavinia's idea to take some Polaroid snapshots of her in costume the night before the photo session so that adjustments to the setting, camera angles, lighting and poses for the model would be tested in advance.

They had set the studio with many plush symbols of decadent sensuality reminiscent of Storyville's brothels in their heyday. An overstuffed, antique, French couch. A gilt mirror. A large parlor palm. A hurricane lantern. An oil painting of the Riverboat, Robert E. Lee. With decadent, almost funereal, silken drapes in the background.

Designed to coax beer-drinking Southern gentlemen into buying six-packs and cases of Storyville Draft for consumption when they golfed, fished, barbecued, played softball, and watched college and professional sports on the idiot box.

The tagline written by the ad agency for the product was:
QUENCH YOUR THIRST FOR LIFE.
WITH STORYVILLE OLD STYLE DRAFT.

She emerged from the dressing room in 19th century clothing, which was abundant but utterly provocative. Evoking the sensational qualities of her beauty. As he suspected, the camera loved her, which was no great shock since the cameraman was mad for her. Her radiant coquettish smile almost struck him senseless as he peered through the viewfinder.

"I feel pretty strange in these clothes," she said.

"Be beguiling," he suggested. "But let's not make the wives, who buy beeh foh their husbands, too jealous. Let's go foh simple classic   beauty."

"Hey, do you think I could have kept the wolf from the door turning a trick or two. In Storyville back in the good old days?"

"The best thing about the good old days is that they're gone," said Aeneas. "Please make yourself comfohtable on the couch."

"Daddy warned me about men like you," she said feigning Southern innocence. He surprised her by shooting this pose while lights blazed.

"Okay. Left leg up. Hand on your knee. No, the otheh hand. Shouldehs back. Head up. Look straight ahead. A little defiance. But not too brazen. Good. That's it," Aeneas said.

He took the Polaroid and then adjusted some studio lights casting an unwanted shadow.

"This time, show me Storyville. With bedroom eyes. And see how fah we can push it," he said.

She instinctively produced the expression he sought and it seemed to work.

"Excellent," he said. "That's what I want."

He captured her with a click of the shutter. Then he shot profiles of her lounging on the couch. He had planned to process the film to evoke sepia tones reminiscent of the photography of Bellocq's era. And just the right touch for the old style, draft beer label.

Lavinia looked stunningly sensual. They tried other classical poses and photos. The animal grace emanating from her stirred him. Her physical presence, at times, nearly overwhelmed him. She graciously accepted his direction as she posed.

He told her that she looked lovely. He moved around her clicking the shutter in search of every possible new perspective.

Then he abandoned the Polaroid and considered, as she looked so compelling here and now, that he might actually be able to make the shoot now. And surprise the client with more finished black-and-white prints.

Aeneas was hungry for her. He wanted to capture the artistry of the supple curves of her body. To affirm the essence of her beauty. She showed becoming poise and discipline. Each click of the shutter became a kiss. A meeting of her beauty in his eyes.

He felt compelled to touch her. He simply had to bring himself nearer to this source of loveliness that engulfed his consciousness. His touches lingered as he directed her. His instruction became rather more commanding. She quietly responded with astonishing instinct as he photographed. Presenting humility amid gentility.

Her long chestnut hair hung loosely down naturally drawing the eye to the sensuous décolletage framed by her tresses. He noticed the shadow of her full breasts beneath her thin creamy cotton chemise.

"You look pehfectly seductive, my deah," he affirmed, clicking the shutter repeatedly.

She possessed not only the tranquil spirit of a mystic. But also vulnerability. Her depth of substance gave the full effect of an aura, a mantle to her photos. She *was* utterly radiant.

Her loveliness performed a silent coup. At that point the will of Aeneas Jam seemed to belong as much to her as to himself. Desire for her built within him. Until, like spring floodwater spilling over a *levee*, he bent down. Looking into her gentle inviting brown eyes. And he warmly, sensually kissed her.

She did not speak. Or show objection. But rather appeared to seek more of their intimacy. As Aeneas took in with his eyes her long slender legs stretched upon the couch. Her lovely breasts tugged at the full folds of the bodice. He kissed her again with more authority. Almost as if he owned her.

"Am I to be your harlot?" she asked with a gentle smile.

"You are my Creole lady," he returned. "And every propeh Creole lady has a little of the hahlot in her."

Symphony Fantastique of Berlioz played upon the stereo. And then Aeneas experienced her sweet, Southern, sensual opulence.

            Though
            the music
            was
            a symphony
            in his soul
            he was
            whistling
            Dixie.
            * * *

CHIMERA II:
The Sack of Troy

"You must escape, son of the goddess. You must save yourself from these flames. The enemy is master of the walls and Troy is falling from her highest pinnacle . . . Look for a great city to   establish after long wanderings across the sea."
— *The Aeneid, Book II*

High Cotton

By his vision and labors, Andrew Jackson Palmer became a rich, self-made man. Living proof that the American Dream could be realized. Early in life he discovered his uncommon personal powers. Raw talent which, like sugar cane or a barrel of crude oil, he refined into a commodity in demand. Pulled up by his own bootstraps. Ever a realist.

He graduated *summa cum laude* from Tulane. An All-American receiver, he caught the winning touchdown pass in the final minute of the Tulane-LSU game in the Sugar Bowl in 1940. A fiercely loyal Greenie. Who sometimes drank to excess at frat parties.

In World War II he rose to Commander of a destroyer in the Pacific. Decorated with medals. Once he nearly drowned when his ship was torpedoed. Forced to jump from the flaming vessel into the cruel sea. Went down for what could well have been the last time. "This is it," he thought. Then struggled to find a lifesaving rope. Unwilling to meet his Maker just yet.

The Navy dried him off, assigned him a new uniform, put a new medal on it and sent him back out to sea on another battleship to confront the enemy. And he emerged from the Big One a true war hero.

On the GI Bill, he studied at the University of Virginia to graduate among the top of his class with an MBA. A hardworking and diligent student. Respected for intellectual strength by classmates. He had a flare for business. And a taste for bourbon.

Andrew's father owned some swampland – a few hundred square miles – near Baton Rouge. A widely derided acquisition during his lifetime. Andrew's father was a respected but rather modest success in supplying oil field equipment to pioneer, coonass oilmen.

When he died, he left Andrew the land and the business. The former on the Tuscaloosa Trend. Beneath which much natural gas was discovered.

Andrew pumped the royalties into the production supply company along with his business acumen. Palmer Production Supply rose to become one of Louisiana's major oilfield equipment companies. Making Andrew a millionaire many times over by the time he was thirty.

Having built his Fortune, he decided to marry a fine, cultured, New Orleans debutante named Arabella, who came from "old money."
Her father was a senior executive at the Whitney Bank and was active in the Mysticke Krewe of Comus.

Andrew and his wife honeymooned in Savannah, Georgia – a jewel of a city. Which Andrew once said resembled New Orleans. Except that Savannah was smaller and cleaner. Their trip to Savannah was one of the best parts of the whole occasion.

Andrew and Arabella moved into a million-dollar Greek Revival on Millionaires Row near Audubon Park. Andrew bought a Rolls Royce Silver Shadow. And a summer home on Pass Christian on the Mississippi Gulf Coast. Which he always pronounced "Guff" with the "L" silent. A year later Arabella gave birth to a healthy baby girl whom they named Lavinia Savannah.

Arabella was a kind, gentle, loving mother. The little girl's hair blew like the golden reeds of a savannah at that age. Whenever she played in the sun upon the beach at Pass Christian. For a while they lived in quiet luxury.

But when life is overgenerous in matters of Fortune, it often recaptures the source of it in a sum zero game. Andrew once said he was almost afraid for every act of benevolent hap that had come his way, earned or undeserved. Because waiting in the wings in the drama were heartbreak and sorrow. And the greater the happiness, the deeper the sorrow. In the end it all balances even — more or less. Which meant to him that even as he stood at a pinnacle of his powers as a businessman, husband and father, he was sowing the first seeds of his own decline.

Such was the nature of life. Neither good nor bad, life was just a nice clean ellipse. A sum zero touched by the finger of God, the weight of which shaped an ellipse.

There was an upside to this brand of ultimate realism. Above all, Andrew was a realist blessed with vision and adequate talent to build foundations under his grand designs. And the upside was that nothing sorrowful, no matter how tragic, is permanent.

Life certainly isn't a straight line but is more like the stock market chart of a Fortune 500 Company, moving up to Olympian peaks and down to Stygian depths.

In every defeat is sown the seeds of a new victory, a resurrection or a renaissance. And in the history and religions of mankind, Andrew believed, one could see the great ancient ellipse, the sum zero. A twist away from infinity. Struggling for significance in a vast absurd universe.

One midsummer night after a party at their neighbors in Pass Christian, Arabella and Andrew had drunk a bit too much Dom Perignon.

She wanted Andrew to walk with her by the sea. And perhaps take a dip, as well, in the warm Gulf beneath the galaxies of the clear, ebony sky of the Deep South.

When Andrew stated his regrets and preference for sleep, she changed into her bathing suit and went for a swim alone. Leaving her husband asleep in their summer home.

Early the next morning surf fishermen found her body left gently by the Gulf tide upon the sugar white sand beach. Lavinia was only two when her mother died and, hence, had no memory of her.

Andrew then began to drink to excess. He blamed her death upon himself. Only bourbon, he believed, would hold insanity at bay. The mad torment and bitter wrenching of his soul. Because Arabella was the only woman he was born to marry. Ultimately, his work became his salvation. After Arabella's death, Andrew worked from dawn to dusk. He was a quietly driven man and this greatest sorrow of his life fed his ambition and fueled a magnificent career.

Andrew's office comprised an entire floor high atop One Shell Square on St. Charles Avenue downtown. From this *campus martius*, his lofty corporate fortress, he oversaw the French Quarter, the Dome and the River. On a clear day one easily could see Lake Pontchartrain.

He dined at the Boston Club, named after the card game, and International House. He had friends in high places in Baton Rouge. A stone's throw from the political power structure of Louisiana.

An intense, tireless man, he was devoted absolutely to his business and considered it his responsibility to return his good Fortune to New Orleans. He was resolutely dutiful to his beautiful young daughter, who was his only real personal vulnerability. Although he exercised enviable power in New Orleans both personally and socially, he possessed no such claims over his own daughter. Arabella's deliberate demeanor had passed onto Lavinia as a legacy.

Aeneas Jam to see Andrew Pahmeh," he said to the receptionist. A neatly dressed, attractive, younger gatekeeper. With dirty blonde hair who wore glasses. Svelte physique. Clothed for business head-to-toe with a hint of masculinity in a dark, conservative pinstripe suit. She gave him the once-over from top to bottom. A little sign on her desk said:

IDA.

Aeneas smiled at her pleasantly.

Mount Ida?

Dressed in a natty, three-piece suit that his mother had given to him as a going-away present from Filenes Basement in Boston. The receptionist accompanied him to the oak doors upon which in bold gold letters read:

ANDREW J. PALMER
PRESIDENT & CEO

"Go right in," Ida said. "Mr. Palmer is expecting you."

Aeneas pushed open a heavy door to find Andrew sitting behind a dark, hardwood, antique desk with many drawers and brass handles. A man-of-power's desk.

"What do you know, Jack Jam?" Andrew said, standing to offer a crushing handshake. Aeneas almost cried out from the agony of the grip. This particular question was asked often in New Orleans upon introductions. But he had neither a witty nor succinct immediate answer. Which Andrew awaited in the exchange.

"Life is a raft ride down a vast River of Fortune," Aeneas finally replied.

This *repartee* left Andrew slightly at a loss: he nodded quizzically and then smiled politely.

Andrew wore a pinstripe suit from Brooks Brothers. An Oxford cloth shirt with a button-down collar and burgundy print tie. He was in rugged physical condition from jogging daily in Audubon Park. Dark, gray, thinning hair. Broad, toothy smile.

"Nice pehspective of New Ohleans you have up here," Aeneas offered.

"I do enjoy the view of the tankers on the River. Many tankers on the River mean that business is good. Sit down, son," Andrew advised.

"Thank you, sih."

As usual, the letter "R" was heinously slaughtered in his self-conscious indigenous speech among Southerners. As Bostonians only recognized 25 letters of the alphabet. The letter "H" in dialogue improved upon any "R." Heeding Thoreau's unlaconic admonition from his cabin on Walden Pond: "Simplify! Simplify! Simplify!" Why thrace?

Andrew's Tulane BA and University of Virginia MBA hung in gilt frames upon his office wall. His framed Purple Heart garnished his diplomas. With its purple and gold ribbon, silver shield and golden profile of George Washington. Photo of Andrew in a Green Wave football uniform posed to catch the passed pigskin for a big gain.

The Wall Street Journal, Harvard Business Review and *Fortune Magazine* among business publications in a pile to one side of his credenza.
More photos of Arabella, little Lavinia and him. A Navy photo in bright white officer's garb with legions of medals. Photo of a racehorse named High Cotton. An old oil of the French Quarter before the Louisiana   Purchase.

A spacious sofa surrounded with rich, leather, big easy chairs. All of which focused upon an heirloom, cherry coffee table like those Aeneas had admired in antique shop windows on Royal Street. Obviously, Andrew was a man who attended the counsel of his advisors. Antique armoire converted to a wet bar. Banker's Club Bourbon and two crystal glasses awaited toasts of victory. Executive toilet adjacent to his suite. Andrew's own thunderbox on the 51st floor.

"Let me tell you why I've asked you to come here this morning," Andrew said becoming rather serious, indeed, almost grave.

"I assume that it concehns our fohmal pahtnehship agreement," Aeneas interrupted.

"Yes, but before we get into that -- Lavinia is obviously taken with you, Johnny."

"And so am I with her."

"For reasons that elude me."

"Well, I seem to have noticed that all straight men desihe your daughteh . . ."

"Her attractiveness to other men is no mystery, son. It's *her* attraction to *you* that I just can't begin to fathom."

"Oh, I see. Of course. I respect your candoh, sih."
The throat of Aeneas became bone-dry. He broke into a prolific sweat. And thrashed to loosen his tie in a neurotic panic.

"Your engagement came as sort of a surprise. Considering you aren't even divorced yet," Andrew stated firmly.

"That, sih, is simply a legal fohmality. With a waiting period defined by this quaint, ancient Napoleonic law. That you still have down here in Louisiana. Foh some odd reason."

"Like the Louisiana Purchase?"

"If you want to get technical."

"It is the custom here. And elsewhere, I'm told. For couples to wait until the ink dries on a divorce decree. Before they sign a new marriage license."

"I love your daughteh, sih. I want to marry her. With what remains of my broken heart. When fohmalities pehmit."

"You're rushing it."

"It's the real thing. We both know it. Waiting would only delay the inevitable. It would sehve no puhpose."

"Lavinia tells me that you take pretty fair pictures. In fact, she claims that you're the best photographer in New Orleans right now," Andrew said, turning his chair to gaze over the city.

"I am."

"Good. Glad to hear it. Because if you were to take care of my little girl, you'd need to make lots of money. I know that from experience."

"We shall live on profits from our studio."

"That won't be enough right now," Andrew said. "You'll need all the prosperity you can stand. Before you'll earn enough to keep Lavinia happy."

"I won't be poor forever. I'm a damn fine photographeh. I know my aht well. I love Liv. That's enough for us right now. I'll make it on my own. I have a promising future as an *ahtist*. Or if you prefeh, an *aesthete*."

"Is that so? *Artist?* Now, there's a career with a lifetime of financial security. And what the heck is an *aesthete?*"

"An aesthete is a person concerned with the intrinsic problem of the metaphysics of the beautiful."

"Oh, really? I may bust a gut laughing. Heck, son, you're every father's worst nightmare."

"Sih, I must say that I object to your tone of voice . . ."

"Lavinia has no concept of sacrifice. She is simply unpracticed in it. Do you think that love, by itself, can conquer all things?"

"That's not really a fair or kind question to ask someone in the predivohce stage of one's life, Mr. Pahmeh."

"Love hasn't saved you from divorce. Why would it save you now?"

"Love that is shared by two people can conqueh anything on eth. I believe that as a reflection of my optimism. Despite hahsh and painful pehsonal experience to the contrary. I know this is true."

"Son, love needs more help than most people can give it."

"She's crazy about me, sih. I can't explain to you why she is. I'm as suhprised as you are. Maybe more so. You'll have to ask her that yourself. Since we're being frank here. The timing foh the engagement is more her idea than mine."

"You're having second thoughts then?"

"Not about Lavinia. Not about us. Not one. Not foh one second. Am I making myself cleah?"

"So you would be prepared to wait. For the good of you both."

"I have already told her as much. You needn't convince me. Get her to buy it. I am a patient man."

"In my entire life I never thought she'd fall for a Yankee," Andrew asserted.

Respectful of his potential father-in-law, this comment infuriated Aeneas, who fought his own sentiments. He *hated* the Yankee appellation. He was a Bostonian and despite of lifetime of utter futility, a devoted Red Sox fan.

"I'm not exactly a pestilent beggah, sih."

"I sure do hope you ain't pestilent on top of being broke," Andrew said. "I always assumed she would marry an Uptown boy."

"She has met a lot of them, sih. Through deb balls and the like. As we say way down here in Dixieland, Lavinia doesn't seem to *cotton* to Uptown men. She finds them shallow, materialistic, egotistical and not pahticulahly smaht. Present company excluded, of course, sih. Which is why she broke off with that totally arrogant egomaniac, Pehcy Tuhneh."

"Percy is no fool, Johnny. He has a lot more to offer her than you."

"Oh really? Like what?"

"First off, he comes from a wealthy New Orleans family. His daddy owns car dealerships all over town. We're both well acquainted through Rex."

"So what? Lavinia isn't marrying Pehcy's fatheh."

"Secondly, Percy is well connected. He's plugged into capital. He has contacts. And he knows how to use them. He recommended my chief financial officer, Evan, who's sharp as a whip."

"Big deal. I know people . . ."

"Thirdly, he's making a good living. He's independently wealthy. He owns a home on Dumaine in the Quarter. He has money in the bank."

"I'm *independently* poor. I wohk hahd at it . . ."

"Fourthly, he has manners. Education. And culture. He's an active member of New Orleans society. And respects its traditions. Now, let's see. How does that stack up against you?"

"You underestimate me, sih . . ."

"Do you really want me to continue on the subject of Percy? Because I could go on. For quite a while, in fact. There's really no comparison from where I sit, Johnny."

"But Lavinia disagrees, doesn't she? I have been through this before. In Boston. Among people who underestimated me . . ."

"There's a lot to underestimate in you, son."

This comment touched ugly scars of deep and painful wounds.

"Well, sih, you weren't born wealthy. You're a self-made man. Risen from the middle class. If a son of a bitch like you can make it big-time and keep Lavinia's love, so can I."

Andrew smiled for the second time. A fleeting, involuntary smile.

"I don't know if your talent will make you wealthy. I don't even know if you're the best photographer in New Orleans. But I can make you a success. Or break you. However, I damn well please."

"What loving fatheh would not wish his daughteh every success?"

"My daughter is in a position *to marry* success."

"You know what I say? . . . Let's team up. Why not? Foh Liv's sake."

A long, uncomfortable silent period ensued.

"How would you like to become one of New Orleans' best upscale portrait photographers?" Andrew finally asked. "You already do a lot of portraits. Only of poor people on Bourbon Street. You're working the wrong end of the social spectrum. There's no money in it."

"I would consideh being locked into pohtraits of high society as hideously Philistine. I wouldn't wish it on my wohst enemy. Its challenge and creativity would be *severely limited*. It would lead to disgrace in the end. Foh what? To degrade my Muse to a whore?"

"You're from Boston. So you must know the paintings of John Singer Sargent."

"I saw them often at the Boston Museum of Fine Aht. In the Fens."

"His portraits in oil are magnificent. So are those of Velazquez. Rembrandt. Hans Holbein. Gainsborough. Sir Joshua Reynolds. Copley. And Cassatt. All world-class artists.

Each is immortal. And all painted portraits of high society. Museums are full of examples of such fine art."

"Yes, I see your point. But I can't picture that approach wohking foh me. Not in New Ohleans. Personally, I would rather die first. I mean, what a bore."

"You'd rather live on love? Be an *aesthete*? And photograph the reprobates, degenerates and miscreants of Bourbon Street? For *chickenshit*?"

"Yes, I'd *much* rather, sih. You see, I am an *ahtist*. Lavinia understands. But I can't seem to get this across to you. Aesthetics abound in simple life. *Simplex sigullum veri.* Simplicity is the seal of truth. Where the manifestation of beauty offers hope. Rather than skepticism."

"Your credit record is abysmal. I checked it. You owe money all over town. Not a penny in savings. No home. Your business is nearly bankrupt. Credit cards cancelled. Overdue on the rent. Creditors and the IRS are chasing after you, all worked up into a frenzy. Now, *you* want to marry *my* daughter. Work as an artist. And live on love. Come on, boy. It don't work that way. You must be realistic about your financial circumstances."

"Realism alone does not lead to progress. Vision does. And realism cehtainly accounts foh less in mattehs of the heart. Lavinia has every confidence, and so do I, that we will make a successful pahtnehship. Togetheh."

"I tried like heck to talk her out of *any* business deal, *at all*, with you. Of course, *you're* destined for better Fortune. As long as you're aligned with her. But don't you realize what a comedown it would be for *her*. That just wouldn't be right. She's used to better. *Much better*. I'm sorry if that hurts. But it's the God's honest truth."

"She loves my Yankee ass, sih. That must count foh something."

"It doesn't count for enough. Not with me. This is *my daughter* we're talking about here."

"It counts to her. And that's really all that mattehs."

"No one lives on love alone. Ask any broken-hearted bum on Camp Street. He'll tell you between swigs of cheap wine."

"I undehstand that it must be hahd foh a fatheh to be rational about the man his only daughteh wants to marry . . ."

"Listen, you do seem genuine. But love won't pay the rent. She'll get unhappy quick. And grow to resent you. I promise you, son. I'm telling it to you straight. The finances alone would ruin your marriage."

"I consideh my business in a turn-around. We're already beginning to experience it. Like a junk bond that is upgraded by Moody's or Standard & Poor's . . ."

"With the emphasis on the Po'."

"That is unkind, sih."

"For the sake of argument. Let me play devil's advocate. And share with you an idea that would *guarantee* you success in your business. In your own line of work. The profession for which you were born."

"I'm listening."

"New Orleans needs a good, upscale, portrait photographer. I know them all. And there isn't a really good one in the bunch. Their prices are exorbitant. And they're slow as cold molasses."

"Yes, I know."

"You could handle only portraits of the well-to-do. Krewe kings and queens. Debutantes. Mardi Gras Balls. Executive portraits. Uptown family portraits. Catch my drift? Make 'em look good. And pay a premium for the justice that you do to them."

"Even at the expense of the injustice that I do to myself."

"Christ, you oughta be rich with your talents. There's a strange justice in that. Wouldn't you say so?"

"My business outlook is promising. Headed foh an uptuhn. But the sooneh the betteh. If you think it will make a difference in Lavinia's happiness, well then, I must be all foh it. And so I am."

"Now, you're talking. The beauty of it is this, son. I can put you in touch with the right people. That's the real world. For starters talk to this friend of mine. He's principal of the biggest ad agency in New Orleans. He's done one hell of a job for my company. I'll give you the ad budget you need through Lavinia. In my tax bracket I can always use another write-off."

Aeneas scanned the card. Then he tucked it away. Into his thin, dusty, torn, trampled billfold devoid of greenback currency. Hoping soon to boost earning power sufficiently to acquire a new wallet.

"Next, you need to upgrade your office space. Where are you now?"

"Decatuh Street."

"De-catostreet? Jingo's crickets! . . . Here are the keys to some prime French Quarter office space. On Bourbon Street near Esplanade. Quaint. More suitable for your new clientele," Andrew said, dropping a set of keys into the hands of Aeneas. "I own the building. Lavinia can help you set up your new digs."

"That's really quite generous of you, sih."

"It's business. And we're partners. And this turnaround had better be highly profitable. Because I don't buy turnaround businesses that stay dogs. I either convert them quickly into cash cows. Or I sell 'em. And move on. Understand? I am a believer in the power of leverage."

"I understand."

"Now, you'll own 33 1/3% of this highly profitable business . . ."

"One-*thihd*? But I *founded* the business."

"Son, you can have it all, if you want it. All 100%. Just walk out this office door. And never look back."

Aeneas stood up to leave.

"Jingo's crickets! Sit your butt down, son. I'm not finished yet."

Aeneas relaxed.

"Listen. It's okay with me if you walk. You just cut me a check right now for Lavinia's investments to date. All of which represent my money. And total a tad over twenty grand. But let's round it down to twenty grand. And call it square."

"Sih, I don't have twenty grand. I don't even have $20."

"Hah. You know what? That's all right then. We can begin installment payments. I can offer you, with your credit rating, an interest rate of only 23.9% *per annum*. Over, say, ten years? How does that sound to you?"

"Like usury."

"Then *do the deal*, Johnny."

"You don't give me much choice."

"Now don't be gettin' squirrelly on me. This deal is just chickenshit to me. But it means a lot to Lavinia. And 100% of a bankrupt business ain't worth a crap. You've got no capital to turn it around. And no credit to get capital. So there you are. What'll it be? 100% of nothing, which according to my calculations, is zero. Or a one-third owner of a booming business."

"You're asking foh 67%?"

"That's right. Split right down the middle between my daughter and me. 50-50. Or we each own 33 1/3%. And the dynamics of that are as they should be, Johnny. Fully leveraged. Just as I like it. "

"Why would my new minority ownership, in a business that I founded, represent good business dynamics foh me, Mr. Pahmeh?"

"Because as long as you have one ally between Lavinia and me, you'll control the company. We both love Lavinia. And she loves us. But if you cross us both, which I'm sure you'll avoid, we could step in together and protect our investment. Does that make sense to you now?"

"I'm *undeh*-whelmed, sih."

"Then what do you want, Johnny?"

"Foh stahtehs, your pahtnership fee. Of $12,500. In cash."

"*Is* that it?"

"The splits go this way. You and Liv each get 30%. And I earn 40%. I did *found* the company."

"Is that *it*?"

"I want debt forgiveness on what you paid in so fah. So I'm not your slave. And can opt out."

"Is *that* it?"

"Yes. That's it."

"Fine, fine. You drive a hard bargain, Johnny. For someone who dudn't own squat."

"Thank you, sih."

"Well, we're business partners now. Use your new capital wisely. If you need more camera equipment, buy it. And be sure to get the best. Jingo's crickets, go get yourself a new Hasselblad, if you all want one. I don't care. Have the bills sent to me. Get whatever it takes to do the job right. Anything worth doin' is worth doin' right," Andrew said. "Now, bust your ass. And make me a genius for accepting the risk."

"I shall."

"I didn't mean to come down too hard on you, son. Lavinia, well, she's kind of a blind spot for me. She's everything that means anything. Even with all this. Without her I'm nothin'. She's all I got left of Arabella. And everything else is just bull. In the end only love makes any difference."

"Love always seems to win, sih. Afteh all is said and done."

"You ain't the son I had in mind, Johnny. But you'll have to do. I'll have my attorneys draw up the final papers for your signature. According to the terms we have agreed upon today."

"Sounds fair enough."

"Just two things, now. I want you to give only the best of care to Lavinia. And quit sirrin' me to death."

"I will do my best, I promise, to justify all of the pehsonal and professional good faith you've shown. And I'll try not to call you 'sih' very often, if you'll quit 'sonning' me befohe my time."

"That's our second deal today, Johnny. Now, I want you to meet some future clients over lunch. Would you prefer to dine at International House? Or the Boston Club?"

"The Boston Club."

"I thought so. Now, just one more thing," Andrew said. "You'll manage better if you show more respect for the letter 'R' when you speak to New Ohleanians."

"I have this small speech impediment. When it comes to the letter 'ah.'"

"You all are hoitin' my ears, son."

>Guarded
>to lean hahd
>upon his
>"Rs,"
>he was
>the only
>true Bostonian
>in the
>Boston Club.
>* * *

Alligator Soup

On the walls along the entrance a long line of framed logos of clients read like a *Who's Who* of New Orleans' business.

As soon as Aeneas walked into the advertising agency, he felt at home.

Alligator Advertising wore an external shell of professional conservatism beneath which he sensed a core of jocularity careful to contain itself. It was almost as if the agency were at a cocktail party at the Plimsoll Club with an outrageous joke it was afraid to tell.

Aeneas liked the ambiance, which seemed germinal to creativity.
People displayed their creative work on their office walls. Photography, graphics, posters, ads as well as affirmations of industry and public acceptance of their work in certificates, diplomas and awards.

The account executives were attired in business suits. The creative people were informally fashionable. The two factions seemed gripped in light-hearted but competitive banter brought on by virtue simply of the dichotomy of their functions. The account executives seemed somehow unmistakably Republican in their demeanor. The creative people seemed to give the impression they hadn't registered to vote.

The ad agency manifested a rich intellectual atmosphere with an abundance of burgeoning plants growing like ideas hanging suspended in the halls and office windows.

Intermittent laughter emanated from sundry offices. Humor inextricably married to the birth of advertising. The agency could boast of a rare collection of wit and talent. Which never strayed too far from a resignation that advertising was ultimately a business as well as a creative outlet.

"Jack Jam to see Chahles Chahbonnet," Aeneas aennounced.

"Raht this way, Mr. Jam. He is expectin' you all," the receptionist replied.

Aeneas followed her unable to tear his eyes off the woman's bikini line beneath her tight skirt.

A strand of a bra revealed through a luminescent blouse. Her waist was as trim as it could be.

"Mr. Jam is here for his eleven o'clock with you," she said.

A charming gentleman with *café au lait* skin donning a suit straight from the display window of Rubenstein Brothers. An incredibly youthful face. Almost childlike. In his mid-thirties, perhaps.

Wearing a bow tie, he pulled a pipe from his mouth with his left hand. He blew out an aromatic wisp of smoke. And twisted his mouth into a broad smile.

Then he threw out his right hand and said, "Charles Charbonnet. A pleasure to meet you. Thanks, Cassie."

The receptionist smiled and asked, "Can I get you some coffee, Mr. Jam?"

"Please."

"Pure. Or chicory."

"Chicory."

"Two Louisiana crudes, please," Charles said. "Cream and sugar?"

"Black."

"Mine, too."

Cassie left with a genuinely friendly smile having taken Aeneas from the Chaos of the outside world and performed with aplomb connecting him with Charles.

"Sit down, please," said Charles, smiling.

His hand gestured to an empty chair. His office was alive with a tasteful, intriguing collection of old advertising posters. They contrasted sharply with samples of his ads posted on brown corkboard. He had won many awards for his work.

Aeneas was impressed that the agency had apparently offered him their ringer.

"The ad agency has a nice feel to it," Aeneas said.

"We're the biggest and, more than likely, the best agency in New Orleans," Charles said confidently. "But we work as if we were still up-and-coming. Which, of course, we are. Despite our accomplishments and long standing in the community. We get the job done. And we have some fun, too."

Aeneas was always amused by the stress placed by business people in New Orleans on having fun. In the Northeast people always wanted you to know that they died a thousand deaths on your behalf.

"The agency comes highly recommended," Aeneas said.

"Why, thank you. That's always nice to hear," Charles said. "And we intend to immortalize you."

"Haha."

Cassie arrived with two cups of chicory. Aeneas searched the office wall for a framed diploma.

"I see that you graduated from the University of Pennsylvania, Chahles? In 1974?"

"Yes."

"From the School of Communications?"

"Undergrad. Then from the Wharton School in 1976."

"I'm impressed. Are you *from* the Nohtheast?"

"Hell no. I froze over six winters in the City of Brotherly Love. I understand you're from Boston."

"You aren't going to ask me to say, 'Pahk the cah in the Hahvid Yahd.'"

"Not redundantly."

"What a relief."

Aeneas couldn't detect much of a deep Southern or New Orleans' dialect anywhere in his speech.

"Your photography for the Storyville Old Style Draft Beer account was excellent. The client loved it. They experienced a sharp up-tick in sales. So they want to expand the campaign. To a national reach. Which we love to hear."

"I would ratheh be lucky than smaht."

"Now about the advertising for your studio . . . We read the marketing plan written by Miss Palmer?"

"Yes, she wanted to be here. But was called out on a modeling assignment with Sibyl Helene, the women's boutique Uptown. And we had a schedule conflict."

"The plan was well devised."

"She is a dangerous woman, Chahles. Brains and beauty."

"Exclusive portraits, I understand."

"Yes. Mostly. Now."

"You'll have to do one for me, my wife and my little girls."

"I'd be delighted."

"The plan indicated that your reach is primarily local. Targeting Uptown."

"Yes."

"And you need a new logo."

"Yes."

"New stationery and business cards."

"Definitely."

"Brochures. Transit signs on the St. Charles Avenue streetcar. Well placed billboards. Ads in the Sunday *Times-Picayune*. Go four-color in *New Orleans* magazine. *Playbill* theatre and symphony programs. I've put together a schedule for you. Your budget is certainly adequate."

"It all sounds good," Aeneas said, reviewing the Gantt Chart of the medea schedule.

"We'll keep it strictly Uptown. Feature your photography in every ad. Keep the copy simple. Dignified. Upscale."

"Fine."

"Time goes by. The birdies sing. The music plays. And you're immortal."

"Ah, the poweh of a few well-placed symbols. It always amazes me. Suddenly, I'm both rich and famous. Until your bill arrives, eh? Then I'm only famous."

"The invoicing, I'm told, is going to Mr. Palmer's company. Directly. Is that correct?"

"Why, yes. It certainly is."

"The Storyville Draft Beer launch was a homer. So the agency plans to farm out more of our photography to you."

"Oh?"

"Yes, we prefer to do business with people who give their business to us."

"I certainly appreciate that," Aeneas said. "Connections are everything in this town. More so than any otheh town I've lived in."

"Connections run New Orleans. Short of our advertising, no better way to do business exists in this town. We've got some powerful connections, too. Hell, we ought to. We've been in this business in New Orleans since God was a boy."

"What exactly is your title here at the agency, Chahles?"

"Ah. Here's my business card."

Charles presented the card. Which he pronounced "cod."

Nicely designed and printed, Aeneas read:

ALLIGATOR ADVERTISING
CHAS. E. CHARBONNET, MBA
PRESIDENT.

Raising his eyebrows, Aeneas smiled and stuffed the business card into his ancient, dusty, disintegrating wallet.
"You hungry?" Charles asked.
"Sure am."
"How about lunch at Antoine's?"
"Sounds good."
"Have you tried their specialty?"
"What is it?"
"Alligator soup."

Suddenly,
everyone
is throwing
rose petals
before my
footfalls.
* * *

Elysian Fields

No other options existed for Aeneas at this juncture, except to face the family priest prior to nuptials. Lavinia and her father were lifelong Catholics.

Aeneas tried every conceivable blockade and defensive tactic and his alternatives simply vanished.

The concept inspired outright dread in his mind. In New England he had been raised forthrightly Methodist.

He believed that one need not unleash legions of holy intermediaries, a worldwide bureaucracy built upon untold wealth, to keep God from a sound night's sleep with holy petitions.

But love can drive a man to desperate deeds in its name. And this meeting counted as a sound measure of the outer limits of love's divine power.

Charles attempted to tutor him the previous night in the fine points of Catholic communication.

Wary of the damage that could be done in God's name, Aeneas listened sagaciously to the experience of Charles, gained at the expense of years of training in Christian Doctrine.

The appointment with Father Latinus was set for 9:00 am sharp at the rectory of The Church of the Blessed Virgin Mary of the Immaculate Conception on Elysian Fields Avenue.

Unfortunately, Charles' tutelage had kept the men out until daybreak.

Incredible discussions of theology and theogony had gone on for hours. Facilitated by the drinking of much red wine at Napoleon House.

When Lavinia pounded on the door of Aeneas at 8:30, his head jack-hammered unmercifully, clouding his consciousness like a bale of cotton.

"Jackie, sweetheart, we're late to meet Father Latinus," she said nervously. "It's time to wake up."

"Join me in the sack, Liv," he mumbled sleepily. "Do we *have* to go?"

"I don't *have* to do anything. Except die. And make love to you."

"Is it really time to see the priest? Already, Dreamface?"

"Rise and shine, darlin'."

"Some pahts are more ready to rise than othehs."

"Would you, please . . ."

"I'll mend your 'would' with a Jackscrew."

Lavinia laughed, disrobed and jumped into his bed. Unavoidably, they made love madly like a betrothed couple.

When Lavinia first sensed that time had darted on the wings of a dove, it was 9:30. Whereupon, she launched Aeneas out of the sack with a potent push. To send him sprawling to the floor beside the bed. Looking up, he read the ragged tag beneath the box spring:

DO NOT REMOVE.
BEAUTY REST MATTRESS CORP.
TROY, NEW YORK.

Rip off the tag. Sacking the sack of Troy. What a fiasco! Can celibate Father Latinus conceive? How pre-nuptial desires may detain conjoined couplets?

Aeneas telephoned Father Latinus to explain that they were running late. Attempting thusly to score few papal points for the Protestant.

"Hello, Fatheh Latinus?" Aeneas said in a raspy voice. He hoped that signs of hangover were sparse and obscure.

"Yes."

"This is Jack Jam. Hey, Notre Dame sure looked good against those Puhdue Boilehmakehs yestehday, didn't they?"

"I don't follow sports. Didn't you have an appointment here this morning?"

"Uh, well, yes. That's why I'm calling. We're on our way. But running a tad behind," he said, pinching Lavinia's sweet, little, naked bottom playfully.

Suppressing a major guffaw and the gaffe that would follow, Aeneas said, "We have become rather consumed by the uh . . . Wholly Spirit. And it's come to give us pause . . . Pausanias, as it were . . ."

"When shall I expect you then?"

"We're on our way. Your rectory is on Elysian Fields?"

"Yes. Near the cemeteries."

"Must be like having an office in your own back yahd."

"When should I expect you?"

"Half an hour. Tops. Excuse me, Fatheh. Which ordeh are you?"

"Dominican."

"The Dogs of God."

"Pardon?"

"Dominican. God's Dogs . . . Please fohgive our tahdiness."

"See you soon."

The pair rushed to the rectory on Elysian Fields in a dazed, disheveled state. In an ungodly downpour. Which Aeneas read as a harbinger.

The rectory, a barren and humble ancient place, reminded Aeneas of the movie, *Boys Town,* starring Pat O'Brien.

Much dark wood and religious artifacts, the symbolism of which largely escaped Aeneas. Many bloody and morbid scenes in paintings hung in ornate gilt frames. The crucifixion. Deaths of martyrs. Interventions by angels. A modest sculpture of Laocoon and sons entwined by two serpents.

Holy card stands filled with touching pictures of the saints lined the corridor. Christ beamed down upon them as they awaited Father Latinus. Hoping for the best, she blessed herself with holy water from a marble font on the wall.

Hung-over, Aeneas did not feel 100%. Father Latinus was a pleasant, direct and courteous Italian in his mid-thirties. He wore the cleric's coal black uniform with its stiff little hoarfrost collar. His black shoes with a nice clean sheen. Everything about his garb was black-and-white. Which was how Aeneas presumed the priest saw the outside world.

The priest spoke with affection toward Lavinia and called her a child of the Catholic Church. Blessed with a rich life of faith. Which deeply moved Aeneas.

"So tell me about your Christian life, Lavinia," the priest inquired.
Aeneas admired his beautiful fiancée sitting prim and cheerfully articulate, answering the questions of the Dominican with measured, cautious and intelligent responses.

The alimentary canal of Aeneas croaked in protest as she spoke.

He twisted in his chair, unable to control his groaning gut.

He apologized intermittently for his uncommonly obnoxious but involuntary condition.

Then the priest turned with a bright hunger in his squinted, ice blue eyes.

"My son, have you ever had any occasion when you were engaged and did not go through with it?" asked Father Latinus.

"Absolutely not, sih," Aeneas said politely.

He should have truncated his reply. Charles had advised factual brevity with priests and adversarial attorneys. But Aeneas rambled on unfortunately to add: "But there was one time when I went through with it. When I wish that I hadn't."

Lavinia buried her head in her hands.

"I see," said the priest.

"Out of a sense of duty and devotion . . ." the syntax of Aeneas dispersed into absolute nonsense. "And so on."

"You mean, my son, that you have divorced previously?"

"Actually, sih, I never did quite consummate the divohce," Aeneas advised.

"You're still *married* then?" the priest said with a bite in the observation.

"You've got me on a technicality. Not much gets by you. I can see that."

"I assume you do intend to remedy that one small detail."

"Uh, yes, sih. Absolutely. I don't put much stock in polygamy. . ."
Lavinia couldn't believe it.

"I'm anti-polygamy . . . An anti-polygamist . . . If it please the chuhch."

"He's waiting for the *waiting period* to expire," Lavinia clarified.

"That's right," Aeneas replied. "As soon as the waiting period expires, I'm free. To wed this babe of God."

"And the waiting period expires soon, I trust?"

"A matter of weeks. Or months. I really need to check. Can I get back to you on that one, Fatheh Latinus? I don't want to mislead you."
Just then, one of Aeneas Jam's contact lenses, unforgiving of his bloodshot eyes, flung itself into the Hereafter.

The blessed lens bounced off the table, landing with a clink on the spotless hardwood floor of the rectory. Muddled, due to hangover, he crawled humbly on hands and knees in search of this instrument of vision.

Aeneas attempted gamely, in what must have appeared almost as an act of contrition, to field the priest's thorny questions from under the table. From whence he perceived an involuntary shot up Lavinia's dress. Who in the rush to Elysian Fields did not sport undergarb.

FOR THE LOVE OF GOD!

The priest's many barbed questions drove him mad. Queries only a celibate man might ask in an extreme state of repression. Presumptuous. Much too personal. Condescending. Perverse even. From an authority that Aeneas did not recognize or seek.

In his Protestant soul he protested. With riot and siege.

"Were you married in the Catholic Church previously?" the priest persisted with the interrogation. As if first-degree murder had been committed.

This was a key point of the Inquisition, as Charles had advised.

The priest would have preferred that Aeneas proffer an answer in the negative.

For the unholy life of Aeneas, he could not remember the tutored answer.

"Let me see," Aeneas began.

"Was the cross on the altar occupied or not?" Lavinia interceded.

"By God, I think it was."

"Which parish?" the priest asked.

"I have not the first idea of the name of the chuhch. They all sound so similah. BVM . . . Immaculate Conception. Something, something, something."

"That's this church, my son."

"See? I rest my case. Not too original."

Still engaged in his crusade for the renegade lens, he bumped his elbow roundly against the stout leg of the table.

Aeneas shouted: "GOD'S TEETH! Fohgive me, Fatheh Latino. I took a wicked whack to my funny bone. On your ancient table. I know not what I do. Saints be to God."

"I will need to talk to the parish priest. Can you speak with your wife? And ask in which parish you were married?" queried Father Latinus.

In his Protestant heart of hearts, with his exploding intestines, blind eye and nearly broken elbow, the request of the bachelor Father did not seem Christian.

"It was in New England. But my wife and I aren't on speaking terms, Fatheh . . . so that's a non-stahteh we have here," Aeneas said.

"Can you ask her parents?" the Dominican pressed.

"If I'm not speaking to her, why would I be speaking to them?"

"I can't help you until I know which church," the priest said firmly.

"Lavinia, if you marry this man, you should be aware that you will be ex-communicated."

"Ex-communicated?" Aeneas asked incredulously. "Foh what? Marrying me? An act of pure love? And that's a hellenic immortal sin, is it?"

"What can we do about it?" Lavinia asked intelligently.

"Get his marriage annulled," the priest said to her. As if he weren't there. *Persona non gratis.* To Father Latinus.

"Null and void it?" Aeneas asked.

"You both will need to attend a weekend retreat. To work out some other religious matters," Father Latinus explained icily.

The abdomen of Aeneas played again like a mad bassoonist. And he arose like a purblind beggar for a pittance from under the table.

Staring at the priest with his one good eye. Having abandoned all hope of correcting his vision. Because of his lost weapon of acuity. His sacrificial lens.

"About how much would the chuhch chahge for this?" Aeneas asked.

"Is it very expensive? I mean, I don't know if I can affohd a costly or time-consuming religious retreat right now. As much as I might need and want one. With my divohce proceedings. And legal bills. And all."

"It's free, my son," Father Latinus said, rolling his eyes at her.

"I see," said visually impaired Aeneas, peering at the holy man with a pitiful glare.

His abdomen utterly bellowed.

"I wohk on weekends."

"In your case, we may require two or three such weekends," the priest surmised. "Possibly more."

"I don't suppose that a nice donation to the chuhch from her fatheh would help all this move along, would it?"

"It certainly would *not*."

Aeneas became incensed by the bewildering ritual he did not understand.

"Fatheh Latinus, let me ask you this," Aeneas began. "In round numbers, now. What do you suppose is the net wohth of the Catholic Chuhch? Including real estate and aht appreciating since the Middle Ages. Slave labor. And tax-exempt status. Alcohol and music concessions. Pooh boxes and fees foh candles and holy cahds. Donations foh priests foh funerals and weddings and papal audiences and absolutions and dispensations. And tuition to seminaries and parochial schools and CCD. Magnificent medical institutions in big cities. And great univehsities with football teams on national TV. And charitable contributions flooding in from billions of followehs, rich and pooh, on every continent. Plus stock and bond and money mahket investments wohldwide . . ."

"That's enough, Jack," Lavinia said, obviously scorched.

"The church is a non-profit institution. Money in equals money out."

You can see the benefit of 2000 years of Catechism. They've got all their answers straight, haven't they? I wonder if they've heard this one.

Aflame, Aeneas fired his next inquiry.

"May I ask you anotheh question, Fatheh?" he asked nearly in a Fury. "One of your fohmeh altah boys, and I'm sure a damn good one, and I made a small wageh last evening on the outcome of your anseh."

"Oh?" the priest acknowledged. "And what's the question?"

"Is God good?"

"Of course."

"Is God all-powehful?"

"Absolutely."

"Then why do we have so much evil all over the stinking planet?"

"Man is weak, my son."

"If God is good and evil exists, He must not be all powehful. Or he would not permit evil to continue to exist. He would intehvene on the side of good."

"Man is free, my son."

"If God is all-powehful, as you say, and evil exists, which is unmistakable, then He must Himself not be all that He's cracked up to be. Othehwise, why would He let evil exist?"

"God *is* omnipotent. And free. He *may choose not* to exercise his power."

"Or if He is both good and powerful, there must be no evil in this pooh, tyred world of ours. Which is it? Because all three can't exist concurrently," Aeneas expounded. "Or perhaps man exists alone in a godfohsaken cosmos . . ."

Lavinia was mortified by the atheistic apostasy of Aeneas to the wholly Father, which lacked even a single shred of common sense.

"That's a fairly pagan sentiment, Mr. Jam," the priest advised.

"I can fully appreciate His mass confusion over the human race," Jack raved. "God created us flawed, dumped us like broken puppets and told us we were free. Then he abandoned us foh saneh corners of the univehse. And who can blame Him? The planet is a phrygging lunatic asylum! Pahdon my Creole."

"It's a matter of *faith*," the priest said. "Either you have it. Or you don't."

"I owe Chahlie ten bucks, sweetie."

At the close of another three hours of intensive, demaining ecclesiastic tribunal at the hands of the good Father Latinus, the following conclusions could be drawn:

- If she married Aeneas, then Lavinia was ex-communicated.
- She could not marry in a Catholic Church.
- Communion would be denied her in perpetuity.
- In the eyes of this church a fiery perdition awaited her *in saecula saeculorum*. And Aeneas was most definitely hell-bent.
- Whenever she faithfully attended services, she should be seated at the posterior of the church.
- Lavinia and Aeneas would need to commit two months of weekends away from the studio at a Dominican retreat, creating a financial crisis in his new line of photography.
- He must request of his ex-wife-to-be, or her parents, the specific name of the parish church in which he was previously married.
- Aeneas should get his marriage annulled.
- He would need to sign a document stating that his children would be raised in the Catholic Church of which his new bride would become an official ex-communicant upon her wedding day.
- Aeneas could convert to Catholicism if he underwent years of Catholic Doctrine – but all still would not be forgiven.
- Never bear the gift of a bone to a dog of God for safe passage.

Exiting the rectory, Aeneas surmised that there was no way on God's green earth that the Catholic Church wanted to take any chance whatsoever that he might actually join it. And he respected the church for this.

Why would he want to belong to any church that would admit him as a member?

"That went betteh than I expected," he said. "Like hell."

"If I marry you, I'm the scourge of God," she said. "Let's set the date."

"I live to fight another day. *Bellum ad internecionem*. A war to the end. Against Latins with odd hats," he ranted, lost in his rage. "It's the hats . . ."

There was
a Methodist
to his madness.
* * *

CHIMERA III:

The Wanderings

"I was an exile taking to the high seas with my comrades and my son . . . When we were out to sea and no longer in sight of land, and all around was the sea, I saw a dark cloud come over our heads bringing storm and black night, and the waves shimmered in the darkness. The wind soon whipped up a great swell and the storm rose and scattered us all over the ocean. A pall of cloud obscured the light, rain fell from the sky we could not see, and lightning tore the clouds, flash upon flash. We were thrown off course and drifted blindly in the waves."
— The Aeneid, Book III

Fisherman's Paradise

Speak the two words that admit fisherman to paradise: *Delacroix Isle*. The name trips lightly off the tongue even in the perverse French of the natives, who pronounced the name of the Cajun town as "Dellacrow."

Aeneas wondered what grudge the good people of South Louisiana bore against the French to massacre pronunciations so painfully.

The French religious derivations of *Delacroix*, of the cross, seemed transformed in mispronunciation to a kind of Cajun swamp fowl. Instead of the genius who led the Romantic Movement in art. The master painter of *Liberty Leading the People*. And *Dante and Vergil in Hell*. And *The Shipwreck of Don Juan*.

Nevertheless, Delacroix was a fisherman's paradise. A village with its cabins roosting upon stilts. Situated on a *bayou* that flowed into the Gulf of Mexico.

Charles drove his red Cadillac Eldorado pulling a 26-foot Mako on a trailer. In the early morning before sunrise, Aeneas fought off sleep.

He laughed aloud at a crudely painted sign, which read:

SCHWIMPS

1 Mile

"What time is it?" Aeneas asked, yawning.

"4:45. But as Adam Zydeco says, 'If you not in de Gulf when da sun she comes up, den you awready too late,'" Charles said in a proper Cajun accent.

"The things men do foh fish," Aeneas observed.

"And women. Ah garontee," Charles said as his dialect lapsed into Creole.

"Foh a few fish, men will lose most of a good night's sleep. Spend a small Fohtune on a boat and fishing geah. Fight off clouds of bloodsucking bugs. Get bit by live bait. Hooked. Lose toes and fingehs to big fish boated too green. Risk drowning. Getting struck by lightning. Exposure. Christ, you couldn't *pay* most sane people to do what fishehman do foh free. All the time. Foh *fun*."

"It's considered bad form, Jack, to make fun of the sport on the drive to the boat launch," Charles said lightly. "Besides, sport builds character."

"If that's the price you pay to build characteh, I'm content not to own any stock in it."

"That's obvious, Jack."

"'Dost thou think that because thou aht vihtuous, there shall be no more cakes and ale?'"

"Fat Jack Falstaff."

"Fat Jack's. That's a bah Uptown."

"Big on Fat Tuesday."

"By the way, where is the damn Riveh?"

"Jack, the word is *bayou*. So don't go 'round askin' 'bout no rivers. You'll confuse us natives."

"You mean the same natives fishin' foh schwimps?"

"Jack, the word is shrimpin'."

"You mean schwimpin'?"

"Close enough."

"Why is the only Riveh named on the roadmap the Mississippi?"

"It's a concession to Yankees. Through whose states the *Mississippi Bayou* also flows."

The two-lane road turned beside a calm *bayou*. Where a modest argosy of Cajun shrimp boats floated. With butterfly nets standing at attention.

"What do all these people do? When a hurricane comes up from the Gulf?" Aeneas asked.

"Evacuate."

"Hence, the stilts?"

"Correctomundo. The stilts also keep out the nutria and water moccasins."

"What's a nutria?"

"You never seen a nutra rat? Adam's got one. I'll show you. Later on," Charles said. "It's a sight that will live forever in your memory. Ah garontee."

As they approached the village, they suddenly encountered a traffic jam. A hundred cars with boats on trailers. Branching off to form shorter lines at the few boat launches.

"Christ, Chahlie. Where did all these people come from? At this ungodly hour?"

"N'Awlins. To fish."

Charles drove past three launches to Adam Zydeco's. Charles asked Aeneas to drive. He bolted in a saturnalian gait. A flash in a quest for ice and bait.

Aeneas advanced the Eldorado in spurts. Just before their turn, Charles returned with three, massive, clear plastic bags of ice plus a bucket of jumbo, market shrimp. He set the bait into the belly of the Mako.

The sky to the East brightened. Charles assumed the wheel. Positioned the Eldorado adjacent to the boat launch and then shot off. Like a man attacked by harpies. To launch his engine of siege. Aeneas had never seen Charles so lively.

Adam Zydeco was a shaggy, filthy, bearded man with a scar connecting his forehead to his right cheek. He wore a black eye patch over his sightless eye. Hoisting immense, expensive boats from launch to *bayou* with only one good eye.

The music of *Buckwheat Zydeco*, with wild fiddles and mad accordions, blasted from an ancient boom box.

Wearing a top of thermal underwear with sleeves cut ragged at the elbow. And filthy tan workpants and boots. He reticently slipped the straps of the electric hoist beneath the hull of the Mako and reattached the loose end to his hoist's hook.

Adam worked the control gingerly. Quickly lifting the massive Mako from its trailer. Swinging it in jerks and jolts. And fits and starts. Down into the calm *bayou* below. Charles had complete confidence in Adam.

Although Aeneas once shouted aloud as the boat seemed to surge in its descent into the *bayou*. Charles parked the car. And the two seamen hustled into the Mako.

"Ready for the most beautiful sound in the world?" Charles asked.

He broke wind on command. Impressive deciibels. A real tiller shaker.

Pax proboscis. Peace to the schnozzle.

Then Charles turned the key. The diesel immediately turned over. With a powerful, guttural, precise, rhythmic grumble.

"Chahlie, that is beauteous. A woman in ecstasy."

"This is even better. It lasts all day."

"My friend, that may depend on the woman."

Charles steered them adeptly out into the winding *bayou*.

Aeneas liked Charles and their friendship had grown out of business. Charles was highly talented, creative, professionally infallible and a quick wit. A spirited man who loved life. He had justly earned his   prosperity.

On the *bayou* they passed Cajun cottages. With dock signs   reading:
DEAD SLOW and
NO WAKE

Good signs for the dock of the Delacroix Funeral Home.

A maze of waterways, Charles followed the *bayou's* main   channel, a twisting maze from the village. On either side marsh grass grew at an almost perfectly even height. Aeneas noticed an occasional snow-white egret grace the canals in solitary grandeur.

Three miles out from the launch they overtook a shack on stilts with a rusty tin roof and rickety dock of wooden slats with four old tyres at the front.

"Who would live here?" Aeneas asked.

"A for-real Cajun."

"What do you suppose a *foh-real* Cajun lives on?"

"Schwimps. And a little nutria now and then."

Charles pulled two baseball caps from doors of the Mako's   console.

"For-real Cajuns wear hats like these."

The cap bore upon its crown a badge, which read:
CAJUN COUNTRY.

And sewn with a little crimson crawfish.

"Do I have to?" Aeneas asked.

"It'll keep the sun outta your eyes."

Aeneas doffed the Cajun Country cap. Like an authentic Cajun.

The boat overtook one sign, which read:
NO DREDGING.

But paint of the letter G was chipped off. Probably from someone who had thrown a Dixie or a Jax Beer bottle at it. Another sign:
GAS PIPELINES.

"Some gas undehneath this land, I bet," Aeneas said.

"The Tuscaloosa Trend."

"Christ, Andrew Pahmeh probably owns half this god fohsaken swamp."

"The Tuscaloosa Trend goes from East Texas to the Mississippi state line. Lots of gas and oal. Only Texas has more gas and oal than Louisiana. That it happens to be godforsaken is its charm."

Aeneas found himself anticipating the opening of the *bayou* into the Gulf, which he had never seen. He imagined one of the world's great seas.

The Gulf. Its currents caressing the Yucatan. Air bussing the south coast of Texas. And French kissing the liquid wanton lips of Mrs. Sip. Whispering sweet nothings one day at the Alabama and Mississippi Gulf Coasts. And hurling profane hurricanes the next. Streaming and stroking the august phallus of Florida.

This should be a vision. The Gulf. Brimming with billions of schwimps. Chock full of delicious trout and pompano. Fierce king mackerel and wahoo. Half-ton marlin. Leaping tarpon torque at us as silver aquatic warriors. In the Grand Isle Tarpon Rodeo. All riding its stream. Home to great sharks. Its currents warming New England, Newfoundland and Ireland. Gas and oil in its shelf. Its liquid heat feeding voracious tempests. The Gulf of Mexico must be rich, as seas go.

The *bayou* finally made a yawning turn, widened and opened into the Gulf. Which was not what he expected.

Oil derricks, platforms, pipes and storage tanks. Intruding upon the water. Muddy water. No clear aqua color. Heaving leviathan oil tankers. And schwimp boats with twin arms dragging closing nets around unsuspecting schwimps. Strange bedfellows. Shrimpers and roughnecks.

The sun lifted itself from the crumpled bed sheets of the Gulf.
Charles headed toward a barren hump of an island a mile offshore.
The air was as wet as a steam bath. Already 80 degrees. Breeze soothing.
From the brisk clip of the Mako. Its trim hull shearing two-to four-foot
swells with the throttle wide open.

"Life's a goddam jungle," Charles said. Looking stalwart at the helm and console. Gleaming silver and glass gauges.

After twenty minutes Aeneas spotted a school of dolphins. Arched backs bouncing silver wings of sunlight. Blowing carbon dioxide and inhaling oxygen. Like humans. Then surging. Admirable admirals. Deep into the Gulf Stream.

Charles pulled to within 50 yards of the island. Proximate to an oilrig. Cutting the engine. He dropped the anchor and set its metal blades into soft bottom silt. To minimize drift.

The fishermen tied on leaders with surgeons' knots. And shad rigs in tandem. Impaling jumbo shrimp onto each bronze hook.

"If we don't catch any trout, can we sauté the bait?" Aeneas asked.

"What bait do you use to catch trout in New England?"

"Ethwohms."

They cast for distance their ungainly fishing rigs. Amid oilrigs. Into the Gulf.

As soon as the bait hit the water, Aeneas felt a strike and set the hook. Briskly, he reeled in a two-pound, mule, speckled trout.

Charles reeled in a double or two smaller school trout.

They re-baited and re-cast and immediately hooked more trout.

Charles had another double.

"Take your time reeling in," Charles advised. "Trout see the hooked fish and think it's after the remaining bait. And hit the bait. Purely out of greed. That's the secret to catching doubles."

Aeneas slowed his retrieval. And soon he began to reel in doubles, too.

"We are into some fish," Charles observed.

"Son, it's a fisherman's paradise."

Within an hour and a half, they filled an igloo icebox with meaty, mule trout after throwing back the smaller school trout.

"Want a Dixie?" Charles offered.

"A beeh? You *must* be kidding. I neveh drink before . . . 8:00 am."

"You got to. That big ole sun'll soon be beating down on your lily white ass. And the only thing between you and dehydration is a couple of Dixies. Go ahead. Pass it up. Turn into a prune if you want to. It don't matter none to me. People will think you're my grandfather."

"Got a Jax Beeh? Or Storyville Old Style?"

Aeneas fished through the ice, smiled and pulled a Storyville Old Style Draft Beer from the cooler. He grimaced, held his nose between his thumb and forefinger. And threw the first brew down the hatch.

After an hour of constantly boating trout, the line raced out and the drag screamed within the new Shakespeare fishing reel of Aeneas.

"I got something wicked big," he shouted, as the drag of his reel screamed.

"Well, play him. Give him all the line he wants."

The fish leapt. A long silver gleam. Then it dove deep and swam in long runs from side to side. Refusing to come to the boat.

Aeneas played the fish skillfully and reeled in line only as the fish grudgingly allowed.

Charles caught a glimpse of the fish as it ran alongside the Mako.

"King mackerel. He's good size. Maybe 15 pounds," Charles said.

The fish raced out to sea. Then turned and made a fierce swift run directly at Aeneas. Who stood in the stern, legs apart for bracing. And for balance in the slight chop of the Gulf.

The sleek, vicious, streamlined fish leapt from the sea at the boat.
Causing major panic as three feet of fish flew. Mouth agape in mid-air.
A spear of fish flesh in flight. Straight toward the crotch of Aeneas.

The king mackerel sailed cleanly between his open legs. And landed with a dull thud upon the floorboards of the Mako.

If the fish had vocal chords, it would have snarled. Wounded and flipping unresigned upon the deck of the boat.

"Watch your feet, barefoot boy. That sucker's mean," Charles advised.

"Who you calling *boy*?"

"That ole boy's got teeth."

"He went foh my live bait. My vitals foh his vittles. My jumbo shrimp. My lure. My troll foh wenches."

"Did you see your whole sex life flash before your eyes?"

"Hell, yeah."

Aeneas exhaled sharply to force the adrenaline to subside. The experience strengthened the bond of friendship.

As the morning drew on, the pace slackened and just before 10:00, Charles caught the first catfish.

"Time to move. The current has changed. The water's getting muddy. Want to pull up the anchor?" Charles asked.

He turned the key and the Mako surged to life. The intense July sun bore down upon them as they headed to sea. Aeneas felt as if he had been awake forever although it was just before noon. His stomach groaned. He reached for a chicken of the sea sandwich and another beer from the ice of the Igloo. Offering more of the latter to Charles:

"Moweh beeh?"

They cruised and dropped anchor off an island of scrub brush. To which a shrimp boat was moored. Bearing on its weathered stern the name:

BONTEMPS
DELACROIX, LA.

A deeply tanned Cajun husband and wife worked on-deck as two Acadian nymphs swam in the refreshing water of the island's brief beach.

"How was your luck?" Charles shouted to the Cajun.

"We doin' real good. Den de trawl, she catch up some rock. Tore her up bad. We goin' home. Can't get no shrimp wid one big hole in you trawl," the Cajun returned devoid of even a trace of dejection in his voice.

"How big is the hole in your net?" Charles asked.

"Big as a gumbo pot. We fix her up. Real good. Den we try her again."

"How large was your catch?"

"T'ousand pound maybe. Maybe jus' a little bit more."

"How long have you been out of Delacrow?"

"T'ree o' foh day."

Charles smiled, waved and resumed fishing.

The idyllic scene of the Cajun family shrimping together moved Aeneas. Arousing an inexplicable sense that real refuge existed. That the madness could be kept at bay.

His father once told him, "There's no justice in this world. Just a little mercy now and then. For those smart enough to find some."

Aeneas would accept all mercy offered from benevolent gods and goddesses.

The Cajun family enjoyed a state of grace. Which Aeneas temporarily shared. Knowing that mercy is a brief window. He relished it.

The fishing slowed. The fishermen talked, slaking their thirst from the harsh Southern sun with drinks of Dixie.

"You ever fish for tarpon?" Charles asked.

"No. You?"

"Once. In Costa Rica. In the last fall season. Tarpon are real fighters. God, are they ever? A fish worth watching. You fly into a fishing camp way out in the jungle. A guide takes you out in a small, flat bottom boat. You use twenty-pound test line. Max. The fish run more than 100 pounds. The world record from 1957 is 283 pounds. Caught off Venezuela."

"That's spohting."

"Hooked tarpon run harder than any fish I've ever seen. They take out line so fast the reel smokes. If you don't grease your reel, the gears can burn out when the fish makes a long run," Charles recalled.

"Silver kings?"

"Yes. Silver kings. *Megalops atlanticus*. And you haven't fished until you've seen six feet of silver king fly out of the sea. Dancing on its tail. A *danse macabre*. Gills rattling. As it tries to shake the hook from its jaw."

"Man alive."

"The fish runs out a hundred yards. You work like a slave for 20 minutes to bring him in close. He sees the boat. And runs out another hundred yards. This happens five or six times, depending on the fish. Every muscle in your arms aches. You bring him in again. Then bam. He's gone on another long run."

"Sweet Jesus."

"You say to yourself, 'He can't be doin' that again. He can't be that strong. Or that proud.' But he is. And when you think you can't fight the fish any longer, you fight only with sheer determination. You become one with the fish. A brother. Linked to its spirit. With a slender thread."

"I understand."

"You feel the fear. The pain. The strength of the tarpon. I wish I could have told him everything would turn out all right. I fought a 90-pound tarpon for an hour and a half. Got him up close. He was almost as long as the boat. The guide lifted him up gently by the gills. Carefully removed the hook. He took a quick photo. And then we released the fish."

"A fish like that deserves to live. Swim free. Poetic justice."

"The zenith of fishing. You should try it."

"Someday, I will."

By mid-afternoon they were drunk as lords. They hit a school of redfish running about ten pounds each. The two men ineptly pulled in the reds. Landing nearly a dozen. And losing just as many.

The Cajun family left just before suppertime. When the shrimp boat had sailed far enough away, Charles declined to use the Mako's privy and peed off the bow. Strangely to resemble a bizarre ship's figurehead.

"May I compliment your distance?" Aeneas asked.

"Prowess in the prow. Learned as a frat man at Penn. In the salad days of my youth. When I was a wisp of a lad. More than once I pissed off the roof of the frat house. Onto Walnut Street."

"Delta Thi?"

"I Phelta Delta Thi."

"No doubt."

"In his whole life a man can never have too much of Delta Thi."

"I propose a toast to Delta Thi."

"Gentlemen, we join Mr. Jam in toast."

"For Delta Thi, we must partake,
John Barleycorn, frat son divine.
Long may we flash the secret sign
And thrill them with the mysticke shake."

"Ah, the mystic Delta Thi shake. How well I remember it. Took me damn near forever to master it."

"It's all in the hips."

"So many co-eds fell by the wayside. Lovely willing nymphs. Trying to he'p this Phelta frosh. Master the mystic shake," Charles said swigging a Dixie.

"Rumor has it that you nearly died trying to get it down right. But you figured at least you'd die with a smile on your face."

Inebriated ebullience ensued. With animated laughter.

"And then you met Bahb," Aeneas continued. "Whose greatest virtue is her patience. Am I right?"

"Barb was a godsend. Annually, I empty my coffers to Kappa Kappa Kappa."

"You're drunk. And getting redundant."

"Am I getting redundant?"

"You're getting redundant?"

"Are you sure?"

"Yes, I'm sure."

"In college I preferred Phig Pi."

"At first, I only dated Delta Queens. Then as a senior, only Dairy Queens . . . Whom I only once desehted."

"When did you desert?"

"Afteh suppeh, of course."

"Why? Was she pickin' up the tab?"

"Nah, one of the Delta Queens tuhned out to be . . ."

"A sternwheeler?"

"Bewahe of Greeks bearing gifts."

Heaping helpings of hilarity. Mad backslapping. Guffaws in the Gulf.

The trout began to bite again at dusk. The fishermen landed exceedingly few. Because they were drunk and incapable of reeling briskly, they inadvertently hooked mostly doubles.

When they lifted their lines attempting to boat the fish, the trout would bounce against the side of the Mako. And drop back into the Gulf. Spared by default by virtue of the fishermen's inebriated incompetence. But trout, too, will accept all the mercy they can get.

"Saves takin' 'em off the hook," Aeneas rationalized. "I don't mind catchin' 'em. But I'm getting damn tyred of takin' 'em off the hook."

"Then you're gonna love filleting 47 trout, 12 reds and a king mackerel."

The chore of filleting proved sobering. They abandoned further fishing. And began to filet their catch. It would sustain them for tonight and future suppers. And remind them of this day upon the sea.

"Nothing in this world is better tasting than fresh-caught, shrimp-fed trout right out of the Gulf," Charles said working the filet knife, a gift from his wife with a fine leather sheath.

"Better than the sign in the restaurant that says, 'The trout you eat this evening was swimming in the Gulf of Mexico this morning.' Ours were swimming in the Gulf this evening."

Aeneas lifted another Storyville Draft from the Igloo. Admiring the photo of his beloved Lavinia on the label.

"So, how's your love life, Jack?"

"I'm mad foh Lavinia."

"What's a butt ugly dude like you doing with a babe like Lavinia anyway?"

"I'd rather be lucky than smaht. But what about you? How do you like being married? Since I'm about to tie the knot. Again."

"Marriage has a nasty habit of playing this practical joke. A man marries, in part, to get it regular. But brides burr up."

"Buhh up?"

"Hell, every now and then I have a little heart-to-heart with Barb. I tell her: 'Barb, you just gotta get them burrs outta your private parts.' "

Just then, as Charles was filleting the last trout, the filet knife slipped out of his hand. Going overboard into the Gulf. To give the trout a Pyrrhic victory. And the last laugh.

"Goddam it," Charles shouted and reared up in anger.

Then he threw the leather sheath into the Gulf after the knife:

"May as well have it, too."

"Is that some kind of Cajun sacrificial rite? To bring more good luck. And appease Neptune. For all the fish we stole from the Gulf. Am I supposed to throw in my filet knife, too?"

"Goddam twenty-dollar filet knife."

"Chahles, about your filleting finesse: it needs wohk."

Charles offered Aeneas some Red Man Chew, which he declined.

"Come on. Try it," Charles cajoled.

"No way."

"Try just a pinch between your cheek and gum."

"What the hell does an Ivy League MBA know about chewing tobacco?"

"At Penn I was more of a WASP than the WASPs. *I studied them*. And learned their mannerisms. Until I was better at it than most of them. I knew the right clothes. The right fraternities. The right society. And the right speech."

"You're a hell of a lot whiteh than I am. But about this Red Man Chew . . ."

"Come on, now. It tastes real . . . minty. You'll like it," Charles said extending an open pouch of Red Man Chew.

Reluctant with skepticism, Aeneas set a pinch inside his cheek. His salivary glands responded with alarm. His tongue and lips ignited spontaneously.

His cheeks burst with foul, bitter juices. His taste buds brutally assaulted by the thug tobacco. His teeth too big for his mouth. Labial paralysis ensued.

Charles briefly studied the expression of Aeneas. Then broke into hysteria.

"What do I do with this crap?" Aeneas inquired.

"What else? Spit."

From the stern, Aeneas expelled the juicy chew. And found himself face-to-font with the craft's name:

DIXIE DREAM.

A tall clear bottle of liquid gold, like maple syrup, with a white, gilt framed label appeared from a hold. Charles took a long tug on the bottle with the nice name and passed it to Aeneas.

"This'll he'p yawl. It tastes slightly . . . caramental," Charlie advised.

Aeneas gaped at the homey brand with a grand Southern mansion on the River. A Riverboat like the Natchez floating by River Road. A two-horse carriage bearing three gents headed in the opposite direction of the Riverboat:

SOUTHERN COMFORT

The Grand Old Drink of the South.

Originated on the Banks of the Mississippi
in New Orleans, Louisiana, U.S.A.

Aeneas accepted a shot. Which fueled and fanned the fires. The worst injustice ever committed to his mouth. The burning endured too long.

"There's no damn comfoht in Southehn Comfoht," Aeneas said.

Between the filleting and the preparations for dinner, the fishermen regained little semblance of sobriety. Charles cooked like a *sous chef* even while drunk. A gourmet in the Mako's extensively equipped galley. Mixing his momma's fish fry batter. To fry thick trout filets on a gas stove. In the belly of the Mako. Choosing prime filets. Intent upon freezing the rest for another day.

Charles prepared pecan rice. And uncorked a Parducci Petite Sirrah '79. Favoring the hearty California reds.

Amid agonizing, rich aromas from the galley, Aeneas spread a bleached linen cloth on the table. Followed by folded white linen napkins, fine bone china and sterling silver. A brass kerosene lamp set in the center of the table. The two fishermen feasted like ancient kings on their catch. In the boat on the tranquil waters of the Gulf Stream. Drunk, happy and tyred.

"This makes the day rich," Charles said with a satisfied smile. "Out here in the middle of the Gulf. Dining as if you were at Arnaud's."

"It's a victory to savoh."

"Man at one with nature."

"That's very transcendental, Chahlie. I just wish I could taste this trout. But if you say it's tasty, I'll take your wohd foh it."

"You're kidding."

"First, with that tongue-bite Red Man Chew. And now we know why the man is red . . ."

"You're putting me on. But you loved the Southern Comfort. Right?"

"It bites like the crocodile of the Nile."

"Don't sugarcoat it, Jack."

"I can't taste a phrygging thing," Aeneas said, cutting the tender trout with his fork. "Not sure I eveh will again. But it sure looks nice on the plate."

"You're blowin' smoke."

"Know what? I *thought* this trout tasted tough. But I've been chewing my own tongue. And didn't even know it. With this tongue-bite chew. And all."

Charlie dropped his sterling silverware. Staring Aeneas straight in the eye.

"Jack, tell me you're raggin' me."

Aeneas stalled brutally.

"Chahlie, I *am* raggin' you all."

"Really?"

"Really. It's wicked pissah."

Both men laughed as night descended. After dinner, Charles poured chicory coffee. Then a nice glass of Grand Marnier. And Aeneas proposed a toast:

"Let's lift our vessels. To honoh the greatest landlady of all. Here's to the fohmeh Miss Minnesota, Mrs. Sip. Long may she pour. But never empty."

"To Mrs. Sip! A more I-popping mistress you'll never lay eyes on."

Both fishermen were exceedingly tyred. Enjoying the warm glow from the grand old drink of the South.

As they cleaned up the galley, all of the sun, early rising, fishing and alcohol got the best of Aeneas.

"Chahlie, I need to lie down. I'm whipped. I feel suddenly so . . . drusi."

"If you're drowsy, take a nap."

"Do ya mind?"

"Hell, no. There's the bunk below deck. Knock yourself out."

Aeneas abandoned his host for the bowels of the Mako.

He climbed into a modest bed. Exhausted. The boat bobbed indolently in the tranquil Gulf.

The stars were beginning to glimmer through an open hatch. In the blackening night. With Southern constellations he had never noticed until then.

What about my engagement to Lavinia? Is she right for me? Is she the One? After the first marriage went wrong. Have I committed myself too
soon? Are we really compatible? Can any marriage fulfill and endure for
life?

His exhaustion expelled fleeting worries. He drew up the bed sheet. On deck Charles kindly completed the chores of the galley. Singing old Dixieland jazz numbers. *When It's Sleepy Time Down South.* Imitating the gravelly voice of Louis Armstrong. And *Dream a Little Dream.*

Willfully, the temperate, limber fingers of a Gulf breeze lifted from him all final vestiges of anxiety.

The sea rocked him like a newborn babe in a cradle to the tender verge of slumber.

                Sleek soothing swells
                of the gentle Gulf
                lapped on the hull
                of the *Dixie Dream*
                like the yawing yawls
                of Marblehead Harbor.

* * *

Fool's Paradise

Tamely sedated to fitful sleep amid the tranquility aboard the *Dixie Dream*, Aeneas drifted in the Gulf of Mexico.

A Stygian delirium from a conspiracy of excesses. Brain chemistry askew. Weary from the day at sea. And wishing he were home.

Aeneas dreamt of his wake:

Awakening. I am dressed in a tuxedo. What? Impersonating a stiff? The sweet fragrance of fresh cut spring flowers spread atop me. Enclosed in a casket. Floating in the suffocating, sulphurous, pitch black.

Crossing over. A levitation. Then a descent amid dim Dixieland jazz and revelry.

As Lavinia weeps. Jazzmen sing. And painted voodoo priestesses blow tin whistles. Amid shrill screams. And wails of heartbreaking agony.

Futilely, Aeneas pushes upon the cover within the casket. Almost out of oxygen. Mourners intend to bury him alive. As *Big Chief* by the ReBirth Brass Band plays.

Acutely now, the sensation of the *Dixie Dream* rolling in ground swells of the Gulf. Then a gentle cradling. The lull before a child drifts into sleep.

He dreams his casket is carried atop men's shoulders. On the way to the open gulf of his grave in Lafayette Cemetery. Near Commander's Palace. Where the headstone reads:

AENEAS JOHN JAM.

If he does not soon escape, they will bury him alive.

Then a premonition of the sound of distant thunder from an approaching storm at sea.

The spearing of spades shoveling dirt, which rains upon the hallowed, hollow roof of his Doomsday home.

His anxiety ebbs and flows. But he feels his body drifting. Which means, perhaps, he has a chance.

He shouts:

"I'M ALIVE!"

He bangs upon the soft silk lining of the casket.

"Who dat?" a pallbearer bellows.

"IT'S ME, JACK JAM! FREEEEEEEE MEEEEEEEEE!"

"Gawd Awmighty! I thought I hoid the stiff. Knockin' from inside the casket," a man mumbles.

Then Charlie's distant voice, "The man's just drunk. Stiff as a stiff."

Abundant acrid anguish and anxiety.

Expressions and shouts of utter disbelief.

"I could use a good rest. But not quite so long. Not quite yet," Aeneas shouts and kicks.

"The dead man's alive," a pallbearer says. "I ain't carryin' this no foither."

The casket topples to the street. He jumps up. Like a Jack-in-the-Box.

Mourners flee willy-nilly. Screaming at his second coming.

Thus, he ruins his own jazz funeral.

Aeneas sat up straight and rigid as a corpse.

Disoriented. Until the familiar surroundings of the *Dixie Dream* settled him down.

His head pounded without mercy. He had fallen asleep with his contacts still in his eyes. His vision failed him. Again.

But something *was* wrong. The boat was clipping along briskly.

The wind blew over the hatch in a torrent. The engine hummed grotesquely light and airy. Surreal like his dream.

Charlie's not at the helm. Bloodstains on the deck. Runaway boat! What else could it be? He has fallen overboard. I'm flying alone all over the Gulf. Waiting to collide with an oil derrick. Or freighter. Or landfall.

Then he noticed the largest, raunchiest rat he had ever seen. Standing frozen in its tracks and scowling from the stern.

The boat flew wildly through the night. The sky black like Louisiana crude. As jagged fingers of lightning flew from storm clouds. The
air much cooler now. The threat of a storm at sea. To churn the Gulf
with whitecaps.

In the streaming lightning strikes, the rat appeared bright white.

"HAAAAAHHHHHHH!"

Aeneas threw both arms up to attempt to frighten the monstrous vermin. Between him and the steering wheel of the boat.

"Chahlie? Where are you?"

No answer.

"The biggest goddam rat I ever saw. In my whole phrygging life. Is on board," Aeneas shouted into the privy.

Still no response.

"Is the boat a runaway? Or what?"

No reply. The rat refused to budge.

Charles obviously had been thrown overboard. And the boat was racing through the Gulf out of control.

Aeneas decided that greater danger would emerge from collision with an oil tanker or rig in the Gulf than from ratbite. Swallowing the lump in his throat, he leapt out of the sack.

He saw an ancient, dull, filet knife. And huge, gumbo ladle in the galley. And approached the rat armed thusly.

Wary but expeditious in this crisis, he confronted the great, white rodent. The rat was easily the size of your average Texas coyote. Aeneas threw the ladle at the rat. Which seemed to sneer, hissing with fangs bared.
Adding to the Chaos, the wind and now large drops of rain brought tears to his bloodshot eyes obscuring his vision.

Get the rat. And toss it overboard. Easier said than done. As always.

Aeneas tried to clear from his hungover head the nimbus clouds of a deep, deathly, opium sleep.

Aeneas stalked the rat. Approaching it deliberately with the blunt filet knife raised murderously high. His adrenaline pumped. Heart pounding.

Head pulsing in pain. Vision distorted by wind and rain.
The great rat had glazed beady eyes. Returning a low, guttural growl.
Bravely, Aeneas charged the beast. Flailing at it with the filet knife.
Expecting a leap from the beast to his jugular.
The first thrust penetrated the rat's hide. Like a knife through pecan pie. The wound bled pure white, feather petals. Which were swept cleanly behind the swiftly sailing Mako.

Stuffed.
Aeneas focused. Blinking in the storm.
It's a phrygging, stuffed, giant, white rat.
Ignoring the rat, Aeneas rushed immediately to the helm. Where the wheel rotated freely back and forth.
He noticed the vague shape of trees in the flashes of lightning.
We must have entered a cove. Christ! I'm a dead man.
Firmly, Aeneas took the helm. As the rain soaked him to the skin.
But the boat failed unfortunately to respond to his turns of the wheel.
The steering is gone. Must have hit a rock. Perhaps, the size of a gumbo pot. In the unlucky Cajun's shrimp net.
He looked for the key to the Mako. He would shut down the engine. But from the bow, the golden boat key was gone.
Chaos reigned supreme. Calamities piling up.
Then Aeneas noticed odd lights off the bow amid the downpour. Perhaps, a distant lighthouse. That might guide him to land.
Tail lights. A Louisiana, license plate that reads:
FISHERMAN'S PARADISE.
On Charlie's Eldorado. Thank you, God!
The Mako floated upon its trailer in tow down the weaving road to New Orleans alongside the *bayou*. They passed the same Cajun town he vaguely remembered in the pre-dawn drive to Delacroix.
"Hey, Chahlie. Pull ya ass over. Will ya?" Aeneas shouted.
But the Eldorado traveled on its determined path home.
Aeneas found the foghorn of the *Dixie Dream*. And blew it.
Charlie slowed the Cadillac to a halt on the shoulder of the heaving two-lane road.
Jumping down sprightly with a serious adrenaline rush from the boat to *terra firma*. Aeneas climbed into the front seat of the Eldorado. Dripping wet.
"What in the name of hell is going on?" Aeneas asked.
Charles swigged a bottle of Dixie from a bandaged, bloodied left hand as he drove with his right toward New Orleans.
"That storm came up *some* fast. I could feel the cool front moving in. So I checked it on the short-wave radio with the Coast Guard. Just after you dropped into sleepy time down South."
"How do you feel?"
"Wide awake drunk."
"What happened to your hand?"
"I cut it on broken glass."

"Bad?"

"Not *too* bad."

"What broken glass?"

"Back at the launch."

"Pulling the boat out of the *bayou*?"

"Um, no. Adam did that."

"Wasn't he closed aftch dahk?"

"Actually, yes, he *was*."

Charles shook his head somewhat sheepishly and said, "I had to go to Adam's house. I found him just starting to eat dinner. Hunched over a nice, big, steaming plate of *boudin* blood sausage. And jambalaya. *Mardi Gras Zydeco* blasting away. By Nathan and the Zydeco Cha Chas."

"You're kidding."

"Wish I was. You missed a hell of a moonlight ride down that *bayou*."

"Until the stohm came."

"I can't believe you. Sleeping the whole ride in."

"I was truly whipped. And drunk. I sleep like the dead."

"I guess you all *do*."

"What did Adam say when you knocked on his dooh in the middle of suppeh? Did he invite you in foh *boudin?* And a little *fais-do-do*?"

"Hell, no. I thought he was gonna to chew my head off."

Aeneas laughed at this vision.

"Adam answered the door wearing his greasy ole workpants. Suspenders flappin' in the breeze. Not botherin' to zip up his fly. With a mean look on that ugly face of his. The lightning over my shoulder kinda lit up his *bayou* of a scar. He was some pissed," Charles explained.

"Man alive!"

"I told ole Adam that I just had to get to N'Awlins."

"What'd he say?"

"He said that his boat launch was open at foh-thirty. And he told me to come back then."

"And you said?"

"I told him it was life or death. There was a big storm comin'. And you were deathly ill. He thought a minute. Grunted, groaned, belched and farted. He told me it would cossus plenty. Then we went to his launch."

"Shiiiiiit."

"We hauled the boat outta the *bayou*. You were off in some other world. So I told Adam that you took sick in the Gulf."

"Which was true."

"I told him you had a rare blood disease. And needed medical treatment. In N'Awlins."

"What blood disease?"

"*Flatulence terminus*."

"Adam *bought* this?"

"In his whole life old Adam Zydeco never heard of *flatulence terminus*. But he wanted to know if it was *catchy*. And he was some pissed. Because his dinner got cold. Emergency or not. Then he ate up a small Fortune in cash. That one-eyed oaf charged me an arm and a leg."

"He knew you were bluffing. Adam Zydeco is no Rhodes Scholah. But Cajuns are big on *flatulence tehminus*. How much did he set you back?"

"You gotta understand how Adam charges. It varies. Widely. One day it's five bucks. The next day twenty-five. Just for the launch. Depending on if he's havin' a good day or not."

"Like the stock market."

"The commodities market maybe. You tell him you owe for bait, ice and beer. And he just picks a number outta the air. And speaks it like the Pope. Usually between twenty-five and fifty bucks."

"And tonight?"

"It cossus a hundred bucks. Cash."

"Oh really, us? Mahk us down foh 100 smackers, did he? Adam was catching doubles tonight. And you and I were on the hook."

Aeneas plunged his right hand into his back pocket to fish for his archaic wallet and dropped $50 on Charlie's lap.

"It's only spohting to share expenses," Aeneas offered.

"Thanks. I appreciate it. So after we get the boat on the trailer, Adam knocks on the car window. I roll it down. He looks *some* mad."

"What'd he say?"

"He told me *never* to *darken* his boat launch, again."

"And you took umbriage?"

"I waited and watched him walk into his cabin. I was pissed. Paying 100 bucks in an emergency situation. Having to listen to that crawfish crap."

"So what'd you do?"

"After he left, I stole his pride and joy. His *albino* nutria. From the glass display box on his launch."

Charles sucked at the phrygid, bronze tit of a bottle of Dixie.

"And you hid it in the gut of the Mako?" Aeneas asked.

"Right."

"As I suffehed. Unconscious. At death's dooh."

"Damn straight."

"He'll miss the great white rat. First thing. And he'll know who took it. Maybe he'll come afteh you."

"It was only a ridiculous albino nutra rat."

"Hey, Captain Ahab of the South. It's Adam's pride and joy."

"I bet it's insured. Adam's never left St. Bernard Parish in his entire life. He doesn't know me. Or where I'm from. Besides, I may just mail it back to him. After we get back home."

"I threw a gumbo ladle at it. And stabbed it. With a filet knife."

"You nutria poacher."

"I thought it was real. I only poach eggs."

"Generally, we don't filet our nutria down here. Only fish."

"It's different up Nohth."

"And, as a rule, we use our gumbo ladles during or after the cookin'. On the ingredients. But not before."

"I see."

"And we almost never use our gumbo ladles in self-defense. Against either wild game. Or stuffed game. As the case may be. Just so you know."

Aeneas recounted his dream and tale of the runaway Mako for Charles.

"Barb'll have my ass for coming home in the middle of the night," Charles said warily. "Like this."

"Bahb sounds like a wicked tough customeh."

"I'd rather take on Adam any day. Than Barb."

"You just did."

"Adam is child's play next to Barb. She'll have my ass. When she sees my bloody bandage. Times goes by. The birdies sing. The music plays. And my hiney is Barb's. Hell's bells. I'm dead."

> Nutria
> may come
> and nutria
> may go.
> But
> to tour
> Delacroix
> one needs
> Zydeco.

* * *

CHIMERA IV:

Dido

"Love is a cruel master. There are no lengths to which it does not force the human heart . . . Why are his cruel ears closed to what I am saying? Where is he rushing away to? Ask him to do this one last favour to the unhappy woman who loves him and wait until there is a following wind and his escape is easy . . . What I am asking for is some time, nothing more, an interval, a respite for my anguish, so that fortune can teach me to grieve and to endure defeat."
— *The Aeneid, Book IV*

The Admonition of Ambition

Totally ravishing, Lavinia slipped her sensual tongue into the ear of Aeneas. Nibbling gently upon the lobe. As she sat upon his lap.
Arms coiled round his neck. Facing him with her lovely breasts at his eye level. In their studio on Bourbon Street.
"Do you love me?" she asked.
"Why do you ask so often?" he responded.
"Because you don't say it enough."
"I think it all the time."
"I'd be satisfied if I could read your mind. Since I can't, I need to ask."
"Fair enough."
"You never seem to want to talk."
"I'm laconic."
"I'm afraid I'm losing you."
"Why?"
"Love doesn't last."
"Sometimes, you're better off if it doesn't. But not in our case."
A sad, distant expression overtook him.
"I could just kiss your face off, Jack Jam. You're so adorable."
"I am?"
"With those flashing, green Irish eyes. That gorgeous brown hair.
With the auburn streaks. Tall and strong. You're yummy, Jack."
"I'm glad you think so, Liv. But I'm the Lucky Dog. If you ask me. To have a Dreamface when I wake every day."
"You really believe that?"
"If life is *zero sum*, I believe that you are my long-lost upside. And I'm expecting amazing heights afteh the bottomless depths I've wandehed."
"How many babies should we have together? I was thinking maybe five or six. What do you think?"
"Speaking of vital statistics, my love, did you reach our CPA?"
"She was at lunch when I called."
"Would you try her again, please?"
"Later," she said. Dropping some contact sheets. To constrict arms around his neck. And drive him wild with intimate whispered desires.
Tempting him into play during business hours.
"Sweetheart, I have *tons* of wohk to do," he said. "We might be too good at this business. It's making me crazy. Trying to make sure this
company succeeds. Foh you and your fatheh."

"I can't concentrate on business right now," she said. "And as minority share-owner I give you permission to fool around. As long as it's with me."

"I love that you feel this way. Really, I do," he admonished. "But there's too much wohk now. The timing is a just a little off. At the moment."

"If this is the price of success, then let's fail."

"No deal."

"I just knew you would be a great success, Jack."

She touched him intimately.

"It's because of you. You made all the difference in the world. You saved me, Liv. From a lifetime of searching. Foh all that I have found in you."

"I love you, my sweet Jackie Jam."

"Success is odd: just when we think we have it made, that uninvited guest, Ambition, visits. Tuhning Jacks into jackasses. Unsatisfied with what we have, we want more. So how do we *know* when we're a success? The damn process is neveh finite. As long as we live."

"Success is no sin."

"It's as empty as the wind. Filling our sails with blusteh. And driving us like slaves. God only knows where."

"Success is a matter of definition."

"I define success as dreams that you make real."

"What if you don't follow your dreams?"

"But people do. Don't they?"

"It's your best hope for happiness."

"But the question is whetheh a dream is wohthy."

"I care more about living. Than making a living."

"You've never stahved."

"I don't understand you, Jack. Now that we're doing well, you're taking it all too seriously. Life will pass you by. If you let it."

"Have you got something against being rich?" he asked.

"Money means a lot to the rich: without it most of them would be failures."

"Try becoming a success without it."

"People succeed without money. Besides, our business is booming You're booked up months in advance. How can that be bad?"

"It is."

"What do you mean?"

"I feel cheated, Liv."

"Why?"

"Two reasons. First of all, it was so damn easy. All I had to do was give up my aht. I'm selling out, sweetie. Can you see that?"

"No, you're not, Jackie. You're adjusting to reality."

"You and your fatheh made the studio boom. Not me. Hell, I was nutria shit before the two of you came along."

"No, you weren't, dear."

"Let's be real. My business nearly went under."

"Daddy's only part of it, Jackie. It's your work, your talent that people want. How could your work be in such demand without taking into account your own skill? Give yourself a little credit," she said sympathetically.

His vulnerability appealed to her. She identified with it. And understood it implicitly. Because underneath the surface, she knew that she was acutely susceptible to injury.

Percy had wounded her deeply, both publicly and privately with his pre-marital indiscretions. He had been too demanding. Domineering. A tyrrhent. And he had betrayed her. She was right to move on despite Percy's many virtues. She had given him enough of a chance.

Enough time to prove himself worthy. But, involuntarily, she wondered whom he was seeing now.

"Do you have any idea how many of the last dozen sittings came from your fatheh?" Aeneas went on.

"No."

"All of them."

"How do you know?"

"I asked our new clients how they first heard about us. They were all eitheh referrals directly from your fatheh. Or the result of your mahketing plan. At your fatheh's agency through Chahlie's advehtising. Paid in full by your fatheh."

"You were wise to make him your business partner, sweetie. It seems to me you should be grateful to him."

"I am, Dreamface. I am . . . I'm sorry. But he's just such an incredible man. He has achieved so much. How can I eveh stack up against him?"

"Don't you dare try. Hear?"

"You're right, of course. I don't mean to seem like an ungrateful ass."

"You do."

He said nothing.

"Jack darlin', your stature is rising fast. Give it enough time. I believe in you. That's one of the reasons I love you so. And I want to be with you when it happens. When you make it, it'll be because of *you*. Daddy never took a decent photo in his whole life. Your success has already begun."

"Thanks, Liv. I needed to hear that. It's all . . . new to me. I don't really quite know how to handle it."

Then he retreated into pensive silence.

"What's the second reason? Come on. Out with it," she asked.

"I hate the wohk. It leaves me empty. Emotionally. And intellectually. There is zero creative satisfaction. And most of the people are hideous. Egotistical. Bloated in their self-esteem. Blatantly materialistic. Impossibly shallow. Fixated on status. Society. Recognition. Money. All of which, in the end, mean nothing, of course. Zero. Zip. Zilch."

Lavinia had no answer for this. She sensed that he was losing sight of the gift of opportunity – a rose of myriad, rich, fragrant petals. A gift in her power to offer. Selflessly provided in good faith. Because there was little remedy if her gift with his immense neediness proved inadequate. And she could never make him happy. If she couldn't satisfy him in this way.

"Listen. We both worked hard today. Let's take a little break together," Lavinia advised.

She checked the appointment book.

"Because of a late cancellation, we have an hour free. Gee, too bad. Come on, Jackie."

Lavinia placed the "Closed" sign in the studio window and pulled down the shade.

"Sweetheart, I love you foh this. But I'm trying to run a respectable business . . ." he started.

"You're a good screw. And I respect you for it."

"You know, you could have an advanced case of nymphomania."

"Lucky you."

"And I could be the cause."

"It's all your fault."

"I may just be too sweet in the sack."

"A hard man is good to find, Jackie. Now, spread some Jam on me."

They both smiled. And looked deep into each other's eyes. And lay down upon a sofa in the studio. Much kissing and hugging and lusty groping ensued. Followed by tearing off clothing. Hot breathing. Sighs of pleasure erupting. Eyes closed in earnest pursuit of the satisfaction of unleashed desire. Down to undergarments.

Then a harsh knock upon the front office door.

"Don't answer it. They'll go away," she said. "Let's make love."

"It could be a client rescheduling. Or with the wrong appointment time. Or some walk-in business," he said, leaping to his feet and throwing on his clothes.

The phone rang.

"Don't answer it, Jack," she implored. "Let them wait."

But Aeneas flew from the couch. And left Lavinia to cool sensual jets ready for take-off. She heard him answer the phone first. Asking the caller to hold. And then he answered the shop door. But she couldn't make out the brief, polite conversation.

He returned with a colossal flaming arrangement of ruby, yellow and peach roses. Enormous perfect blossoms. Graced with dewy baby's breath. A milky glass vase sculpted with grapes. FTD card with golden sprinting Hermes.

"They're foh you, of course," he said.

"From Percy. He always sent me this mix of roses. Who called?"

"Chahlie."

Ceremoniously, he dumped Percy Turner's roses to accept the call.

"Chahlie, your timing is about as bad as it could be," Aeneas said.

"That's not real friendly, bud."

"I'm sorry, Chahlie. I realize how important being friendly is to Southehnehs."

"Damn straight."

"I don't mean to offend you. But you caught me, uh, us at a ratheh . . . inoppohtune time."

"Making hay on company time?"

"When you called, we were filling up the silo."

"Do the people at the top know about this?"

"I'm sleeping with the boss's daughteh. So I hope not."

"Sorry to make haywire. But it is rather urgent."

Charlie's tone of voice darkened.

"I'm here foh you, Chahles, my friend."

"Thank you, Jack. I really need someone to talk to. Can I buy you a steak at Crescent City Steak House? Tonight, maybe? I know it's lastminute."

"Tonight, I'm afraid, is just too last-minute, Chahlie. Can I take a rain check?"

"For when?"

"I'll have to get back to you on that, Chahlie. I'm booked up. Days, nights, weekends. Unless someone cancels. Then there's a waiting list. I'm deluged with wohk. It's bizahhe. But we'll wohk something out. Can it wait?"

"It can wait."

"Are you sure? It sounds serious."

"It is."

"Business or pehsonal?"

"Personal."

"Sorry to hear it. We'll have dinneh soon at Crescent City. And talk."

"Thanks, Jack. Just let me know when you're free."

"Will do. We'll have a wicked big steak the first chance we get. See ya."

"Bah. And thanks, again, Jack. You're a friend."

Aeneas hung up. And the phone immediately rang, again.

"Aeneas Studios."

"Is this the Jackson Street Asylum?" the caller asked.

"There's no asylum here."

"I must have dialed the wrong number."

"Apparently. Good day, sih."

Aeneas yanked the phone cord out of the wall. And returned to Lavinia who icily glared at him as she finished dressing.

"What?" he asked. "You're leaving?"

"You just don't get it. Do you?"

"Get what?"

"Your most important *business* is *me*. Don't you understand?"

"It was Chahlie. He has *big* trouble."

"Sorry, Jack. I'm no longer in a sympathetic mood. You shouldn't have answered the phone. Or the door."

"Were the flowehs from Tuhneh?"

"So what if they were?"

"That guy doesn't know when to quit."

"That's smarter than someone who doesn't know when to try."

"Is that supposed to be a shot? Because I resent it if it is. I'm busting my ass to make this deal wohk. Foh your fatheh. And you."

"Well, maybe it isn't supposed to be so difficult."

"It *is*, Liv . . . So don't be a brat."

"A *brat*? . . . I have given you everything in my power, Jack. And it's still not enough for you."

"I'm just trying to be responsible, Liv."

"I can't give you any more. And you're still unhappy."

She brushed her hair. Perfumed both wrists and the nape of her graceful, swan's neck. With *Bal a Versailles*. And started to exit carrying her blazing bouquet of roses. From Percy Turner. Her former fiancé.

Flashes of unwelcome pictures in the mind of Aeneas enraged him. He could not control their vivid intensity. Images of Lavinia intimate with Percy, pixels of skin naked to the touch, drove him wild.

"It could just as well have been a client instead of the florist. Or Chahlie. Who has serious pehsonal problems."

"Don't we all."

"I'm just trying to run our business. Professionally."

"You make me feel like such a slut."

"I won't let the business fail. I can't let it happen."

"Too late. You just did."

"What do you mean?"

"I'm leaving."

"What? Me?"

"You. And this gallery."

"But why, Liv? I'm lost."

"I have nothing more to offer you. I'm exhausted. And all that I've given isn't enough."

"I don't know what to say."

"You don't need me anymore, Jack. You have what you want. It isn't me."

"How can you say such a thing?"

"You can have all this to yourself. Work out the details with my father. I'm history."

"I want *you*, Liv."

"No, Jack. Percy wants me. Desperately. Without any cause for hope. And yet, he does. Still."

"I do, too."

"You want something else desperately. And it has nothing to do with me. Except indirectly."

"I'm sorry. You've lost me, again, Liv. Completely."

"Call me when you figure it out, Jack."

"It's a riddle then? A mystery?"

"Not to anyone with an iota of common sense."

"Liv? It can't be that easy. To walk away."

"Watch me."

Lavinia yanked off her engagement ring. And dropped it with a rich, little ping. Upon the newly arrived, oak desk of Aeneas. From an antique shop on Royal Street.

In a flaming flash his Fortune fled through the front door. Carrying the fiery splash of roses. And slamming the door so hard that the glass rattled. Which sent a sign to the studio floor. Staring up at him, the cheerful sign read:

CLOSED. PLEASE COME, AGAIN, SOON.

Thus, Lavinia became single, again. Perhaps, off to show her appreciation to her former suitor. Now, her new suitor.

"Many
a man's
tongue
shakes out
his master's
undoing."
* * *

Napoleon at Camp

Happily, each number matched at last. One set on a column of a camelback at Camp and Marengo Streets near Napoleon Avenue. The second scrawled almost incomprehensibly on the back of an ad agency business card by Charles. Who kindly lent the Eldorado to help make a good first impression.

Aeneas stuffed the card into his jacket pocket. Hoping this rendezvous and a blind date with Deirdre Bontempo, advocated by Charles as an antidote to weeks of the blues over Lavinia, would truly prove therapeutic.

As she refused to return a legion of contrite calls. Flowers, cards, gifts went unacknowledged.

He further trusted he would not have grounds for a lawsuit based on misleading advertising. That her "sense of adventure," per Charles, was not a bent for the bizarre. Nor a skew to the insipid.

Aeneas popped a wintergreen lifesaver into his mouth. Took a few quick swipes at his hair with a comb missing several teeth. Checked his fly. Small wrapped package tucked under one arm. He swaggered up to the inviting brink. Like an untested recruit upon tasting the bitterness of battle.

So here you go, again. Off to the cosmic war with the opposite sex. On Charlie's advice. Because I am unloved by Liv. And can't bear it any longer.

With aplomb he gustily rapped the golden doorknocker shaped in the two faces of Janus, a common schizoid icon of Mardi Gras.

A little dog barked a shrill, high-pitched, fitful warning to her mistress.

What are you searching for? What brought you here? Have you lost your mind? As well as your way? How could you have driven so far off course?

Aeneas flirted with outright bolting but held his ground. Hoping that Charles would not lead him irretrievably astray. As lightning flashed in the night sky of June followed by the rumble of thunder. The wind beginning to kick-up off the River.

A trim woman in a long, purple, slinky dress with soft brown hair and sensual olive eyes greeted him. In her early thirties, her full breasts tugged at the straps of her silky gown. An inviting serpentine gold necklace.

Stunning cleavage. Spring buds of nipples. Blossom from her bosom. Under the soft fabric of her fabbiius evening dress. Flat tummy. Trim hips. Nice tan. Exquisite legs. Small firm seat. I just gotta get to the bottom of this.

After looking him up and down, she extended her hand to Aeneas. With a warm smile. Revealing lovely, bleached teeth. Dimples at the corners of her inviting lips. The hazel windows of her soul flashing bright with a hint of approval. Spirited eyes that caused a twitch at his crotch. Barely able to keep under wraps the turmoil in his underworld.

My God, I know her! The woman who picked me up at Napoleon House. Where Charlie practically lives. And then the night at the Royal O. Mutually purging demons. After she dumped her husband. And I got dumped. On Black Saturday.

With surprise but not panic, he clung to the trusty veneer of friendly civility.

"Hello, again . . ." he began.

"Haven't we already met?" she asked with a shock of recognition.

"Yes, I'm Jack Jam. Friend of Chahles Chahbonnet? We've met before. At Napoleon House. You remembeh?"

"Well, sure, I do. I'll be damned," she pushed her hair back with her hand, as it began to pour down rain. "I'm Deirdre Jean Bontempo."

"But your friends call you Didi. Right?"

"Right as rain, Jack. Ain't life just a stitch sometimes?"

"It's a pleasure to see you, again, Didi. Sorry, I'm late. But I got lost."

"Don't worry about it."

"I took a wrong tuhn. And ended up crossing the Riveh, if you can imagine. I wandered all over Algiers on the West Bank. I have no sense of direction."

"Well, you're here now, Jack Jam. And sweet as marmalade. Do come in outta the rain."

Her greeting almost created a bonafide gaffe of the groin.

A silken gray puppy with a furry frost-crested chest and streaks of tan running down her front legs. Sporting a tiny crawfish red bow to keep hair out of her eyes. With a deafening piercing yapping that sneaked into the far reaches of his cranium.

The pup snapped at the nattily attired ankles of Aeneas. With new socks from Brooks Brothers Clothiers and new Bass Weejuns from Terry-Judens. Tearing loose a cuff from its well-tailored shank of gabardine.

"What's her name?" Aeneas asked.

"Peek-ann-tee. I'm always telling her my life story. She listens real good. One hell of a lot better than most men. She's so loyal. And cunning," Didi said.

"Peecan-tee?"

"You know, like the hot sauce. From Avery Island. She's such a dear."

"Ah, yes, *Piquante Tabasco Sauce.* Which breed is she? Schnauzeh? Shiatsu? *Gesundheit!* Hoho."

"Cockerpoo. Half cocker spaniel. Half poodle. Did you ever see such a cunning face? Sometimes, I just call her plain ole Pee. Or Annie.
Or Peecan . . ."

Half-cocked, Piquante promptly peed upon his brand new loafers.

"She gets a little excited. When she meets new visitors," Didi said.

"Let's hope her mistress does, too."

Aeneas knew that proper protocol dictated that he should show some friendly gesture of good faith toward her prized pet. So instinctively Aeneas reached down to pat Didi's pet upon the head.

Whereupon Piquante bit Aeneas with a vengeance on his middle finger. As he quickly withdrew his doggedly friendly gesture.

"PHRYGGINGBITCH!" Aeneas screamed.

Then he kicked in an involuntary, classically knee-jerk reaction.

Brushing the pup with a modest uppercut to the butt. Causing Piquante to cry pitiful, plaintive, puppy whines.

"I'm sorry. I didn't mean to do that. Just a reflex. I *do* apologize," Aeneas said.

"She's only just a cute little puppy," Didi replied defensively.

Aeneas blushed.

"A little *girl* puppy. Once, again. I am deeply sorry."

His finger started to bleed. Diplomatically, without inviting Didi's attention, he quickly sheathed his wounded digit in his pants pocket.

Where it bled.

"Piquante, bad girl," Didi admonished. "Be good. Hear?"

The pup stared back in wide-eyed oblivious innocence.

As Didi cordially offered to closet his Navy blazer, he wondered if it might be impolite to ask his blind date, if Piquante was up-to-date on her rabies shots. Or would she mind terribly if he requested that the little pooch be examined for any symptoms of canine distemper?

Which is more lethal to the psyche? Dog of God? Or God of Dog?

As Didi removed his coat, Aeneas felt the pressure of her eyes. As she casually and discreetly summed up his well-toned physique.

"May I use your rest room foh a moment, please?"

Aeneas felt blood trickling and soaking his pants' pocket.

"Of course. It's right over yonder."

"I appreciate it."

Aeneas bowed politely and calmly marched for the bathroom in search of a bandage to bind his bleeding dogbite. On a closet shelf he found a pad. Which temporarily sufficed.

If the bleeding doesn't stop soon. The blood will ruin the pockets. And I may need to replace the crotch.

He plundered her medicine cabinet. Dislodging fleets of pills, mascara, vitamins, cold creams, nail polish, eyebrow pencils, contact lens caelian solution and lip-gloss. Landing with a vast plastic clatter. Masked by thunder.

Finally, he located a box of Band-Aids in which remained only one extra-large Band-Aid suitable for stanching wounds from double-edged swords and battleaxes. Reluctant to seize it, because it might come in handy later. The way this night was going. Gingerly, he applied the giant Band-Aid to his favored but now tender right middle finger.

Aeneas emerged smiling bravely. Recovering almost cheerfully from the temporary setback of this foray. In the camelback home on Camp Street.

Then he maneuvered to a comfortable antique couch. Near a coffee table upon which casually lay exposed rather explicit and libidinous gentlemen's magazines. A butcher-block platter with crackers, cheese and a formidable uncut *boudin* blood sausage. Coveted by Piquante who regarded it with longing eyes and cocked cockerpoo countenance.

Imitation Oriental rug faintly stained from prior cockerpee and cockerpoop. Piquante's chew toy victims haphazardly strewn all over the camelback home.

"What can I pour you for a libation?" Didi asked. "I can offer you red or white wine. Or a cocktail, if you prefer."

"Red wine will do nicely, please."

Didi exited for the refreshments.

Piquante wandered into the living room. With the first bloodstained bandage of Aeneas in tow. Aeneas gazed at the sodden, winged strip of gauze.

"Piquante, give me that! You little sack of shit!" Aeneas whispered.

Gamely, Aeneas chased the puppy around the room. Until he tore the bandage from the pup's maw risking his only good hand. Just before Didi returned with a nice friendly bottle of Mondavi, a corkscrew and two Waterford crystal wine goblets. Powers Court, he noticed.

"Would you do the honors, please?" she asked.

"Of course."

Adeptly, Aeneas uncorked the cabernet. And poured them each a glass of the ruby mead. Shimmering in the deep silver cuts of the crystal.

From the corner of his eye, he observed that Didi stared at his profile as he fixed vittles. Wetting her lips unconsciously with her tongue.

"Cheese? Or sausage?"

He gallantly offered the snacks that she had provided.

"Blood sausage."

"Well, you might have to fight Piquante for it."

She looked at him suspiciously.

"Haha. Just a joke."

As Aeneas tried to oblige Didi by slicing the sausage, Piquante made a bold, almost heroic lunge at the giant *boudin*. Sinking her teeth into the blood sausage. And growling. Refusing to let go. As Aeneas played a game of tug-of-war with dogged little Piquante.

Didi intervened.

"Maybe I oughtta just put her in the other room," Didi advised.

"That might be wise."

After she crated Piquante in the next room, the dog started to bark her head off. With skull fracturing, mind rending shrieks.

"She'll stop in just a few minutes," Did counseled.

Aeneas sliced the business end of the blemished *boudin* with the gentle but deliberate touch of a cantor at a bris.

"I love your house," he said.

"I like your looks, Jack Jam. You do keep yourself pretty fit, don't you all?" she said.

"I keep in shape lifting weights. And boxing," he explained.

"It shows, baby. Keep up the good work. Hear?"

"And how do you keep fit?"

"Making love. Often. The more, the better."

She smiled and her eyes boldly looked right through him. He began to feel like a pork loin at the Piggly Wiggly on Saturday morning.

The dog howled. Relentlessly. Mindlessly.

"Don't you think my Piquante has a *cunning* face?" Didi asked.

Didi likes that word. Cunning.

"The pup certainly has good elocution," he replied.

"She's just so . . . cunning."

"A cunning linguist, Didi?"

She blushed. He had no idea why. Another silent period.

"So, how do you know Chahlie Chahbonnet?" he asked.

"I met him at Napoleon House. He is *always* there. And at Snobs. We met through an introduction by a mutual friend."

"May I ask who? Perhaps, I know Chahlie's friend, too."

"Percy Turnip."

"Pehcy Tuhneh? . . . Pehcy's dating my ex-fiancée. So rumoh has it."

"Well, anyway. Charlie's a real sweetheart."

"He has a refined eye foh the ladies. I must confess that, when Chahlie described you, I was intrigued."

"How nice of you to say so."

"Did you, uh . . . renovate this place yourself?"

"Pretty much."

"I like what you've done. The ceiling fans. Hahdwood floors. Antiques. You have a nice touch."

"Are you *very experienced*?"

He paused to reflect upon his *repartee*.

"Compared to whom?"

"I suppose it's like being asked if you're rich. It's all relative, isn't it?"

Aeneas nodded. An awkward silent period ensued. He sliced cheese.

"This is pissah cheese," he observed.

"Roquefort."

"Really. It's wicked good."

"Ditto."

Didi poured the young Mondavi cab. Aeneas lifted a glass gamely to break the phalanx of tranquility from suddenly silent Piquante.

"Toothsome cheese, we toast thee!
With Piquante's proxy vote
To accept God's sole apology
For making us the goat."

Didi laughed outright.

"I just *love* a man with a sense of humor."

It's all downhill from here. The Mondavi was having its intended effect. That furry bag of piss next door finally shutting its mad yap. Finger no longer spilling my lifeblood into my hip pocket. Wonder if it will scar. All is quiet on the southern front. By Napoleon at Camp and Marengo.

Aeneas reached for a hefty slice of *boudin*. As the night sky thundered.

"How did you hurt yourself?" she asked.

"What?"

She caught him off-guard.

"Your finger? How did you hurt it?"

"Self-inflicted wound. To the triggeh fingeh. I just banged it up. It's nothin'."

"What a doggone shame. Well, let's just get to know each other. We didn't talk much that night at the Royal O. And since we lost touch. Tell me what you all do, Jack."

"I was an *ahtist*. And *aesthete*. Now, I take pictures foh a living. And re-touch. Society pohtraits."

"Pitchers? You don't say? Free lance?"

"Only when I'm shoht of clean boxehs."

Didi laughed, again.

"You crack me up, Jack Jam."

"I run a studio in the Quarteh. In fact . . . where is it, now? Ah . . . here we go. I brought you a little gift. Of my wohk."

Didi opened a framed black-and-white photo of a poor black and white boy fishing together from a bridge over an inlet to the Gulf.

"That won an awahd, actually. So did some of my wohk foh UPI. Which maybe you've seen in the *Times-Picayune*. Periodically," he   explained.

"Where was that pitcher taken?" she inquired.

"Atchafalaya Bay."

"Near Houma?"

She pronounced it as if he would have said, "Homer."

"Yes, near Houma."

"I just love that part of Louisiana."

"It's quite beautiful. In a unique and sometimes surreal way . . . But, now, have you . . . do you travel much, Didi?"

"We lived in Garmisch. My ex-husband, Dallas, was stationed there for two years. Back when we were first married."

"Really? The Alps are stunning. I almost wept the fihst time I left them. Heading into the flatlands of France."

"You're such a sensitive man. A real artist, aren't you?"

"How kind of you to notice."

"Say, do you all like jazz? Billy Holiday? Cole Porter? And, of course, Duke Wellington?"

"I love them all. Especially, Duke Ellington. Music fit for the gods."

Didi slipped on a tape of Duke Ellington's big band music. *Battle Royal* played first.

"So how long have you and Mr. Bontempo been apaht?"

"Off and on a few months. But it seems longer. We keep trying to make it work. And we break up. Then we make up, again. It's bad news."

"Then you are still Mrs. Dallas Bontempo. Fohmally?" Aeneas queried.

"Yes, I am . . . Technically," Didi answered.

"And you haven't decided to make your break pehmanent?"

"No, not yet. We still have great affection for each other. In some ways. But the relationship just dudn't work. So this is a lonely time for me. And I welcome your company."

"Ditto, Didi. Ditto . . . So how long was your husband in the sehvice?"

"Four years. The army. Infantry. A crack shot."

"A crack shot?"

"He's nuts about the NRA. Deer hunting. And all that bull . . ."

Dallas may pack a dwarf rod. A pigmy peashooter. Light weaponry. Obsolete ordnance. Low ammo. An inept implement. A witless weapon. A recoilless rifle. A godforsaken firearm. Or a seized engine of destruction. And overcompensates. With a juvenile machismo fixation on six-shooters.

"Is he . . . under-sized?" Aeneas asked.

"Six-six and 266 . . . Where was I? . . . Oh, then we moved down here."

"Are you a deeh hunteh, Didi?"

"I shoot clay pigeons. And hunt dear men. Like you. Do you hunt?"

"I only hunt Deirdre."

"That's a good one."

"What is your husband's vocation?"

"He works a tug."

"My *avocation* is to wohk a tug."

"I know what you mean, Jack."

"How exactly does he wohk a tug?"

"He's a River pilot."

"A Riveh pilot?"

"He works ships on the River with a tugboat . . . But enough about him. Why don't we set ourselves down for dinner?"

Didi shifted them to the dining room and served dinner. The table set with exquisite, gold encrusted, ivory china. Newly polished silver. Freshly pressed linen. Many German artifacts from a tour of duty abroad.

She lit ivory candles in silver candelabra. Dried flower arrangement upon the table. Creating a warm, pleasant, little glow of home. Exiting with a satisfied smile to the kitchen. As soft sexy jazz played upon the stereo. Returning with a large wooden bowl full of generous tossed Caesar salad greens and chipped cheese. Giant wooden spoon and fork protruding. Didi served him attentively.

"This is lovely, Didi. Really."

"I enjoy entertaining. And indulging my guests. My home is their home. If you know what I mean."

"You do it with grace."

After the salads, Didi brought on fresh vegetables, homemade linguine and a chicken dish.

"What's your chicken recipe, Didi?"

"Chicken marengo. Specialty of the house. I also make a killer Beef Wellington. I'll just have to rustle one up for you next time."

"How nice."

"I made the pasta myself. It's *homemade*. 100%."

"Nothing like . . . *cunning* linguine, eh?"

"And they say Latin is a dead language. You naughty boy, Jack."

What on earth does she mean?

As they dined and drank, the conversation became personal.

"You're bright, attractive and very capable. Why did you separate from your husband?"

"It was the sex."

"Pahdon?"

"Sex in excess."

"Some men are insatiable . . ."

"No, I mean . . . well . . . my husband has trouble keeping up with *my* . . . uh . . . urges. He said I almost killed him. Because I wanted it so often."

"Is he an oldeh gentleman?"

"Dallas is a child of the River. And mostly just plain juvenal."

"Dysfunctional?"

"Well . . . every now and again."

Jack Jam, you Lucky Dog. Déjà vu all over again.

"Dallas also has a tendency to . . . imbibe . . . just an iddy biddy too much. If you know what I mean," she replied, tipsily.

"How repre-hen-si-bubba," Aeneas slurred.

After the main course, Didi served chicory coffee. Aeneas respected her honesty and candor about her feelings. She cleared away the dishes and Aeneas went to the hutch to admire her selection of Hummels.

When Didi reappeared.

"You have an impressive collection here, Didi."

"Do you collect?"

"Photos . . . Do you collect other . . . collectibles?"

"Experiences."

"Ah, yes."

"*In*tense ones."

"Really?"

"It's the secret to life. And eternal youth."

Didi smiled and led Aeneas by the hand into the master bedroom. Femininely decorated. Lace intricate as the craft of Jack Frost on a Boston bedroom window on a winter morning. A collection of crystal perfume bottles graced a wooden antique dressing table. Baskets of verdant plants flourishing on a window seat. The scent of hyacinth. A Hunter ceiling fan circled lazily. On a bedside tape player the pulsing rushes of *Fingal's Cave* by Mendelssohn. Copious candles lit by Didi emanating the faint spice of vanilla. Candlelight golden against her smooth, tanned skin. Big brass bed. Plump with pillows.

They drank more wine. The head of Aeneas reeled. He felt Didi's hands upon his privates. Attempting to take them public.

"Hello, again, big boy," Didi said.

I come to bury Caesar. Not to praise him.

Soon Didi stood before him sensuous and lusty and unclad. Flawless body. Bursting eager breasts. Narrow waist. Firm behind. Slim thighs. Slender legs. Petite feet with toenails painted to match crimson fingernails. Brown hair flowing gracefully over her shoulders. Warm, gentle eyes.

She approached him. Entangled her arms around his shoulders. Looked him straight in the eyes. And kissed him with tenderness that turned into warmth and then passion. With gentle ardor, she drew him into the sack.

"Be firm. And slow," she advised. "Like last time. Hear?"

Aeneas knelt beside her as she lay before him in all of her ladylike loveliness. A sweet Southern song. And caressed her. She threw back her head. Closed her eyes. And purred sensuous, feline sounds.

Diligently, Aeneas focused his hands upon her. Deliciously deliberate. Compelling and suspending. Tarrying. To tease gently. Building intensity and rhythm. Attending her rhapsody for what pleased her. Inventive. Careful to be firm and slow and strong.

"Jack, in the drawer. There's something you need."

He yanked open the drawer to a broad assortment of protection from which he chose his brand. Aeneas tore open the package and tossed the wrapper on the bedroom floor. He slipped into a Trojan. And spontaeneously they winged. Somewhere over the rainbow. To a land they dreamed of.

He waited patiently for her. With diverse intimate styles. All of which suited her. Until the high-spirited performance of Aeneas came to fruition. As the grand golden gong clanged inside her head. Accented outside by thunder and lightning. Shivering and quaking. The pulsing rhythms of her moans evolved into hesitation and then frank, bold streams of ecstasy. And a rich afterglow.

"My *God*, Jack Jam. Where *did* you learn to be so tender?" she asked.

"In the paradise foh prigs. Beantown," Aeneas answered.

"You're just too sweet for words, lover man."

"I'm not usually this good."

"The hell you aren't. But your modesty is so cunning."

"I guess you just inspire me, Didi."

"May I have more please?"

So Aeneas sought her pleasure again. With endurance that astonished even him. Partly deferred because he was sheathed. But also because he wanted her to love the experience of being intimate with him. The secret to a woman's desire. Downstream.

She became fulfilled with such surprising ease. With reverberations possibly heard across the River. Over and over again. In the camelback on Camp and Marengo Streets. Until he could no longer defer. And spent his pleasure with abandon that ended in a final surge of her satisfaction.

Didi kissed Aeneas appreciatively.

"God, you make sweet love, Jackie Jam. You make me feel so much like a woman. I could just about dance on the ceiling," Didi cooed.

Aeneas felt at peace, too. Fulfilled. Happy. Content.

"When are you coming, again?" she asked.

"Pahdon?"

"Back to see me."

"I hope to come, again, soon."

They basked in rich contentment. Sharing small talk. Touching and kissing and smiling at each other.

The doorbell unexpectedly rang. Like the harsh dirge of a harpy.

"Who could *that* be? At *this* hour?" she asked.

"I'll bite."

The doorbell sounded again, impatiently. Followed by a persistent, punishing, pounding upon the doorknocker shaped like Janus.

"Let me in, Deirdre Jean! God damn it!"
A harsh, deep, rugged, angry, bass voice.
"God, it's Dallas. He's more than likely *some* drunk."
"Shall I answer the door foh you?
"You got a gun on you?"
"No. But I'm fast with my fists . . . Why?"
"He does."
"Right. A crack shot."
More hammering, shouting, threats and fist pounding.
"Open up, Didi! I gotta talk to you all. I *know* you're in there."
The rather enraged husband of Deirdre Jean almost pummeled down the front door with his fists.
"You better hide. If you value your life," Didi quietly advised Aeneas.
"Where?"
"Any port in a storm."
Then a thundering, splintering discord. As the front door of the camelback at Camp burst off brass hinges into smithereens. Mr. Bontempo's idea of a good time on a steamy summer Saturday night. All liquored up. And packing heat. Admitting the resonant rush of gutters and downspouts overflowing from rainwater.
"DEIRDREJEAN!" Dallas bellowed amid jagged bolts of lightning and thunderclaps. "DE-IR-DRE-JEAN!"
"I'm coming, dear. Just a minute now, sweetie. Don't go gettin' your shorts in a bunch."
Didi pulled on a robe and a pair of high-heel slippers.
Buck naked, Aeneas grabbed his clothes. And scrambled beneath the bed. Upon which he so recently had so pleasant a romp with the good Mrs. Bontempo. Squeezed undignified by shallow headroom. Amid much shouting in the living room. Beethoven's bold *Emperor Symphony* stirring in the background.
"Have you got a man in this house, Didi?" Dallas asked bellicosely.
"Whatever gave you *that* idea? Why you're soakin' wet, Dallas dear."
"Whose tomater red Eldorado is parked out front?"
"More than likely someone visiting the neighbors. That's all."
Suddenly, Piquante appeared in the bedroom. Freed by pure hap in the fracas. Aeneas could see the bottoms of her short legs. As she attacked a chew toy. Begging for mercy in little squeaks. As Aeneas may soon be forced to do.
"It would kill me. If you had someone in *my* house. When I wudn't around, Didi. I'd shoot his balls clean off. That's just what I'd do. And you *know* it. Cause a man's home is his goddam castle."
A gunshot unexpectedly was fired. Shattering the glass of a gilt mirror. Scaring Piquante shitless. And freshly staining the imitation Oriental rug.
"Dallas, now put away that Magnum. Before the neighbors call the NOPD."
"Someone's been here. Eating dinner at *my* table. And bringing you presents. And all. I can *smell* him."
Dallas simulated big sniffs.

"I had Dottie over for dinner. From next door. She left about an hour ago. She bought me this new, framed pitcher from some old photographer down in the Quarter. Wadn't that nice of Dot?"

"It's a stupid pitcher, Didi."

"I know. But it's the thought that counts, sweetie."

I'm so unamused. How my Artemis pans my art amiss.

"Oh, hell. I'm sorry, Didi. But you know how crazy I get. Whenever I think about you. Gettin' sexy with someone else. I just go nuts."

"I know, sweet potato pie. I know."

Piquante's face appeared under the bed. Staring at Aeneas. And clutching in her jaws a Trojan wrapper.

"Piquante, you phryggin' mutt. Come here, girl," Aeneas whispered.

But Piquante scampered jauntily from the bedroom with her new spoils.

"Didi, I just gotta get a little. Right now. It's been a *long* time."

"Has it, sweetie?"

"Hell, yeah. At least, since yesterday."

"That long?"

Silence. Footsteps. Like a couple of bad dancers. Heading this way. Mr. and Mrs. Bontempo crashed upon the bed beneath which Aeneas hid. Much rolling, wrestling, kissing, heavy breathing, oohing and ahhing.

Springs whistling Dixie like a choir of harpies. Beneath the mattress he read the dingy box spring tag:

DO NOT REMOVE.

KING KOIL MATTRESS CORP.

CARTHAGE, ARKANSAS.

I just gotta improve my outlook on life. I am a witless wonder. A connoisseur of mattress tags. On the soiled side of merry ole King Koil.

Peering from cramped quarters. Aeneas noticed that Piquante had dropped the condom wrapper in plain view on the floor at the bedside.

A long arm's length away. As the pup pulled a half-eaten Mars Bar from the pocket of Dallas's jeans. What good Fortune!

Carefully, Aeneas reached from beneath the bed in a valiant and daring effort to recover the offending Trojan foil.

Extending his bandaged hand he felt the foil at the tip of his fingers.

Then Didi's high heel as it descended rather squarely upon his troubled trigger finger.

Aeneas nearly cleft his own tongue in two. Attempting with the other hand to muffle his screams of sheer agony. Fortunately, drowned out by the classical music, thunder and commotion directly overhead. As Dallas pulled Didi back into bed.

The sound of a belt and zipper coming undone in a big rush. Huge, wet, muddy, oil stained and incredibly foul smelling cream-colored socks in heavy work boots thudded to the hardwood floor. With just a hint of Dr. Scholl's. Then a giant's jeans. Monstrous soaked denim shirt. Colossal Jockey shorts. Profoundly pungent. Lastly, a shamrock green, baseball cap with a label that read:

JOHN DEERE

NOTHING RUNS LIKE A DEERE.
Above him panting, groaning and kissing.
Phrygging Pyg!
Didi back for an encore encore. And Aeneas fantasized about what vengeance he could wreak upon Charles. For this blind date gone amuck and amiss.

The bed shook vigorously and rhythmically, heaving in three-quarter time. At the crescendo of the *Emperor Symphony*. As the married couple porked furiously. Didi trying to seem as engaged in the heat of passion as Mr. Bontempo. As the cuckold cuckolded Aeneas.

No golden bell rang for her. As Dallas was too quick on the draw.
A sixty-second six-shooter. Selfishly leaving her suspended and gasping and unfulfilled.

After his hearty amorous hoots and catcalls, the great bell of Dallas sounded. A sonic mix of panic and distress. A death rattle from a slaughterhouse. And he just as quickly fell asleep. Sawing a forest of swamp cypress. In his deep, drunken, satisfied stupor.

Didi's fingers snapped in front of his face. And pointed to the door.

Time for Aeneas to beat a hasty retreat. And git while the gittin' was good. Make a getaway. Giddy up.

After gingerly tearing off the King Koil Mattress Corp. tag, he crawled fluidly, like a mime exiting a mine. Marcellus Marceaux. From the dark regions under the railings that supported the connubial bed.

Witnessing the huge brutus, dead asleep upon his *femme fatale*. Getting his beauty rest.

"Call me," she mouthed. And held her hand to her ear. With pointer and pinkie extended. Thumb upon tall and ring men. Like a telephone. Or a Texas alum giving the hook 'em horns hand gesture.

With impossibly wrinkled, tangled and knotted clothes in tow, Aeneas exited in a brisk trot. Stubbing a big toe upon Dallas's loaded revolver. Sending it spinning across the hardwood floor. Slipping upon one of Piquante's squeaky toys and falling painfully upon it with his bare posterior. With a great death squeak from the tortured toy. Barely avoiding broken glass and ragged wood fragments underfoot.

Aeneas tried to evade Piquante. Whose canine teeth latched onto his draped white flapping boxer shorts. And ran away with them growling into the bedroom. A souvenir of all the fun. Leaving him no choice but to go commando. As he pulled on his pants and wrinkled permanent press shirt. And foraged for his Navy blazer from the front hall closet. His entyre attyre, as the Cajuns say, *en dishabille*. Sprinting through the splintered portal.

I'll tell you what kind of artist you are, Jack Jam. You're a phrygging escape artist.

Exiting into lakes of mud puddles spoiling the new sheen of his Bass Weejuns. With his capacity to produce offspring intact. His shirt misbuttoned. Pants' fly half-zipped. Boxerless. Hair askew. Beltless and sockless. Stained, spoiled, scented and territorially inscribed by cockerpiss.

Even a Pyrrhic victory is better than none.
Thus, Jack extricated himself from yet another jam. And battle royal.

Aeneas relished
the pungent scent
of gunpowder reeking
in his nostrils
like Napoleon
at Camp
at Marengo.
* * *

CHIMERA V:

Funeral Games

"They were soon coming near the Siren's rocks, once a difficult coast and white with the bones of drowned men . . . When Father Aeneas sensed that he was adrift without a helmsman. In mid-ocean in the dead of night he took control of the ship himself, and grieving to the heart at the loss of his friend, he cried out: 'You trusted too much to a clear sky and calm sea, and your body will lie naked on an unknown shore.'"
— *The Aeneid, Book V*

Crescent City Steaks

Every true beefeating *connoisseur* in New Orleans knew that the Crescent City Steak House secured its prime beef from Minnesota. Its wine from France. Its retired owner from Brooklyn. And an erudite headwaiter from Princeton for the summer.

Despite its imported qualities, it was a venerable, Crescent City institution. As Durgin Park is to Boston.

The Crescent City simply offered the best steak in New Orleans. Yet it rarely became overcrowded with customers. Aeneas assumed that the reticent, rotund, superaennuated owner ran this business as a retirement pastime.

Incredible sniffs of mushrooms and grilling beef. The hiss of flame against tender red meat. Yeasty aroma of breads baking. Cigarette and cigar smoke tinted the air with its blue haze. The smell of spilled beer lingered in the carpet.

The zydeco of *La Danse de Mardi Gras* by Steve Riley and the Mamou Playboys playing unobtrusively on a tape deck.

Charles was already perched forlornly in a private booth when Aeneas arrived. His shirt collar open. His tie loosened. Looking tyred, gaunt, mentally strained and uncommonly serious.

"It can't be that bad," Aeneas began with a smile as he sat.

"It is," Charles replied, downcast.

"What's wrong, bud. Has someone died?"

"Yes. Me."

"What do you mean?"

"Barb has filed for divorce. She packed up and moved away to her mother in Lafayette. She took my little girls with her."

"When?"

"She moved out weeks ago. Things weren't going well between us. But I didn't think it would be permanent. Then, today, she filed for divorce. It's the shock of a lifetime."

"Trust me, Chahlie. You're still in this life. You're just confused about the afteh-life because a Crescent City Steak is a little bit of heaven on eth."

Charles did not smile. Aeneas hoped that Charles would retreat into the safe harbor of his own sense of humor. To emerge with minimal damage. As humor keeps one's sanity intact. When one calamity treads upon the heels of another. Coming in battalions. When the absurdity grows overwhelming. And despair advances on every front.

The best weapon is simply to laugh. After a chance to blow off steam. Laughter is the only true javelin a man can always hurl at the jugular of the absurd. The only way to defeat such a talented, inventive, relentless adversary.

"Why did she leave, Chahlie?"

"She said she just wasn't happy."

"But why?"

"I'm not real sure."

"She'll change her mind. There's a waiting period, you know."

"She sounded pretty definite."

"Few things are irretrievable in this life, Chahlie."

"She moved everything she owns," Charles said, as tears welled. "I came home from work. And my house was nearly empty."

"Steady, Chahlie."

Aeneas patted his friend on the back.

"Chahlie, she may be unwohthy of you. You Big Swinging Ivy League Dick. And you might be betteh off without her. Have you considehed that?"

"I love her, Jack. I can't stand thinking of her with someone else . . . What will I do without my little princesses? The younger one just started ballet. The older one is taking horseback riding lessons. I can't bear it."

Charlie wept. His lower lip trembled. And he just broke down.

Mourning the loss of such precious stakes. Crescent City patrons staring. Waiter wearing a worried grimace.

"She's been with someone else. She told me so," Charles explained.

"Buck up, Chahlie."

"I worked so hard to give her a good life. A nice home. Beautiful children. They are *such* a miracle. So smart. And sweet."

"I know, Chahlie. I know."

"I gave Barb love. Affection. Security. What more could she want? If I had known, I would have found a way to give it to her. And now she sleeps with strangers. Christ, that hurts, Jack. It hurts so much . . . What's the point of even trying? What am I killing myself for? I'm driving myself to drink."

"You're just trying to get ahead in this wohld. Like everyone else."

"I work like a slave, Jack. I'm working my ass into an early grave."

"All this is just a *temporary* setback. Trust me. A shock to the system. The pixels have ovehtaken the big picture. So it's out of focus. And the depth of field feels wrong. Changing pehspective. But you're a strong, young man. You'll adjust. And this, too, will pass. I'm cehtain. And I'm here foh you until it does."

"It wasn't good for her in bed. She wasn't hungry for me. But how could she give to a stranger what she couldn't give to me?"

"It happens, Chahlie. Don't ask me why. It just does. I don't pretend to understand women. I just know we can't live without them. So we'll just make a few adjustments. Tweak the lens into a new focus."

"All I did was love her, Jack. So what did I do to deserve all this agony?"

"She's probably upset and confused, too. You can bet on it. As long as there's still love, Chahlie . . ."

"Our love had more light than heat. I haven't had any . . . in a year."

"A *ye-ah*? . . . Heat is impossible without light. Things may wohk out yet."

"This isn't supposed to happen to me, Jack. I'm too smart. Too Ivy League. Too young. And I work my ass off. What's the point of a life of struggle?"

"You're an inspiration, Chahlie. Honest."

"I've had more opportunity thrown my way than any other Creole in New Orleans. Scholarships to Penn. My own business. Property. Money well invested. But I killed to make it all work, Jack. I carry the future of my whole race on my back. Willingly. Because every white man in this town wants me to lay down and die."

"That's quite a buhden, Chahlie. It's too much foh anyone."

"But it's not gonna happen, Jack. Never. No how. No way."

"I believe you. You'll bounce back. This is just a little rough spot. You'll see."

"You think so?"

"Yes, I do. This dahk night of the spirit is not biggeh than you."

Charles did not reply.

"It happens a lot, Chahlie. More than you know. And it's a damn tragedy. But how you handle it makes a difference."

"I take no consolation. That the problem is common."

"Take comfoht in the bounty of the solution. There are plenty of fish in the sea."

"I just want Barb. But I know that she's gone. I have to face it."

"If she isn't right foh you, there are many beautiful, intelligent, sensitive women in New Ohleans."

"Really?"

"It'll all come out in the wash, bud. And wohk out foh the best. Take my wohd foh it. If anyone should know, it's me."

"Thanks, Jack. You are a true friend. I don't have anyone else to talk to who understands. I was on a fast track. With Penn. And my own business. Racing to the top. Then this blindsided me. It came out of nowhere."

"I read you loud and cleah."

"I didn't mean to drop all this on you. But I knew I could count on you. Thanks, again. I am grateful for your loyalty."

"These things happen in life, Chahlie. It's not the end of the wohld. It could always be wohse. Perhaps, it's just the staht of a new adventure."

"A new adventure . . ."

"You're a stuhdy sail looking foh the wind, Chahlie."

"That's well said."

"And we'll sail where the wind takes us. And that will be our course."

"Of course, wherever the wind takes us."

"I'm not one to offeh advice, Chahlie. But right now, it's cleah you need two things. A big steak. And a little sex. And you'll have both before the night is oveh."

"I'm up for the beef but . . ."

"No negativity now. We need abundant flesh foh consumption, Chuck. And you'll have it. Before the night of the mystic Mrs. Sip calls it a day."

"God, Jack . . ."

"Shed a whole new light on things. You'll wake up a different man . . . Waiteh?"

"Yes, sir."

"Two of your most substantial sirloins, please. Of the black ancus beef. Sautéed mushrooms. Baked potatoes with butteh and sour cream. Waiteh, may I have a Jax Beeh?"

"Sorry, sir. We don't carry it."

"I can *neveh* find a Jax Beeh in this town. Fine, then, Dixie will do. Does that sound all right, Chahlie?"

"Yes, medium rare."

"I prefer mine ray-eh. Red in the middle. And bloody."

The waiter smiled, nodded and left with their orders.

"Jack, how are things going with you and Liv?"

"Nothing new since she quit the gallery weeks ago. And threw her ring in my phrygging face."

"What have you heard from her father?"

"Nothing so fah. But he may put me out in the street any day now. I live in utteh dread of it. It would be hahd going back to the kind of povehty I've known. Afteh a taste of the good life."

"If he does, the agency will find work for you."

"Well, I'm not so sure about that. It's Andrew's account with the agency. Remembeh? But I do like your spirit."

Charlie managed a brave smile.

"So what did you think of Didi Bontempo?" Charlie asked.

"I was lucky to escape with my life."

"She keeps calling me about you, Jack. So you must have made a big impression on her."

"You mean like the big impression her husband almost made on me with his Magnum."

"What?"

"Her husband, Dallas, almost gave me a free vasectomy. Louisianastyle."

"Your voice does seem an octave higher. So what do I tell Didi?"

"Tell her I became a priest. It's my only refuge. But what chuhch would eveh have me?"

"The Temple of Doom. The Shrine of the Sacred Cow."

"Hedonism is our best sanctuary, Chahlie. One can't feel good and bad at the same time. It's a physical impossibility. The heaven we make is our only haven. It'll give us a new outlook on life. Time away from the hubbub. To renew our strength. And rebuild our dubious Fohtunes."

"We must be doing something *really* wrong, Jack. Look at us. Our lives are in shambles. We're human sacrifices. To gods. Women gods. Who for some reason, despise us. Did we piss off Mrs. Sip some how?"

"Chahlie, the loves of our lives have tohched our sailing ships. And left us stranded on a hapless isle. To fend foh ourselves in a fens. A swamp of a thousand quagmires. We're a couple of resourceful guys. So what do we do?"

"We need a new strategy. A brave new game plan."

"It would renew our sunken spirits. And we could fohge ahead. Like *men*. By God!"

"By God!"

"Let's cook up a new course. More to our taste. As gentlemen of quiet dignity. *Panem et circenses!* Bread and circuses!"

"They're all a man really needs in this life."

"*Carne et Circen*. Flesh and sorceresses. We're doomed as it is. So we may as well die laughing. And cheat the Grim Reapeh. This calls foh our Muse. The lusty and curvaceous, Mrs. Sip."

"Of course, who would know more about altaring. Than the meandering and sodden Mrs. Sip?"

"Sex and steaks. We'll delight in both. Before the sun kisses good morning to our fickle mistress. That pixie of Dixie, Mrs. Sip. As sure as I'm sitting here."

As an antic to cheer Charles, Aeneas fell off his chair. Nearly tripping an overburdened waiter. Who emerged to reward their patience with the greatest steaks of the Crescent City. And drafts of Dixie. Evoking toasts to the Muse of the Mississippi. To gratify one appetite. And whet another.

>Joys
>of the
>tongue
>are oft
>left
>unsung.

* * *

Uptown in an Eldorado

Disco! The pulsing, sensual beat of climactic dance music hit Aeneas solidly upon the chest. Assaulting eardrums more accustomed to classical music and jazz. As he and Charles strode through the front entrance of Snobs past the white-coated doorman into the poshest club in New Orleans.

"Strategically, the courtyahd bah is the smaht place to pehch," Aeneas said.

He navigated them through a bevy of beauties to the bar.

"We're early. But soon this place will have more beautiful women per square foot than any other place in the known universe," Aeneas proclaimed. "I swear upon my fatheh's grave."

"You swear to God?"

"I swear to Zarathustra."

Come! Let us wander now! The hour has come: let us wander into the night.

A slow song from the Isley Brothers played upon a state-of-the-art sound system:

"Every time I meet a dream
Life is so sincere
About what it means . . ."

The clientele was strictly Uptown and dressed to kill. To die *le petit morte*. Penultimate gamesmanship in the offing. Much gleaming gold and silver and pearls donning necks, wrists, earlobes, fingers and ankles.

Blatant displays of designer labels. Many Brooks Brothers' suits, shirts and ties with the logo of the sacrificial sheep. The latest cuts of hair. Polo after-shave. Bally loafers and Rolex wristwatches. Calvin Klein ties with Dior shirts.

Meaningless status games. To ignite the libido of the demure, lovely ladies of New Orleans. Feline and feminine and high minded. And encourage advances by sophisticated, wealthy and handsome young men with aspirations of conquest.

The ladies wore chic designer cocktail dresses of silk and linen and rayon from Nieman-Marcus, Talbots, Sakowitz and Sibyl Helene. Legs well exposed. Close fitting, tailored, clinging. Wherever curves could be accented. According to the advantage gained and the degree of a woman's bodily blessings. To play up the strong features. Conceal the weak.

High heels from Nine West were doing justice to the calf. Sundry undergarb to accommodate sultry necklines lavished with necklaces and earrings forged of precious metals and glinting stones. Flowing feminine coiffures like lions' manes adorned sensual, trim figures. Well sculpted by jogging, biking, tennis and racquetball into tip top shape. Colognes from Paris and New York emanated nice spicy scents.

All worked a conspiracy of the senses to bolster men to advance over the stretch of real estate separating them from intimacy with beauty. With only one's self-importance to risk crashing on the rocks of rejection. Driven by hope that a witty remark and dashing smile would suffice to sweep a beauty off her feet. To launch an evening of indulgent sensuality and perhaps a lifetime of bliss to make one's spirits soar. Abide with the gods in Elysian Fields. The forbidden lotus of heaven on earth.

So many suitors and Helens seeking darlings. To say kind words of affirmation and fulfill primeval urges. Men and women were never more cultivated, accomplished and coy. Careful to keep churning passions under lock and key. And prevent an ill-turned phrase from leading to estrangement. What could be more devastating than the contempt of beauty?

Many people danced, as lights flashed. Bacchanalia amid the pulse of music. Dancers initiating and imitating intimacies. Hips twisting, buttocks boomeranging, bursting breasts bouncing in public display.

Torsos extended and retreated rhythmically. Privates in chic bikini briefs snug and smug. Feet shifting deftly and hands touching. Expressions of grimacing men and women with eyes closed. Heads tossed back with cool pain painted on their countenances. Eyes searching for secrets of the souls of their partners. In various degrees of abandon. Making calculated decisions about the lengths to let oneself go. What could be finer than the figure of beauty expressing spirit with abandon in dance?

Superceded only by amorphous visions of ecstasy.

A sensual, blue-eyed blonde in a cardinal red sweater. With imposing curves and the face of an angel. A model, perhaps. Gently, she touches the arm of a handsome man. Who converses with another gentleman beside him. Ignoring her.

She tries to gain his full attention. Grooming his hair with her fingers. And fixing his shirt to open the collar. To expose more of his broad, manly chest. She tilts her head. Lightly leaning against his shoulder. But the gentleman rebuffs her.

A sin for such loveliness to go wanting. Why do women respond so fervently to men who cannot do them justice? And vice versa? Do they perceive infatuating strength in such denial? And therein the aphrodisiac of power? Inviting negativity, rewarding it and perpetuating a cycle of   disillusionment. Wanting only what cannot be had and scorning as worthless what can. With the misconception that what is attainable lacks value. Never really having what one seeks. Sad, quixotic pursuit in the hunt for true love.

Yes, I'm game. Doomed from the outset. Noble futility. Because the odds are so against it. What soul resides within such a frame? I long to know. For I could love you. And I would be kind to you. If I thought you might love me. And be true.

But, of course, I'll do nothing. Except wonder what might have been. And she'll never even know. Because she wants him and no other.

"I am *stunned*," Charles said. "What an eye-opener. I feel like I died and went to heaven."

"One could do worse than to be footloose and fancy free. Here in good old N'Awlins," Aeneas observed.

"After-shave, work your magic."

"I use *Evening in Algiers.*"

"Personally, I prefer *Eau de Atchafalaya*. What does the wine list offer?"

Snappily, Aeneas picked up a menu. And withdrew from his jacket pocket a penlight. To shed new light on the subject of California reds.

Perusing, contemplating a cold Jax Beer, then ordering a glass of Beaulieu Vineyards Merlot. As Charles ordered Mondavi Pinot Noir. Aeneas doused the penlight.

Overhearing drink orders, he observed that the clientele requested premium brands and exotic mixes. The ambiance at Snobs living up to its name. Excessive pride. Snobbery good for the night club's commerce.

No humble Dixie longnecks. However, a half-empty Storyville Draft bottle with Lavinia on the label stared at him from the bar in mockery. He turned away the label of the bottle.

"Consideh all the lovely women here, Chahles. And bear in mind that 90% of them came here to meet a dappeh, engaging, intelligent, sensitive stud. A man of the wohld. A Bigswingingdick like you," Aeneas aennounced.

"If God were lonely, She would dance here."

"Chahlie, your morale *has* improved. Already."

"I'm beginning to see life in a new light. I was always loyal to Barb. This is all a . . . revelation."

"A friend of mine is a playboy. He once told me that he neveh understood why a man would want to spend all his life with one woman. There are so many truly magnificent ones. It's selfish. An insult to the grandeuh of the gentleh gendeh."

"'A man married is a man marred.'"

"I remembeh once strolling down Michigan Avenue in Chicago. Late one brisk fall night. Amid a galaxy of lights. I calculated that in the city of fouh million, probably a hundred thousand were making love in the course of my walk of one mile."

"How did that make you feel?"

"Lonely."

"Jack, I see the new love of my life. Smiling at me."

"At the fah end of the bah? Your optics are off, Chahlie. She's smiling at me. But I'm prepared to be cavalieh. Talk to her."

"She's too . . . beautiful."

"No such thing. Are you a man or a mouse?"

"A nutria."

"'Every talent must unfold itself in fighting.' All you have to lose is your dignity. And your self-respect."

"But I have so little right now."

"You can do it."

Charles abandoned his better judgment and safe stool. Quietly, wine in hand, he approached the beckoning creature with grace, dignity and humility. Aeneas discreetly observed as Charles was out of earshot. They spoke briefly. She shook her head positively and then negatively. Crushing out a Players cigarette. She ignored him. And he returned to his stool somewhat dejectedly.

"At least, you tried, bud. What'd you say to her?"

"I asked her if she liked vulnerable men. She said that she did. But not pathetic men."

"A bitch grammarian, Chahlie. A word-mincer. How can you be vulnerable without *pathos*? I ask you. *Ut desint vires tamen est laudanda voluptas.*"

"This is no time for dead language, Jack."

"'Though the poweh is lacking, the lust is nonetheless praiseworthy.'"
"Never mind. I *suck* at this."
"You're just out of practice. The pursuit of beauty is a Nantucket sleigh ride hahpooned to a spehm whale. Once you've done it, you neveh fohget how. But that fihst time . . . it's a killeh."

Then a svelte, young woman came to the bar beside Charles with an empty glass holding an unlit cigarette. She was confident, elegant, well dressed and smart. Sexy inviting smile. Perfect teeth. Trim with long legs and a sweet physique.

"Hi. My name's Donna."
"I'm Charles," he said, offering a light. "What are you drinking, Donna?"
"*Crème de menthe* and soda. With a twist."
"May I order you another?"
"Oh, yeah. You may. Definitely."

Charles ordered her a drink. She worked for the airlines and lived in the Quarter.

She was from Miami, loved the Caribbean and had traveled extensively to South America. The two of them clicked spontaneously.

Aeneas left for the men's room. Briefly skirting the dance floor, upstairs to another bar and dance floor past people playing Backgammon, chess and card games.

Upon reaching the last table before the sanctuary of the men's room, Aeneas beheld Lavinia. Wearing a short, basic black, cocktail dress. White hose and black, patent leather pumps. With a string of pearls and pearl earrings. Exquisite *parfum* from Sibyl Helene's Boutique.

Sitting with a well-heeled, young, extraordinarily handsome, welldressed, Uptown, golden boy. Ralph Lauren polo shirt. Khaki pants. Navy jacket. Bass Weejuns without socks. Rolex President. Gucci wallet. Slouching, not crisply sitting, at the bar. Cool and casual. Flamboyantly Uptown.

A formidable presence. Phrygid, long neck bottle of Storyville Old Style firmly in his grip. LSU class ring flashing gold with a purple stone. Ellis Ewe. Resolute to captivate.

Oddly, she seems to spurn rather than spur him. Eyes averted. Body language shouting disengagement.

Then her eyes briefly met those of Aeneas. And her attention upon her suitor grew more ardent, almost rapt. A smiling visage. Turning square and leaning toward him. Her hand upon his arm now. Encouraging.

Aeneas approached her directly. In part, because he longed to be near her. But also because she blocked his desperate course to the men's facilities.

"Aeneas John Jam," she said. "Have you met Percy Turner?"
"Pehcy."
"Jack."
Cordial hands for shaking were withheld.
"Where in the *hell* are you *from*?" Percy bellowed, smirking.
"Boston."
"You ever consider speech therapy?"
"You eveh consideh holding your tongue?"
"Sounds like you got shit in your mouth."
"I discourse in the idiom of Pilgrims."

"Well, Aeneas John Smith. Yawl are a bit off-course from Plymouth Plantation. But only by two seas. And half a damn nation. Can you even say the letter 'R' three times fast?"

"Ah-ah-ah."

"You sound like Bluebeard the Pirate."

"You aspihe to be a man of the wohld. It must have struck you that millions of Americans speak as I do. So what's your point, Pehcy Tuhneh?"

"The name is *Percy Turner*. Not *Pehcy Tuhneh*. Can you say Percy Turner without insulting my good name?"

"Pehcy Tuhneh."

"Haha!"

"Your own tongue insults your good name. Fah betteh than mine eveh could. You take all the fun out of it foh me, Pehcy."

"That's some speech impediment you have there. But it doesn't seem to hold back your tongue much. Not as much as it should."

"You eveh listen to yourself? Do your own wohds make sense even to you?"

"Here alone, are we, tonight?"

"Really, Liv, you desehve so much betteh," Aeneas replied.

"So she was just telling me, Jack."

"That's odd, I used to hear that quite a lot about you, Pehcy."

"Things change, Jack. All for the better."

"So they do, Pehcy. So they do."

"I want you to leave her alone, Jack."

"Why should I?"

"Because I *said* so."

"Back-off, Pehcy."

"She's mine, you tongue-tied dunce."

"Pehcy, I couldn't care less about you."

"I'll drag you outta here. And whip your ass."

"Anyone eveh tell you that you got a shoht fuse?"

"Cool your jets, boys," Liv intervened. "Yawl are makin' a scene."

"Liv, what do *you* say? Does he *possess* you? Do you *belong* to him?"

"I don't know what I want, Jack."

"Come to your senses, Liv . . . Excuse me, please."

Aeneas exited this brief vehement encounter to use the men's room and then breezed past them after exiting. He paused to collect his thoughts on the edge of the crowded upstairs dance floor.

A hot, sexy woman walked onto the floor and danced solo. Consumed in self-absorbed frenzy with her back to him. To the clean throbbing strains of *Take the Long Way Home* by Supertramp.

Percy asked Lavinia to dance. And she accepted.

On the fringe of the dance floor, Percy abruptly pushed Aeneas brutishly aside. And into the flailing bacchanalian arms of this zealous, erotic dancer. Who in her abandon swung a hand behind her. Just as Percy deliberately shoved Aeneas into her. And thus she inadvertently thwacked Aeneas. An arrow to the bulls-eye of his retrenching vitals.

As a first response, Aeneas played the stoic. As the pain shot through him. But he could not help folding in the middle. Legs together. As creases of anguish etched upon his countenance. Hands submissively encasing the scepter of a man's peerless pleasure. Now a cudgel of absolute pain.

Standing as he was, he saw Lavinia on the dance floor. A Janus smile of sad sympathy on her lips. Perhaps, delight in her wide eyes and arched eyebrows. As Percy howled and hooted impolitely like a madman. And pointed derisively at the misfortune of Aeneas.

Then Percy expertly maneuvered her in dance. With all of the manly grace on God's green earth. As Aeneas lumbered away in wooden retreat.

He returned to Charles, who was getting on famously with Donna. Both laughed from an exchange of wit he caught midstream. Getting the punch line without the setup. Like the epic practical joke of his existence.

"Jack, say hello to Donna."

"Hello, Donna."

"Hello, Jack."

"Donna, please excuse me. Chahlie, I have to go. But I can catch the streetcah. You stay with Donna."

"We just got here. Donna and I were just getting to know each other."

"Liv is upstaihs with that unholy snake, Pehcy Tuhneh."

Charles could see the lost expression upon the vacant visage of Aeneas.

"Donna, I hate to do this. You can't know how much. But I need to leave with my friend, now. May I please have your address and phone number? I would very much like to call to invite you out for dinner. Could we do that?" Charles asked.

"Loyalty is a trait I admire," Donna said, smiling. And she wrote down her name and number on a cocktail napkin for Charles.

"I *really* hate to leave," Charles said. "Jack, do we *have* to leave?"

"You don't. So stay. I can fly solo."

"But I'm driving."

"I'll just take the streetcah, Chahlie. It's no big deal. Just sit tight. And get to know Donna. I insist. I'll see you both."

Aeneas retreated toward the door. Once outside, he felt a sense of betrayal overcome him.

His good faith toward Lavinia and Charles had left him literally out in the cold. To his own devices. Abandoned. To anticipate the St. Charles Avenue streetcar just outside Snobs. Since they were engaged in the pursuit of new conquests.

As Aeneas awaited a streetcar heading toward Bourbon Street, Charles emerged. Driving his Eldorado.

"Hello, sailor," Charles said from the driver's seat. "Want a lift?"

"I appreciate this, Chahlie. You're a good man."

"I'm not ready for Donna yet. She's cool. But she's not Barb."

"Still, I owe you, Chahlie. You're a true friend."

"If Barb doesn't work out. I don't know. Donna seemsinterested."

"Good foh you, Chahlie. There's no love lost then. And you have options. Which make a man free."

"I *do* have a conscience. And thought it would just be selfish to stay. Considering everything. I'm just as sorry as I could be about Liv."

"Let's get stiff, Chahlie. Wohk our way down to Bourbon Street. Maybe bring the evening to a climax at *Lucky Pierre's*. Perhaps, we'll have an early breakfast when the sun also rises. Over our blessed Mrs. Sip. God love her."

"I'm with you. It's Jack Jam, right or wrong. Even if it kills me. And it may."

"It may change your outlook on life foreveh. But, I promise, it won't kill you. Let's shove off, then. To God only knows where. To meet, God only knows, whom. God only knows when."

"For, God only knows, what."

"The sweet mead of victory, my friend. Off we go in the Eldorado. It can't feel good and bad at the same time."

They ate oysters at Tyler's. Where a live band played inspired blues. And they drank Dixie longnecks. After which time Lavinia and Barb were sirens dimly howling.

The sailors drifted in the Eldorado amid a dark pall of fog. Distant from soul shattering rocks from which sirens aspired to cast mystic charms upon them.

   O,
   let
   my
   flame
   roil
   as
   long
   as
   my
   wick
   sips
   oil.
   * * *

CHIMERA VI:
The Underworld

"The Sibyl gave her warning in few words: 'Night is running quickly by, Aeneas, and we waste the hours in weeping. This is where the way divides. On the right it leads up to the walls of great Dis. This road we take for Elysium. On the left is the road of punishment for evildoers, leading to Tartarus, the place of the damned.'"— The Aeneid, Book VI

Demon Bourbon

Ride Rebel Yell Bourbon into hell! Damn the devil's uncivildrink! Bottoms up. The home wrecking homebrew of Beelzebub.

The overzealous and ungenteel lotus of Lethe. The potent pick-up potion of Persephone. The trashy sour mash of Tartarus. The bitter dregs of Dis.

Unlike wine which is fine at first sip. And offers a bouquet for one's judicious sniffer. Bourbon assaults the nostrils before it touches the tongue. More fun as one gets more numb. Ah, Dixie's the drink. Damn demon bourbon. I wish I was in Dissie. But I am, by God. In Dissieland I'll make my stand.

They cruised down St. Charles Avenue while listening to a tape of Wynton Marsalis prodigiously playing a classical piece of Haydn. *Concerto for Trumpet and Orchestra in Asia Minor*. Charles parked the Eldorado at a garage within the entirely ivory carapace of One Shell Square on Poydras Street.

The two friends disembarked toward the French Quarter and attempted to make a crossing at Canal Street. Portage fraught with peril from their alcohol-induced narcolepsy. Forsaking elegant Uptown for the madcap mayhem of the French Quarter on Bourbon Street.

A shaggy, filthy, ragged and reeking homeless man seeking spare change promptly assailed them. The fabricus of his life torn to shreds. A human sty limping along steadied by two, battered, walking styx. And an unkempt German Shepherd mix. Accosting for cash the Uptowners and tourists who breached the Quarter at Canal and Bourbon Streets. Only blocks from the brink of the levee of the Mississippi enshrouded by fog.

Claiming a need of fare for the streetcar ride Uptown. Bottle of Rose of Sharon Irish Whiskey only two good swigs from empty.

Aeneas smiled in a wobbly trance forking over a silver dollar. Gleaming alms, which Aeneas conveyed in his pocket to dispense, upon request, to homeless souls. Remembering his nightmare of lean times. That could descend at anytime without warning. Leaving one trapped and tapped-out. To roam the streets.

The homeless man displayed a brief, flash of a smile and badly decayed teeth. Settling accounts with raving advice about where to find the best restaurants and cabarets in the French Quarter.

The pair accomplished their precarious crossing of Canal into the *Vieux Carre*. Dodging St. Charles Avenue streetcars and Canal Street buses. Past the Orpheum Theatre at which *Camelot*, starring Richard Burton, was performing. A street musician played jazz on the trumpet for spare change. Blasting out *Between the Devil and the Deep Blue Sea*, a favorite Louis Armstrong tune.

Aeneas tossed another silver dollar into the musician's gaping, grape velvet carrying case. Stubbing a toe in the transaction on a curbstone.

At an unexpected handicap parking spot.
Wham! Holy shit! Pain . . . in the forehead! Christ! Owww! Phrygging nose . . . Is it bleeding? Hurts like bloody hell.
Aeneas stared down at the wet, raven, pockmarked pavement. Scraping his honker on the rough macadam rind of the horn of Bourbon Street. Eye-to-eye. Finding there perfectly smooth, round, crimson droplets of blood.
Where's my goddam handkerchief? Pants dirty. Shirt all wet. Loose change scattered over the macadam. Sober passersby staring rudely. Get up, boy!
"Jack. Here. I'll help you up. You've had a little too much Dixie."
"Pixilated on Dixie, am I?" Aeneas asked rather rhetorically.
"Imagine that."
"Don't 'dis' me now, Chahlie. Just because I'm a Yankee. With a naturally low tolerance foh Dixie. Never bohn foh the Deep South."
"How's your sense of smell?"
"Senselessly scents less. But still better than my sense of direction."
The friends took a sharp right from Canal staggering onto Bourbon Street. Soon they were navigating a predominantly gay neighborhood of the Quarter.
Wasn't it here? Bourbon and Dumaine? At the last Mardi Gras. The eccentric spectacle of a gay beauty contest. Monsieurs outfitted as outrageous demoiselles. Parading and posing before judges. Who chose a queen of queens.
They passed a public telephone on Dumaine, which unexpectedly rang. Charles retreated to answer it.
"Ghenghis Kahn's Pleasure Palace. Name your pleasure . . . Uhhuh . . . An ex-Kahn? . . . Uh-huh . . . One moment, please," Charlie said, placing a hand over the mouthpiece. "It's for you, Jack."
"Aeneas John Kahn, the Great Kahn, speaking. How may I be of sehvice to you today?"
A deep man's voice on the other end:
"I'm looking for some nice dick."
"This is Jack, not Dick. And I'm not nice."
"I want some *big* dick."
"Is this a Kahn game?"
"Do you want to talk to me?"
"Sorry. I only have 14 inches."
Then Aeneas hung up.
"You just can't please everybody all of the time, Chahlie."
They strolled aimlessly into the Quarter. Turning onto Bourbon, again, toward Canal. At the distant end of Bourbon, tourists paraded *en masse.*
Jazz faintly filtered onto Bourbon Street from cabarets. *Lazy River, Heebie Jeebies* and *Ain't Misbehavin'* entangled in perverse discordant cacophony.
They passed the overhanging sign of a porno shop advertising:
MAR*T*IAL DEVICES.
"The sign painter made a Freudian slip," Charles perceived.
"Sic 'em, Chahlie," Aeneas said.
Charles barked like a mad Dog of God.

"Could have instructive literature foh wives on self-defense against lusty husbands," Aeneas argued. "Or vice vehsa."

"All men sooner or later in the pursuit of the gentler sex hit the Wall."

"Hit the Wall?"

"You find the woman of your dreams. In an intimate little place. Show scintillating wit. Candle lit dinner. Soft music. Intimate exchanges. A cordial. Retyre to the couch. Amid encouraging signs. Await proper timing. Make advances. Kissing and fondling. Only to hit the Wall."

"The Great Wall."

"She becomes a thrash of arms and legs."

"Burrs up."

"You just think you've overcome the Wall. And you hit the . . ."

"Bahbwire?"

"Haha . . . And the Dobermans."

Charles barked, again.

"Chahlie, we could probably use some of these mahtial devices."

They entered the porno shop to explore the ordnance.

The shop offered walls of magazines tidily wrapped in plastic serranus wrap. Catering to a wide range of exotic tastes. And preferences.

Electronic devices. Private booths streamed tactless sound tracks. Erotica for a quarter in the Quarter. A derelict at the cash register. Fantasies for sale.

A ragged sign read:

NO LOITERING.

How is one supposed to engage. In the business of this elite establishment. And keep moving?

"Let's leave. Now," Charles advised.

"We just gotta get some mahtial devices. I'm just relieved to know that we're not expected to satisfy a woman with only the tools God gave us."

"What could you possibly want here, Jack?"

"Let's see if they got any mahtial arts stuff. An all-silk karate suit. To help us oveh the Wall. And we need Milk Bones foh the Dobehmans."

"This is all very, very instructive but . . ."

"So this is the competition, eh?"

"Never fails to fulfill. Says so right here."

SATISFACTION GUARANTEED. OR YOUR MONEY BACK.

"No wondeh we're losing the wah. The competition's brilliant."

Charles exited. Aeneas followed. Staggering like drunken sailors.

Past Acadian arcades in the arcane haze.

A grocery market advertised lottery tickets:

ALOTTALOOTLOTTO.

Grand prize of a million bucks. Paid as a lifetime annuity. Monthly amounts until death. Which may be, oddly enough, any minute. The winning odds a million to one. More likely to be hit by lightning. Only a buck apiece. Perchance, I feel lucky. I'll take two. Improving the oddities.

They tottered down Bourbon Street to *Lucky Pierre's*. Where Aeneas made a left turn into the front door of an unpretentious and quiet bar past a coal black iron gate.

In the front room to the right, Frankie Ford played the piano and sang *This Masquerade*:

"To understand the reasons why
We carry on this way,
We're lost inside
This masquerade we play –
Lost in a masquerade."

Aeneas pressed ahead toward the back to another French Quarter courtyard bar. High dark ceiling, many tropical plants. Wrought-iron tables and chairs. Facing a *faux* two-storied Quarter edifice with stairs to a pallid wooden balcony. At which sat many sensual, alluring sirens, who smiled as the men entered.

A waiter in a short burgundy jacket with black satin lapels and a shiny black bow tie escorted the gents to a table. He was a little man with greasy hair, a mole on his left cheek and a whisper of a mustache trimmed like David Niven's.

"Is this a brothel?" Charles asked Aeneas.

"No. But hookehs come here to unwind."

An extremely sexy woman at the bar turned on her stool winding up a big smile flashed at Charles.

"If you smile back, Chahlie, it'll cost you plenty," Aeneas counseled in a stage whisper.

On the verge of returning a shimmering grin, Charles caught self midway and converted it into the incensed, psychotic glare of a serial killer. The way one stares down a coiled rattler in one's path. Which got him off the hook. And off the hooker, as it were.

"Every woman here is . . . delicious," Charles observed.

"Just be careful not to be eaten alive, Chahlie. Remembeh: they hold the poweh. Not you. And they know this."

"In my life I never even heard of *Lucky Pierre's*."

"You've been wasting too much time wohking. Living and making a living are different, you know? Many people are confused about this."

"I'd bed any one of these women."

"Beau-ti-ful dream-eh, wake unto me . . ." Aeneas jammed off-key.

"You'll wake the dead."

"*Wake the dead*? What a medical miracle, Mr. Finnegan."

Piano bar music drifted unobtrusively soft and sensual into the patio.

"We're both too afraid to say,
We're just too far away.
We're lost inside,
This lonely game we play –
Lost in a masquerade."

The waiter came to take their order.

"Demon bourbon. Fighting Cock on the rocks," Charles said. "A double."

"A Jax Beeh?" Aeneas asked the waiter.

"We don't gut no Jax. Where you been? The Jax Brewery shut down years ago," the waiter said, rather surly as he flopped down two cocktail napkins upon their table. "We gut Dixie."

"Dixie, then. By all means."

The waiter grunted assent and left.

"What's eatin' that Beelzebubba?" Aeneas asked. "That guy wohks in paradise lost. I mean, what a schmuck."

"That's Unlucky Leo. Lucky's twin brother. The headwaiter."

"He waits in the head."

"Leo brightens up our *potty*."

Charles enunciated it as Aeneas would pronounce "party." Both parties misunderstood.

"Well, someone here must be paying off the right people, Chahlie."

"The right people more than likely come here often."

"Think so?"

"I see a Councilman at the bar. A judge at a table in the corner. A bank executive over my right shoulder. Try not to stare. A big oilman just walked in . . ." Charles advised.

Aeneas became rather indiscreetly bug-eyed.

"Holy cow, there's the head of the Orleans parish archdiocese. See him? Talking to a politician from Jefferson Parish? On your left," Charles continued.

"Really? . . . You're pulling my leg."

"I leave the pulling of your leg to you."

"You appaulus . . . Is his mission to conveht sinnehs? Or to sin?"

"I have no sense of his missionary position."

"Let's have nun of that."

The headwaiter brought drinks. Charles proposed a toast:

"Here's to beefsteak when you're hungry
To bourbon when you're dry.
To greenbacks when you're busted.
And heaven when you die."

"Ah, Dixie's the drink."

They imbibed. And Aeneas lifted his glass, again. He felt the presence of Mrs. Sip surge through him. Maybe, it was just the bourbon. Or Bourbon Street. One way or the other, spirits immersed him.

"Who'd want to be a bee and sip,
The nectar from the lotus lip.
I'd rather be a roach and steer,
Kaplunk into a Dixie Beer."

They consumed their brews and the waiter reappeared.

"How about an *apéritif?*" Charles offered.

"Fine. Southehn Comfoht. On the rocks."

"That sounds . . . comfortable. I'll have one, too. On the rocks. Just like me."

The waiter left abruptly like an automaton.

"I know how to tell if that wholly man is a priest," Aeneas advised.

"How?"

"Ask him a simple question. Which any priest could answer."

"What question?"

"Could God create a rock so big that He Himself could not throw it? If He couldn't create such a rock, why not? And if He couldn't throw it, why not?"

"Or better yet: do you think He could pass it for the Saints for a thousand yards in one season?"

"Remember you're talking about the deity who gave us mosquitoes, plagues, droughts, floods, rattlesnakes, earthquakes, rats, tornadoes, hurricanes and canceh in children. *Ad infinitum*. He must despise the hell out of us bloody miscreants."

"Think He just made the Big Clock? And lets it tick?"

"I get the impression that He wouldn't give us the time of day. And who can blame Him? He's the head of a lahge dysfunctional family. God is asleep and dreaming."

The waiter returned with their after-dinner drinks.

More toasts. Charles, first:

"I drink to your health when we're together.
I drink to your health when I'm alone.
I drink to your health so often,
I'm worried about my own."

Then Aeneas:

"Here's to Mrs. Sip's welcome, most cordial.
And to her cordial, most welcome."

They drank and Charles asked, "Where's the head at?"

"Good God, man. Don't you know the King's English?"

"Who dat? Ah nevah hoid dat. When did *dat* happen?"

"A *Penn* grad. And an *ad man* to boot? Shame on you, Chahlie. Neveh eveh end a sentence with a preposition. But if you ask, like the educated gentleman that you are. And properly rephrase your interrogatory. I know where the gentleman's facilities are located. And will conduct you to them."

"Fine by me . . . Where's the head at, jackass?"

Aeneas sensed that Charles might have feared somewhat. Being left to his own devices among the sirens of *Lucky Pierre's*. Hence, he arose to join Charles at the john, a euphemism that Aeneas execrated.

"I thought that only women went to the powder room in tandem," Charles said.

"Like trout?"

"That's an insulting observation from a chauvinist pig."

"Again, Chahlie. Don't *dis*respect me. Every hog has his day."

They walked past the brigade of hookers at the bar to the men's room. They peed side by side at the stand-up urinals. Onto little boy blue Spartan brand urinal cakes.

Aeneas read a crude handmade sign from the management:

PLEASE BE ACCUARTE.

Sic me. I'm God's phrygging urinal cake. And what an incredibly righteous pisser He is.

Charles shook the one-eyed eel and was about to slip it into his pants.

"How many *times* did you shake it?" Aeneas asked.

"What?"

"How many times did you shake *it*?"
"I wasn't counting. What's it to you?"
"If you shake it more than twice, you're playing with yourself."
"Haha. Sometimes, I swear, you're just so . . . aenal, Jack."
"You know what's wild, Chahlie?"
"Wild Turkey Bourbon?"
"Aces. Deuces. And one-eyed Jacks."
"Jumpin' Jack Jam is damn-dame-damned."
"You're dis-sing me, Chahlie. Cease and dis-sist."
"I'm not. No way."
"As they say in Texas, I know when someone's pissing on my boots. And telling me it's raining."

Stereo flushing of impressive, immaculate, shoulder-high stand-ups. Many women's names and phone numbers in unsteady scrawls on the walls above the facilities.

Aeneas considered adding Lavinia's number. And Barb's. But with rare forbearance, he refrained. As he could find no pen. And momentarily was stunned by an Achillean bull roach the size of an average Texas armadillo.

Scarab. Dung beetle. Beelzebug.

Charles returned to the table to turn a phrase dedicated to this ancient, abundant bug. Claiming that poetry was his true and destined genre. Seduced by a new muse. Engulfed in the creative fervor that consumes mystics, mullahs and minor poets.

In the meantime, Aeneas sought a public telephone. He called the highly accommodating Royal Orleans to secure a last-minute room reservation. From a friend at the hotel's front desk.

Aeneas returned to the courtyard table and Charles. Who intensely read his latest creative venture to Aeneas over a double, straight-up, Jim Beam on the rocks:

To the Roach
Here's to thee – humble prolific pod.
Antennae searching, eyes too dim to see.
Wanting the merest gleam of vitality,
E'er in flight of man's mighty plod.
As man's inclined to thee,
Thus, toward man, is God.

The poem, Aeneas said, was a minimalist neo-Romantic gem in the school of Blake. Pleased with himself, Charles downed his double.

"So, who looks good to you? At the bah?" Aeneas asked.
"See the two nearest the door?" Charles queried.
"With chaihs on the Pehsian cahpet?"
"Yes . . . I'm torn between the two ladies."
"You must favoh one."
"I like them both. Equally."

Two elegant, sexy, tall, well-dressed, voluptuous ladies smiled at Charles. And he returned their pleasing gaze. Oblivious that it could cost him plenty. They were simply irresistible.

Aeneas adjusted his tie. Nervously buttoned his jacket. Waited silently for optimal timing. Cleared his throat. And discreetly approached both women. Clandestinely slipping each legal tender in hundred dollar bills. Speaking in hushed tones.

He returned devotedly to his friend. To whom he owed a sweet luscious breakfast of Lucky's charms. Because of his missed connection with Donna. One woman left. Then, the second followed suit.

"Jack Jam, you rascal," Charles said.

"Listen to me. Go to the Royal Ohleans . . ."

"The Royal O?"

"Yes, the Royal O. Ask foh Hectoh at the front desk," Aeneas said, pulling out a business card and more legal tender. "Give him my cahd. And this tip in cash foh his sehvice. I've reshevved Room 428. The women will be there in about 15 minutes or so. The room's paid by credit cahd. Don't say I neveh did anything foh you."

"*Women*?"

"Right. Redundancy is good. In glasses of vintage reds, Cuban cigahs and women in Room 428. The Royal O. Hectoh at the front desk. Got it?"

"Hell, Jack, I'm not sure I'm *up* to this."

"I bet you ah."

"That's very . . . decent of you, Jack. What will you do?"

"Ordeh breakfast. I'll call you lateh. I'm booked foh lunch and dinneh until Mahdi Gras. But let's meet foh breakfast soon. At the Camellia Grill. The Royal O will be *monumental*, bud. Go for it."

Aeneas handed Charles a fistful of Trojans. As if they were chess pawns.

"Optimistic. Aren't we?" Charles asked.

"Betteh safe than sorry."

"Martial devices? In mass quantities."

"I hope it's your brand. Anyway, you've been living like a monk. Your reproductive chemistry is all backed up. It's unnatural. And unhealthy. So go spoil yourself."

Charles stood shakily, slapped Aeneas on the back heartily and wandered gingerly forthwith. Without contributing toward the bar tab an iota, iona, IOU or iambic pentameter. He flashed a big thumbs-up. With a determined but rather besotted smile. From the doorway he stumbled onto Bourbon Street.

Why, so often, are our chimeras so sordid? So sad? Is life so incomplete, love so unfulfilled?

If life were not all of these, what need would we have of dreams? And who can live without hope?

You've a hard road ahead, my friend. This midnight of fantasy. This walpurgisnacht *will purge some demons. And fortify you.*

Or what is Mardi Gras for?

> "Lovers
> and madmen
> have such
> seething brains
> such shaping fantasies

that apprehend
more than
cool reason
ever comprehends."
* * *

Fires of Joy

Eager, expectant River Road alongside the Mississippi at this December dusk felt impishly brisk. Cajuns were already beginning to build their *feux de joie*. Fires of joy. On the *levee* along the River.

Driftwood, cypress limbs, reeds, bamboo and sugar cane stalks stacked. To shape great *bayou* pyres. Which after dusk on Christmas Eve were set ablaze. To guide Papa Noel, the Acadian Santa Claus, in his night flight. To the homes of Cajun children. Living amid swamps of the *Mississippi Bayou*.

Relaxed in flannel shirt and jeans, Aeneas was ensconced snugly in his Garden District apartment. Fire in the fireplace. Dreading the onslaught of the holidays. And impending move into a new home on St. Charles at Octavia.

Listening to Vivaldi. Glimpsing at pictures in *Vivant* of the *Times Picayune*. Nibbling Carr's biscuits, Jarlsberg and sipping a Parducci Petite Sirrah. Like King Scipios sipping and dipping sippets into his mead. The simplicity so rich.

An article about the *feux de joie*. These bonfires were to New Orleanians at Christmas as snow was to Yankees. Then an engaging ad with photography featuring Lavinia in sleep attyre. Above intriguing body copy the headline read:

SUGAR DADDY NIGHT AT *THE GOLDEN BOW BOUTIQUE*.

Lavinia posed, in soft focus, in a sensual, soft, slinky teddy. In voluptuous femininity perched upon a fountain's edge in a French Quarter courtyard. A decent but not exquisite photo. Stunning, nevertheless, in its effect. The photo credit listed Percy Turner. Aeneas saw red.

The ad invited men to rediscover the romance and personal attention of the antebellum South.

At The Golden Bow Boutique. Where "sugar daddies" can shop for intimate apparel. For wives and mistresses as holiday gifts. Richly rewarding both recipient and giver. With a gift that keeps on giving.

The Golden Bow Boutique . . . an adventure in timeless femininity.
Coupling classic taste in fashion. Presented with impeccable attention to service. Beer and wine served. Jazz by Pudd Brown. Tonight. Starting at 9:00.

Lavinia looks great. I see her everywhere now. Photos in magazines. On billboards along St. Charles Avenue. Transit posters on the streetcar. And at Moisant International Airport by the lake.

When evening came, Aeneas rode the streetcar to the corner of St. Charles and Carrollton. A short stroll past the Camellia Grill, a Haagen-Dazs ice cream store and the Winn-Dixie. Behind the strip stores *The Golden Bow Boutique* was nestled in a quaint garden alongside the *levee*.

The aesthetically lovely *Golden Bow* display window. With tasteful dresses, hats and lingerie in pleasing scenes. Also a sign in the display window for Sibyl Helene's celebrated and social "Sugar Daddy Night." Nice clean type. With a golden *fleur de lis*. Upon which a dove nested.

At the front door of *The Golden Bow Boutique,* a tall model with lovely long legs greeted Aeneas. Perfect hourglass figure. Wearing a fox jacket and lizard shoes. Donning a necklace with a gold *fleur de lis*. Her own golden bough.

An epiphany of the first order. Peering beneath blonde bangs framing sensitive, sensual, intelligent brown eyes. Aeneas had also seen her photo around town on *Golden Bow Boutique* billboards and posters and ads in *New Orleans Magazine*. Immortalizing the fox jacket she wore in the ads. And herself.

Politely, this beauty asked Aeneas if he had an invitation. When he said that he hadn't, she recorded his name and address in a guest book with a golden *fleur de lis* blind-embossed upon its cover. And then she directed him past three New Orleans policemen sitting upon a couch together.

The three officers of the law nibbled chocolate truffles. Talking up a storm. Heads snapping back and forth in conversation. Yacking in loud voices and warily surveying Aeneas. To ensure that he belonged among the elite Uptown clientele. And was not some uninvited gate crasher.

"Hell, I invited the Captain," one policeman said to his partners.

"But his wife wouldn't let him come tonight."

Gales of laughter from all three heads of this odd merry cerberus.

Aeneas ventured into the boutique. The music of Pudd Brown, as promised, cheered him with classical jazz standards. Like *Way down Yonder in New Orleans*. Or *Smoke Gets in Your Eyes*. And *That Old Devil Called Love*. Mixed with jazzy renditions of festive songs.

Initially, Aeneas felt shy and ill at ease. The last purchase of such evening attyre having been a gift for his *ex*.

The boutique impeccably tasteful and feminine. With the ambiance of an Uptown home. And the feel of a woman's bedroom. Crowded with self-proclaimed sugar daddies. Gawking without shame or forbearance at exceptionally pretty models strolling around the store. To show off and sell the boutique's exclusive lingerie.

Men thinking impure thoughts. Frantically searching through racks for sheer, silky, revealing lingerie. Then asking the models to oblige by please trying it on. Which they pleasantly and in good humor agreed to do. Stirring the randy appetites of sugar daddies.

All of these men think they're buying the models. Instead of the lingerie. A brilliant marketing strategy. And wise way to part willing men with their abundant funds.

A smiling model with a buxom body brushed by in a sheer night gown and bikini panty. With her scent of hyacinth she reminded Aeneas of Didi.

Saleswomen dressed as Papa Noel's elves. Rung up big sales from lines of sugar daddies in pin-stripe suits, silk ties and wingtips. All purchasing gifts of sweet nothings. Amid touches of scarlet and emerald and golden garnishes that adorned the store as wreaths, garlands and ribbons.

At a niche that offered women's shoes, Aeneas found Sibyl Helene.

She sipped white wine in a narrow passageway. Strikingly dressed in a frost white gown with much lace and silver trimming. And a regal, snowy hat with more lace, silver trim and little tendrils of white in front.

Raven hair and warm, gray, welcoming eyes. Confident and gracious. Trim and sleek. Proud, modern and thoughtful. A veritable vision. This Beatrice of the Delta budding in her realm. An April rose. A newlywed, he thought he had read in *Vivant*.

From the counter she lifted a carnival, *papier-mâché* mask, which was for sale, and hid her face behind it. A puckish mask. Behind which she laughed as she viewed herself in the mirror.

"It's the real you," Aeneas advised with a smile.

She unmasked and pleasantly extended a fragile flower of a hand, which Aeneas shook. A firm, aristocratic, lady's handshake.

"I'm Sibyl Helene. I don't believe we've met. Call me Siby."

"Mrs. Siby, I'm Aeneas. But most of my close friends just call me Jack. I run Aeneas Studios on Bourbon Street. I'm a photographeh."

Aeneas handed Sibyl his business card.

"How do you feel about our photography?" she asked.

"It could be betteh."

"You wouldn't believe the agony we endure. For our ultimate creative results."

"I would. That agony resides in all wohthy aht."

"Let me show you my store."

Gently, she escorted him by the arm.

"Over here we make our hats," Sibyl said with warm accessibility.

Many shelves of undecorated hats and hatboxes. Ribbons, feathers and French silk flowers. Highly lifelike.

Then an area that exclusively sold make-up. Her own line of perfume. Which she sprayed upon her slender wrist and extended sublimely for a sniff.

Onto the lingerie section. Where throngs of sugar daddies lurked. Shoulder to shoulder. The power elite of the city. Politicians, executives, entrepreneurs, financiers, lawyers, bankers and surgeons. Professional football players from the Saints. Who wore golden *fleurs de lis* upon their helmets as they played like hell. Even Mardi Gras krewe kings. All men.

Aeneas recognized among the crowd a rogue's gallery of supremely talented and rich scoundrels. Many of whom he had photographed in his studio on Bourbon Street. Eyes popping out of their heads at scantily adorned models. Feasting upon fine white wines of France. In this world of unders. And undress.

"When I was a little girl, I helped my mother sew silk underwear. Which an order of nuns sold to affluent, Uptown ladies. To support a boarding school," Sibyl explained. "Now we have all this."

She waved to an impressive display of fine lingerie.

"Would you say that you appeal to the Southehn decadence of New Ohleanians?" he asked, smiling.

"I would *never say* such a thing," she said.

Her mystical smile reappeared. Naughty. Sweet. And smart. Her boutique exuded vibrant vitality, like her own mantle. Of sensual, elegant and discreet fantasy.

"Be sure to stop at the bar for a libation," Sibyl said, pointing in the right direction.

"Thank you foh the tour. You've been a most generous hostess."

"Select something nice. For someone you love. For the holidays."

"I cehtainly will."

Although I have no mistress at the moment. Not a soul to love me. I am alone. Eternally, infernally alone. Except for the muse of Mrs. Sip.

She waved. And became immersed among a horde of men. A woman of amiable grace.

Aeneas navigated deliberately to the bar. Anchored, he ordered a glass of Olde Bourbon by J.W. Dant on the rocks. Adjacent this island of womanly sensuality. Where Uptown sugar daddies came to buy lingerie from perfect ladies. For girlfriends, fiancées, wives and mistresses.

"Jack Jam. Nice to see you," said a young insurance executive, whose name escaped Aeneas. Flinging a hand into the face of Aeneas. Flashing a big business smile. Iron grip. Fit and trim. Elegant navy blue suit. Conservative regimental striped tie. Shiny cordovan loafers. Five o'clock shadow. Breath smelled of pipe tobacco. Inadequately masked by peppermint Lifesavers.

"Why, hello. Nice pahty. How is business at the Etna?" Aeneas asked.

"Magnificent work on the photography for our regional advertising.

My boss at the home office in Hartford loved it. It's better than the national ad campaign."

"Why thank you. We'll have to do it, again. Soon."

"Call me."

"I will. Afteh Mahdi Gras."

Both men nodded smiles and then speared in different directions through the surging ranks of sugar daddies.

Aeneas spied Lavinia modeling a scanty salmon mousse pink bra and matching high-cut French thong beneath a sheer bridal white dressing gown. Among many tongue-tied, bug-eyed admirers. Including Percy Turner nearby. Whom she seemed to ignore totally, Aeneas noticed, as if he didn't exist. Despite his persistent, obnoxious efforts to corner and engage her in dialogue.

A feeding frenzy fired by the libidos of ardent sugar daddies arose in its pitch and intensity. As gentlemen in the holiday spirit sipped too many fine wines and spirits. Evolving slowly but surely into swine.

"May I see you in this, please?" a hungry banker asked. Extending a luminescent, expensive, silk bra and panty set on a coat hanger to Lavinia.

"Sure thing," she said, smiling.

The rich interest of the banker escalated usuriously. As she accepted the attyre. With its sumptuous price tag. And disappeared to change.

Aeneas considered approaching Lavinia but decided against it. The timing was all wrong. She was working the crowd. Who couldn't get enough of this Uptown goddess. The more prudent course was to await a better opportunity.

What could she possibly have to say to me, anyway?

After finishing a glass of wine, he decided to leave. And wandered through the mass of males to the exit.

Outside the men's room, he observed Sibyl engaged in conversation with Andrew Palmer. Whose numerous phone calls Aeneas had not yet returned. So he quickly ducked undetected into the men's room.

Hearing their voices pass the door. When the coast was clear, he beelined for the boutique's front door.

Before leaving, the gorgeous blonde model beamed. Sweet gatekeeper of a world of unders. In her jacket of fox she stole the heart of Aeneas.

"May I ask your name, please?" he inquired.

"Virginia."

"Thank you foh admitting me without an invitation, Vihginia."

"You're most welcome. Would you like a truffle?"

Virginia offered him a small box of chocolates wrapped in gold foil.

"Ah, Tuecer's Chocolates. How sweet of you to offer. Yes, thank you."

"Sibyl buys them in New York. At the Plaza."

Aeneas selected a rich, delicious, champagne chocolate truffle.

"You may as well leave with a yummy taste in your mouth. Because we want you to come back."

"It's divine. Like you."

"Something tells me we'll see more of you. Won't we?"

"I'll come, again. Soon. I promise."

Virginia smiled divinely. And Aeneas exited onto Hampson Street, heading toward the St. Charles Avenue streetcar stop.

Must we say good-bye. So soon after saying hello? My flower of life.

The winter air was phrygid. At the streetcar stop, his eyes followed the grassy bank of the *levee*. Along which upriver the Cajuns built their pyres.

Virginia lit within him a *feux de joie*. Although it was too soon for plump Papa Noel to arrive.

> The
> air
> smelled
> surreally
> like
> snow.

* * *

CHIMERA VII:
War in Lathium

"Great king, son of Faunus, it is not black storms that have driven us to this land of yours, nor have we lost our way by mistaking a star or a coastline. It is by design and with willing hearts that we sail to this city, driven from our own kingdom . . . Since that cataclysm we have sailed all those desolate seas, and now we ask for a little piece of land for our father's gods, for harmless refuge on the beach, for the air and sea which are there for all men. We shall not bring discredit to your kingdom. Great fame will be yours . . . I swear by the destiny of Aeneas."
— *The Aeneid, Book VII*

No Instant Grits

Assiduously, Charles expressed his generous gratitude to Aeneas for an uncommon existential encounter.
"I'll never forget, as long as I live, the Royal O," he said. "I mean to tell you. What an experience."

"It was meant to be one."

They ate a late breakfast at the Camellia Grill. Charles devoured pecan waffles as Aeneas consumed a substantial Swiss cheese omelet and grits.

"How' evrathing, gentlemen," a young waiter wearing a white coat with flat feet asked them. A bundle of nervous energy. Cheerful smile. A professional in love with his humble trade.

"The waffles taste so fresh. Not like those Golden Grain storebought frozen dealiebops," Charles offered.

"Great grits!" Aeneas added.

"We doane use no instan' grits, foh sure. Them instan' grits ain't no good. We use dem hominy grits what take an eternity ta make. Unnestan'? Cain't get 'em afta 'leven AM. Not heyuh. Chef close down da grill on grits at 'leven. You jus' made it undah da wire on da grits. You doane want dem instan' grits an' dats foh true," the waiter explained.

He discoursed for some time on the virtues of slow cooking grits.

"Cane syrup, please?" Charles asked. "It's the ambrosia of the gods."

"You got it, captain," the waiter said, reaching down the counter and with a single, smooth, sweep, slid the bottle of syrup ten feet toward Charles.

"Would you please pass the jam?" Aeneas asked.

The young waiter responded immediately. Bouncing a small jar of jam off his left elbow and catching it with his right hand. With a flourish to present the jam to Jack.

"Please pass the Tarquin's Tartar Sauce," Charles requested.

On the bottle label, always in good taste, noble Alexander I of Russia prominent upon a rearing Arabian stallion. Signaling to attack with a raised blade of sword. Encircled by red stars which motto read:

THE CZAR OF TARTARS.

"Tartar sauce? Foh peecan waffles? Are you nuts?"

"It's pah-kahn, Jack. Peecans are toilets. Shushup, now. And watch."

"Didi's dog is nicknamed Peecan. How *apropos*. Maybe, she's path Peecaenese."

"She calls me once a week about you, Jack. I hate to waffle. I'm running out of lame excuses for you."

"You're not alone, Chahlie. So am I."

The waiter performed similar stunts with Tarquin's Tartar Sauce. A veritable man of a thousand hands. They watched in awe of his digital dexterity.

"I love this place," Aeneas said.

"I bet he makes good tips," Charlie observed.

"So the Royal O was okay?"

"Just what the doctor ordered. I'm a new man. I swear it."

"You've got to blow those demons out of you," Aeneas said. "Lost souls of the dahk spirit. You got to puhge them. Fight fihe with fihe. The fihe of spent desihe. Otherwise, you end up walking around halfdead. Emotionally crippled. No good to anyone. Especially, yourself."

"My head is clear. But, sometimes, I just feel . . . *totally* lost."

"I understand. I'm there, too."

The two men ate the liberal portions of their breakfast with relish.

Charles attacks his waffles. Like Piquante with a chew toy. The man is a savage beast. God, what an appetite? I'm full already. Gorged. And that phrygging cane syrup tastes like hell compared to real Vermont maple syrup. Man, I'm gonna need a Tums after this.

"Hungry, are we?" Aeneas asked.

"Starving. It's so late, I could eat the plate."

"I honestly hope you never know the true meaning of stahvation."

"My days of starvation are long gone, bud."

"Stahvation assumes many fohms."

"Anyway, after the Royal O. *Carpe deum*. There's one you can cross off my list."

"Foh today."

"But there's something we need to do for you, Jack. Because our friendship is a two-way street. *Quid pro quo*."

"What's that?"

"A 'coming out.' In the New Orleans debutante tradition."

"What do you mean?"

"A second coming."

"Like Yeats? 'The ceremony of innocence is drowned.'"

"No, I mean, a deb ball."

"An introduction to society?"

"Correctomundo."

"Why on eth would society have me?"

"We'll give it no choice."

"What makes you so sure I'll have society?"

"No man is an island, Jack."

"I'm Thoreauly unamused by society. Donne with it."

"You're a peninsula."

"Only privately. I'm a misfit. No good to anyone. Not even to me."

"You're my best friend, Jack. That must count for something."

"Does that mean you're picking up the tab foh once?"

"Let's go Dutch."

"From you, Chahlie, that sounds odd. Foh some reason."

"I got brothers in Haarlem."

The two men ate voraciously, as if there were no tomorrow.

"We'll place a notice in the *Vivant Section* of the *Times-Picayune*," Charles advised. "I got connections there."

"Ah, yes, the *Living Section*. I constantly get pretty invitations in the mail to quaint parties for tea."

Confusing as Aeneas pronounced "pahties" as Charles would say "potties."

"I can see it all now: presentations, luncheons, teas, cocktail parties, formal and informal dinners, dances and other sundry *divertissements*," Charles said.

"Culminating, of course, in Mahdi Gras *bals masques*."

"Or possibly even climaxing in the meeting of Rex and Comus. At midnight on Shrovetide. Jack, you could be the first *demonsieur* of New Orleans."

"Why should *demoiselles* have all the fun?"

"We can take a photo of you at the helm of the *Dixie Dream*. With the headline: AENEAS JOHN JAM –
DEMONSIEUR WITH A SENSE OF DIRECTION: UP."

"The only three potential problems are: 1) I have no sense. 2) I have no sense of direction. 3) Lately, things haven't been looking up."

"We could put a notice in the Sunday paper with other debutante announcements. Among the bumper crop of debs coming out of their cocoons. Or how about something more understated:
DEMONSIEUR ADVENTURER
PURSUES UNEXPLORED PLEASURES."

"Neveh to return, Chahlie. Lost in the funhouse."

"We could throw in some stuff about whitewater rafting . . ."

"A real wonderbuoy."

"Running with wild wolves in Alaska . . ."

"More like dancing with Uncle Remus in *Song of the South*."

"Playing first violin in the symphony . . ."

"I'm too base."

"Visiting those at death's door . . ."

"I need my own asylum."

"Rappelling . . ."

"You mean repelling."

"Stalking wild boars . . ."

"Wild bores is closeh."

"Safaris . . ."

"Hunting dearies. At Snobs."

"Riding in the hunt. Horsemanship is key . . ."

"That reminds me of Napoleon's great toast:
*'Here's to good women and good horses
And to the good men who mount them.'"*

"Napoleon would have made a *Demonsieur par Excellence*. Could have made something of himself. Born too soon. Also from the wrong Orleans. The old one. A crying shame."

Aeneas ordered another cup of chicory coffee.

"Then you're *for* the idea? You'll be the goddam Queen of the May. What do yawl think?" Charles asked.

"That dog won't hunt," Aeneas replied. "As they say here in the Deep South."

"Why not?"

"First, you must become a *sub*-dem."

"I can't picture you as a junior dem."

"I may be too senior. Too fah gone. Past the point of no return."

"You have to come up from the right club. Pendennis. Society of the War of 1812. Bienville. Essex. That's just the way it's done. Otherwise, you'd be spotted as a fraud in no time. Ruin everything. Hell's bells, Jack. It's just plain ole bad form."

"Let them eat cake, Chahlie."

"King cake?"

"I'm all foh it. Just foh the spoht. Except foh one small detail."

"What?"

"Foh a *dem* or *sub-dem* I also might be too married."

"Don't be coy, Jack. I've seen that reluctant debutante routine a million times in this town."

"My cocoon is long gone. Torn to shreds. By every fickle wind that blows."

"But as butterflies go, you're a monarch, Jack. Born to reign."

"I was born to snow."

"As the first *demonsieur*, you get to write the rules. For generations that follow. Think of what it could lead to."

"I shuddeh to think, Chahlie. Marriage. Betrayal. And divohce. *La petite morte verite*."

"Don't forget rebirth, Jack."

"We'll come back to life yet, Chahlie. It may be a crooked path we tread. But by hook or by crook. We'll make it out alive. Find our way. Somehow."

"I say put on your lucky underwear. Damn the cocoon. And come out standing tall."

"I've seen more social buttehflies escape more cocoons than Houdini."

"Social butterflies never die. They just become sober."

"They flit from one lotus blossom to the next."

"Paradise regained."

"Paradise of fools. Call it what you will. To me, it's just home."

Charles suddenly became rigid as a pillar of salt. He stared transfixed at a striking, young woman. As she entered the great ivory painted door of the Camellia Grill. Accompanied by a rugged, bearded, young man in an L.L. Bean chamois shirt and gabardine slacks. The couple assumed seats at the far side of the diner.

"Chahlie, you look like you've seen a ghost."

"That woman . . . She's a dead ringer for Barb."

"Is she Bahb?"

"Dear God, no. I see Barb everywhere I go. She haunts me. That woman is even wearing a gold serpentine necklace. Like one I gave Barb on her last birthday."

Although neither man had finished his coffee, Charles touched his napkin to his lips and said, "Let's go."

Charles paid the tab and Aeneas left a generous tip. They walked outside into the bright, blinding sunshine of Carrollton Avenue at midday.

Charlie is bummed. Deer God, a barb to the heart. Try small talk. Rally the troops. He needs something and someone to take his mind off her.

"Would you mind dropping me at St. Chahles and Erato Street, Chahlie?" Aeneas asked.

"What's at Erato?"

"The love of my life."

"No, really."

"I need a cah. I take the streetcah everywhere. Not that I really go anywhere. Whenever I drive, I get lost. I was a half-hour late foh my date Uptown with Didi. Lost somehow on the West Bank. So, you want to help me pick out a cah?"

"New or used?"

"Practically new. Or hardly used."

"Now that the big bucks are rolling in, Jack."

"*E pluribus unum*. I just got a nice check foh the down-payment. From some mutual funds recommended by Evan, Andrew's financial wiz kid."

"Which fund group?"

"Janus."

"As long as you're happy, Jack. Are they no-load?"

"Low-load . . . But about my new cah. Rumoh has it that Satuhn is a good deal. There's a new dealership on Erato. Want to come along?"

"Sure. Hey, have you ever considered a Mercury? Maybe, a Zephyr?"

"I had an ancient Mehcury Grand Marquis. It always broke down. Cost me a Fohtune. The Pahking Authority auctioned it off foh $50. I just need a basic cah. Foh around town."

"Hey, Percy Turner's father just opened a big Saturn dealership out in Bridge City. At the foot of the Huey P. Long Bridge. The sales tax may be cheaper in Jefferson Parish."

"Out in the swamps? By Jean LaFitte State Pahk?"

"Jack, everything in New Orleans is near a swamp . . . I'll drive us there, if you want."

"Why would I do business with *anyone* associated with Pehcy?"

"I see your point."

"Pehcy's a blind spot. Just the mention of his name . . . I can hahdly say it. Without going mad."

Charles strolled silently with his hands in his pockets to the scarlet Eldorado. As they embarked into the front seat, Charles inserted his key into the ignition and turned over the big, smooth, Cadillac engine.
Charles pushed into the sound system a tape of legendary jazz and *For All We Know* played:

> "*We may never meet, again.*
> *Before you go,*
> *Make this moment sweet, again.*
> *We won't say good-bye*
> *Until the last minute.*

> *I'll hold out my hand.*
> *My heart will be in it."*

They cruised down St. Charles toward the Saturn dealership on Erato. In the University section approaching Tulane, Sophie Newcomb and Loyola.

"When are you going out with Donna? From Snobs?" Aeneas asked.

"I'm not."

"Why not, Chahlie?"

"I'm not ready yet."

"You're ready. Call Donna. She likes you. She's a babe. She wants to spoil you rotten, Chahlie."

"It's no good, Jack. I still love Barb. I can't hide from it. Or blow smoke. I still love her. When I saw that gold necklace, I was sure she was Barb. I'm so screwed up, Jack."

> *"So love me tonight.*
> *Tomorrow was made for some.*
> *Tomorrow may never come*
> *For all we know."*

Charles began to break down. He couldn't contain himself any longer behind his own sundering perimeter of stoicism. The music just got to him.

At the advice of Aeneas, he steered the Eldorado to the shoulder of St. Charles. To catch his breath and collect himself at Audubon Park. Across the Avenue from Lavinia's home on Audubon Place. Andrew's Silver Shadow slowed to a stop in the drive of his Greek Revival mansion.

Ah, there goes my beauty. Out for a drive in her daddy's Rolls Silvius Shadow. Maybe, I'll catch a glimpse of her sweet face. God, I miss her. I know how Charlie feels. I see a vision of Lavinia at every turn, too. At work. At night. In relentless dreams of her.

My wife, too. Once at Sibyl Helene's. While shopping for Liv. I thought it was she. Distant pictures. Incoherent ragged pixels. Images fuzzy and out of focus. Phantasms shot through the fisheye of lost love.
I hope Liv doesn't see us in Charlie's fire engine red Caddy. And jump to the conclusion that I'm spying on her. Or worse yet, stalking her. It would make Liv livid.

The driver opens the front door of the Silver Shadow. I see her now. Looking prettier than ever. Carrying shopping bags from Sibyl Helene. Her hair is styled differently. Shorter. But nice. Lavinia is such a knockout.

But someone else climbs out from the Rolls, too. A man. But not Andrew.
It's him! She's gone back to him!

> *"This may only be a dream.*
> *We come and go*
> *Like a ripple on a stream.*
> *Love me tonight.*
> *Tomorrow may never come.*
> *For all we know."*

* * *

Private Battles

Mercurially, his phone intoned, as Aeneas lay abed in his Garden District apartment. Midway through reading a new prose translation of Virgil. And listening to old jazz. Duke Ellington's classic *Tulip or Turnip* on PBS radio in the background. Sipping the remains of a bottle of husky Fetzer Merlot.

"I want you back, Jack."

A silky smooth woman's voice. Slow and soothing. Tinged with desire.

"You do?"

"Yes. I do."

"Why?"

"I miss you, that's all. Do I need a reason?"

"Yes."

"I miss being with you."

"That's too bad."

"Now, be good, Jackie. My sweet boy."

"I thought you were . . . involved with someone else."

"I'm not. If I were, I wouldn't be calling you, now. Would I?"

She's too dangerous. Too wild. She'll eat you alive. But, God, it's good to hear her voice. And I miss her desperately. Play it close to the vest. Or you'll be the loser.

"Tulip or Turnip?
Rosebud or rhubarb?"

"Are you there, Jack?"

"Um, yes."

"Then talk to me."

"What about your loveh?"

"Who?"

"You know who . . . The buffoon."

"You have nothing to worry about."

"You gave me up foh him. As I recall."

"I did no such thing. There's nothing going on between us. That's all in your head."

"I don't think so. I have the battle scahs to prove it. Afteh you abandoned me foh weeks. You treated me like diht. And I gave up hope on us."

"What battle scars?"

"I have them. Never mind where."

"Jack, are you playing hard to get?"

"No, I'm truly concerned. And with good reason. Anyway, playing hahd to get is your game."

"Did I hurt you?"

"What do you think?"

"I'm so sorry, sweetie. I miss you terribly."

"Me, too. But why did you break it off? So suddenly."

"I made a mistake. And I'm apologizing. I want you to forgive me. You can, can't you?"

You're about to walk through a great gate. The door of opportunity opens. Heaven or hell on the other side. From which there may be no turningback. The woman of your dreams. Gird your loins. She knows where you live. And what makes you tick. But she could eat you alive. In a New York minute.

"Tulip or Turnip?
Moonbeam or mudpie?"

"Jack?"

"I'm thinking."

"I'm only asking you to forgive me."

"It's not that simple. My life is so fragile. I could lose everything in a blink."

"I won't let you, Jackie. I want to be your partner."

"You're the cause of my Chaos."

"We can work it all out, can't we?"

"I just don't know."

"There's nothing bigger than you and me together."

"You're so damn beautiful. You're every man's dream."

"I want to be your private dream."

"Beauty betrays."

"I don't know about all that, Jack. But *I* didn't betray *you*."

Look at the premium men pay. For admission to beauty. The lengths they go. Seduced. And made suckers. It's so damn disillusioning. So empty. In the end you're a fool for trying. And the only thing worse is not trying. Because you might as well be dead. Than give up. But why must beauty betray? As it does, so relentlessly.

"Tulip or Turnip?
Bankroll or IOU?"

"Talk to me, Jack. We haven't given ourselves enough of a chance."

"I feel empty."

"You do?"

"Unfulfilled."

"You just need me to love you."

"I'm running around New Ohleans like a maniac. Fighting off demons. Left and right. Trying to fill what can never become full."

I must be some strange Quixote lost in Dixie. Bashing my brains out in foolish quests. Running as fast as I can. In pursuit of pure fantasy.

Love. Sex. Women. Money. Business. Success. Material wealth. Social status. Professional prestige. And I'm going nowhere. Smashing brutally into reality at every turn.

Bleeding my spirit dry. What do I really want? It must not be so complicated. But what is it? I have no idea. I should feel more at home with it. Whatever it turns out to be.

"You've come a long way, Jackie. With miles to go before you sleep, honey. But I can take you to the promised land. It's within our grasp."

Ripeness is all I seek. But each pecan I pick from the tree is no good. It rots in my hand as soon as it parts from the live branch. Inedible. Or worse, poison. What vast angry force of life holds me in its grip? Thrashing me so cruelly?

"Tulip or Turnip?
Rosebud or rhubarb
Moonbeam or mudpie
Bankroll or IOU
What am I to you?"

"Tell me what you're thinking, Jack."

"I'm afraid of you."

"Why?"

"I just am. I desire you. And feel deeply foh you. I respect your intelligence. And your competence. But you scare the hell out of me. I can't take too much more hurt. My life is a clown act."

"No, it isn't, Jackie."

"I'm ready to commit myself to the Jackson Street Asylum. The insane place madmen call me about. At all hours of the day and night. I'm a lunatic magnet."

"You're being too hard on yourself, dear."

"I'm afraid to let you in close. Do you understand?"

"You can't just walk through life. And ignore what's important to you. That would deny life its meaning. And be too sad."

"But it would be safe. And keep me intact."

"Playing it safe isn't your style, Jack. It takes courage to love. And you're a true artist."

"Am I?"

"Of course, you are. I believe in you. My daddy once told me that if you have a choice between experiencing something in life and not, you should always try to experience it. As long as it doesn't hurt you. Or anyone else. That's what living is for."

Aeneas was mute.

"Shoot, Jack, you're the one always taking pictures of loveliness. Of life. I love that about you. And look at all the beauty you've discovered. In your travels. I wanted to know you. To love you. When I saw your art. I wanted to know the man who saw so much in life. Who could share my life with me. So that we could find the beauty of life together."

"You mean it?"

"Jack, beauty is your business."

"My photos never betray. They endure. That's why I photograph."

"Of course, *possessions* don't betray. That's why so many people with money surround themselves with nice things. Uptown New Orleans is full of rich people who possess everything. Except real love. Their possessions can't save them. Can't fill up the emptiness. Can't make them whole. I know this much is true. Believe me."

"It takes a hell of a lot of guts to love a woman like you. I'm not good enough foh you. You desehve someone better. Much betteh."

"I only want you."

"I'm flattered. Really. But unfit foh you. We aren't equal. We live on different planes. I can't keep up with you. You're way over my head. You seem to be within reach. But you're not. You're an exquisite chimera."

"We're kindred spirits, Jack. Don't you give up on us. Hear?"

"I would love to believe that."

"It's true . . . But speaking of different planes. I do have some news . . ."

"So . . . let's hear it."

"Well, I showed some of the head shots you took of me. To the head of a big modeling agency in New York . . ."

"Which one?"

"The June Wilhelm Agency."

"They're wicked good. Fihst rate."

"Sibyl knows June. Because Sibyl's always going up to the Garment District. To buy for the boutique . . ."

"So?"

"June was visiting Sibyl. June was at *The Golden Bow* on Sugar Daddy Night."

"So what?"

"So I met June Wilhelm. At the store . . ."

"And?"

"She asked to see my portfolio. So I showed her the work we did together."

"The head shots? The studio wohk? The ads?"

"All of it."

"What did June think?"

"She loved it."

"Get out!"

"It gets better. She wants to fly me to New York. To discuss a contract."

"So you're going?"

"Yes. I plan to. It may turn out to be nothing. But I've got to give it a shot. Know what I mean?"

"If they weren't serious, they wouldn't invite you to New Yohk. Way to go!"

She's gone. I've lost her. Not that I really ever had her. But I was right. She was too far beyond me. And Andrew was right, too. I would have held her back. She's going to split the Big Easy for the Great White Way. Good for her. It's what she wants.

"It could be a dream come true. Because of you," she said earnestly.

"I'm grateful to you, Jackie."

"I didn't do a damn thing."

"June Wilhelm just *loved* your photography."

"Of *you.*

"She has a *ton* of contacts in New York. Big ad agencies. Corporations. Magazines. You name it."

"They would be extremely fohtunate to win you."

"So would *you*."

"I know. But that's really not the question. Is it? . . . Would you move up Nohth? If things wohk out? New Yohk's a great city."

"I don't know, Jack. I love New Orleans. And daddy . . . well, he just doesn't know what to think right now. He's seriously conflicted."

"I bet."

"But I'd fly up to New York all the time. And travel around the world. On photo shoots. I'll know more after I visit New York."

"Wow!"

"I know. It's hard to believe. But it really could happen."

"I don't know what to say."

"We're good together, Jack. We make a good team. And the opportunity at the June Wilhelm Agency just proves it."

"You're giving me way too much credit."

"You were the one who told me in the first place. You said I was on the wrong side of the camera. Remember?"

"Hell, I feel like a jackass."

"Why, babe?"

"You had all this great news. And I bahely gave you a chance to tell me. I was rambling on like an idiot . . ."

"How about if I just come over?"

"What? Now?"

"Sure. Why not? We could celebrate. I'll bring a bottle of DP."

"But I'm in bed . . ."

"Well, then. Don't you dare move."

"I won't, Dreamface."

I'm
caught
in
another
gale
of
Fate.
* * *

CHIMERA VIII:
Aeneas in Rome

"This is the home that is decreed for you . . . Do not give it up. Do not be intimidated by the threat of war. All of the angry passions of the gods are now spent. But come now, so that you may not think what you are seeing is an empty dream."
— *The Aeneid, Book VIII*

Pictures of Happiness

Serendipitously, business boomed at Aeneas Studios on Bourbon Street. Aeneas had reinvested a healthy portion of revenues into new equipment. And redecorated to provide an enhanced ambiance, which his wealthy clientele would find both comfortable and appealing.

Andrew Palmer had given him a *carte blanche* that Aeneas was reluctant to deploy. Determined to make good on his own.

He rapidly established a reputation in New Orleans as a hot photographer. Sought-after by wealthy Uptowners for family portraits.
Executives in top corporate echelons demanded him for marketing, advertising, PR and investor relations' photography. And for their portraits displayed outside Board Rooms.

He was contracted exclusively for cover photography for *New Orleans, Southern Living* and *Lagniappe Magazines*. He still accommodated Andre Boudreaux at UPI, whenever possible, for old times sake. Because Andre had kept the wolf from the door during the hard times.

Kings of the most exclusive Carnival krewes resorted to strongarm tactics in booking. The appointment book of Aeneas was full. As the Carnival Season was at hand. Shot in festive, regal costumes for posterity to remember. He was pressured into shooting weddings at St. Louis Cathedral, which he later began to refuse.

He weighed hiring more employees, which now he could easily afford. But his clients demanded him behind the Hasselblad. No substitutes would suffice.

Aeneas was reluctant to relinquish control over the quality of his art. He did all of the creative work – the shooting and developing — personally.

He declined sittings rather than overbook. His waiting list grew embarrassing long. Whenever he was forced to turn away work, his polite decline inadvertently served to heighten demand for his photography.
His photo sessions evolved into a status symbol.

This surge of popularity created an uncomfortable situation. He hiked his fees to the brink of unreason. To limit the quantity of his work so that he would continue to provide superior quality. But despite the
exorbitant fees, the wealthy had no qualms about paying dearly for the immortal images that he created so masterfully for them.

Strides in personal income, and Andrew's connections in banking and real estate, enabled Aeneas to secure a substantial mortgage at close to the prime rate. He bought a lovely, Louisiana center hall cottage on St. Charles Avenue near Octavia.

Increasingly, he was invited to Uptown *fetes*. A party for the governor. Debutante balls. An affair at Commander's Palace for a guest conductor of the symphony. A dinner

party for Senator Russell Long at the Plimsoll Club. A tea for the opera directors at the Pontchartrain Hotel.
Forum borium.

He attended most social events with Lavinia. They were good for business. And frequently people commented upon what a fine young couple they made. Occasionally, their photo appeared in the society pages of the *Times-Picayune*. And they were mentioned in Betty Guillotte's column entitled *Lagniappe.*

Andrew used his influence to admit Aeneas into Rex, a major feat for such a young man who was *nouveau riche* and of foreign, indeed, Yankee origins. The successful intervention of Andrew was a major *coup* for Aeneas. And from Rex it was a logical leap into the Boston Club.

Aeneas consented to be dragged off to pretentious affairs at the insistence of Lavinia. At first, he was reticent and uncomfortable. But Lavinia helped draw out his wit and sense of humor to delight the erudite aristocracy of New Orleans.

His accommodating, self-deprecating sense of humor with the stunning, charming and finely dressed Lavinia at his side came to represent a welcome social encounter.

And so it went in this golden age that, years hence, he might look back upon as his heyday.

Mardi Gras advanced relentlessly. The balls, which began after Twelfth Night, heightened in social importance as Fat Tuesday approached.

Parades drew the city onto its streets. With all the revelry and spectacle of Chaos for which Mardi Gras in New Orleans was world-renowned.

With the arrival of Carnival Season, the workload of Aeneas became a thrash. At times, he felt a victim of his own business success. Stung by the infringing pressures of a hectic social and professional life.

After late nights several times each week and inevitably arriving at the *Café du Monde*. Eating *beignets* and sipping *café au lait.* Armored in his tuxedo from Brooks Brothers. Sterling silver studs in his white starched shirt at the buttons and sleeves. Silver tie and cummerbund. Socializing until the wee hours.

Even after those Carnival Balls he did not work. The energy required by his work became elusive. To survive the turmoil of the Carnival Season, he evolved into a social soldier of Fortune. There were some mornings when the mere click of the shutter sent shudders surging through his cranium.

As the Season progressed, the Mardi Gras Balls seemed inexplicably redundant. Despite the individual grandeur each strove so hard to project. Every reigning krewe king similarly gamboled, paraded and waved his scepter in the glaring spotlight on the floor of the Municipal Auditorium. Before an adoring formally attyred crowd and masqueraders.

Amid bright, lavish stage settings. Prior to ascending his throne. In repetitious ceremonial pomp.

At times, it grieved him to think that so many sleek, gleaming Uptown brides and grooms, whom he had photographed, would become alienated and divorced. And moon with pangs of heartbreak at their dearly bought wedding photos. That ultimately just gathered dust in dark drawers.

Once during Carnival Season he photographed the chairman of the board of a great Southern insurance company at the pinnacle of his career. Aeneas imagined this captain of industry in his less fulfilling and imminent forced retirement. Whose portrait of prior corporate grandeur would mock and heighten a sense of decline. A man whose vision and energy and shrewdness built a small regional company into a multinational Fortune 500 corporation.

As pretenders and usurpers in league for his ouster climbed the highest rungs of the corporate ladder. To replace him and for his troubles offer a golden parachute. As they hastily and heartlessly ushered him out the door.

He saw this hideous scenario repeat itself. Through mergers, stockswaps, acquisitions, strategic alliances, marriages of equals, initial public offerings and a myriad of corporate power plays to which he became witness in his position of influence. It disgusted him every time he saw it.

But what life gives with one hand, it takes with the other.

Periodically, Aeneas felt himself gripped with cynicism. He and Lavinia sometimes talked about it. His art took a sudden, uncontrollable downturn. His love for his occupation drained from him. He began to hate coming into the studio every day. But in his new standard of living, he had become enamored of luxury. After so many years of abject poverty, perched on the marshy brink of the quicksand of insolvency.

Aeneas had been happier photographing the age-old jazzmen. Trumpet players with callous lips. Sax players, piano men, clarinetists, bass players and jazz guitarists. With their white socks, short-sleeve shirts and archaic implements of construction.

The humble pecan farmers in the French Market. The hookers and barkers and strippers of the Quarter.

The tap dancers and street artists.

The sundry tobacco and souvenir shop keepers.

The Cajun chefs, barmaids, oyster shuckers and waiters.

Such life was authentic. And such art had truly positioned him to weave intimately a rich real tapestry of life. A meaningful offshoot of his profession.

Secretly, he perceived his new wealth as another trap, which his poverty first set for him. He had sold his soul in a Faustian trade. And after the novelty began to wear off, he resented the bargain of which he had been the artificer. Wishing he could shape waxen wings. And fly out of the labyrinth. Like Daedalus. Even if the wings should cost a Fortune.

Lavinia convinced him that he should become more diverse. And carve out time to photograph purely aesthetic treatments to meet the artistic demands of his soul. It was good advice that he resolved to follow.

One day, happily, Sibyl Helene called. She was displeased with the workmanship of Lavinia's former beau, Percy Turner.

Percy still called Lavinia despite her consistent, clear rejections. He was haughty, demanding and domineering. At intervals, he called with macho displays of unbearable ego. Making bizarre or impossible demands. That she rejected. Futilely sending flowers daily. Impertinent and persistent.

Sibyl sought the next level in photographic composition. For a new advertising campaign for *The Golden Bow*. A logical business decision. For him it meant a nice change from krewe kings, executives, rich brats and dowagers.

She insisted that Lavinia pose as the model. Perhaps, trying to secure photography before Lavinia became a hot property in New York. As the trip to New York had been a success for her.

Lavinia, Andrew, their lawyers and financial adviser, Evan, were negotiating as a team the deal points of the contract with June Wilhelm. Who confided that a new ladies intimate apparel catalogue named *Virginia's Fantasies* was interviewing a short-list of models with her elegant appeal. For national reach.

Aeneas speculated that June had confided as much to Sibyl. In return for Sibyl's role in connecting Lavinia with June in the first place.

Sibyl was too smart to break such business confidences if that scenario were accurate. And at the moment it was a speculation that aspired to be Rumor.

Nevertheless, in gratitude to Sibyl the couple agreed to the photo shoots. Aeneas never denied an old ally, a business practice that Lavinia also valued. And Sibyl sent the lingerie by courier for the first of a series of photo shoots. A translucent silk bra and panty.

"You're sure your fatheh won't mind?" Aeneas asked.

"Pretty soon, this sort of shoot will be small time. He better get used to it," she replied.

"I suppose you're right."

"Why? Do you? Mind, I mean."

"I don't know. How would you feel if the tables were tuhned? What if, as your fiancé or husband, my picture appeared half-naked on billboards. In trains and buses. And magazines?"

"Gee, Jack. I don't know what to say. We need to talk this out."

"We do. But not now. We accepted this assignment for Sibyl. At least, I control the images. The poses. The setups. The lighting. That won't be the case for June Wilhelm."

"No, it won't."

"I'm sorry, Lavinia. I'm only human. Any guy would feel the same."

"You don't own me, Jack."

"I don't want to. Honest. I do love you so."

Aeneas brandished a small velvet box, which she accepted gleefully.

"Open it," he said.

"Oooooooh!" she replied. "Jack, I just love it. Help me put it on."

Gingerly, she inspected a silver necklace and *fleur de lis* pendant with three nice diamonds. One glistened like a dewdrop at the tip of each petal. And she held up her lovely, shining hair as Aeneas fastened the delicate silver clasp.

All smiles, they kissed sweetly. The mood nicely set, they plunged into the photo shoot. Aeneas had sold Sibyl on a concept that would capture the loveliness of Lavinia as well as the feminine allure of *The Golden Bow* lingerie.

Charles had arranged with City Park to borrow a dozen, downy ducklings. Lavinia dressed in the fine lingerie. Then Aeneas directed her to sit back upon her knees upon a fleecy milky blanket with her back erect, and her legs and knees together. A pose that Aeneas considered eminently feminine.

The soft, peeping and tender ducklings wandered aimlessly. Huddling and flapping short downy wings. In the propinquity of the sensual woman, they provided a dreamy aura. Their feathery texture lent poignancy to the silken lingerie. The downy ducklings alongside Lavinia's skin epitomized her soft, gentle femininity.

The ducklings peeped and rushed curiously in circles around Lavinia. She held a few of them in her hands, close to her face. They seemed to welcome the warmth, the full softness of her body. Beneath three well lit
silver studio umbrellas, Aeneas began to circle Lavinia. To capture the essence of her. She laughed and played lovingly and petted the ducklings. Through the viewfinder she was sexy and natural. His lovely flower of life.

Aeneas adjusted the f-stop attempting to maximize its potential to capture nuances in depth of field. Selecting the right f-stop to determine the penetration of focus was critical in pulling off the soft, sensual effect that he first shot in his mind a week ago. The f-stop brought the wholeness, harmony and radiance of the subject into perspective. The f-stop was key to his art. The camera became an extension of his eye. A faithful instrument of his vision.

After an hour-session, first getting the shot and then experimenting for new looks, the ducklings were placed in comfortable, spacious overnight accommodations on the papered studio floor. With plenty of food and water until their morning return to City Park.

Lavinia had graced his art with refreshing spirit. To renew his enthusiasm for his work.

"Should we walk to the Chart House for dinner? I just know you have your heart set on a nice, bloody steak," she offered.

"A steak doesn't meat my needs."

"Then what does?"

"I have a taste for Italian," he replied. "You know how your mouth watehs for a certain cuisine? And you can't shake it. Until you devour what you crave."

"How about *La Louisianne*? I love their crabmeat Caesar salad.
The Romaine hearts always taste fresh from the French Market. And the crabmeat is yummy."

"Maybe we should invite your fatheh to join us."

"That's so sweet, Jack. But he's up in New York. Visiting the parent company of a steel mill he's thinking about buying in Baton Rouge. He says we may as well own the mill that makes the pipe for our energy business."

"New Yohk City?"

"No, Rome, New York. Upstate. Between Ithaca and Troy."

"Does he fly into Syracuse?"

"He sure does."

"In Syracuse, he'll be a roamin' Catholic among throngs of Orangemen. But when in Rome, do as the Romans. Which company is it now?"

"The subsidiary is Vulcan Steel."

"I don't know that name. Who is the parent?"

"Rome America Enterprises. They're a multi-national, Fortune 500 conglomerate."

"How did your fatheh connect with them?"

"Through Evan, daddy's financial advisor. Evan's a real genius."

"He must be."

"But don't call your broker just yet. The deal's not done."

"I wouldn't think of it."

"Any how, thank you for asking about daddy, sweetheart."

And she kissed him appreciatively.

"You know something?" he asked. "Foh the first time in a long while, I remembeh how much fun it can be to take pictures. I love you, Dreamface."

"I wasn't upstaged by the duckies?"

"They brought out your best. Which presented the client's product in the finest possible light. Tonight couldn't have gone betteh. You're a natural, babe. And the world will beat a pathway to your door. If you let it."

Lavinia dressed and they closed up shop. As Aeneas locked the front door and turned on the burglar alarm, Lavinia pointed to a staggering, meandering, disheveled man in a rumpled business suit. Braying and howling with laughter.

"Is *that* Pehcy Tuhneh?" Aeneas asked.

"I'm afraid so," she replied.

"I've seen him like this more than once. Staggering down Bourbon Street."

"Should I say something?"

"Nah. You busted him up pretty well, babe. He was neveh this bad. Until you left him."

"I feel sorry for him."

"I tried to offeh assistance before to the poor guy. And he refused. Too proud for his own good. He got mad. Embarrassed to be drunk and alone."

"He could get robbed."

"Where does he live?"

"On Dumaine Street. Here in the Quarter."

"Then he hasn't very fah to go. It's a pity to see him like this. But I undehstand it. There, but foh the grace of God . . . And you."

"The wonder is that everyone in this town isn't an alcoholic. Not to change the subject. But I have wonderful news for you, Jack. Daddy
expects to be named Rex this year. He thinks that it's pretty much a done deal."

>Bow down,
>popes,
>presidents
>and saints,
>to true royalty.
>Rex,
>the Kingcake Eater,
>wants
>God's job.

* * *

Proteus and the Jester

Outrageously surreal, in this dream Aeneas stands dressed like a court jester in the front row of the Municipal Auditorium.
He awaits the presentation of a Mardi Gras masked ball in a motif entitled *Tales from the Roman Empire*.

A packed house of seated Uptown ladies in formal gowns wear sparkling silver and gold jewelry. Flashing big diamond wedding rings.
Myriad fur coats upon ladies whose faces are pancaked and painted to mask old age.

Uptown gents don ebony tuxedos and stiff collars of bleached shirts with pearl buttons and white ties. Medallions hang from shrimp-colored ribbons on their chests and Rolexes festoon their wrists. Cummerbunds bulge among grim graybeards. Notably numerous baldpates.

Men wearing gloves and sporting blood red carnations on black, satin lapels.

A microphone drops from the ceiling to a waiting overweight, middle-aged man with fiery red hair in a gray tuxedo. He advances into a spotlight like an announcer before an Atlantic City title bout. Italian lyres and flutes play the background music of Pan. As the announcer strains tiny eyes through thick glasses on his script. Reading with loud, melodramatic and bellicose overtones.

"Ladies and gentlemen, now we take you to Rome, Italy in its early days. Before the arrival of the Caesars. To the birth of the Republic on the banks of the Tiber. The Krewe of Proteus proudly presents:
TALES OF THE ROMAN EMPIRE."

The mike and announcer vanish.

A mother wolf runs in circles chased by two men in diapers. Intermittently, they suck and flap their lips and wail.

Romulus is played by Percy. And Remus turns into the cartoon figure of Uncle Remus from *Song of the South*.

Venus and the Sabine women, dressed in short togas, strut upstage.

The wolf-suckled babies about-face and pursue the Sabine ladies. Ardently whistling like construction workers. Or juvenal delinquents. And shout, "Oh, baby. Give it to me hot. And wild. Let's go over to your place. Or come over to mine. Give it to me now, baby. Oh, yeah. Oh, yeah. Oh, baby, baby."

Uncle Remus hunts the Sabine women. Offstage screaming. Leaving Romulus and Venus alone.

Romulus drops his diaper. And his manhood becomes a Leica camera with a colossal zoom lens.

Venus loosens her toga to pose. In lingerie from Sibyl Helene.

Venus assumes the face of Lavinia. Percy's strobe upon his Leica throbs with fitful flashes. His Leica likes her. He furiously adjusts his telephoto lens. Growing impossibly imposing. Tripping the shutterbug's shudder.

Venus twists in the turbulent agony of hot rapture. Posing with cool desire on her face. Making love to the camera. Her torso twisting in tortured torque at us. Then a dance of vogue motions. As covers of magazines flash behind her from *Cosmo, Glamour, Elle, Vanity Fair, Esquire, Playboy* and *The New Yorker*. Frank Sinatra sings *New York, New York*.

The scene dissolves with Percy's strobe failing to flash. And he has no spare Ever-Ready batteries. Running offstage with both hands pulling out his hair. And howling like a wolf.

"*Hahaha,*" Aeneas laughed in his sleep. "*Fool.*"

Alone, Venus beckons to the jester. Smiling sweetly seductive. A King Koil king-size bed ascends from the floor. The backdrop changes to a villa upon Roman hillsides. The pleasure palace of Octavius.

A classic, Broadway, blinking marquee drops from the ceiling that reads:
CAESAR'S PALACE
Atlantic City

Casino one-arm bandits shoot up from the floor. Tony Bennett sings *Arividerci Roma*. Jackie Gleason makes a surprise appearance and famously shouts, "Great Caesar's ghost!" Then he dances comically offstage to a little travelling music by Sammy Spear and His Orchestra. The marquee and slot machines cleanly withdraw from the stage floor and ceiling respectively.

Venus again smiles inviting him to join her. But the jester can't move.

She now transforms into his wife. They are on a honeymoon in Granada, Spain. Inside the palace of the Alhambra. Amid monks within the monastery of San Francisco.

Abundant fragrant gardens flourish. Oranges and grapefruits grow upon trees. And roses blossom amid playing fountains in the courtyards. Sweet scents of perfume. And he wants to lie with her. To sleep where royalty had lain. And Moorish kings had loved. To drink from a shallow goblet and taste in a brief draught the grapes intoxicatingly sweet like sangria. And she lay upon the bed. A garden. An Alhambra rose in bloom.

He can see from a turret, a battlement, the beaches of the Costa del Sol. With the blue Mediterraenean and Africa intriguing and mysterious and beckoning and vast on a distant shore. In this mist he envisions ancient armies. Moors marching. Led by Don Quixote riding with Sancho Panza across rich, raven, new-plowed plains. And fields scattered with peasants picking grapes.

The jester attends a bullfight at the coliseum in Torremolinos. When the last bull, sleek and jet black and raging, breached the high inner walls. To scatter a battalion of toreadors sheltered behind it. A short, gaunt, young bullfighter wearing cactus flower pink stockings and an olive green toreador uniform slays the brute, bleeding beast with grace and craft.

A dissonant blast of Middle Eastern music in the ballroom floor heralds a rushing bevy of harem dancers with veiled faces. They dance barefoot on the hardwood floor. Wearing tight silver sequined tops and lobster bisque pink sheer pantaloons.

The krewe of Momus. Cleopatra tableau.

Alexandria, Egypt. Roll the great actium movie between Cleopatra and Octavius. With bronze ships amid silken golden sheets as gleaming waves of sea. Egyptian warriors enter robustly with swords like crescent moons. And headpieces like Ramses. Bare chests, loincloths and sandals with serpentine leather thongs encircling their legs. Janus smiles.

Cleo's Antony emerges with the visage of Percy stepping into a Roman bark rowed by slaves. And Venus has become Cleopatra. Transformed into the Queen of the Nile. A group of belly dancers enters as the Middle Eastern music reaches a crescendo. Their hips and flat tummies shake erotically. They wear silver turbans, silver tops and silver briefs. Celebrating the fleet's departure for battle with the Romans offshore Greece.

Time goes by. The music changes into Duke Ellington's *Creole Love Call* with Cleo Laine. Janus frowns.

Cleopatra clasps asps in Alexandria. After her furious, wretched retreat to the delta of the Nile. Following infamous Actium.

A crowd of sooty-suited, Spanish classical guitarists with Mexican hats plucks fat guitars emerging into the tableau.

"*Ah, Endymion,*" Aeneas murmured in his sleep.

A male flamenco dancer in tight, black pants, vested, with thickheeled boots, white ruffled shirt with billowy sleeves. Upstage he dances flamenco. Joined by Venus who transforms into a scarlet, low-cut, dress.

With a coal black lace shawl and fan. And the face of his wife. She lifts her skirts to dance passionately with the Spaniard. They stomp together in syncopation. Clicking passionately their heavy-heeled, flamenco, tap shoes upon the dance floor with a formal, dignified, spirited sensuality.

Each dances for the other a ceremony of passion. He dances first with hands gripping his vest. Elbows pointed out. Head thrown back. Legs together shaping a V at his crotch. His long and lean, trim hips shifting artfully. As his feet explode onto the hollow wooden floor.

Then she dances. Skirt open to reveal long, firm, black stocking legs with little crimson ribbons on her high, black, patent leather, tap shoes. Eyes closed, with castaenets she clicks out a love song to him. Her face in ecstasy. They leave the floor in a rush holding hands.

Peasant girls, wearing hats made with fruit, in full cotton chemises. Long, heavy, thick, dresses. Hips shaking. Weaving amid the Spanish guitarists.

All players exit.

Venus, as the Queen of the Krewe of Proteus, enters. A refined matron with Medici collar. And gem-encrusted gown with *fleurs de lis*.

Wearing long gloves, her scepter studded with brilliants. She parades past the crowd. The face of Arabella. Led by boy attendants dressed as princes in white. And holding the ends of her ermine train. Escorting her to a throne. And a handsome young Duke with the face of Percy bows and presents her dozens of a fiery mix of rich mustard yellow and garnet roses. She smiles a heavenly aura. And knights him with a touch of her scepter.

The music becomes solemn and regal as King Proteus struts upstage. Stern faced with a long, frosty false beard and hairpiece. Upon which rests a pointed crown of diamonds. Throwing brilliant fingers of white light from the spotlight focused on him. Cloak of pure white ermine, white gloves, and silver tapestry bodice with ermine trim at the sleeves and waist. White leotards and knee length boots. Sipping from a flask of Old Grand Dad Bourbon. One arm extends a diamond scepter.

Pointing at the hushed respectful crowd of onlookers. Proteus highsteps pompeyously full of the lust of his own power.

Proteus struts regally in circles around the jester. And then ominously points his diamond wand directly at Aeneas.

Proteus looks with phrygid, gray, serious, bloodshot eyes directly into the jester's. And speaks grim words in a stage whisper meant for all to hear.

"Soon, Fool, you will be visited by Death," Proteus pronounces.

"I sent him no invitation," the jester replies with a foolish smirk.

"Laugh while you can. It won't save you."

"Stop. Before I die laughing."

"Soon enough. You will."

"I could use a good rest. But not so long. And not yet."

"Give me five."

The jester raises one hand to celebrate. Unmet by the other hand of Proteus. The sound of one hand clapping.

Stern Proteus waves his scepter. And with it touches the jester at his crotch. When, to the astonishment of all, a bulge the size of a pomegranate appears. The crowd sighs in collective amazement.

The jester reaches into the front of his leotard with his right hand.
And pulls a magnificent, live, golden çodfish from his sodden çodpiece.

"Who dat?" Proteus asked, laughing.

The çodfish surging and sucking and squirming. With a $5 bill attached to the single whisker dangling from the çhin beneath in its gaping, bony cheeks.

"I hereby grant you a new çrotch!" Proteus proclaims.
Sailing the crowd, even Proteus, almost pissing their pants into stormy gales of Hesperian hysteria.

Proteus is transfigured by his own laughter into Bacchus.

The krewe of Bacchus. Great motif. Took a dozen roles.

The goat man. With grape adorned horns, shaggy rust loins, legs with cloven hooves and a bread pudding crust blush in his cheeks.
Continuing the howls of Proteus. Then he becomes transfixed as a statuesque bust for a Mardi Gras float.

The adoring crowd goes wild with applause. As the krewe carries the idol of Bacchus off the floor.

At the side of Aeneas, Lavinia silently weeps. Knowing she can't save him. Who then? Or what will spare the jester? From a most unwelcome guest?

Andrew emerges wearing a hardhat. In a steel mill with glowing red-hot steel flowing from great cast iron caldrons into molds. The jester dials in pantomime his broker at Merrill Lynch with a buy-order. Because that financial genius, Evan, says we are on the verge of a Pamplona of a bull market.

Lavinia's father comforts her. With all his wealth and power, Andrew can not save the jester. But he holds out a great apple for the jester. The shape and color and scent of the fruit please him.

"What kind of apple is this?" the jester asks.
"A Rome Beauty," Andrew says.
"Ah, my mother made the best pies of Rome Beauties."
With a touch of his scepter, Proteus transforms the apple into a hot, steaming pie. *Mmmmmmmmmmmmmmmm.*
In his sleep Aeneas licked his lips:
"May I have a nice, big piece, please?"
"You may NOT!" Proteus admonished.
"Then what may I have?"
"Nothiiiiiiiiiiiiiinnnnnnggggg . . .
Nothiiiiiiiiiiiiiinnnnnnggggg . . .
Nothiiiiiiiiiiiiiinnnnnnggggg . . ."

The bedside Princess telephone startled Aeneas. A harpy's scream in lotus land. Aeneas fell out of bed.

His undershirt was soaked with perspiration. The wet bed sheets wrapped around him twisted from fitful turning in disarray like a toga.

Hair matted and tousled. His face swarthy with stubble. Heart thumping like a kettledrum. In shock from the power of his nightmare.

Eyes stared disoriented at the bottom of his new bed at St. Charles and Octavia. To its clean, white, new mattress tag:

DO NOT REMOVE.
SLUMBERLAND MATTRESS CO.
ROME, GEORGIA

The telephone revived Aeneas to reality. Like smelling salts to a fighter down for the count. And saved by the Bell.

At first, he felt paralyzed from the vivid dream. And he couldn't move. His digital clock radio blinked a bloodshot 12:58 am.

The PBS radio station softly played the final bars of a recording of a live performance of jazz renditions by Cleo Laine with Duke Ellington. Followed by applause.

Finally, Aeneas summoned the strength to tear off the mattress tag. Then weakly reached for the phone. Wiping a brackish tributary of perspiration from his forehead.

"Who could this possibly be?" Aeneas asked.
"Aeneas John Jam?"
It's either another inquiry from an inmate at the Jackson Street Asylum. Or someone who should be committed. Like me.
"Chahlie? Tell me this isn't you. At this hour."
" . . . This isn't you at this hour . . ."
"Then who is it?"
"It isn't you . . . At this hour."
Aeneas said nothing. Afflicted. Indisposed. Unamused.
"You awright, bud?" Charles asked.
"I'm sick."
"We know that."
"I've had a feveh foh two days. I'm exhausted."
"Then you weren't making hay?"

"Hahdly."

"Even International Harvester takes a break. Every now and then."

"Haha..."

"The flu?"

"I ran myself into the ground. My resistance was low. It's nasty stuff."

"I've been looking all night for nasty stuff with low resistance."

"You sound stiff, Chahlie. Are you?"

"Hold the line. While I check."

The sound of a telephone dropping.

"No, Jack. I'm flaccid. At the moment. But thanks for caring."

"I meant drunk."

"I've made some toasts. If that's what you mean. To that magnificent polluted broad. The sodden Mrs. Sip. The toast of Dixie. And to the best mounts of Napoleon. Here at Napoleon House... Has Liv nursed you back to life?"

"She left a couple of hours ago."

"So... Do you feel any better?"

"Maybe a little. The feveh just broke."

"Let me tell you why I've called. At such an ungodly hour."

"Please do."

"I've decided to revive an old krewe. I knew you'd want to join."

"Chahlie, it's well afteh midnight..."

"Jack, think about it. You've slept through one-third of your phrygging life. Even Rip Van Winkle only slept for 20 years."

"So what's the point, Chahlie?"

"My krewe is called the Phunny Phorty Phellows. With a Ph up front. Like Ph.D. I phound phive phellows so phar. All phunny. The original krewe goes back to eighteen-ninety-phive."

"I want to go back to sleep."

"This year... we're toasting... a great New Orleans' institution..."

"The Wall?"

"Haha. The Wall. That's Great. By the way, one of our Saudi Arabian Phunny Phorty has a new approach to the Wall..."

"Instead of crampons, rappelling geah and dog biscuits foh the Dobehmans?"

"Exactly... BeingonewiththeWall."

"Transcendental."

"That's the idea. Transcend the Wall."

"So which institution are you toasting?"

"The Whore of Rome. Latin's last refuge."

"*Pax vobiscum*, sweet prince. I'm hanging up my Princess."

"Do you want in, Jack?"

"It's been phrygging phun."

"We're philling up phast."

"Chahlie, I'm not interested in any social club that would admit me. Besides, aren't you a big shot in Zulu?"

"So what? I can still lead the parade down Bourbon Street. I've been dubbed Sir Knight of the Tooters."

"Very apropos, Chahlie. Considering your talent foh breaking wind on command."

"Jack, you need a krewe. For Mardi Gras. To get into the right spirit."

"I'm already in Rex."

"To hell with Rex. You could be Da Boss."

"Da Boss?"

"King of the Phunny Phorty Phellows."

"Goodnight, Sih Knight of the Tootehs. Can you see me hanging up?"

"Wait . . . Before you go . . . Guys! . . . Come over here! Abdul? . . . Sir Turnip? . . . Francesca! . . . Let's all lift an ale to ailing Jack. And cheer him with our motto. All together now."

Phive Phunny Phorty Phellows phumbled onto the phone to phrase:

"A little
nonsense
now
and then
is relished
by the
best
of men."
* * *

CHIMERA IX:
Nisus and Euryalus

"Euryalus was held back by the weight of his booty, and in his fright he lost his way. But Nisus escaped . . . In the moment of his own dying he cut off the breath of his enemy. Then pierced through and through, he hurled himself on the dead body of his friend and rested there at last in the peace of death. Fortune has favored you both! If there is any power in my poetry, the day will never come when time will erase you from the memory of man."
— *The Aeneid*, Book IX

Beignets and *Café au Lait*

Feigning anonymity, a Valentine had arrived for him at the studio. Aeneas sipped *café au lait* while sitting at a wroughtiron table on the *banquette,* or sidewalk, of the *Café du Monde*. He opened the çoddin' card.

Graphically, a sheep was crudely drawn. Revealing the artistic talent of a first-grader. With hearts ballooning from its woolen head.

Rose are red.
Violets are blue.
The sheep are all nervous.
Thanks to you.
XOX,
Baaaaabs

Aeneas laughed, set down the card and reached for a powdery, white, warm *beignet*. The French Market doughnuts were once his sole solid food in lean days before Lavinia. For months thereafter, he couldn't eat one. When his Fortune turned, the sweet fried dough reminded him of the heights he had scaled with his dough in New Orleans. Now, he relished and savored them.

Charles was late, as always. New Orleanians lacked respect for real time. The one constant was tardiness. The remaining question: how late?

Aeneas gave Charles a half-hour's lead-time in all appointments to minimize the wait. He had decided to close his shop early. A cancellation left him free for the balance of a lovely, warm, February afternoon.

He needed a brief respite of peace and quiet.

The bright sun shone in the lucid sky of royal blue. Magnolia buds bravely unfolded tight, tender, pink baby fists. Azaleas ready to burst.

Mardi Gras just around the corner. Spring would appear in full bloom in only two weeks.

Before he knew Lavinia, he sometimes left the gallery and spent an afternoon at the *Café du Monde*. To gain a better perspective of the wild, whirling pixels of his life. And watch the world pass by him. Stand back and assess the big picture with the great Southern leisure that New Orleanians embraced with conviction as essential to good living.

He hadn't come to sip *café au lait* on the fringe of Jackson Square in the throes of a lovely afternoon in months. Not since moving his gallery to Bourbon Street.

Lavinia was in New York, again. Finalizing her modeling deal with June Wilhelm.

"Baaaaaaaaaaaaaaaaaaaabs!"

"Chahlie, you are stealth itself," Aeneas accused. "You bleating heart!"

"Isn't love grand? I once had a friend at Texas A&M. An Agra-American. Sheep never did anything for him. He idolized cows."

"A bovinophile."

"Quite a sacrifice for him. Because bovinophiles have problems, too."

"For instance?"

"For instance, you have to lie on your back to fondle her teats. And then run around to the front to kiss her."

"I prefer foxes."

"Speaking of which, maybe it's Valentine's Day. But I *am* in love, Jack. I thought you should be the first to know."

"Maybe *she* should be the first to know."

"She's beautiful. I'm moonstruck."

"You're smitten?"

"Straight through the heart. She's built like a Greek goddess. Long dark hair. And the eyes of a deer."

"You're not going to lapse into bestiality, again, are you?"

"She has a sweet, gentle face."

"What's her name?"

"Francie. I think she likes me, too."

"Where did you meet?"

"Napoleon House. She's a Phunny Phorty Phellow."

"Then the joke's on you, Chahlie. In the French Quarteh a guy can't be too careful. Not the first time a Francie turned out to be a Frankie."

"I'm leaving."

"Hey, I'm sorry, Chahlie. Sit down. Waiteh, a *café au lait* foh my fatheh."

"You're pushing it, Jack. I spill my guts about the first woman I've met since Barb left . . ."

"You're right, Chahlie. I *am* sorry. *Truly.* Now, tell me more about her. I'll just listen."

"She lives Uptown. She's divorced. I can't believe anyone would ever want to leave this woman. I call her Francesca."

"She sounds . . . exotic. So she's your Creole queen."

"Exotic, as hell, Jack. To me, anyway. She's everything Barb isn't?"

"Is she Creole, too?"

"What if she wasn't? Would you have a problem with that?"

"Hey, I'm a Yankee. Remembeh? An outcast. A misfit. Here in the land of cotton . . . So how is she in the sack?"

"Hell, I don't know, Jack. Beat around the bush, why don't you?"

"That's my question."

"I have no answer for the Wall."

"Have you tried *BeingatonewiththeWall?*"

"Abdul is an idiot."

"Use the great aphrodisiacs."

"I *am* the great Afro-disiac."

"I refer to the existential aphrodisiac. Of a man who has lived."

"Been there. Done that."

"Poweh is the second great aphrodisiac. Poweh breeds trust. But in that trust, there must exist enough strength to lay out your vulnerabilities."

"I'm not giving *anybody* the power to walk all over me, bud."

"Women see vulnerability as a sign of strength. As bizahhe as that may seem to guys."

"But aren't they afraid that . . . if they love a man for his weaknesses, they'll never see the end of them?"

"No. They see it as a link . . . A connection . . . Common ground. All men are idiots about women. More or less. So what? Women want to ensure they can live with the baggage that exists. In any particulah man who interests them."

"This vulnerability thing fascinates me. Because I have so much of it. Especially, if it represents some kind of bizarre edge."

"When a woman gives herself to a man, it's a great gift. You must honoh the sanctity of that gift. Lavinia told me it created a bond foh life between us. I told her that I hoped so."

"I tell you what. It seems to me that men want sex. Then friendship. And women want it the other way around."

"The logic of platonic relationships with beautiful women escapes me. The dialogues are exehcises in masochism. *N'est pas?*"

"*Faux pas,* Jack. *Faux pas.*"

"*Mea culpa.*"

"But let's have more great aphrodisiacs then."

"The mentor aphrodisiac. Between a woman and a man who is her mentor," Aeneas said, shaking the confectionery sugar from a doughnut.

"Do beautiful women know the power they possess?"

"Women write off men as fools overdosing on testosterone. Maybe they're right. Most of the time. Beauty is poweh."

"Francesca is so lovely. She needs only to intimate that she wants something. And if I think I'll get her by doing it, I see that it's done."

"Men are absolute slaves to beauty. But beauty betrays. You take a chance. Because the alternative is even worse."

"I lust to know more aphrodisiacs on St. Valentine's Day."

"Fantasy."

"There's one with substance. What do you mean?"

"A woman likes to feel that a man recognizes her greatest possibilities foh fulfillment. As *she* sees them. Love thrives on fantasy. The selfrealization of potential. Foh which a man can be the . . . engine."

"I *am* a love machine, Jack."

"If you say so, John Shaft. I do have one last resort foh you, Chahlie. When all else fails. It's the greatest of all aphrodisiacs. Normally, it's classified. Banned to our gendeh. Because it's . . . well, it's just plain dangerous."

"Name it."

"True love."

"True love?"

"It melts all Walls. High or low. It's a miracle. Because the only really intimidating aspect of a Wall is that it exists inside your head. You know what Robert Frost wrote? 'Something there is that doesn't love a wall.' "

"I don't know, Jack."

"Do you feel intensely about her?"

"Yes."

"Is it real? And deep? And true?"

"Absolutely."

"Does she know?"

"Not yet."

"She needs to know. When are you going to tell her?"

"When we're both ready. Remember, I'm rusty at this."

"You've got to buck up, Chahlie. And take your best shot. If it's real. And mutual. Just tell Francesca that you care deeply foh her. Touch her with tendeh words from your heart. Let her act fihst. You have no chance if you don't open up to her."

"I'm working on it."

"Speak the language of sincere affection. Utteh words of tendehness to Francesca. If you really mean them, she'll melt like butteh on grits. If she feels even close to the same way you do. It'll push her over the edge."

"What if the affection isn't mutual?"

"You're betteh off knowing sooneh than lateh. Trust me."

"My Wall is higher than yours. Because . . . race is a factor."

"But you're . . . *café au lait*."

"You tan up nice and dark. For a powder sugar, Yankee ass . . ."

"I didn't mean any offense. We're friends. Right? I can tell you anything. And it would be all right. Even if it came out wrong."

"My mother was half Creole. A strict Catholic. And half Uptown WASP. My father was half Cajun. Acadian. Baptized Catholic. But not devout. From Nova Scotia. And half Uptown WASP. So bottom line . . . I'm half Uptown WASP. And at Penn, I out-whited whitey. So the WASPs couldn't sting me."

"You mean out-witted?"

"No, the truth is that I out-whited whitey. To my wit's end."

"My grandparents are both from Canada. Otherwise, I'm WASP. So our Walls may not be so different."

"Maybe not."

"Maybe, even the same."

"I don't know. Maybe . . . We always laugh, Jack. Whenever I'm with her. I'm nuts for her!"

"The seed of a good joke hides in there. But damned if I can find it."

"I'll give it a chance, Jack, with Francesca. I appreciate your counsel. I can find my way now."

"Chahlie, here's the bottom-line. So pay attention now. *Whatever you do* . . . my best advice is: do *not* take any advice from *me*?"

"Don't worry, Jack. I won't. I just wanted to know what you're doing. So I can do the *exact opposite*. Considering how screwed-up your love life has been. How can I pay you back for this? I owe you, bud."

"I may be just a candle in the galaxy. But I'm there for you."

"Gee, thanks, dad. Can I have my allowance now?"

"I've already given you more allowance than you deserve. Now go out there. And, damn it, son, make our gendeh proud. Die *le petit morte*. And rise to fight anotheh day."

"Geezum! The time! I'm late!"

"No great surprise there, Chahlie."

"I'm supposed to meet Francesca at Napoleon House. I just got to go. But you've inspired me, Jack."

"To do what?"

"To mount her Walls. By conquering her heart. After writing about the art of love. Inspired by Mrs. Sip. See you. I gotta run. Bah."

"Bye. My best to Baaaabs."

Charles gulped down the last of the *café au lait* of Aeneas. He pilfered a *beignet* and marched briskly out of the *Café du Monde* across Decatur Street.

Then the inky iron gates amid the palms and gardens of Jackson Square obscured Charles. And he was lost behind the great stone base of the statue of General Andrew Jackson.

So much nonsense about Walls. Their defense. And breach. I do not love them.

> *But*
> *even*
> *Mrs.*
> *Sip*
> *abides*
> *levees.*

* * *

The Bed Is the Battlefield

Aesthetically inclined, Charles had presented his scrawled essay to Aeneas. Inspired by his Muse, Mrs. Sip, he had penned a concise manual for men on the fine art of love. An immediate critique was requested.

He not only aspired to publish it in *Esquire* or *Vanity Fair*. But also, just as importantly, he sought to uncover what women *really* sought in men. How could men, by understanding the needs and desires of women, better connect?

Aeneas tried to keep a straight face during the transfer of the manuscript. But he couldn't wait to learn the discoveries of his friend in the art of love.

A brief perusal projected a mix of recommendations.

Some seemed outrageously baroque. And others were earnest. The challenge would be to ascertain when Charles was serious. And when he was not.

A daunting task, he approached it in good faith to benefit his friend. Aeneas postponed a focused reading of the manuscript until late on the evening of its acquisition. He lounged in a comfortable chair. Grandfather clock ticking. A fire warming the hearth. To take the chill out of the wet, late-winter night. And warm the ghosts of drafts within his palatial new home at Octavia and St. Charles.

The saxophone jazz riffs of Grover Washington, Jr. played on the stereo. Southern Comfort on the rocks. The maid had gone after cooking dinner. With Lavinia in New York and not returning for two more days. He felt the bachelor *par excellence*.

Aeneas opened the manuscript to its title page:
LESSONS FROM THE LOVELIFE OF AN AD MAN.
Haha. This should be good. He knows even less about women than I do. If that's possible.

The subhead read:
A SURVIVAL GUIDE FOR MEN WOOING MODERN WOMEN
OR
LESSONS I HAVE LEARNED THE HARD WAY.

Ah, what an honor. He has dedicated his opus maximus *to me. The most spectacular failure among straight men ever to have loved women since the origin of being. Well, then, let's see what can be learned on the subject.*

After all, Liv will be the beneficiary of new tactics learned. Poor darling woman. I can't wait to kiss her sweet face.

CHAPTER I – WHY AD MEN?

"Nearly all enlightened suitors recognize that advertising men have superior love lives. They communicate in deep and meaningful expressions that are attractive to women and know how to package themselves.

A recent survey among young single women revealed a consensus that ad men were better lovers. This logical conclusion is the result of the creative powers which ad men possess and to which women respond with appetite. Now you, too, can learn the techniques and philosophy that will lead you to bed the contemporary woman of your dreams."

For someone who has been on the make so short a time as Charlie, he's certainly giving himself a lot of credit for expertise in the art of love.

CHAPTER II – APPEARANCES

"Always present a suitable image. This is the advertising man's *modus operandus*. It's basic, good, common sense. Women of quality rarely trust ill-kempt men upon introduction and shy away from them. Transmit nice sniffs and be scrupulous in your choice of after-shave. Get a decent barber, preferably a woman with good taste.

Balzac once wrote that good French tailors made more men successful in the Paris of his heyday than any other body of individuals.

Modern women prefer broad-shouldered, firm-buttocked, wellchiseled, strong-chested fellows. Many ad men don't fit this prototype.

They aren't unloading ships or building bridges and roads or roughnecks drilling for oil out at sea, after all.

But the ad man's bulging finger muscles and firm wrists from substantial writing and typing are physical attributes that today's women seek. So build up that wrist and finger strength. Women are watching you and they value digital dexterity . . ."

Aeneas lunged for the blue pencil.

Be careful not to let this sensitive topic get out of hand, Charlie.

"Always keep fit. The law of the jungle applies. If you are good to your body, your body will be good to you. Women notice when you're looking muscle-bound and well manicured. If you chew tobacco and must spit in unisex toilets, always remember to put down the seat.

Although I have never fallen backward into a toilet bowl, apparently women do all the time and they seem to resent it."

Aeneas scratched out most of this section.

Lots of spitters in Louisiana, Charlie, but Yankee readers won't benefit much from this advice.

"If you really look good, you'll soon learn that other men, as well as other women, may notice. My personal opinion is one of gratitude and respect: for every gay man, there's a woman gone wanton."

Aeneas skipped ahead a few pages, which he would re-read in full later.

CHAPTER III – TAKE THIS BEFORE YOU GO TO BED.

"Women love ambiance. Most cannot get enough of this particular aspect of the art of love. Give them all of it that you can stand.

Never skip the preliminaries – you'll be the loser. Linger at the risk of overkill in your efforts regarding the 'prelims.' Even at the risk of dragging them out. She'll tell you when she's had enough. Know the signals and move on only at the right time. Under *no* circumstances *ever* rush a woman in situations pertaining to love.

Pay attention and learn all you can about the art of seduction. If your woman doesn't respond to the prelims, don't proceed. You have obviously chosen a woman who is *too good* for you. Or a sexy woman taking you for a ride down the Yellow Brick Road. Who could be just as broken-hearted with disillusionment over *you*.

If she loses interest in you after you signed the Diner's Club tab at an exclusive restaurant, you may have misunderstood her hunger. She may only have wanted a hot meal.

Or if she starts yawning when you arrive at her apartment after an expensive night at the symphony, theatre or a comedy club and tells you how early she must awaken the next morning, sorry. She probably only wanted to hear Wagner or Sibelius or Mendelssohn. Or experience the quiver and thrill of *A Streetcar Named Desire*. Or have a good laugh at your expense.

Don't blame yourself for being a fool! You're in good company as this basic, frequent deception is skillfully perpetuated upon men by infinitely more talented players. Many women just don't buy the food for fooling around trade-off with the unbridled optimism that men think it justifies.
Try to represent your gender nobly. When that is not possible, just try to represent it competently. Good communication is essential to the art of love. Only give your love to a worthy woman. And consider yourself fortunate if she accepts it."

Add lengthy disclosure about precautions.

"Try to be as subtle as possible. Because women can sniff any hints of anxiety in a man ten miles away. They have finely tuned radar that's so sensitive it could be used to track hurricanes, tornadoes, tropical storms, cloud cover and high tides.

Conversely, women respond with interest to men's disinterest. I don't have the faintest idea why. But mine is not to reason why. Only just to do or die, Gunga Din."

Aeneas turned to a later chapter entitled:
THE BED IS THE BATTLEFIELD.

"Because of her vastly superior intelligence, a woman will *always* know, before you do, if you have any shot at getting lucky on any given day.

If the improbable should happen, just remember — as they say in Texas — that the post always goes before the post-hole.

Satisfy your lover first: this is the cardinal rule of love. Place her pleasure before yours and you'll be generously rewarded. Nothing breeds more loyalty in a contemporary woman.

Be a good warrior. Fight the good fight. Put on your armor. And die *le petite morte*."

Aeneas turned ahead in the manuscript to:
MARRIAGE CONSIDERATIONS.

"When you find the woman of your dreams, should you marry her?

Of course, only you can know for sure. Or think so. Because nothing is certain in the art of love. In the end it may just be a crapshoot but you can't win if you don't roll the dice – even when the odds are against you. And, of course, they always are. But life's a great risk against impossible odds anyway. So what's the big deal?

Many men never realize, until it's too late, the cost benefits associated with mistressing *rather than* marriage. It's certainly much cheaper in the long run to take a mistress than a wife. Mistressing *after* marriage is a fool's paradise."

I understand the economics, as you point out. But absolutely do not objectify the more tender gender.

"I have learned that all love is temporary. Ultimately, if it runs deep, it will tear your heart out sooner or later.

You can contain love for short periods but inevitably it vanishes like a dream. That's just the nature of the beast. So it's bad form to go moping around and pissing and groaning and making everybody else's life miserable when this happens, as it will. Just move on. There are plenty of fish in the sea.

Odds improve when you may honestly imply that you are the 'marrying kind.' While we *never* espouse false or misleading advertising, if you can't make such claims in good faith, you have a better chance of getting hit by lightning or winning the big state lotto than reaching intimate serendipity.

Women are made with miraculous accouterments to perpetuate the human race, whether mankind is worthy or not of perpetuity. Females almost always want to run these habiliments and experience childbirth if they can.

Of course, today's conventional women want a half-dozen children, a five-bedroom colonial in the burbs, a Mercedes and the presidency of a multi-national Fortune 500 Corporation. And why not? Women could hardly do worse running the planet than men. And besides, it's their turn.

Women respect honesty. Even if it hurts. You owe it to them if they place a bet on you. So they aren't wasting precious time. Because, God knows, love's a risk. And a fool's game. But every soul gets a chance to play. Against the odds. People hit the Jackpot. Every day. And the firstclass fool is one who won't play. As winning is worth the high price of admission. And losing is unacceptable. God suffers fools gladly who, in good faith, give all to the heart. It makes little sense sometimes. But it's the essence of being alive.

Take courage and heart. Be a real man. Carry your sword and shield with honor. It may be your good Fortune to live with the same person to see your golden wedding anniversary. Qualifing you as a genius. And your partner, too.

Above all, today's woman wants an existential partner: someone with whom to share the abundant richness of life. Therefore, if for no better reason, by all means *live*."

Aeneas closed his best friend's absurd composition on the mystic art of love.

Haha. Charlie may be a jester. Donning the foolscap for laughs. Perhaps, more than a touch of truth, too. Making grand banter of bitter experience.

The heart of his art. Or the art of his heart.

For all I know, he's a patron saint of shipwrecked souls like me. The next Kahlil Gibran. When in doubt, for God's sake, don't be serious.
It all simply begs some questions. I'm beginning to say all *too often. Like*
Dixielanders.

The child is the father of the man. And what does that make me if not a fool, too? I may not have a clue. But surely I know more than he does.

Let me see.

Do I have the potential to live brilliantly in love? What have I learned from the teaching of my own suffering? Like poor Charlie.

Where does his self-searching gibberish leave him? Can I lead him to roam out of his dark night of the spirit? Or myself for that matter?

Is Lavinia my true love? Is my love shared? Will she abandon me in New Orleans for New York? Would Percy Turner follow her there? Is he in New York with her now? Don't get paranoid.

Does the ideal mate await elsewhere? How can I ever know this? How good it would be to find my true love. How sad to have found my soul mate. And lost her. On such distant soil. With the spoil of my soul.

> *As*
> *the song says:*
> *"And when*
> *I grow*
> *too old*
> *to dream,*
> *her love*
> *will live*
> *in my*
> *heart."*
> * * *

CHIMERA X:
Pallas and Mezentius

"Pitiless Mars was now dealing grief and death to both sides with impartial hand. Victors and vanquished killed and were killed and neither side thought of flight. In the halls of Jupiter the gods pitied the futile anger of the two armies and grieved that men had so much suffering, Venus looking on from one side and Saturnian Juno from the other, while in the thick of all the thousands raged the Fury Tisiphone, pale as death."
— *The Aeneid, Book X*

The *Bon Vivant*

Elegant nonsense prevailed, as usual in New Orleans, and Aeneas ranted while the studio became a madhouse only a few short weeks prior to Fat Tuesday. Perhaps, it was simply too much of a good thing. As the first street parades rolled down St. Charles Avenue. Navigating Uptown in the evenings with the crowds and traffic that preceded the parades proved problematical.

The pace of the city heightened by degrees since the beginning of the construction of the reviewing stands by the city alongside the parade routes. New Orleans' roads were perpetually in disrepair. The public schools were in shambles. The drinking water consistently was polluted. But the reviewing stands for Mardi Gras always went up like clockwork.

The professional and social life of Aeneas assumed the persona of the city. He longed for the tempo of the Louisiana holiday to ease. And longed for a sense of normalcy.

He had observed to Lavinia that he thought he had forsaken a brutal, life-shortening, Puritan, work ethic in Boston. She advised him that you never really leave behind an ethic – it stays with you forever. Like your conscience or guilt. And if he ever left his conscience behind, she would help him recover it.

Aeneas further perceived, ever since the birth of religion, that ethics, guilt and conscience have been sapping men's spirit. Making it difficult to live a full life.

The next appointment in the book simply read: Mrs. Bee.

She arrived in the midst of his changing film and re-arranging the studio lights for her head-and-shoulders portrait. She entered the inner sanctum of the sunless room where Aeneas photographed his subjects.

Jack was all business on this extremely jammed day. He simply pointed to a stool, without acknowledging her, and said, "Please have a seat, Mrs. Bee. I'll be right with you."

Without speaking, she moved toward the stool and perched upon it. Aeneas closed the door to the studio and drew a curtain. Shutting out distraction and permitting him to concentrate on his art.

He changed lenses, adjusted the telescope legs of the tripod and peered through the blurry viewfinder.

"Let's see if today aht shall be or not be, Mrs. Bee," he asked. "Or if we shall instead suffer the slings and arrows of outrageous Fohtune."

"Um, Bee is only my . . . last initial. The letter B," she politely corrected.

"Oh. And what does the B stand foh?"

"Bontempo."

"Well, as the Cajuns say, '*Laissez les Bontempos rouler!*'"

"I couldn't agree more."

"I'm sorry I'm running behind. With my schedule, it's not easy keeping . . ."

As he focused the lens, he discovered a striking young woman in a black velvet dress. Open in the front to the waist. Baring naked shoulders and a voluptuous bosom.

" . . . abreast of things."

Then his eyes traveled North to her face.

"Didi?"

"I'm glad you all *finally* noticed."

Aeneas hid behind the civil wall of his professional equipment: Hasselblad, lenses, camera, tripod and lighting umbrellas.

"I've had one *hell* of a time finding you," she said.

"Well, I moved. I bought a new house on the Avenue. Near Octavia."

"Lucky you, then."

"Yes. Lucky me."

"Fate is being kind to you, Jack. I saw a pitcher of you all in the *Times-Picayune* . . . In the *Vivant Section*. You must make a real nice living."

"Yes, well . . . notoriety just comes with being a *bon vivant*. I photograph so many of them. Sometimes, I stumble into the line of fihe. And get caught in other people's frame and Fohtune."

"I connected the name in the paper with the studio. I remembered that you had your own studio in the French Quarter."

"Ah, yes. From my visit to your home at Camp and Marengo. The studio address was on the back of the photo . . . the one I brought as a gift."

"Dallas trashed that pitcher. A while ago. So anyway. It took me forever to get an appointment. I had to pull a few strings. And tell a few itty-bitty white lies. Like wanting to pay yawl's fee."

"Haha."

"I mean to say, your fees are outta this world, darlin'. I hope you don't mind some minor indiscretions."

"I'm more worried about the major ones. Always have been."

"I've been waiting a long time to see you, again," she said, gently easing out of her velvet dress altogether. To sit upon the stool clad only in French cut, black, satin panties, garter belt and black silk stockings.

"So what are you waiting for?" she asked. "The Canal Street bus?"

Trying to hold his composure, Aeneas shot a few frames of film.

"I didn't really come here for pitchers, babe. But now that I'm here, I suppose we might as well take some."

Mrs. Bontempo moved with feline grace from the stool and posed with her hands holding her hair off the back of her neck. Lifting her incredibly lovely breasts. Enticing him. Stirring his desire.

"Didi, what about Dallas?"

"Dallas is dead."

"Dead? . . . When did this happen?"

"Dallas is not really dead. Just Dallas's, you know . . ."

"Dallas's phallus?"

"The po' dear. He's such a fast mover. And I want a lover with a sllloooooow hand. And an easy touch."

Adeptly, Aeneas unscrewed the Hasselblad and held it vertically.

He distanced himself from her and tripped the shutter erratically. Unwittingly to buy time by creating erotica.

She approached him one step at a time with each new pose.

Aeneas retreated involuntarily as if his viewfinder were a glass wall separating them.

"I bet you take hot pitchers all the time," she said.

"Uh, no."

"But you'd call them art."

"I'm just a humble public sehvant. Framing immortality foh my clients. At my peril."

"And what would you call *these* pitchers?"

"Trouble."

"Do you think I ought to pose for some of those men's magazines? Like *Machismo*. Dallas reads *Machismo* all the time."

"Um, Didi . . . we need to talk."

"Let's send *Machismo* a few of these black-and-white glossies. What do yawl say?"

"Didi, since I last saw you, I became engaged. I have a big wedding coming up. At St. Louis Cathedral. In June."

"I bet you would just *love* to see me in *Machismo*."

"Well, don't be so sure about that. My fiancée is in the next phrygging room. Sitting at a desk. Just back from New Yohk. Helping out here in the studio. During our busy season."

"Just consider this a little wedding present then. Part of the bachelor party. If that makes you feel any better."

"It doesn't. My fiancée wouldn't approve. Would she?"

"I've fantasized about this, you know?"

"It does seem fantastic *per se*. A fantastically bad idea."

"Except that in my fantasy, you're naked, too."

"You're not listening to me, Didi."

"I love living my fantasies. Don't you? They make me happy."

"Fantasies are so . . . what's the word?"

"Dangerous?"

"That, too. In this case. But I was thinking more . . . unreliable."

"When it comes to fantasies, I just know I can rely on you, Jack."

"Come now, Didi."

"I'll come. But not yet."

"I didn't mean it that way."

The Hasselblad of Aeneas exposed the whole roll of film. As Aeneas bared his future to the three Fates. The shutter refused to open.

"I thought we'd never get through that ole role of film," Didi said.

She addressed him and then undressed him. Camera first.

"I ain't leaving this place, honey. Until you make love to me," she insisted.

Didi draped her arms around his neck. Dropped a long, liquid kiss.

She drew her half-naked body close. His resistance melted. And absconded with his conscience.

God made women too beautiful. What chance does any man have against such beauty?

His reason acquiesced to her talent for seduction. And her overwhelming drive for satisfaction.

Didi led him to the couch in the corner of the studio. Upon which he had photographed legions of stalwart Uptown families. And Lavinia during the Storyville Draft Beer and *The Golden Bow Boutique* photo sessions.

She unbuttoned his shirt.

"Damn it, Didi. This won't wohk," Aeneas edified her.

"Hush now. And make love to me."

"I can't do this."

"Tell it to your dick."

She tugged at the belt and fly of his pants. In an instant, shoes, socks and his briefs flew into a little pile of forlorn laundry. Landing heaped upon his Bass Weejuns like a flock of starlings.

Aeneas could hardly believe his state of affairs. Too fantastic to be reality. Good and bad at the same time.

A quick knock on the door into the studio settled the dichotomy between fantasy and reality. Causing great confusion and inner turmoil as to how to extricate oneself from this swamp of circumstance.

Lavinia entered into the studio leading a portly man of the cloth dressed in full religious regalia. A dignified, Italian gentleman in his early sixties. A trimmed, salt-and-pepper beard framing a tranquil face. With a prominent classically Roman nose and no trace of wrinkles. Except tiny smile lines in the corner of his mouth. The stale smell of tobacco smoke on his breath. And tea-and-cream fingernails on colossal, smooth, folded hands.

"Jack, Archbishop Mezentius is here for his appointment . . ." she began. "Christ Awmighty. What in *hell* are *you* trying to do?"

"Jumpin' Jack Flash," Didi answered.

"Lavinia, deah, you really shouldn't sweah in front of the Ahchbishop," Aeneas answered.

"Isn't *he* a big boy?" Didi asked rhetorically.

Aeneas felt like the village idiot. In the town square. Pants down. Everyone staring. One's private life now in the public domain. *Flagrante delicto.* With disbelief stricken upon all faces.

The archbishop was impressed by this baring of Didi's soul.

He and Aeneas blushed crimson. Lavinia flushed white-hot. Mrs. Bontempo calmly wore peaches and cream.

The archbishop in his pointed cap looked very much the up-andcoming pontiff. He made a brisk sign of the cross. Transfixed with a ridiculous smile upon his face.

"We seem to have caught you . . . at an inopportune time, my son," the archbishop said.

"Who is this bitch?" Lavinia asked.

"Your *language*, deah," Aeneas said, drawing up his designer unders.

"Whose idea was this? Yours? Or his?" Lavinia asked Didi.

All eyes focused on Didi.

"It takes two to *fais-do-do*."

"My kingdom foh a mount," Aeneas said.

"Here's, possibly, an apt phrase," the archbishop interrupted. "Take my wife, . . . please."

The wholly father, the archbishop, laughed aloud alone.

"Just trying to add some humor to the situation," he offered, with his hands folded. Embarrassed that his *repartee* didn't connect.

"In my whole life I never met an archbishop yet. Who could deliver a punchline," Didi indiscreetly uttered.

"You *unholy bimbo*. How *dare you* insult the *archbishop*?" Lavinia fired back.

"It's all right. I've heard that before," the archbishop said.

"When, may I ask, do you hold confession?" Aeneas asked, pulling on trousers. The quick zip of his fly punctuating his question snappily.

"Today. From two to four."

"At St. Louis Cathedral? Next dooh?"

"Yes, my son."

Aeneas checked his Rolex President.

"It's almost two now. Hey, maybe we could all go. I know it's been a while between confessions foh me."

"But you're a Protestant, Jackie," Didi observed.

"You little whore," Lavinia proclaimed in a whisper, as she lunged at Didi.

Lavinia was enraged: clawing, punching, biting, screaming and pulling hair. Aeneas tried to control her. To keep this photo session from becoming an all-out catfight. As the archbishop remained fixed. Hands crossed. In cold, distant tranquility. Out of harm's way. Remote amidst the fracas.

"Can you give me a hand, Your Holiness?" Aeneas politely beseeched.

"I'm neutral, my son."

So the archbishop declined. Brandishing an ancient ash spear, his cross, born amid his vestments. As Aeneas tried futilely to separate the women.

Much harsh wrangling as the women screeched and tore at each other's hair. Toppling studio lights. Creating great white blinding flashes.
And the shattering of long glass bulbs. A slam of metal tripods and cameras. An odd electrical burning smell but only a little smoke. Drapes impaired. Chairs crashed.

Aeneas imagined this holy man wholly in street clothes. Devoid of his sacred costume. He wondered, given his own apostasy toward the Church, where they could possibly have met in the past.

At last, the battle spent itself. Lavinia furious but defensive of Aeneas.

As Didi threatened lawsuits for assault and battery. Citing million-dollar damages against the studio. New leverage for having her willful way with handsome Aeneas. Too good-looking for his own good. Big man on cameras. Stud of the studio.

"Perhaps, introductions would help," the holy man offered. "And humanize the situation. Defuse it."

"Good idea, Fatheh . . . Lavinia, this is Didi. Didi, this is my fiancée," Aeneas offered.

"You mean, Jack. This is your *ex*-fiancée."

Once, again, Lavinia threw her engagement ring into the blinking, disbelieving face of Aeneas. She stormed out of the studio.

Didi slipped on her black velvet dress.

"Call me, Jack. Now that you're a free man. Your office has my number."

In front of the archbishop, she pressed a long, wet kiss upon Aeneas.

Then she sashayed out the studio with a sexy smile of victory.

Leaving the two men alone in an awkward silence. Until Aeneas ventured to break the ice with a question for the archbishop.

"By any chance,
has
Your Eminence
eveh been to
*Lucky
Pierre's?*"
* * *

Halcyon Hallucinations

Nestled above two cool glasses of straight bourbon on the rocks, Aeneas and Charles had personal business to conduct. Over a glass table at Commander's Palace surrounded by a lush leafy jungle in the Garden District. Ivory wrought-iron chairs positively comfy.

A sanctuary, a refuge, an Eden Uptown. The evening air cool and pleasantly brisk for a February night.

The fan palms and elephant ears, broad and leafy, drooped heavy with the prior afternoon downpour. The aqua Victorian mansion with white trim bustled inside. About six weeks before Mardi Gras. But Aeneas and Charles had the garden to themselves.

he Maker's Mark Bourbon went down easy. Sharp and incandescent and glowing as it flowed to the center of his being. Lotus lava.

Aeneas finished nervously smoking a long, silky smooth, *Cohiba Esplendido*. He crushed the perfect circular ash of the *Habana* into a glass ashtray displaying a logo of Rex.

Charlie's manuscript lay upon the tabletop unopened. Their conversations seemed headed in different directions. As one man saw reason for hope and the other saw justification for despair. Because oneman had just lost his Dreamface. And the other had just found one.

"So what did you think of the manuscript, Jack."

"Hell, I don't know, Chahlie. I'm a photographer. Remembeh?"

"Did you read it?"

"Of course, I read it."

"And?"

"In the main I thought it was nonsense, Chahlie. I respect you as a writeh. But I thought the ahticle was super . . . sila . . . ous."

"Supercilious? The first draft was super . . . scicilia. But I edited it."

"Listen, I'm no good at critiquing other people's aht. I just try to see the flaws in my own wohk. Before otheh people do."

"I understand."

"For all I know, it could be great. And I could be dead wrong."

"Know what the funny part is, Jack?"

"What?"

"I worked it all through in my own mind. Advice I would give to me. If I were my own friend. And separate. You know?"

"Schizoid?"

"Objective."

"And did you take your own advice?"

"Yes, Jack. I did."

"And did it wohk?"

"As a matter of fact, yes. It did work. It helped me win Francesca."

"You're kidding?"

"No, Jack, I'm not. The manuscript is supposed to be, as you say, *pixilating*. You understand that much, right?"

"Of course. And pixilating it was. Even enlightening in places. Hey, maybe some magazine will buy it. What do I know?"

"You mean, some magazine like *Esquire*?"

"Yeah, I suppose so. Strangeh things have happened."

Charles smiled a broad smirk. And his shoulders started to heave.

"What? . . . Don't tell me, Chahlie . . ."

"*Esquire* bought it. Today. For three grand."

"*Esquiyeh?* Get outta here, Chahlie. Congratulations! That's pissah!"

"Thanks. I re-wrote it. Cleaned it all up. And sent it to the editor at *Esquire*, who was my professor at Penn. I was counting on your hating it."

"Because the wohld contradicts its misfits. And, therefohe, the wohld loved it. Because I didn't."

"You're my true antipode, Jack. Reality is everything that you say it isn't. And isn't anything that you say it is. That's why you're so damn reliable. And valuable. You're a sundial read under a full moon that's always exactly accurate."

"Man, you're on top of the world. Between the *Esquiyeh* deal. And this new lady friend of yours . . . When are you going to tell me about her?"

"Fill me in about what happened between you and Lavinia. And I'll tell you about Francesca."

"I don't want to rain on your parade. But it was bad, Chahlie. It was one of those ray-eh times when it couldn't possibly have gone wohse. I've lost her foh good. I'm sure of it. I've neveh seen a woman so mad . . ."

"She's the best I've ever had, Jack. Remember the night at the *Royal O*. After *Lucky Pierre's*?"

"Of course."

"She was the equivalent of the two women in bed. I swear to God."

"I knew it was dead wrong, Chahlie. But I just couldn't help myself. God made women so damn beautiful."

"Amen."

"Didi looked so hot. I wish you could have seen her through the viewfindeh. I'll show you the prints when they're ready. You won't believe them. She wants me to send them to some men's magazines. And she'll probably end up a centehfold. Maybe *Esquiyeh* needs a coveh girl . . ."

"If so, they would choose someone like Lavinia."

"I guess you're right."

"I never thought a woman like Francesca would end up with me. Maybe I feel a little unworthy. Hell, I don't know. But when Barb up and left with the girls, I felt empty. Francesca has put together the pieces for me. I can't explain to you how strong I feel. You know the feeling that some women inspire. Like you could take on the world. That's exactly how I feel right now. Pixilated. I'm reborn. Reincarnated. I reinvented myself . . ."

"The saddest paht, Chahlie, was that underneath the angeh, I could see the huht in her glorious eyes. She fought foh me. Blaming it all on Didi. Didn't even question me. This beautiful, loving woman fought over an idiot like me. With my pants down. And Didi . . . Holy Christ, what a disgrace . . ."

"I never knew how proud I could feel of being a man. I feel like a demigod. Simply for making love. As she deserved. The epitome of femininity. She makes Barb seem like a hag. And a fool . . ."

"That Boston guilt. You know, you neveh eveh shake it. The old New England guilt eats at you like a tapewohm. The things Didi can do. I was about ready to crawl up the Wall. Afteh all these years, I still can't believe how God built women."

"My Francesca knows what she is about. I know what you're saying. She must have slept with some men before me. Not that I care about ancient history. I like a woman who knows what she wants."

"That's the new woman, Chahlie. The woman of our age. Self-assured, confident, strong, sexy, smaht and capable. A lady outside the bedroom. And a whore inside it. I've lost the best woman I ever had, Chahlie. I can't believe I eveh let her get away from me."

"Imagine the loser husband who let Francesca stray. What kind of a buffoon do you suppose he is?"

"Some people just don't know a good thing. When they have it."

"I told her that. Any man who would let her get away must be a fool. I told her I would never, of my own will, let her leave me. Know what? She cried when I said that. A tear came to her eye. I don't know why. But I saw her eyes well up. And she brushed a tear away. Just as it started to roll down her cheek. Her soft lovely cheek. Much too used to tears."

"Maybe she was abandoned."

"Maybe she never had somebody who said they'd stay. No matter what happened. In the battle of ordinary life. No matter what wounds. Or scars. Or defeats. And she has known all of these. I know she has."

"Lavinia and I, since we've been togetheh, have known only good times. The tide tuhned in my life when I first saw her in the flood. I guess we were neveh really tested. Now, she's gone, too."

"This is your first test, Jack. If it's meant to be, it will be. If it's good, love stays. There is a certain pragmatic justice in love. Take it from me. I know. When love ought to go, it does. And it's just as well. Like knowing when to leave a good party. A question of timing. And the grace of your exit."

"Our love should have enduhed, Chahlie. I handled it badly. Clumsy. And foolish. With the finesse of a bounceh in a Bourbon Street strip joint. I'm sick to death about it."

"Tell her, Jack."

"*How?* . . . How do I explain my behavioh to Lavinia? In front of Ahchbishop Mezentius. Andrew was making arrangements foh him to pehfohm the wedding ceremony. At St. Louis Cathedral. I have humiliated Lavinia and her fatheh. Before their chuhch. Before God."

"Have you talked with Andrew?"

"No, not yet. But it comes at the wohst possible time. Our busiest season of the year. I just sent free-lance photographehs to my bookings foh tonight. That's a fihst. But I can't handle them. I'm coming apaht at the seams."

"Well, Andrew didn't sell the business the first time you and Lavinia broke up. Maybe he won't this time either."

"He's getting a great retuhn on his investment. The business is a cash cow. It just needed adequate staht-up capital."

"Jack, I heard a Rumor. And it's only a Rumor. But I want you to be aware of it. So you aren't caught off-guard. Or ambushed."

"Spill ya guts."

"One of my graphic designers picked up from a typographer at a financial printer that Percy Turner is out for you."

"You mean Pehcy is afteh Liv? Or out foh me, professionally?"

"I don't know about what feelings or ambitions he may have toward Lavinia."

"Pehcy neveh got oveh her. Now, I know why."

"He has the ear of some cash rich, venture capitalists. Mostly regional entrepreneurs. Like Andrew. Angels, as they're called. People who invest by buying businesses. Percy has shown them a formal business plan. Based on the business model of your studio with Andrew's deep pockets."

"Pehcy has no intellectual capital. As a photographeh."

"Not in his opinion. He has his followers. And *mucho* business connections. Everybody who's anybody in this town knows your turnaround story. It's a classic case. Almost textbook on how cash infusion and new management can turn around an undercapitalized business that has the right concept. And with the Oil Boom in this town. Quite a few folks are cash rich. And looking for other companies in New Orleans to buy. Or they overpay the tax man."

"So what are you saying, Chahlie? I'm confused. What's the Rumoh?"

"The Rumor is that Percy and his venture capitalists have already talked to Andrew. Percy wants to buy out the majority ownership in the business from Andrew and Lavinia. With his venture capital group. And leave you twisting in the wind."

"Liv and Andrew own 30% each. Iona 40% share. So if they join forces, they determine my destiny."

"Percy could be your new boss soon."

"He'll have to deal with me first. Man to man."

"Hell, Didi just may have cost you a corporate empire."

"I don't think so. I mean, let's get . . . ah . . . assyrious. It just happened. I screwed myself. I alienated my business pahtnehs. And my family. I betrayed them. And myself. I am such an idiot. I have no one else to blame. But me."

"Well, it is still only a Rumor, Jack. But you need to know what's going on behind your back."

"Nothing will happen befohe Mahdi Gras, at least. Business is too good until then. But aftehwards, who knows? Especially, the way things tuhned out between Lavinia and me. I wish there were something I could tell her. To make it right with us."

"Tell her it was just the *juices*. Nothing more or less. Nothing personal."

"*Nothing pehsonal?* Come on, Chahlie. It was *too* pehsonal. That's the problem."

"Didi was stalking you, Jack."

"So what? I qualify foh an insanity defense?"

"Why not?"

"Liv'd never believe it."

"She *wants* to believe it. She knows that men are idiots about women like Didi. Hell, Lavinia is an expert on the subject herself. How many men has she sent over the edge personally? Including Percy?"

"And maybe me."

"You can't let that happen. You gotta talk to her, Jack. Or she walks. And she stays gone. She can't come to you, now. Can she? Her pride won't let her. So you need to go to her. If you love her. Am I wrong?"

"Unfohtunately, no, my friend. I was so damn cavalieh about it. With some lame comment about taking confession with the ahchbishop at St. Louis Cathedral."

"Any port in a storm, Jack."

"But it really was so . . . *surreal*. Two dreams at once. Committed to one. Unyielding temptation on the other. The Achilles' heel of hedonists. It happens to me all the time, Chahlie. Doesn't this soht of thing happen to you often?"

"No, it doesn't. Except in Francesca's case."

"I suppose it all depends on the opportunities you get."

"Life is all about choices, Jack."

"But there is also Fate. Destiny. Cihcumstance. Greateh powehs. God. All out of our hands."

"They all change. If you give them a chance. And there's your own will, too."

"I handled it like a hedonist, Chahlie."

"Maybe so."

"Thick skin or thin. Black skin or white. Scratch a Bostonian and you'll find beneath the discipline and the wohk ethic and the guilt . . . a hedonist."

"Liv loves your ass, man. She'll forgive you. If you ask her. And you know you have to ask her. Be gentle. Sincere. And give her reasons to forgive you."

"God, Chahlie. You're such a true friend. I owe you my life. I'll think about it some more. About how to approach Liv."

"What's going on in New York? With that big modeling agency Up-North?"

"She's ready to sign a contract. They want her. And they're willing to pay her big money. June Wilhelm is already lining up photo shoots. Including the *Virginia's Fantasies Catalogue*."

"So Lavinia could cash in her chips. Take cash from Percy's venture group for the studio. And get cash flow from June Wilhelm in New York. Then what's to keep her here, bud?"

"She may not leave New Ohleans. As long as her fatheh is alive. When he goes, that's a different story. But that won't be anytime soon."

"You risk underestimating her, Jack. New York is logically where she should be right now. If she is a world-class model. As June Wilhelm seems to think. June's instincts are never wrong."

"But Liv won't base her decision on pure logic alone."

"In that case, it could be even worse. She has the money to fly back and forth to New Orleans, whenever she wants. To see her daddy. Who flies to New York all the time on business. She has Sibyl Helene as a travelling companion. And her relationship with you is history. Why would she want the strings attached to the studio? She sells out. And moves into Manhattan. To a nice brownstone on Park Avenue. Checkmate. Endgame."

"I am so screwed, Chahlie. I can't tell you the pain."

"The pain is telling you to choose another path. To be a realist. It inspires creativity. It's a spur to re-group. Seize the opportunities that change brings. 'Fortune favors the bold.'"

"I need to change myself. From the inside out. I have the will. It's more a matter of wherewithal. I don't know what's right anymore."

"You get three chances when you make a decision, Jack. You could be smart and simply choose the right decision and it works. Or you could execute and stroke and finesse it to work. Or you could get lucky enough so that circumstances change and it becomes right. And works downstream. The last scenario makes you a visionary. A seer. A prophet."

"I suppose you're right."

"You need to figure this all out. Fast. It's time to dig deep. And pull the wherewithal up from down inside you. You can do it."

"Would she eveh in a million years take me back, Chahlie?"

"If she were sitting here with us. And she heard everything we said, she might. She just might."

"Do you, honest-to-God, think so?"

"You bet. But you gotta talk to her. Soon. Don't let her stew long. Time is your enemy. Get to her right away. Or she's gone. Maybe, for good."

"Shall we lift a glass in toast? My devoted pal, as we said, Chahlie . . . Here's to the juices. Our lifeblood and poison swirl in the same Pimms Cup."

"To the juices. And to my lusty Muse, the mighty vast Mrs. Sip."

"To the Penn of esquiline esquires. And deep down in Dixie Pixie, Mrs. Sip."

Both men consumed their piquant, piercing bourbon and turned over their glasses with clumsy ringing clinks onto the glass tabletop.

"Enough about me. Tell me all about this Francesca, your Acadian queen," Aeneas said.

"I have been. Weren't you listening?"

"I'm outta whack, Chahlie. Outta focus. Pixilated . . . So tell me more. You have my full attention now. Tell me *all* about her."

"She is that most dangerous of woman: she is a true beauty. She is incredibly bright. And she is sweet. We met at Napoleon House. I love her. Deeply. More deeply that I have a right to. She's a Yankee, too…"

"So she respects that you graduated from Penn?"

"I guess. You know, you Yankees ain't *half-bad*. After all."

"When the South rises again, Yankees will be the cause of it."

"Francesca is from New England. Did I tell you that already?"

"You might have mentioned it. Where?"

"Massachusetts."

"Really? Is she from Beantown?"

"Odds are, if she's from Massachusetts, she's from Beantown. Right?"

"Poor lost soul."

"Maybe you know her name. I think she comes from a fairly famous family. They live near Charles Street."

"Have you impressed her with your command of Longfellow?"

"Funny, Jack."

"Back Bay? Or Beacon Hill?"

"Don't know. But I'll have to ask her."

"Boston's about the same size as New Ohleans. But it's also a small town. It's whom you know. Right?"

"Never mind. Forget it."

"No, come on. I used to know a few Boston Brahmins. In another life. When I lived in the Back Bay. *You* probably know the most famous Boston names. The Lowells, Kennedys, Harrimans, Cabots, Lodges . . ."

"Holmes."

Insensate Aeneas gaped at the table. Then nausea shocked him with its indomitable grip.

"Like the poet, Oliver Wendell Holmes," Charlie continued.

"What's her full name?" Aeneas asked, eyes blinking, threatening to fling a rogue lens.

"Frances Holmes."

Aeneas turned flush. Like the belly of a catfish. He said nothing.

"Hey, bud. What's the matter?"

In bitter silence Aeneas stared back.

"Talk to me, Jack."

He tried to speak. But couldn't.

"You *know* her?" Charles asked.

Aeneas nodded in the affirmative.

"I'll be damned," Charles said.

Aeneas was almost catatonic.

"You know her *well?*" Charles probed.

Another affirmative nod. Aeneas was somber as a grave.

"If it's bad I gotta know. Out with it," Charles pleaded.

Aeneas shook his head negatively.

"Speak to me, Jack. If she did something horrible, I need to know.

The words can't hurt me. Because I love this lady. She's my heart. And I won't give her up. No matter what."

Tears formed in the corners of the eyes of Aeneas John Jam. He tried to clear his throat but simply couldn't.

"You're scaring the hell out of me, Jack. Did she perform some kind of *criminal* mischief?"

Aeneas bowed his head in assent.

He lifted a Waterman fountain pen from his suit pocket. And wrote on a cocktail napkin in a shaking hand in the garden of Commander's Palace:

Once,
she
married
me.
* * *

CHIMERA XI:
Drances and Camilla

"We do not have to look too far for our enemies – they are standing all around the walls. Shall we advance to meet them? You hesitate? Where is your martial spirit?"
— *The Aeneid, Book XI*

The Passing Parade

Estranged egregiously, he perched upon the curb of St. Charles Avenue. Lonely Aeneas awaited the *entourage* of the Krewe of Momus.

Traditionally, the Momus parade down St. Charles provided splendid floats, bands and maskers throwing beads and doubloons. The lively crowd began to line the Avenue sipping Dixie and Storyville Draft Beer, and eating Popeye's fried chicken.

Many parents erected ladders atop which, in makeshift wooden seats, small children could see the parade above the throngs. The streetcars had stopped running.

On such a Friday night, normally he would hang out at Tipitina's. Listening to the music of Irma Thomas or Professor Longhair. Or to disco at Snobs. Or to jazz or the blues at Tyler's. But tonight he felt utterly isolated. An island of grief in a sea of revelry. He hoped the bacchanal of the passing parade would cheer him. So far, this pragmatic tack got him nowhere.

First, he had lost Frances. Then he had ruined his relationship with Lavinia. Percy was launching a hostile takeover. His business relationship with Andrew was at risk. And he had alienated Charles at Commander's Palace.

Aeneas simply couldn't bear the thought of Frances sleeping with such relish with his former friend. It was different if she had slept with strangers. Such a nightmare had only one face. But the vision of Charles and her together intimately was simply beyond his ability to cope.

He could not shake the recurring, haunting, carnal images of them jointly. They harped at him with a Fury that was relentless without mercy. They came without warning and lingered until he was thrown into an abyss of formidable despair. The smallest reminder of this relationship sent him reeling into the deep, wretched agony that assumes dictatorship of the mind. To grip the heart and wrench the spirit from it.

He now fully fathomed that money provided no guarantees of personal happiness. He had thought, as a poor man, that rich men were full of pelican dung who had said, "Money can't buy happiness." But rich men, too, were irresponsible. And they paid a price for it. Money was virtually irrelevant to the prospect of human happiness.

Poor Charles could hardly understand why Aeneas cared that he continued to see Frances Holmes. Charles pointed out that she did not wear a wedding band. And that divorce was only an impending legal technicality. A point Aeneas had already made to Lavinia's father and to her holy father.

Aeneas wanted to be magnanimous and give his blessing as a peace offering. Instead, he issued an ultimatum: forsake either Frances or him.

Charles, who had found solace in Frances after the debilitating loss of Barb and his daughters, could hardly give her up. Frances seemed mutually engrossed with Charles.

Aeneas could not tolerate the cruel turn of events. Circumstances had so quickly altered the landscape of his life. And no one could do otherwise.

Hence, life assumed the dimensions of a grand conspiracy at which he was caught whirling at the vortex.

"Who knows why life is as it is?" Charles had said at Commander's.

"But you're free to do as you will."

Then his friend sadly left the garden at Commander's Palace. In a shame he had not willingly caused nor knowingly created. And an odd innocence for which he nevertheless suffered heart-rending pangs of guilt.

The sounds of sirens shattered his self-pity. A troop of street merchants pushed shopping carts ahead of the parade. Selling cotton candy, confederate flags and various cheap Mardi Gras mementos. Envoys of Momus.

The dense crowd arose to its feet to welcome King Momus. Except for Aeneas, who roosted despondently upon the curbstone. Hesitant to participate in the Chaos of the revelry. As policemen upon motorcycles gently pushed back the surging crowd with adept finesse. A New Orleans Public Service truck led the parade. Checking for overhanging branches of oaks.

Then the King's float emerged. Pulled by a John Deere tractor.

Upon the float was emblazoned in Latin the motto of Momus:

DUM VIVIMUS, VIVMUS.

Below which read the translation of the great dead language:

WHILE WE LIVE, LET US LIVE.

Again, life went too far in a joke. A doubloon tossed from the King's float landed in his lap. The motto inscribed and staring up at him cast in silver. For him to bring home as a keepsake. As around him the sporadic pings of more doubloons hit the pavement. Reminding him of the rich little pings of Lavinia's engagement ring.

Children scrambled for the doubloons and the necklaces of beads.
So ardently sought. With so little inherent value. Artifacts of Momus. Admonishing one to live.

King Momus passed, ensconced upon his moveable throne, beneath a *papier-mâché* canopy of a glittering, golden crown. Momus waved his wand. Throwing doubloons. And discreetly sipping spicy demon bourbon from a small flask tucked beneath his cape. As his hoary beard wagged upon his chin. In the humid, Southern spring breeze. Regally attyred attendants threw beads and doubloons to the admiring crowd. Everyone really lived it up. Giving credence to the motto of Momus.

Then a buoyant float affably entitled:

THE PEPPERS OF AVERY ISLAND.

Like that phrygging Piquante of Didi.

Maskers dressed as red-hot chili peppers. Full of fiery vigor. Waving and tossing beads and doubloons. Humble servants of Momus. A float drifted by of a godlike, ungainly alligator. Upon which was inscribed:

ALLAH GATOR.

This float might be sponsored by Alligator Advertising.

Then came phalanxes of bands from Kentucky and Florida. Banners held high and rippling in the promising fragrant currents of spring. Marchers manipulated and tossed and twirled false rifles. Strutting martially proud and drenched in fighting school spirit. The bass drum and tuba players exhausted already by the great burdens of their instruments.

The *flambeaux* carriers, traditionally white men disguised in black face as slaves, bore great wooden crosses upright. From which hung blazing wicks fed by tubes to fuel cans. Their lights illuminated the way as they did in the Mardi Gras parades of a 150 years ago.

Many screams of:

"THROW ME SUMTHIN', MISTAH!"

Whispered atop ladders from lips of little children. Whose suppliant cries maskers rewarded with beads, doubloons and little stuffed animals.

Women perched astride men's shoulders and, whenever the parade stopped, approached the floats and seduced maskers into parting with fists full of the beads of King Momus.

The most beautiful women were tossed the most beads. Each masker assumed he had spotted a beauty for the first time. Pointing before tossing his spoils. To capture her admiration. In futile anonymity. In women's krewes the most handsome men caught the bounty. Darwinian principles at work in the natural selection of the endless variety of contests at Mardi Gras.

A float of men dressed as nuns. Wholly mothers of God. *Mummius*.

To whom a bystander shouted:

"THROW ME SUMTHIN', SISTAH!"

Rewarded in his nunsense. With the tin ping of doubloons. Falling not from the gods or heavens. But the auspices of munificent King Momus.

As the Queen's Float passed, Aeneas read its sign:

QUEEN MAUDE E. GRAW.

A lithe and lovely blonde queen. With a sensuous smile. Reminding him of splendid Virginia. Among debutante maidens in satin gowns and long white gloves.

The U.S. Marine Band played *Anchors Aweigh*. In sharp, crisp notes on the brass. To thunderous applause. Wearing white captain's hats with shiny ebony brims and golden cords collapsing upon a golden emblem. Navy blue uniform jackets with scarlet piping and bright golden buttons. White gloves and pressed royal blue pants with a sharp crease and elongated red stripe. Nice shiny black shoes. Strutting proudly with precise steps in perfect formation. Impressive and inspiring confidence in the future of the Republic.

Floats followed with themes on crawfish and shrimps. Which New Orleanian gullets voraciously engulfed. Tasty humble crustaceans saved from extinction only by their delta and gulf ubiquity.

Amid ample clamor from bands. Hordes shouted hysterically for beads and doubloons. Yowls of laughter. The syncopated pulse of the bass and snare drumbeats. Keeping marchers in step. As no one marched to a different drummer.

Greedy onlookers planted feet upon flung doubloons. To protect one's hand from other stepping, claiming feet. In wildly senseless pursuit of the booty of Momus. As if the coins were currency of true value. As, once obtained, they became insignificant trophies. Like the vast stash of cash of Aeneas.

Thus, the parade passed. A great leviathan slithering down St. Charles. Just one cell of revelry. Of the beast of Fat Tuesday's feast.

Aeneas stood upon the curb of St. Charles and headed home toward the corner of Octavia Street. The distance to which did dim the din.

The azaleas flowered in full bloom. In the gardens of Uptown mansions.

His solitary footfall kicked upon the brick sidewalk that heaved from roots of grand oaks. Garden District homes hosted black tie affairs.

Elegant and formal and reeking with rich, Southern gentility. All around hedonists had a field day. In the parties and passing parades before Mardi Gras.

Aeneas never felt so alone amid the great festival that gripped this entyre city on the mighty Mississippi. America's Tiber. Lacking even one friend with whom to share the revelry. An epic party pooper. Momentarily, no true friend of Momus. Despite the doubloon in his pocket.

On the front steps of his home. A woman, wearing many strings of beads, awaited him. Also alone.

It
was
his
ex
to
be.

* * *

Awakening in the American Dream

Ambiguously, he approached her with the pokerface of a card sharp. Unwilling to convey his inner flash of elation. Upon beholding his wife. Supine upon steps leading to his new home.

"Hello, Fran. You look wondehful. You really do," he opened.

"So do you, Jack."

"It's been a while. Almost a year. How have you been?"

"I've had my highs and lows. *C'est la vie*."

"What brings you here?"

"The parade. I was with a friend. I happened to pass your house. I thought I would just stop by and say hello."

"I'm glad you did. Shall we go inside?"

"Okay."

Aeneas took her arm as they walked the steep stone steps. Leading to the grand porch of his Uptown home.

They walked into his living room. Well furnished with Southern and English antiques. Rich gold drapes hanging in the window. Authentic Persian rugs graced hardwood floors. A baby grand piano in a corner by a marble fireplace. Abundant bookcases filled whole walls with the classics. State-of-the-art sound system. Potted palms. A wet bar well stocked with premium labels. Wine rack filled with tilted bottles of vintage California reds. And enlargements of old New Orleans and Boston.

Aeneas ushered her to a plush velvet couch. Upon which rested an open copy of *Ulysses* by James Joyce. Reverently, he moved it to make room for her.

"What can I get you to drink?" he asked.

"Amaretto on the rocks, please."

"Coming right up."

He poured her a drink. And a Booker's Bourbon on the rocks for himself.

"This is very nice, Jack. You must be doing well."

Is she surveying the property? Perhaps, hoping for a nice financial windfall as part of the divorce settlement. Or to sue for peace? Between whom? Her and me? Charlie and me? Or is it just because of Momus that she happened to be in the neighborhood?

"I'm stahting to make a go of it," he offered.

"A fah cry from the days when we used to count pennies. And shop with coupons clipped from the newspapeh," she replied in her Boston accent.

"I remembeh only too well. And not having enough to pay bills. Those were hahd times, Fran. But what followed just afteh. Made them seem like a walk in Audubon Pahk."

"It's a shame it had to be so hahd. Money problems driving us apaht."

"It wasn't the money, Fran. It was us."

"Still, my parents were . . . well-off. They could have made it easieh on us. Maybe we could have wohked things out. If I hadn't been . . ."

"Thrown to the wolves. Out into the cold. Because of me."

"Well, it *was* because of you."

"I was an insolvent ahtist. Bahely suhviving. Therefohe, I must be a social climbeh. Looking foh a mahk. A way up and out. I was a bum. A drunk. Not good enough foh you. Your fatheh's exact words. Wohst of all, I wasn't *him*."

"That's true."

"But you were in *love* with me. Even though your fatheh closed every gallery dooh of consequence in Boston in my face. And you were just a spoiled brat. And didn't know the value of a dollah. Or a day's wohk. So we had a choice. Stahve and freeze in Beantown. Or find a home in the booming Big Easy. I guess he taught us a lesson. Driving us both out of Boston. Losing you in the bahgain."

"Well, Jack, that's all changed now. We have . . . reconciled. Fatheh and I. With mother playing the peacemakeh."

"How do they feel about Chahlie?"

"They don't *know* about him yet."

"They'll like his Ivy League MBA."

"They may *neveh* know about him."

"Well, your secret's safe with me."

"Jack, I didn't come here to talk about Chahles."

"Then why did you come?"

"The divohce papers . . . They were delivehed last night by courieh."

"Did you think they neveh would arrive?"

Silence settled upon them. They sipped their drinks.

"Jack, what happened to us? I want to undehstand. What went wrong? Maybe, I'm just facing up to this foh the fihst time."

"Nothing has changed between us. Except the passage of time."

"A lot has changed, Jack. In both of our lives. From what I heah."

"I suppose that Chahlie has filled you in. On all the gory details."

"He's not spying on you. If that's what you think. It's not, is it?"

"No. I know him betteh than that. At least, I thought I did."

"He's your friend, Jack. He's a victim in this, too. He had absolutely no idea about you and me. I neveh knew that he was your best friend. And a business colleague. Afteh you and I lost touch. How could I know?"

His glass was empty. And hers was low. So he refreshed both.

"So how is your wohk going? Are you still brokering stocks?" he asked, shuttling the drinks.

"I just got a promotion. Anotheh one."

"Is your fatheh sending you business? Now, that I'm out of the picture. And you've mended fences?"

"Actually, he and a few of his friends in Boston are placing trades with me now. And with the Oil Boom here. Everybody is throwing around money. Like there's no tomorrow."

"I'm glad to hear that you're moving up the laddeh. Good foh you."

"And you, too, Jack. I mean, this place is incredible."

"Do you think that your fatheh would approve?"

"He would."

"Even if it's moot. At this point."

"Making money cehtainly takes wohk. Doesn't it?"

"It's a simple matteh of trading time foh money."

"Let's hope it's all wohthwhile."

"Well, the single life seems to agree with you, Fran. Much more so than life married to me. You look fit and trim."

"I took up racquetball."

"You're dressing well. Things seem to be going your way. You really do look just . . . terrific."

"So do you? . . . Are you happy, Jack?"

He averted his eyes. He paused for a shallow swallow of demon bourbon.

"I live a life of quiet desperation," he replied.

"You seem to have everything that a man could want."

"That's the really absuhd paht, Fran. Foh the fihst time in my life, I'm not living hand-to-mouth. As we were, when we were togetheh."

"You're the American Dream come true, Jack."

"I have every material thing that I thought I would eveh need. Things people wohk a lifetime foh. And I'm young enough to enjoy them. But . . ."

"But what?"

"The American Dream is a trick bag."

"What do you mean?"

"I sold my soul, Fran. For a few shekels. Now I have nothing that really mattehs."

"All this means nothing to you?"

"Fran, I have virtually everything I wanted when we were poor. Afteh you made sacrifices. To marry a nobody. I used to *dream* about having the things I now *own*. Maybe I was pushing too hahd to make good. To *prove* myself. Because of your sacrifices. But do you know when the best times were?"

"When, Jack?"

"When I had nothing."

"You have a short memory, Jack. You were miserable."

"It was a struggle. I admit it. We had hahd times."

"The hahdest times I ever knew."

"But the good times, Fran. We had some good times togetheh. Didn't we?"

Frances nodded. A rush of memories ensued. Boston. Spain. New Orleans.

"It should be enough, Fran. Really. I've paid my dues. But there aren't 100 men in a million as lucky as I am now. Where do I go from here? What do I do for an encore? How can a man be so insatiable? So ungrateful. So miserable."

"Maybe, you're chasing the wrong dream, Jack."

"What do you mean?"

"Tell me about your aht."

"I haven't shot a truly great photo in nearly a year. I used to shoot one or two a week. Photos I was genuinely proud of. My wohk with Uptown pohtraits bores me to teahs. But now I can't affohd to abandon it. So I'm a goldfinch trapped in a gilt cage."

"You need to fall in love. Or have you? I don't mean to pry."

"I just lost someone very special."

"I'm sorry, Jack."

"It's my own fault. Completely. And I'm paying the price."

"Is it that pretty, wealthy woman? The model? Lavinia Pahmeh?"

"Yes. Why do you ask?"

"Tell me something, Jack. About us."

"I'm listening."

"Did my family's money make a difference to you? In why you thought we should be togetheh?"

"I loved the idea of your family's money, Fran. The summeh house on Cape Çod. The ski trips to Stowe. The big brick mansion on Mt. Vehnon Street high on Beacon Hill. Your Radcliffe degree. I loved it all …"

"So what are you saying?"

"What I'm trying to say is simply this: I wasn't seduced by the idea of your family's money. But by the idea of you."

"Thank you foh that, Jack. I really mean it."

"But what about you? Was there something about me as a diht poor, Bohemian that appealed to you? As a way to get back at your fatheh. For all his vicious biases against me."

"I saw raw potential in you, Jack. Pure talent. I thought it might make you rich someday. And it has."

"Tell me, did your love life fare better? Afteh we split up?"

"I met some people who cared foh me. I tuhned down two marriage proposals. At least one of which might have wohked out. I've enjoyed fihst-class sex. But I haven't experienced real love."

Her words wounded him. A dagger through his heart. They *were* still married.

As he often did when hurt, he retreated into reticence. Wondering if Frances felt more for Charles than she would admit.

"I'm still not sure, Jack . . . that you and I have tried hahd enough. How can we know this?" she asked.

"We've been through a lot. And the hahd times and the good times neveh brought us close enough. To keep us togetheh."

"But as you said. We did have supremely happy moments. Didn't we?"

"What was then, was then. And we'll always have that. What's now is now. And what is to come has no place foh you and me togetheh. We'll suffeh until we face that fact."

Tears glistened at the corners of her eyes.

"I still need you, Jack."

"No one will eveh love you as much as I did. But if it could wohk, we'd know it by now."

Frances looked into her glass of Amaretto. For strength somewhere in the ruby mead on the cold ice in the crystal glass in the hollow of her trembling hand. Her sad expression resembled a small girl lost in a vast department store. A fist of wretched grief clenched the chest of Aeneas like defeat.

"I cried all last night," Frances said.

"You really haven't come to grips with it yet."

"No . . . Not yet."

"It gets wohse. Then it gets betteh. You have my sympathy. I've already descended into my own private hell. Suffering more than I thought possible. Unbearable agony. But I bounced back from it. And endured. So will you. I'm strongeh now. I have learned from my suffering."

"What have you learned from your suffering?"

"I've learned that some of our deepest wishes are just not meant to be. Like our marriage. But we craft our own dreams. And we must follow them anyway. Even if it means heartbreak. And defeat. It's the risk we take. Foh happiness. It's the price we pay foh being human."

"What else, Jack?"

"You can't bring back the past. Even if you wish with all your heart that you could."

"And do you, Jack? Wish with all your heart that you could?"

"I only know now . . . that we just weren't meant to be togetheh foheveh."

"I have to go. Thanks foh the drink," she said with a brave smile.

"Frances, I wish you all the happiness that you neveh found with me."

"I'll always keep a place in my heart foh you, Jack. Good-bye."

Fare
well,
my
Alhambra
rose.
* * *

Lotus Land

Subsequent to his meeting with Frances, Aeneas hit new personal lows. Haunted by visions of ecstasy in the eyes of Charles and his wife. In utter despair at the loss of so promising an affair with Lavinia. A sense of betrayal soured his love affair with life.

He could not control the visions that flashed through his consciousness like the malevolent nightmares of a lotuseater. He felt victimized by their incessant intrusion. He could neither eat nor sleep and to overcompensate he drank to excess. Demon bourbon. His eyes became hollow globes and he grew lean.

Aeneas lost interest in his work and wallowed in a consuming depression that overcame him. Until, once again, life went too far in a joke.
Hearing the Dixieland bands of a pre-Mardi Gras Day street parade on the Avenue, he walked outside to sit upon the steps and listen.

The street parade mocked and deepened his brooding melancholy.
He envisioned Andrew Palmer's forthcoming glorious odyssey as Rex. And Lavinia basking as matron upon the Queen's float. As usual, she would look stunning in her snowy formal gown and long white gloves. Crown upon her lovely hair. Roses in her arms. Ermine cape. A perfect member of the New Orleans aristocracy. The queen of hearts. A real dream queen.

The reverie was rudely broken as a fire engine red cardinal overhead impressively discharged an immense direct hit of a fusillade that fouled his favorite L.L. Bean shirt.

Life, I love your excesses. In them we have a common bond. I have been shat upon. Yet, again. A cardinal sin. Life, I laugh in your face. You just keep playing your annoying little practical jokes. I get it! Very funny. Enough already. The way up is the way down. Because I'm so low, I live underground.

However, I'm stepping up. To street level where maskers gambol and dance. No more royal screws, please. I am a convert. To the regal will of Momus.

Aeneas wiped the cardinal crap from his shirt with a handkerchief.

Inside his St. Charles Avenue home he cooked himself a steak in a red wine sauce, broccoli *au gratin*, broiled mushrooms and uncorked a bottle of Sterling Merlot.

It became clear, like an epiphany, that Lavinia was key to his deliverance.

Somehow, for the sake of his sanity, she simply must be persuaded to forgive him. He must find a way to win her love. He must tell her everything, as Charles had advised, and make her understand that his fleeting foolish fling meant nothing. And she meant the world to him.

If she would forgive him, then she was truly a woman of divine essence.

If he could not communicate his love and make her understand that they should be together no matter what calamities, self-made or otherwise, it was not meant to be. This *was* a great test of their love.

He must help her through it. By communicating and helping her see that he had learned from his excesses. And they were, in fact, kindred spirits.

Aeneas must trust her affection, which he knew ran deep. It meant accepting great risk. As he promised he would never do again for a woman.

If I were in New England, I would go into the wilderness. To the White Mountains. Or to the desolate lakes of Maine. On a lonely trail or a dirt road. Or upon a bed of rich pine needles. Staring up at the evergreens stirring as they embraced the wind. There I could reach conclusions.

In this dismal swamp. This city surrounded by marsh. There is no such earthly paradise in which to make life-altering decisions. Perhaps, that's why New Orleans created so many fantasies. Evacuation routes for hurricanes.

The immortal Mardi Gras. Fantasy invented to help troubled citizens. Face the realities of life. Odd as it may seem.

Once, before our marriage was ended. I reached a conclusion. To try, again. With Frances. Deciding beneath the giant redwood trees of Muir's woods. Where I saw a child play. Who resembled exactly Fran's pictures. In big pixels of black-and-white snapshots from a Kodak Brownie Automatic.

As a sweet innocent child of three. Like the child we might someday find in our midst. If Fortune would only grant it.

So I tried once before. And lost Frances. All efforts proving painfully futile. Despite our dreams for the future. Of a little family.
Now, I must try, again. And risk all. I know it. However brutal the outcome might prove. Because there is no chance, otherwise. And inaction is an absolute endgame. A total surrender to Fate. Defeat.

Aeneas picked up the telephone. And dialed Lavinia's number.

"Hello?"

An unfamiliar man's voice answered.

"Is this Lavinia Pahmeh's residence?" Aeneas asked.

Then in the background he heard her voice.

"Who is it, Percy?" she asked, barely perceptible.

"Who's calling?" Percy asked.

"Jack Jam."

A hand over the mouthpiece. Muffled pieces of conversation floated through the earpiece. As Percy's hand slid over the telephone receiver only partially blocking his reception.

"It's that loser, Jam . . . I'd tell him he has the wrong number. But he'd only keep calling . . . You can't possibly have anything to say . . . No, don't Lavinia . . ."

Then her voice clearly, as she wrestled her own phone from Percy.

"Hello, Jack."

"Why is Tuhneh with you?" he asked, not setting the proper conciliatory tone he had intended. Percy had definitely thrown him off his gameplan.

"That's none of your business, Jack. Listen, I'm in a rush. I'm off to the airport for a flight to New York for a few days."

"Is he going with you?"

"That's also none of your concern, now, Jack. Is it?"

"No, I suppose not."

"Then why *have* you called?"

"I want you to know that I am *profoundly* sorry about *all* this . . ."

"You're too late, Jack."

"It can't be too late to hope that you might find some way in your benevolent heart. To fohgive me foh what I have done. And the pain I know I have unwillingly caused you and your family."

"I don't think so. You humiliated me. Daddy, too. God, Jack."

"I simply can't exist without you, Dreamface."

"Don't call me that anymore. Hear?"

"I need you desperately. Do you undehstand?"

"Yes. I understand exactly how *you* feel. But you don't seem to understand how *I* feel. God, Jack, in front of the archbishop. With that tramp. Wherever *did* you find *her*?"

"It was the juices, Liv. I didn't mean to do it. It means nothing. And you mean everything. I love you deeply, Lavinia . . ."

"How do I know your overactive hormones won't act up, again? And you'll betray me? When there is more on the line? Than there is now?"

"I can't promise I will never disappoint you, deah. That would not be truthful . . ."

"Jack, I really have to run. Or I'll miss my flight to New York."

"Lavinia, I want you to know that I have learned from all this. I want you back desperately. Simply name any penance. I don't care what it is. I love you with all my heart."

"Jack, it's over between us. That's your penance. Deal with it."

"Please don't say that, Liv." "I'm sorry things didn't work out differently, Jack. But I have other options. You're a really cute guy. And you can be a real sweetheart, when you want to. You'll easily find someone new."

"Please, Liv. Listen to your heart. I live there. And try. Please, try. To fohgive me."

A brief silence. Then Percy's voice.

"Listen, you goddam loser. You screwed-up, big time."

"Put her back on, Tuhneh."

"Stop harassing her, man. With your pathetic pleas for forgiveness. You don't deserve it. Not one single bit. You hear me?"

"Back off, Tuhneh."

"She's crying, now, Jack. See what you made her do? You bastard . . . There now . . . Go and find yourself a tissue."

"I won't fohget this, Tuhneh."

"I'm *warning* you, Jack! Stay *away* from her!"

"This is *not* oveh, Tuhneh."

"But it is. Because I'm buying your business right out from under you."

"Not if I won't sell it. You need *both* Lavinia and Andrew to buy. And I just need *one* of them to keep it."

"And just which one do you think you have on your side? The beautiful woman that you just cheated on? In a public disgrace that's being talked about all over this town. Humiliating her near to death . . . Or her daddy? After your little stunts force him out of the running for Rex?"

"You set me up, Tuhneh."

"You're such an easy target, Jack. I sure do hope Mrs. Goodtime was worth it all."

"You incredible prick!"

"You'll wish you *were* my incredible prick. Tonight. About ten o'clock. In our penthouse suite at the Plaza in New York."

Her voice, again, dimly in the background.

"Give me the phone, Percy . . ."

Click. Dial tone.

The king of Aeneas was just placed in check.

> The question
> is,
> before
> coming up,
> how far
> down
> is
> rock
> bottom?
> * * *

Sir Knight of the Tooters

Incensed as Lavinia abandoned him for her assignment on the Great White Way. With Percy as her travelling companion.

Aeneas hastened to hire a temp named Camilla Yatte to handle the studio's seasonal overload.

Camilla proved to be a talented administrator. A workhorse capable of plowing through mounds of paperwork. In her mid twenties.

Highly interested in photography. With not much of a portfolio yet. He offered to help her build one outside of business hours at his studio.

Street smart. Preppy and shy. Deep, rich, blue eyes and blonde hair. Tall. Five-foot-twelve, she said. Lean with the strong, classic physique of a distance runner. Modest chest. And long, disciplined legs that headed North forever.

She wore tortoise-shell glasses and seemed rather withdrawn, at first. Oddly inaccessible. More at ease in the company of other women.

Pleasant and even tempered. Sense of humor. Very disarming, peculiar accent, which is indigenous to the Ninth Ward of New Orleans. Oddly New York in this powerful dialect. Hard upon one's ears. Like his Boston accent to Andrew.

As he emerged from the cave of the darkroom adjacent to the studio's front door with fresh prints in hand, Camilla stooped over a low file drawer. Fine inviting hiney. Firm flex of legs. At this time of extreme loneliness, the temp looked most tempting.

As Lavinia is lost forever. I am hopelessly single. Yet again. Ah, Camilla.

We really must get to know each other better. More intimately. Someday, soon, I hope. If you'll have me. I wonder if she prefers women. Don't go down that road. You can't afford that fantasy today. You need to concentrate.

"You got some sun this weekend," Aeneas observed from behind her.

"Magawd, magawd, magawd, Mr. Jam! You scared da life outta me."

"Sorry. But the sun looks good on you."

"Thanks, dawlin'. I didn't wanta distoib ya. While you was developin' and all. But Mistah Chardonnay is waitin' foh yah in da foyeh."

"Mr. Charbonnet, you mean?"

"Yeah him. He says it's important dat he sees yah ASAP."

"I don't want to talk with him. I have no time."

"Whaddya want me ta tellim?"

"Tell him I took dead."

"Took dead?"

"It's like one who has 'took drunk.' As you like to say down here. Only more pehmanent. It's close enough foh govehment wohk."

"I'm afraid dat I awready tole him dat you was in."

"Tell him I have appointments to shoot the King of the Krewe of Schwimp. Followed by the Queen of the Krewe of Mudbug. Followed by the Grand Marshal of the Krewe of Cockroach. *Ad infinitum.* Tell him that I'll be tied up all day. All week. Terminally booked. With no time in the foreseeable future."

"I get da pitcher, Mistah Jam."

"Good. Then please pass my message onto Chahles."

Camilla left in a big rush.

Salt of the earth. A few rough edges. Certainly gets right to the heart of the matter. The face of an angel. The voice of Yogi Berra.

Soon she returned.

"Mistah Cabernet. Did I say dat right? Like da wine?"

"Charbonnet."

"I can nevah get my colohs straight. As faw as red and white wines are consoined. Anyhow, Mr. Charbonnet wants ta know, can you jam in Sir Knight a da Tootahs? Whatevah da heck dat means."

"Tell him no."

"I don't think he's gonna take no fah an anseh."

"If you say it like you mean it, he will."

Camilla exited. And almost immediately reappeared.

"Dis man is sumpin' else, Mistah Jam. Said he was frum da Krewe ah da Twenty Funny Fellahs . . ."

"Phunny Phorty Phellows?"

"If you say so. He's demandin' reconnition a da krewe. Says he ain't leavin' 'til you tawk wid him. As faw as dis man's consoined. Know what I mean? I think dis man deprived some village somewhere of an idiot."

"He's an *intellectual*. He only *behaves* like an idiot."

"I seen more brainpower in bait."

"Camilla, this man attended *Penn*."

"He don't strike me as no criminal. What did he get sent up fah?"

"I have nothing at all to say to him. Please ask him to leave. Now."

"I can try. But I can't guarontee nothin'."

"Camilla, please just try your best."

She departed. Shortly thereafter Charles barged through the door leading from the foyer followed by a visibly upset Camilla.

"Don't worry about it, Camilla. I'll handle this," Aeneas reassured her. Camilla left wildly cursing a litany of Ninth Ward profanity under her breath.

"Francie dumped me," Charles said.

Now, you know how I felt. He's devastated. He loved her. Conciliatory. Pathetic. As I must have sounded to Liv. Hat-in-hand aspect on his face. He is reaching out. To his friend. And fellow exile.

"I guess that makes two of us," Aeneas said. "Look, Chahlie, I'm very sorry about all this. But I'm in an impossible situation. I'm ovehwhelmed with wohk. As you can imagine, since Liv left. And Camilla is a new temp. Besides, I have absolutely nothing to say to you. Except that I think we should paht ways on the business side. Which becomes moot if Pehcy takes me oveh. And he may well succeed. I'm prepared psychologically foh the absolute wohst. You might be betteh off aligning yourself with him."

"Of course, a change of agency is your prerogative. Although we're doing damn fine work for you . . ."

"Did you come here to save to the account?"

" . . . And despite our binding contract, which has not expired and will not for another five months, I'll give you an out if you want one."

"I do."

"Fine. You've got it."

"Consideh it a pehsonality conflict. A creative conflict. A conflict of interest. Call it what you will. Now get out, please."

Aeneas pointed melodramatically to the door.

"Francie still . . . cares for you, Jack. You should know it. That's why I'm here."

"I already know."

"Don't you even give a damn? I would. If I were you."

"Of course, I do. But her interest in me is simply . . . platonic."

"Platonic?"

"Our relationship just doesn't wohk. That's all that mattehs between us. And some good memories."

"Very sad. All of this."

The ad man's head hung hangdog.

"Yes. Very."

"I wish I could express to you how truly sorry I am. I just didn't *know* who she was. When we first met. Then I couldn't help myself. After I did know. It was just too late."

"If she hadn't dumped you, Chahlie, you'd still be with her."

"Harsh words, Jack."

"I'm trying to exehcise some restraint. What can I say? Christ, I instructed you in the seduction of my own wife."

"And you did it *well*, too."

"Well enough to read about it in *Esquiyeh?*"

"We're all victims, Jack. You and I. And Francie. All three. But the issue is resolved, isn't it? Certainly, it's not worth killing our friendship over."

"Friendship? You betrayed me, Chahlie. You and she both."

"Is it because I'm black? And she's white? Is that what's eatin' you alive?"

The accusation was a dart to the heart. It hit Aeneas where he lived. Wasn't the grand tableau of their kinship forged at its essence by inventively aligned black-and-white pixels? He paused to think before speaking.

"I loved you like a *son*, Chahlie. You were more than a *brotheh* to me."

"A *brother*? Good one, Jack."

"Whatdya mean? It's absolutely killing me. You betrayed me. As much as anyone possibly can."

"Like you betrayed Lavinia."

"That's a low blow, Chahlie. She's probably just waking up about now. In the bridal suite of the Plaza Hotel in New Yohk. With Pehcy Tuhner."

"I'm sorry to hear that, Jack. When did you find this out?"

"Three days ago. When I called to beg her fohgiveness."

"I'm asking you to forgive me. Even though my actions had no malice in them either. Just as you asked her. Which puts us both in the same boat. Doesn't it? Forgive me, Jack."

"Every time I soften the heart someone runs a javelin through it. I need to guard my Walls betteh, Chahlie."

"Building Walls only shuts out life, Jack. There's no victory in it."

"Everyone, that I eveh love, ruins me. Love will be the death of me."

"Never did a friend so unwillingly let another friend down."

"Chahlie, you slept with my wife. Yes or no?"

"You know the answer, Jack."

"You set me up with Didi Bontempo."

"I played a matchmaker. So what? Before the deal with Turner bubbled up. I had no idea. How was I supposed to know?"

"I trusted your advice. Or rather, your ignorance. Implicitly."

"It was *your* decision to go on the blind date. You were so pathetic . . . emotionally. You set yourself up."

"I'm in ruins. You're a one-man wrecking ball. What else can I say?"

"Say that you're a bigger man than all of this. Whose heart is still strong enough to forgive. And whose head is clear enough. Despite the Chaos all around you. To understand that it's the right thing to do."

"I don't think I can, Chahlie."

"You *can* do it. Just as Lavinia can."

"It's only your ungodly Catholic conscience."

"I can't blame you. I'd feel the same way, too. If you want objective advice from a friend on choosing a new ad agency, I'll give it to you."

"That's good of you, Chahlie."

"I better let you get on with your work. I know you're busy. So long, Jack."

Charles slowly walked to the door.

"I may be a total idiot, Chahlie . . . But I'm also short a few friends. And the bahbarians are at the gates. So let's leave things as they were. Before all this happened. Because it's really no one's fault. And there's no point in making everyone feel wohse than they already do."

"I made that same point in my *Esquire* article. Remember?"

"Maybe that's where I got the idea."

"You are a prince among men, Jack. Maybe even a *king*."

A vital point as an opening still existed for Aeneas in the Phunny Phorty Phellows. Maybe even, Da Boss. According to humble Sir Knight of the Tooters.

In the mind of Aeneas the prophetic one-liner of Archbishop Mizentius flashed past.

"Take
my
wife,
. . .

please."
* * *

The Pleasure Principle

Naturally, he was determined to deliver distinction in the dark room of Aeneas Studios. Before the first morning appointments with sundry clients due for portraits, Aeneas dabbled in his photo lab with Camilla.

He knew that the front door bell would ring audibly. And his clients' voices and their roaming about the studio would signal their entry.

If they arrived without first ringing. As they commuted to the foyer to chat amiably as New Orleanians often do. Lingering for the flash that would aesthetically shape their images for posterity. As he crafted such art with his eyes, hands and Hasselblad.

He had promised Camilla that she could spend some time developing photos in the darkroom with him. But he hadn't lived up to it.

Because the studio had been a lunatic asylum. And he just didn't have time during business hours throughout Mardi Gras season.

Aggressively, Camilla had called him on the carpet for his broken promises to her. And said she never would have accepted such low wages as a temp in this position. If she thought he would renege on his promise as a mentor. She threatened to quit. And leave him in the lurch so close to Fat Tuesday.

Aeneas respected her competence. And didn't want to invest more time in retraining another temp who might not be as capable. He contemplated the advantages of hiring her to a more permanent position. To avoid catastrophic Chaos that would converge if she suddenly quit, he acquiesced. And honored his promise to her.

They processed a role of black-and-whites. Before regular business hours. Photos that she had taken of French Quarter courtyards. Of which professional quality she was most hopeful.

Camilla appealed for the tutelage of Aeneas under the black light. Which he was happy to offer. Insisting that she manage the development and he would only oversee the process.

Together in the darkroom beneath an infrared bulb. A discernible pattern of a bronze statue in a French Quarter courtyard of Joan of Arc, framed by palm fronds, emerged. Onto paper immersed in developing fluids in the pan.

She was exuberant at this miracle of creation of her first print.

Celluloid, chemicals, paper, light. Time passed, the birdies sang, the music played and *voila – metempsychosis*. The transference of a soul into another body.

Aeneas helped her lift the soggy paper onto the dryer. His hands rested and guided hers in the transfer of the precious paper in the dim light. When the print dried, Camilla was ecstatic with her work.

As a gesture of good faith, Aeneas agreed to frame and display the photo in the studio foyer.

The bell of the front door rang. His first client of a busy day.

"Can we please do anodder one? Huh? Please? Dis is *so* interestin'," she begged good-naturedly.

"If you make it quick. But first, please seat Mrs. Borgeois," Aeneas said, standing on principle.

Camilla stepped outside the darkroom and asked Mrs. Borgeois please to make herself comfortable. His client became indignant, indeed, haughty as she was unaccustomed to waiting. Especially as her day was full, too. She lived in a mansion on St. Charles. Her deceased husband had been a shipping magnate. Whose Fortune rose with the growing stature of the Port of New Orleans.

Once Mrs. Borgeois at her poolside party drank too much bubbly with too few *horace d'oeuvres*. And poured an entyre case of Dom Perignon into her pool. One bottle at a time. Much to the indignity of many dignitaries. Thin, wrinkled, gray, immaculately attyred and filthy rich, she would wait impatiently. As Aeneas and Camilla finished another of her courtyard prints.

"You see the stock I place in your learning the art of photography?" Aeneas softly asked. "Who else would give you so much time? On such a busy day?"

"I promise to be brisk as brisket, Mr. Jam."

She chose another print. Which they also proceeded to develop.

Moving along smartly. The front door pealed, again.

"Friends of the Symphony," Aeneas surmised. "A group photo. Very important people. They're early."

Aeneas answered the door admitting elderly women from Uptown and a retired gentleman. Amiably, Aeneas asked them to wait. As he was in the midst of a make-or-break developing stage. A crucial print for the King of Momus.

"*Dum vivimus, vivimus*," Aeneas said. "Immortality refuses to be rushed."

They smiled their assent jointly and politely acknowledged that they had arrived early. Aeneas charmed Mrs. Borgeois and returned to his darkroom.

"Let's get on with it," Aeneas advised. "We have to wrap it up."

Camilla had just dropped the print into the fixer, when the doorbell rang yet again. Aeneas volunteered to answer it.

"The President of the Chambeh of Commehce. Foh his 9:30 sitting," Aeneas muttered. "I'll get it."

He directed the executive to a comfortable chair just outside the darkroom and pleasantly warned of the brief wait. The businessman smiled affably, sat and picked up the *Wall Street Journal* from the coffee table. Turning to the stock indices where he became transfixed. Tracking the Fortune of the Fortune 500. As Aeneas boldly retreated into his darkroom once again.

"Gawd! Dis one's betta dan da last! I'm so happy, Mistah Jam. Ain't it a beauty? I'm so proud. I can't thank you enough."

"It does look fihst rate, Camilla . . . Perhaps, you should stay on here at the gallery. Pehmanently. With a raise in pay. What would you say to that?"

"I doane know how ta thank ya, Mistah Jam. I'd do anything ta show ya how much I appreciate dis. Anything."

Camilla flashed her big, baby blue eyes beneath spangling, long, blonde bangs. And a faint smile crossed her lips.

"That's really nice, Camilla. You are a promising young photographeh. No doubt about it. With the right guidance, you could have a studio like this one. Someday. And make big bucks."

"Ya think so, Mistah Jam? Will ya show me how?"

"Absolutely."

"Gee, I think you're terrific. You da best. I been meanin' ta tell ya how much I like ya woik. I just wish I could pay ya back. Foh all dis. Some way."

"Just keep giving your best effohts to your wohk. That will suffice."

Unexpectedly, Camilla pressed her lips, a flower yielding to light, upon his mouth. A long, highly charged kiss. The impact of which surged electrically through him. Hope beckoned. In this dark, loveless chapter of life. Intimacy.

"I really like da way you tawk, Mistah Jam. You're so Ivory League."

In the darkness under the black light they kissed again. Seized by Camilla's ambition and ardor in his dark room.

He felt her hands undo his fly in an instant. He squeezed her with a strong embrace and his fingers tore at her silk blouse.

Aeneas lifted her brassiere over demure, pear-shaped breasts: tears on a baby's cheek. He kissed them underneath with the shaft of his tongue.

Then he unbuttoned her skirt. And yanked it to the floor. She helped herself out of pantyhose and slip. Then she disrobed of her blouse and unhooked her bra.

As she did so, he loosened his Calvin Klein tie. Unbuttoned his button-down Oxford shirt. And stepped smartly out of his Dior pants. Without bothering in the confined space to remove dark socks or wing tips.

In a Fury of passion, Aeneas balanced her upon the ledge of the sink. Where he removed the final vestiges of her underclothing.

The doorbell rang. Again.

Camilla yelled to the most distinguished clientele of Aeneas Studios: "One a yawl . . . out there . . . wanta get . . . dat?"

Without suppressing the hot, sighing, heaving pleasure of her voice.

Why do these things happen to me? I must be coming up in this world.

If I'm now a target for gold diggers. I'm God's lightning rod. But who else could deliver such desperately pixilating amusement to Him?

Then Camilla whispered:

"Jesusgawd, Mistah Jam. I been pitcherin' dis in my own mind fah days. Dis feels so excitin'. I hope I ain't tawkin' too much. I don't mean ta babylon or nuthin'. But you Yankees really know how ta kick up ya wing-tips."

"True Bostonians neveh make love unshod of wing-tips."

"Der is sumpin' else you better be wearin', too. Ain't der?"

Aeneas yanked a spare Trojan from his wallet. Condoning condoms.

The round shield left an impression upon the leather of his archaic wallet. He ripped the foil to shreds in a Fury. Sheathing his sword in its scabbard. Stabbing Camilla's wound without mercy. As the agony of pure desire engulfed her pained countenance.

"Jam it inta me . . . Doane stop . . . I sweartagawd . . . I'll die if ya do."

Aeneas continued unruffled. As in the foyer one client opened the door to admit another. Someone was overheard to suggest that the new guest take a seat. As Aeneas was devoutly diligent in "delicate developments" in the dark room. For King Momus.

Dum vivimus, vivimus. Thus, I impale her with my pixilated prod.

Two sets of footsteps and then chairs groaned from their burden.

"I'm gonna make love to you until you come," Aeneas whispered.

"Magawd, yes, Mistah Jam. Make sweet love ta me."

Camilla groaned as her passion built. With her arms clutched around his shoulders. He felt the sharp darts of her fingernails bite into the exposed flesh of his back.

She looked lovely in the light of infrared. The small darkroom became steamy as their pleasure developed. Aeneas perspired and felt his wetness transfer to her lovely warm skin.

In his abandon, Aeneas knocked over an empty chemical bottle. Which tumbled headlong to the floor and explosively shattered. But he was shielded from glass shards as he was well shod. Hesiod in Bostonian wing tips.

He positioned her back flush against the Wall for maximum advantage.

As he repeatedly surged to breach her fortress, the Walls of the dark room began to tremble, thunder and quake bombastically.

Clients in the adjacent waiting room began to grumble in a crescendo of clamor. Unsavory and indecent Rumor hissed from the tongues of its masters and mistresses. Like snakes of Medusa.

Camilla whispered.

"Magawd . . . I think I'm gonna come, . . . Mistah Jam."

"That's it . . . Quiet as chuhch mice."

Then louder.

"Jesusgawd . . . I'm gonna come."

"No serenades, please."

Much too loudly.

"I'm comin' . . . Like a freight train!"

"Easy does it."

Finally, without restraint.

"MAGAWDMAGAWDMAGAWDAWMIGHTYIAMCOMING!"

More guttural utterances by Camilla. Like a yak struck by lightning.

The Walls shook in barbarous augmentation. As his pleasure arrived full and deep and rich. He nearly bifurcated his tongue like a serpent's. To keep from articulating the heaving pleasure that wildly possessed and transformed him.

Then the hammering against the Walls ceased.

Briefly, peace prevailed. A truce.

Then Aeneas heard loud grumbling and shouting. Many feet retreating indignantly one after the other to the door. Much muttering and muffled exclamations in harsh tones. Offensive to the sensibilities of a lady and an aesthete.

"King Momus? HAH!"

The retreat complete. The gateway sealed.

Silence ruled the studio.

"Dey lef'. All a dem."

"It's all right. Don't you worry one bit."

"You wondaful, Mistah Jam. Honest. I ain't makin' no Hippocratic oath. You iz just wondaful."

"So are you."

Aeneas parted her warm, wet lips with an affectionate kiss.

"I'm afraid ta go out der. Suppose somebody's still waitin' foh yah. What den?"

"You better wait here. While I see."

Aeneas hurriedly dressed. Cautiously, he drew open the door. His regimental striped tie askew. Oxford shirt besotted with perspiration. Bostonian wingtip shoestrings estranged. Hair apparently arranged in a wind tunnel. From his gaping fly a white flag of Fruit-of-the-Loom in surrender.

Aeneas John Jam was Troy sacked.

In the foyer someone still patiently waited. Sitting alone. Hands folded. Flushed in anger. Intimating intimidation. One more sacking.

Fate waylaid in his wake.

"Son, I think we best have ourselves a little talk."

I am
a feather
for every
wind
that
blows.

* * *

Chimera XII:
Truce and Duel

"The Fates are too strong. You must not delay them any longer. Let us go where God and fortune call me. I am resolved to meet Aeneas in battle. I am resolved to suffer what bitterness there is in death. You will not see me put to shame again. This is madness, but before I die, I beg of you, let me be mad."
— The Aeneid, Book XII

Millionaires Row

Dreadfully, Aeneas Jam knocked upon the imposing portal of Andrew's private residence. A mansion on Millionaires Row at the corner of St. Charles Avenue. The alabaster, pillared, antebellum Greek Revival.

Thriving greenery. Hibiscus, hyacinth, camellias and impatiens. Live oaks. Old hickory trees. And spreading junipers. Manicured lawn verdant as a golf green. The fast fading sun silhouetted the palm trees on the neutral ground.

The Rolls and Mercedes stately in the drive. A vacant space left for Lavinia's absent Cadillac Coupe de Ville. Blue gas tongues licking against the glass lanterns on each side of a formidable cypress door.

Balcony arched and protruding over the front door. With a neat wooden railing for viewing millionaire neighbors. The purple and gold krewe flag of Rex hanging in all its splendor from the balcony railing.

The streetcars passing by Audubon Park at the nexus of the palatine of the next Rex. Once again, they rolled down St. Charles Avenue after the day's street parade.

Aeneas lifted the tail of a heavy brass crawfish. Thudding it thrice. Like a swimming *bayou* mudbug. To say hello.

He had dressed in his best corporate executive uniform. Gray, pinstripe suit. Starched white shirt. Polka dot navy tie. And black Bostonians. Hoping to put his best wingtip forward.

At least, trying to look the part of heir to his own company. Of which he was now only a minority stakeholder. Carrying in sweaty hands a pair of presentation folders of financial information. He meant business.

Dressed like a banker awaiting a big rate cut by the Fed. An appointment with his pecuniary Fate. After tripping up. By getting caught with his pants hopelessly down. Yet, again. He was braced for the worst. Hell hath no Fury like the wrath of Rex.

He heard footsteps on the far side of the door coming to answer. And admit him to the man in whose considerable power his Fortune rested. The man whose good graces had launched the meteoric rise of Aeneas.

Like a gladiator in the Coliseum, Aeneas awaited Caesar's thumb.
After accidentally castrating the lion. Another lesson in abject humility from life.

Raymond, an ancient butler, opened the door. Dressed in white coat and starched white shirt with a little black bow tie like a train porter on the Crescent City Limited. Smiling and polite and dignified, he led Aeneas to Andrew's study.

Rex was enthroned on a high-priced, overstuffed, leather, big easy chair in his silk smoking jacket and cravat. Puffing cyrenely upon a *Habana*. Enshrouded in pungent clouds of cigar smoke. Which combined with tension to trigger in Aeneas a nicotine fit. And he wished he had brought his Peterson bullbent pipe.

he study decorated more like a library with walls of leather-bound books. Original oils of Dixieland Jazz musicians.

A gas fueled fireplace unaccustomed to wood. Over which hung in an elaborate gilt frame an oil painting of a young debutante in an ivory gown grasping a nosegay.

Upon a coffee table rested a Waterford decanter, a half-full glass of Ancient Age Bourbon and an empty one. Andrew's chair faced the fireplace and the painting of the debutante. Whose warm, brown eyes emanated an aristocratic elegance. Like Lavinia.

Exquisite Louis XVI period pieces strategically were placed by an interior designer. Monstrous burgundy Khiristan upon the shiny hardwood floor. Tall windows from floor to ceiling framed by rich velvet burgundy drapes tied at the middle. Antique French desk in a corner near a window.

An empty chair opposed Andrew. Silently, without greeting, with a mere sweep of his hand, Rex bid Aeneas to sit. Andrew paused thoughtfully and stared with a penetrating glare into the soul of Aeneas before speaking.

"Son, whatever am I going to do with you?" Andrew began.

"I have absolutely not the vaguest notion, sih. I trust that's what I'm here to learn."

"Jingo's crickets! Have you any idea of the power of the group of people who fled in horror from your studio? Shortly after I walked in yesterday morning? After you so brazenly ignored all my telephone calls."

"Yes, sih."

"The symphony directors. Frowning like a concert pianist in the middle of a Grieg piano concerto. Who hears that his Steinway is out of tune."

"Yes, sih."

"The President of the Chamber of Commerce. Which I have belonged to for thirty years. And on whose Board I sit. Squirming like a taxpayer. Missing too many receipts during an IRS audit."

"Yes, sih."

"Mrs. Borgeois. President of Pendennis. Whose deceased husband owned 25% of the land in Louisiana upon which Standard Oil had rigs during Huey Long's heyday. Lavinia is now attending a gathering of debutantes at her home on St. Charles Avenue. Escorted by Percy Turner, I might add. You kept this important client . . . waiting an *hour* . . . for no good reason . . ."

The throat of Aeneas clenched. Suddenly constricting. And choking off an apology. Hitherto, well practiced. Glancing at the two presentation folders. Humbly enduring the excoriating paenegyric from the spleen of Rex.

"All of whom from your waiting room could hear *every* word. Every groan. Every cry. Every *whisper*. As you drilled your poor young secretary's brains out. An employee of mine. Who could easily now launch a costly and scandalous sexual harassment suit against us? And call plenty of witnesses to the stand."

More throat clearing by Aeneas. His contact lenses felt dry. Would one fling across the study at any moment? As it did at the rectory on Elysian Fields?

"Havin' sex in the darkroom. During business hours. In front of all these very important people. In fact, the most respected citizens of New Orleans. My friends and colleagues and business associates of many years. Well, son, that's one *hell* of a way to run a business. Wouldn't you say? And here's the part that gauls me. It's not just any business. It's *my* business."

"Yes, sih."

"Heaping one social disgrace upon another. Your little indiscretion, before my saintly daughter, no less. And Archbishop Mizentius. A power in the sacred church of my faith. Whom I had prevailed upon personally to perform the ceremony in St. Louis Cathedral as a favor to me . . ."

"Yes, sih."

"Lavinia's big opportunities way the hell up in New York now look like a sanctuary. A refuge amid such . . . *scandal*. Which practically makes her a refugee in her own hometown. Where she was born and raised. And which she loves. To that god-forsaken Sodom and Gomorrah on the Hudson."

"Unlike this one on the Mississipp?"

"Don't give me that salamis, Jack. I'm dead serious."

"We share similar concerns, Mr. Pahmeh. New Yohk is no place for a young, gorgeous, up-and-coming, rich supermodel, sih."

"Don't get flip with me, Jack. There's more. I did harbor the dream that one day, before I died, I would ride down the Avenue on Mardi Gras Day. As Rex. With Lavinia riding at my side. To shake the hand of and toast the King of Comus at midnight."

"I really didn't mean to sound flip. Or create a row . . ."

"That has been a *lifelong* dream of mine, Jack. One I have worked very hard to turn into reality over a period of *years*. A world-class aspiration I am on the very brink of grasping . . ."

"I undehstand."

"I'm dying, Jack . . ."

"We both are, sih. By the minute. Dying a thousand deaths."

"You placed my dream in jeopardy. Because fellow krewe members at Rex won't vote for a king. Unless that man is truly honorable. He must not even invoke the *appearance* of impropriety. Or place the immaculate integrity of Rex at risk. Rex is above reproach. Untouchable by vice. Or scandal."

"You have a long distinguished recohd to stand upon in New Ohleans. God knows, this town has a shoht memory. And it cehtainly needs one . . ."

"Let me finish, Jack. I have on the table a very generous offer. From a group of credible venture capitalists with deep pockets. A deal lined up by Percy Turner. And guess what?"

"They want to buy our business."

"Very good, Jack. But let's come back to that, shall we?"

"If you wish."

"What can you possibly say in your own defense, son? That justifies all the faith I have placed in your hands. Including a promising business venture. And the future happiness of my daughter. All of which you seem utterly, totally and hopelessly to have squandered."

Andrew became calm. Folding his hands upon his lap. And listening.

Aeneas tried to speak. Words escaped him. He squirmed and gasped and sputtered a comic pantomime. Like his dream of the çod in his çodpiece.

Andrew poured bourbon from the Waterford decanter and offered Aeneas a glass: "Have a sip of bourbon. I know you like it. And steady yourself."

Aeneas accepted the glass of straight Ancient Age. Hands trembling.

Wounded by the direct hits. Every word a dart, an arrow, a spear. Crystal glass and decanter clattering in a racket. He took a big sip that subjugated his throat. But restored the dignity of speech.

"It's all been ratheh humiliating, sih. Fihst and foremost, I want you to know that I apologize deeply. I immensely value your pehsonal and professional trust. And would never intend to do any hahm to you or your business enterprises. I have had the good Fohtune to benefit by your trust. And business acumen. And I deeply love your daughteh. With all my heart."

Andrew sipped silently as he listened.

"I am afraid that afteh my marriage ended. And afteh losing Lavinia, I haven't been myself," Aeneas continued. "I almost went off the deep end. More than once. I have been lost at sea. In a deep, dahk night of the spirit. I have learned valuable lessons. I would give anything to live those two days oveh again. And to justify your faith in me. But nothing of this soht will eveh happen, again. I give you my wohd of honoh."

"Integrity is a commodity, Jack. Don't ever take it lightly. It's your stock in trade. It brings respect. And real honor. And meaning to life."

"I undehstand, Mr. Pahmeh."

"I also understand you, Jack. When I was your age, I was a lot like you. I sowed my wild oats, too. I remember how desire burns hot inside you. And how fresh ambition tastes like a mint julip. When you're young."

"I haven't handled my newfound financial success very . . . successfully."

"In fact, I went through two dark nights of the spirit, as you call them. I almost went off the deep-end myself. Just before I settled down. I was drinking and chasing women all over town. Because I was rich and young and single. Reasonably handsome, a war hero and an MBA. And New Orleans will seduce you. And fill your ears with the whispers of sweet nothings. Chimeras the likes of which you have never known. If you offer her those qualities. I remember it. I've been there."

"What changed you, sih? Into such a pillah of the community?"

"I married that beautiful little lady."

Aeneas sipped his bourbon, which burned hot and husky and clean down his throat.

Andrew shifted his eyes to gaze sadly at the oil painting of the debutante smiling down upon them. In all the fresh and tender beauty of youth. An overpowering resemblance to Lavinia in her eyes and hair and in the shape of her mouth. Judging from the placement of Andrew's chair, it was obvious that he had spent much time contemplating the portrait of his deceased wife.

"Arabella came along and civilized me. I would have burnt out like a swampfire. If it wadn't for her. She set me straight. And there's nothing like a good woman for that. God bless 'em . . ."

The women of my life seem to have set the swamp afire. Rather than extinguish it. But I let Liv get away. And for that, I have only myself to blame.

"I miss her, Jack. To this very day. More than I can ever say."

"I undehstand. I miss Liv, too. Deeply."

"When I lost her to the Gulf in Pass Christian, a second dark night of the spirit descended upon me. Like yours, mine was caused by the end of my marriage. By death. Which more than likely hurts even worse, if you can imagine it, than divorce . . . Did you know Arabella's death was a . . . suicide?"

"I had no idea, sih."

This revelation shocked Aeneas.

"Things are often not as they seem. She was manic-depressive. Born with it. And no drugs, no treatments, not even electric shock therapy helped. With all the medical and financial resources available to me, I was still powerless . . . Totally. In the one aspect of my life that mattered most. "

"I don't know what to say."

"After Arabella's funeral, I almost lost it, again. Became a borderline alcoholic. Maybe even a full-blown one. But drinking for a while got the best of me. My life was an absolute mess. Everyday I looked down into Lavinia's beautiful little face. Crying pitifully, inconsolably, for her mamma. And I saw Arabella in those sad brown eyes."

"And what changed that?"

"I had that little girl. To love and care for. She was all that was left to me of Arabella. A most glorious and beautiful legacy. As great a gift of our love and devotion as God can give to any man. So I had responsibilities to honor. I faced them head-on. Like a man. I saw the wisdom of moderation. I weeded out my excesses. And got down to business. But at the end of the day, it was Lavinia who saved me. From my second dark night of the spirit."

"Son of a gun."

"So I *know* you, Jack. Jingo's crickets! In another lifetime, I *was* you."

"I'm flattehed by the comparison, sih."

"Well, don't be. Because it wasn't pretty. And I'm not proud of it. But I came out from hiding behind the Walls. During my dark nights of the spirit. What are you planning to do? To emerge from yours?"

The wild man pulls the hair of his beard out. That's what makes him wild, no doubt.

"I didn't come here empty-handed, Mr. Pahmeh. I know that we have a business togetheh. And despite the lapses, to which I have already confessed, apologized and promised to avoid in the future, our business has been profitable. Highly profitable, as a matter of fact."

Aeneas handed Andrew a presentation folder. Nicely bound and typeset. With many charts and graphs.

"I'll let you and your financial advisehs read this privately, sih. But let me point out the extent of our rapid growth. Our rate-of-retuhn, sih, has been phenomenal."

"I know it has. That's why we have a buyer lined up."

"In addition, our revenue stream has been extremely generous. As you can see."

"I know that revenues are headed north . . ."

"Our business has provided you with some generous tax writeoffs. Including depreciation and write-offs for equipment under Section 179 of the Internal Revenue Code. As this last cohporate tax return shows."

"Uh-huh."

"Here was your original venture capital outlay foh the staht-up. By tuhning around your business, here's what you would need to earn through otheh investments. In stocks, bonds, T-bills and mutual funds. Just to match the current and projected retuhns from our business. We beat the indices for all of these investment alternatives, all asset classes, over a one-year period. We flew past every benchmark. Exponentially. In only the first year of the turn-around. There was no betteh place foh your money than invested in our business."

"Well-done, Jack. Miracles never cease."

"I give most of the credit to Lavinia for our operating pehfohmance. She has your genius. And your vision foh business management, sih. Liv and let Liv. Haha . . . And Chahles Chahbonnet. At the ad agency. He did a nice job on the presentation. And has excelled in mahketing our studio."

"That's noble of you. You've brought credit to yourself."

"To us, sih. Us. We're a great team. Don't sell us shoht."

"These numbers are better than Percy's."

"Pehcy's numbers are projections, sih. Ours are more reliable data . . . He's low-balling you."

"I'll have Evan take a look at this. He's my financial advisor. I don't think you both have met. But he's dropping by to analyze the latest offer from Percy's investors. Of course, we always turn down the first offer as 'insufficient.' As a matter of protocol."

"I see."

"So, have you done a business valuation?"

"Yes, sih."

"And, bottomline, what would you estimate the business is now worth?"

"Book value is about a million-seven. $1.727 million to be precise."

Andrew closed the binder. And threw the presentation of Aeneas upon his coffee table.

"Percy's first bid was $1.4 million in round figures. But the next one will be much higher."

"I see."

"I like what you've done, Jack. I respect a young man with spunk. With age that develops into a man with guts. If he's lucky and smart. There is a hell of a lot of wimps runnin' around this town. You've got real spunk. And more of a head for business than I thought."

"Despite early mistakes in the tuhn-around, sih, your retuhn on investment is sound. And your revenue stream will really staht to takeoff shahply in our second year. If there is a second year . . ."

"You can see why Percy's group wants to own it, Jack. He buys out the competition. Raises prices. It's a smart move."

"And, may I ask, where does Lavinia stand on this deal?"

"She has a mind of her own, Jack. She is uncommitted. Her stake is outstanding. Does that surprise you?"

"And where do you stand, sih, on this deal?"

"I won't know what kind of a deal we have. Until Evan gets here with his full analysis of their latest offer. I refuse to speculate on hypothetical scenarios. I need to see reality first."

"I undehstand."

"Talent is a commodity, Jack. I hate to see it wasted. In fact, I hate to see waste in any shape or form. It makes no sense. Now, you've shown me you know how to build up a business. And you have built up our venture profitably. You do have great potential. But godammit, son. As far as our future business may be concerned, you have *got* to *steady* yourself."

"You're right, of course."

"And that worries me. Going down the road, son. If you don't steady yourself, you're goin' to lose everything you worked for. I'd hate to see that happen to a promising young man like you. My daddy gave me that same lecture about 30 years ago. When I was a young hellion like you."

"Life takes its toll, sih."

"Life is a blink of a butterfly's wings. Don't blow it, son."

"I very much appreciate your advice, Mr. Pahmeh. I'll strive to follow your good counsel."

Andrew sipped more bourbon and stared at Arabella. The irony and pathos of Andrew's earlier life gripped the photographer.

A firm knock upon the study's door.

"Excuse me, Mr. Palmer. Mr. Evan is here for you," the butler announced.

"Show him in please, Raymond."

The butler left. And shortly Evan appeared at the doorway.

Evan was a lean but rugged young man. High cheekbones with an aquiline nose. Sturdy, compact, no-nonsense. A Ph.D. in Economics from Rice. Impeccably dressed in a business suit and regimental striped tie. Short blond hair immaculately cut and combed into place. Shoes well shined. Milky fingers of a handkerchief flaring jauntily from his suit coat pocket. A youthful face with the blush often found in marathoners.

"Johnny, meet my beancounter, Evan Rohmer."

"Nice to meet you, Evan. Your reputation precedes you."

"Evan, shake hands with Johnny Jam."

"Hello there, Johnny."

Big smile, perfect teeth, sturdy grip. Formalities efficiently dispensed.

"Listen, Johnny, I know this concerns you. But I want to meet with Evan privately first. Before we look at his analysis of the new numbers from Percy Turner's investment consortium."

"Fine."

"Would you all mind coolin' your heels, let's say, for . . . an hour? Or maybe two? Take a little walk or streetcar ride down St. Charles Avenue. Get a cup of coffee at the Camellia Grill. Or some dinner at Pascal's Manale. Dusk is certainly a nice time of day for it. Why don't you call me back in about an hour? And I'll let you know how we're doin'."

"Sure."

Aeneas left the mansion unescorted. And walked onto Millionaires Row for the St. Charles Avenue streetcar. Thinking much about Andrew Palmer.

Except for his daughter, Andrew seemed insulated from real love.

He had disciplined himself completely. And seemed to have driven sentiment from his repertoire of emotions in the course of his evolution.

The last remnants of romance belonged to Arabella.

Lavinia had been the primary beneficiary of the man's tenderness. Which was clasped behind two shells like the guts of an oyster.

Rex, the posh potentate. Fully capable of squashing mortals. Like the deities of ancient Rome.

Will Rex spar with me? Spear me? Or spare me?

Rex, the hellraiser in his heyday. Had he heeded all the lessons of his excesses? Except excessive moderation? Was the mansion on Audubon Place a palace of wisdom for Rex?

Time was passing Rex like the shadow of a thunderhead over a *bayou* upon a midsummer's day. Making cowards of all hedonists. Who eventually learn that the greatest pleasures in life are quiet victories rich with dignity. That touch a River of deep eternal forces. The secrets and mystery of which life is stubborn in yielding to impetuous youth.

He saw Andrew's human side. His fondness took root. Aeneas began to admire him immensely and genuinely. Like a father. With homage devoid of dread.

Poor
lonely
Rex
thinks
everyone
just
loves
his
money.

* * *

Aeneas in Dixie

Inspiring Xanthus never flowed on the plain of Troy more sedately than the St. Charles Avenue Streetcar as it rolled toward the Garden District. The antique engine chugged reliably, reminiscent of *The African Queen*. A nascent annoyance spread within Aeneas of the stiff wooden slats of his seat.

I need a new Saturn. I'm tyred of riding this old streetcar everywhere.

En route to Pascal's Manale on Napoleon Avenue to cool his heels. Dusk descended tenderly upon the *Bayou* City. His mouth watered with a foretaste of barbecue shrimp. And a bottle of Dixie Beer. Anticipating a nice quiet dinner.

Through the window across the neutral ground, an illuminated Rex krewe flag hung from another St. Charles mansion. LSU colors. Except for the crown in the center. Displayed by a crony of Andrew. Aeneas wondered if Andrew's big dream to be krewe king would drown in a River of tears in the Big Easy.

Parked on the street in front of this mansion. Aeneas noticed an out-of-kilter Cadillac Coupe de Ville. Its Louisiana vanity plate simply read:

LIV.

The right front Goodyear Radial Tyre is not right. But decidedly flat. The car abandoned by Lavinia. Too gracious a deb to impose further upon a host like Mrs. Borgeois. Content pleasantly to ride at dusk like a tourist on the St. Charles Avenue streetcar. Before the parades shut it down. And disembark only steps from home. Why not let a man like Raymond manage the change of tyre?

Aeneas pulled the cord above the streetcar window and at the next stop he detrained. And retraced his passage two blocks up St. Charles toward her Coupe de Ville near the corner of Felicity Street. Before which he saw a Storyville Old Style Draft bottle crushed like a swagbelly roach. The culprit tyre slasher.

She must have waited for the streetcar. To ride it home. But isn't that her wallet? I've seen her with that pretentious Hermes of Paris purse. The car door unlocked. Gaping purse plundered of cash. Of which she always carried plenty. Inside mirror askew. Something amiss. And amuck. A brazen thief.

In the clay still wet from afternoon thundershowers along the sodden fringe of sidewalk, he found two sets of footprints. A small woman's high heels. On top the shape of a bishop's cap. Beneath which were heels shaped like a pauper's empty pocket. And a man's Nike ribbed sneakersouls. Leading down Felicity Street on the lakeside into some of New Orleans' worst slums.

Grim, untidy, crowded shotgun singles and doubles. A bad neighborhood from which emerged many felons. Who made their living by stabbing, stealing and shooting the ostentatiously rich so tauntingly proximate to them. Unsafe for any unarmed lady or gent of means to walk after dark.

Driven by his fear that Lavinia had been victimized, his love for her surfaced, too. His heart beat like his feet, which he quickly picked up and laid down upon the heaving pavement. Unwittingly, grisly images took shape in his mind. Instinct drove him as he searched for Lavinia without any idea as to where she could be.

I presume she's safe. But it's wiser to act by assuming the downside.

Uncomfortable with any contrived self-deception, he wandered aimlessly amid the dangerous slums. Willing to prove himself Fortune's fool for her sake. His deb in possible distress. Humbled by a Storyville Old Style Draft longneck. On the way home from Pendennis.

Aeneas passed the small lot of an abandoned, decadent mansion abutting flush against Felicity Street. A notice posted by the city said it was condemned.

In the descending darkness he ambled past a weed-choked vacant lot. Further down the street, residents relaxed on front porches upon swings suspended by chains. Awaiting the nightly street parade down St. Charles.

Aeneas roamed. Vigilant for slight hints and imprints of his Liv's prior passage.

He stopped at a phone booth, defaced with carved, penciled and spray-painted graffiti. The phone book mutilated.

From a pocket he withdrew a worn dime bearing the bust of Mercury. He dropped it with a pleasant ding into the coin slot and dialed Lavinia's number.

"Pommer residence," the butler answered.

"Hello, Raymond, this is Jack Jam. Is Lavinia home?"

"Hello, Mr. Jack. No, Miss Lavinia is not here. She must have got tied up at the Penn-dentist."

"When was she due back."

"About a 'owah ago."

"Is Mr. Pahmeh there?"

"He sure isn't. He's out takin' Chicory for a woke down Audubon Place."

Aeneas imagined Andrew walking the raven Labrador retriever down the safe, secure street.

"Is Evan still there?"

"Yessir, he is."

"May I speak with him, please?"

"Certainly, Mr. Jack."

Evan's voice.

"Jack?"

"Yes, Evan. Hello. When should I return?"

"Not until tomorrow."

"How does it look?"

"Percy's offer is right this time, Jack. Andrew really can't turn it down. Percy and his venture capital group put together one hell of a package."

"What does Lavinia think about the offer?"

"I called her earlier. She hasn't told us yet. But it will seriously increase her net worth. She's smart. I expect her to . . ."

A recorded message from the payphone requested another deposit of ten cents. Aeneas rummaged his pockets for change haplessly.

"Thanks, Evan. Please tell Mr. Pahmeh that I called."
"I will, Jack. I'll call you tomorrow morning. Good-bye."
"Good-bye . . . Oh, Evan . . . Evan?"
The phone clicked dead.

Aeneas hesitated and then hung up the phone. He continued walking down the pockmarked patchwork of macadam with abysmal potholes.
Beer cans, fried chicken boxes and assorted trash littered the street. A candy wrapper from a Mars Bar. An abandoned, pillaged, burnt-out Ford Taurus, from which four tyres and the battery had been stripped.

A fat rat sauntered along the tightrope of a telephone line overhead.

Loud disco music played. A baby screamed. A dog barked. A couple argued. In the distance a siren sounded.

An old man with a curly, snowy beard and kind eyes swayed upon a porch swing.

"Excuse me, sih. Did you happen to notice a beautiful woman with chestnut hair walk past? With a man. She was probably wearing her light tan, London Fog raincoat."

"Lemme see. I seen a *real sharp* lookin' lady. I remember thinking *she* sure didn't belong around *here*. Not this time of night. With a man wearin' a two-faced Mardi Gras mask. One with a happy and sad face. He looked like a flambeaux man. They walked right over theyuh inta that big ole, rundown mansion. Right at Felicity Street."

"The condemned building?"

"Yeah. Dudn't make no sense. But they walked right in. It was hard to see. In the dark, and all. She ditn't seem right. She was unhappy about *somethin'*."

"When?"

"Maybe half a owah ago. Moh or less."

"I'm concehned that she's in deep trouble. In physical danger."

"Want me ta call the *po*-lice?"

"Would you please?"

"Sho' will. Don't know how long it'll take 'em to git here. With all the stuff goin' on this time of year. But I'll he'p yawl. If I can."

"Sih, I can't thank you enough. You are a true gentleman."

In his wingtips Aeneas sprinted a block to the condemned mansion in fear and trembling. At the dilapidated Victorian home, the front door was padlocked. First floor windows had been boarded although individual slats were missing or in disrepair. Paint curled off the scarred, wizen clapboards of the decadent manse.

Wild palms and ivies grew unattended. Rotten posts, dined upon by many insect pests, barely supported a sagging porch roof. Missing many shingles. Floorboards were cracked, bowed and absent in places.

The side door slightly ajar. Cautiously, he stepped inside. Greeted in the dark by multitudes of scattering cockroaches. A covey of blackbirds like inky *gracchi* took flight. And rats that called this decadent mansion home scampered away squeaking.

The house now quite dark, Aeneas pulled out a penlite. Practical for the enlightening perusal of menus in cozy, candlelit, French Quarter restaurants. And wine lists at Snobs. Whenever dining with clients or dates of distinction.

Then a woman's voice crying softly. Heard faintly from a room up two flights of skeletal stairs missing planks and a banister. But which bore longitudinal rails.

A man fiercely growled.

"Yawl are goin' ta get it now, bitch!"

The blade of the penlight aglow, Aeneas approached the stairwell. From the handrail, Aeneas tried to dislodge a protruding post. One stout enough to serve as a weapon. He gingerly urged the post from its stubborn anchor at the rail. It would serve as a club or spear or cudgel.

Warily, Aeneas crept up the first flight of stairs. Brutish, primal, ally juices of survival pumped within him.

"If yawl don't want me to cut yoh poifect face, keep yoh mouth shut. An' strip, rich bitch. Real slow . . . Let's ged on wid it."

"Please . . . Please don't do this."

Lavinia's pleading voice.

Aeneas tightened his grip on his wooden weapon. Climbing another flight of stairs with the silent, feline grace of an African lion.

Giving into the adrenaline.

"Ah jus' love hearin' you all beg. Yawl are goin' to be *sweet*. In your whole life you ain't never made it wid no one like me."

"You think you're the only man with a thing between your legs?"

"Yawl are one cocky little bitch. Take off yawl's blouse. Now! Hear?"

Despite a brief binge of brash bravery, Lavinia now started to weep. Knotting the heart of Aeneas. And heightening his resolve.

"My daddy will get you for this. And my boyfriend, Jack. You'll pay for it. When our lawyers get through with you, they'll lock you in a cell in Angola Penitentiary. And they'll throw away the key."

"But yoh daddy and boyfrien' ain't heyuh now. Are they? . . . *Are they?*"

". . . No . . ."

"And second of all, bitch, I awready spent time in *An*-gola. Now give yo' new boyfrien' a show worth a few mo' years, baby."

Aeneas carefully shifted his weight from one step to the next. Mindful of their creaking. As he continued up the second flight, both voices became clearer.

"You're lookin' real fine, princess. Now let's see what you got foh legs under that little slip. Ummm. You're lookin' *fine*. Just as sweet as yawl can be."

The shallow, narrow, dim luminescence of the penlight of Aeneas fell upon the top, two steps. Immediately beyond, a third story door half-open. These two, top steps were missing planks. Providing a creaky chasm to be overcome. Over which he hoped cavalierly to climb.

"Now gimme yawl's silk stockings."

Aeneas in Dixie. Moving fluidly. Light and smooth. Traversing with agility the boxy abyss. To land catlike in the half-open doorway. Where he quite quenched his penlight.

He peered into a large third story master bedroom overlooking Felicity Street directly below. Devoid of furniture. Cracked and broken wallboards exposed ancient wooden beams.

From his haunches in the dark, dreary doorway, Aeneas obscurely viewed in the dim light a man larger than he. Wearing a black-and-white Mardi Gras mask of Janus over a black ski mask. A dark turtle neck and dusky jeans. With sooty Nikes. Hands adorned in leather driving gloves. Wielding a long, thin, menacing blade. Standing with his back to Aeneas.

The surreal bluish glow from a streetlamp on Felicity Street shone up through a broad, ragged, broken window. The streetlight diffused on the ceiling. Where it bounced to illuminate the brutality of the razor sharp, silver blade of a fishing knife.

A filet knife. Cruelly adept for precision in slicing flesh.

The lovely figure of Lavinia dimly lit both directly by the street lamp off Felicity Street and by its diffused overhead light.

The model undressed to only a diaphanous, snowy, scalloped bra with matching silken thong. Silver *fleur de lis* necklace flashing. She trembled and wept in her extreme vulnerability. Unaware of the aspect of Aeneas in the eclipsed doorway.

His eyes fixated upon her, the assailant stooped to retrieve her thigh-highs.

"Stand in front of this post, baby. Put your hands behind your back. An' doane try nothin' stupid. Just do as I say. Hear?"

Reluctantly, she complied. Weeping mournfully. Mascara staining her dream face. He tethered Lavinia to the post with her hose. First, he bound her wrists and then her ankles behind the beam like a Sabine woman.

He slipped the knife's keen cutting edge under the shoulder straps of her top. And sliced each with a simple, single, clean upward stroke of the imposing blade. She moaned mournfully after each stroke. He unhitched the clasp of her bra at the back. And it fell forlornly to her feet.

Leaving her nearly naked.

Tears leapt from her eyes wide with true terror. As he ripped the *fleur de lis* necklace from her swanlike neck.

"Yawl are my slave, baby. Lemme axe you. How does it feel to be a slave?"

She wrestled against her bonds, which held fast.

"That's it, baby. Set yourself free."

Did the old guy call the NOPD?

The man unzipped his fly. Slowly and silently Aeneas reared in the doorway. Into the band of light cast by the streetlamp. With an index finger to his lips. To signal for Lavinia's stillness.

She saw him rise up in the doorway like an apparition of hope. Her eyes reflected an unrestrained surge of surprise. The element of which was about all Aeneas had going for him. Except for his crude wooden weapon. His penlight. Pugilistic pluck. And his love of her.

The rapist lowered his jeans.

Aeneas made his move. To within a few steps of striking distance.

"You don't need that knife. I'm not going anywhere . . . I'll do what you want . . . Just put down the knife . . ." Lavinia negotiated.

"Beg me for it, baby. I just love hearin' you all beg."

Aeneas drew up behind the man with his club raised high, his foot fell upon a crisply, resounding, squawking floorboard.

"Who dat?"

The man turned his head. Just as Aeneas lowered the boom. Bringing his club down smartly over the man's skull. Breaking the rotten rail post in two. Splitting the porcelain Janus mask down the middle. And thus, delivering a decisive blow. Which Aeneas followed with a jab to the jowls. A roundhouse right to the eye. And an incendiary uppercut to the jaw.

The pain promptly registered in the bloodshot eyes of the hood. Eyes that became squinted slits. Mouth agape. A parody of lust.

The hoodlum collapsed to his knees. Around which his trousers and jockey shorts gathered. Dropping the fisherman's knife onto the dark shadows cast upon the floor. In the course of his demise. Wrestling with his agony.

Aeneas lost sight of the knife in the penumbra. He untied the stubborn silken hitches that bound her. Then he reached out to capture Lavinia's hand.

Hastily, they exited. Aeneas gingerly guided her down the two flights of staircase. Up which, only minutes ago, he had so painfully slowly crept.

Dazed and stunned. But still absurdly far from unconsciousness from the combination punches of Aeneas. The man growled maniacally:

"I'm gonna *kill* yawl!"

The man found his feet. He pulled up his briefs and jeans. Buttoning up and zipping the fly.

Fumbling for the knife in the shadows, he found it.

In frenzy, knife firmly held waist high like a street fighter, the man raced to the door. Halting at the missing top two steps. He vaulted them. His leap's landing burst the putrid stair-step upon which his Nikes crashed. To send him off-balance and tumbling down this ramshackle flight to the second story.

Impaling him on the thin blade of his own knife. The shank of which broke upon impact. As the blade tip resided in the assailant's body. Lodged just below the sternum of his ribcage. The base of the blade and hilt of the fishing knife followed him. Clattering down the stairway to the story below. He was out cold.

Aeneas shielded Lavinia by throwing his pinstripe suit coat over his deb as they exited the shabby manse onto the sidewalk of Felicity.

A New Orleans fire engine and a fire chief in a car arrived with red globes flashing and sirens wailing. Two firemen in full regalia bolted from the engine's rear and unfastened axes. A fire chief and young deputy chief leapt from an emblazoned official car matching the color of the Eldorado of Charles.

"We got a report of trouble here," the New Orleans fire chief briskly stated. "From a neighbor."

"I asked him to call the *police*."

"He did. But the police are stretched thin. They're working overtime. At parades and masquerade balls all over town. And this building's condemned. So the police dispatcher called us to the scene."

"A rapist is injured on the second floor. Stabbed by his own knife," Aeneas said. "He might be dead."

"Tullus what you know, Miss," the fire chief probed.

The chief questioned Lavinia for a report. She trembled almost convulsively. Sporadically, she wept openly. Grieving without restraint.

She was most understandably hysterical. In trauma. And shock. Nearly inconsolable.

Aeneas unbound a nylon trailing from one of her wrists. And held her in his arms. To quell her involuntary shuddering. Then he comforted her with soft words. Slowly, her contortions and weeping diminished.

A few curious neighbors congregated from the ruckus of the fire engine sirens. Aeneas buttoned her up tight in his suit coat.

"I'll go back foh your clothes," he volunteered. "You must feel... naked."

"Thanks, Jack. I feel dirty. And people are staring."

Aeneas escorted her to the fire chief's car for sanctuary and more privacy.

On the fringe of the gathering of neighbors, Aeneas saw the elderly gentleman. Who had steered him to the condemned mansion on Felicity Street.

"Thank you for calling the police," Aeneas offered.

"I knowed you was inta some trouble."

"Sih, you helped save her life."

"Ah just done what anyone would do."

The chief disbursed the crowd. He sent the deputy chief into the manse to examine the fallen assailant. And directed the fire engine to return to the firehouse. Clearly, this was a police matter over which he had no jurisdiction. So he called the police dispatcher and gave him hell.

Aeneas returned to the third story of the decadent mansion to retrieve Lavinia's scattered apparel. His penlight reflected on the porcelain surface of shattered Janus. The elliptical mask split by his blow longitudinally and raggedly down its fragile middle into tragic and comic portions.

He descended past the fallen, still, silent, bleeding rapist on the second story. In the darkness the deputy fire chief struggled to complete a report.

The deputy chief cursed as his flashlight blinked from nearly spent batteries. He held a Gucci wallet made of rich Italian leather and a driver's license.

"Use this," Aeneas said, offering his penlight for illumination.

"What a lifesaver," the deputy fire chief answered. "Thanks."

Aeneas stood behind him. Flashing a spear of snow-white light over the fireman's shoulder onto the form. Upon which was written a description of the unconscious suspect.

Six feet tall. 200 pounds. Athletic build. Age 35. Single. Brown eyes. Dumaine & Bourbon. NO, LA. Race?

The deputy fire chief removed the hood's ski mask.

White male.

Unhooded, the hoodlum hoodwinked Aeneas.

"I *know* this man. You need to call an ambulance. Right away, please. I'll keep an eye on him," Aeneas informed the fireman.

The knife's jagged shaft jutted out a couple inches from the slowly bleeding wound. The blade's breakpoint gleaming like a gash of quicksilver.

"He's lucky it's a puncture wound. Or he might have bled to death. We best let the medics yank out the blade. And let the NOPD cuff him," the deputy fire chief advised and exited to call an ambulance from the chief's car radio. To procure a fresh stock of flashlight batteries. And to check on the dispatch of the NOPD. Forsaking Aeneas.

The assailant stirred.

"Lie still," Aeneas advised.
"Shit! I don't believe it! Christ!"
In shock. Hallucinating. Mad. Wounded. Wincing. Bleeding. Spittle foaming at the corners of his mouth.
"Just tell me *why*, Pehcy," Aeneas demanded. "You were *engaged* to her, foh God's sake."
"Until you showed up."
"But New Yohk?" Aeneas asked incredulously.
"The truth is we slept in separate rooms at the Plaza . . . It was all a façade."
"Why?"
Squinting in pain, Percy tried to calm himself. And assess his condition.
In crisis he needed to talk. As dialogue offered him a chance to regain control. Without which he simply couldn't function.
"She loves you, Jack. But she had to punish you. Because you hurt her so much, you bastard."
"But you were *sleeping* with her?"
"Not after *you* came along. And we broke up. She wouldn't have me anymore."
"Why?"
"She had her reasons."
"I thought you were sleeping with her. All that time."
"I'm sleeping with someone else."
"You lie, Pehcy."
"Ask Liv."
"Haven't you already put her through enough hell?"
"Maybe so, Jack. I'll tell you . . . But come close so I can whisper. I can hardly speak."
Aeneas bent his ear very near Percy.
"Closer, Jack."
Aeneas consented. And he detected the scent of Percy's musky after-shave.
Percy whispered:
"I sleep with . . . Evan."
In shock, Aeneas reflexively withdrew.
Percy laughed madly. After he calmed down sufficiently, he rambled on:
"Liv learned about Evan and me in bad way. She found us in the sack. After she came home in the Quarter. Toting a cold bottle of DP. And two glasses. To celebrate her first big gig with *The Golden Bow*."
"She was *faithful* to me?"
"Even when you didn't deserve it. You were such an idiot, Jack."
"You're sleeping with Andrew's financial advisoh?"
"I walk both sides of the street, Jack. Fact is, I always liked your looks."
"Pehcy, I'm straight as a phrygging *arrow*."
"So I see . . . But when I play with the ladies, I like to play rough. I need to be in control. Evan says I have a borderline personality. With obsessive-compulsive tendencies. Into power trips. Head games. And he's right, of course."
"A control phryg?"

"Power games satisfy me. And women consent. Some of them. To my fun and games. My ravaging Sabine ladies grant my ravage. And, of course, my photography. A high octane, power trip. That's all it was."

"Lavinia never consented."

"No, she never did. She found it . . . queer an' all . . . Those were her words."

"What *were* you thinking, Pehcy? Why would she *ever* submit to it?"

"She was a *perfect model*. Highly born for it. Can you see the tension? The beauty of the contrasts? The darker tones defining the light. Eve after the Fall. The surreal arrest. Of Liv's vim. And all."

"In your godfohsaken dreams, Pehcy."

"The photos were shot . . . exquisitely. There's an art to it. A certain style. I wanted to be the next Mapplethorpe. Capitalized. In your studio. And Lavinia could have launched me. If she had been willing."

"But you couldn't take no for an anseh. You bastahd, Tuhneh."

"Whenever she refused, it pissed me off. Each new rejection sent me into a rage. Because Lavinia is a hot commodity. A real Gulf Coast Goddess. And her photos taunted me. Harping. Showing no mercy."

"But the deal with Andrew . . ."

"When I drove her to Pendennis. She told me exactly in no uncertain terms. Her father's decision to sell to my consortium didn't mean squat. Despite all my arguments. Because of her *irrevocable decision*. As she called it. To vote her share of the company. To *your* side. No matter how high the price. She busted the deal. And that *really, really* ticked me off, Jack . . . I can't begin to tell you."

Percy began to scream. Raving from his wounds. Physical, emotional and psychological. He just lost it.

Percy flies from the car. Ready to explode. Like his deal. Slamming the door. Cursing his Fate. In the descending darkness on St. Charles Avenue.

His reputation now is compromised. As a deal maker and stud financier.

His new venture busted. His failed power play over me a joke. And he's a laughing stock. His financial credibility to build future deals shot to hell. All because of her misplaced loyalty. To an unworthy, foreign-born fool from Boston.

So she promenades in dignity without remorse into Mrs. Borgeois' home. To meet with other debutantes for a few hours. To plan her upcoming debut. Because she has no mother to advise her. At such a consequential time in a budding, young lady's life.

Leaving Percy in a deep rage on St. Charles. Onto which he shatters a half-drunk Storyville longneck. Slicing the hide of her Goodyear Radial Tyre. Near the label of the winged sandals of Mercury. Gripping the jagged shank of the Storyville bottleneck. And planting the shards under her right front tyre.

Then he takes a streetcar to his home in the Quarter. Establishing an alibi with his ticket. He changes his clothes. Seizing a black ski mask. And just to be sure, a porcelain Mardi Gras mask of Janus from Sybil Helene. Returning the same way by streetcar.

Then the flambeaux man lays in wait. Lusting for Lavinia in the dusk. Misrepresenting robbery as a ruse. Planning to breach and deface this goddess. Because he could not possess her otherwise.

She has a dreamface. Maybe, he wanted to transform her. Retouch her perfection. Dominate and diminish and despoil Liv. Just as some people worship perfection. Others are deeply threatened. As a mirror to shortcomings.

Or seek profit, cheapening it. Perhaps, he wanted to retouch her by a traumatic brush with death. To change her into a humbler, more submissive beauty. Who would turn to him in her crisis. And accept his strength and solace. And whose will he might hold some hope to control.

Percy lapsed into a calm. The eye of the storm. As his hysteria tormented him. And the maddening circumstances of the headwall swirled into focus.

"You were a fool. To gamble foh such high stakes, Pehcy."

"But I was stronger. And smarter. Always in control. And if she could kill my dream, then I sure as hell could ruin hers."

A Storyville Beer Bottle on the mad aventine Avenue. In a frenzy to defeat impertinent me. Who adored her sheer photogenic perfection. Her dreamface. And to drive me from the brink. Into an Abyssinian abyss.

"You set me up with Didi, you incredible bastahd."

"What a stroke? I just knew you'd fall for her. She was just plain irresistible. So I made her a wedge. And drove her between you and Liv."

"And you set up Chahlie, too."

"If he was your friend, then he sure as hell was my enemy. So I made him *your* worst enemy. And my best ally. That night at Napoleon House. When you were sick with a fever in bed. Under Liv's care. I could picture her in my mind with you. At your bedside. Fussing over you. And it nearly drove me insane."

In his misery Percy's face became distorted.

"Chahlie was drunk."

"Drunk? Hell, he was *oblivious!* When he called you after midnight. About his confederacy of dunces. And about Francesca. I was there. Filling his glass with Olde Crow double Bourbons. The second it was empty. That ole boy just loved nicknames. I was dubbed Sir Knight of the Turnip. What a laugh . . ."

Percy winced. Coughed. Grimaced. And ranted.

"I introduced them to each other. Eros playing both sides against the middle. I mean, that's a favorite tactic of mine," Percy raved.

"But Chahles was loyal."

"Was he? He had *ambition*. And a business to grow. Ambition pumping through his overachieving heart. And a new lover to impress from Beacon Hill. You know how that goes. Don't you, Jack? But he had more to overcome than even you did."

"What did you promise him?"

"An introduction to Frances. But somehow I forgot to mention she was still your wife at the time. And I never told her that Charles was your best friend."

"You phrygging *pimp*, Tuhneh!"

"I just love to see you angry, Jack. But there's more. I promised him new business. From my consortium. And venture capital downstream. If he ever needed it. Or wanted to go public. Because Charlie was so . . . fallible, I guess is the word for it. So predictable. Driven to win. Or just die trying."

"Like you?"

"You bet, like me. I knew exactly what made Charlie tick."

"You betrayed him."

"His ambition betrayed him, Jack. Ambition does that. I just watched him rush in deeper and deeper with Frances. I knew it would kill your alliance. And him, too. After I no longer needed him."

"Quite a game plan."

"It was *easy*. 'By the way, Charlie. Do you know anyone young and prosperous and single? Interested in meeting a friend of mine? A hot, sexy, recent divorcee from Uptown?' That's about all it took to set you up with Didi."

"I was an easy mahk."

"The setup between Charles and Frances was easy, too. I learned all about Frances. From friends of friends. Then I stalked her. And seduced her. All the easier because she was trying to get over you. When she wanted me, and she did, Jack. I told her I was gay. But I knew someone just right for her."

"You disgust me, Tuhneh."

"Then I set-up the introductions. At Napoleon House. Where Charlie drinks. And I bought him round after round of straight bourbons. A small price to pay. For such a devastating ally."

"You stalked Lavinia, too. Long afteh it made no sense."

"What sane man stalks, Jack? I just couldn't he'p myself."

"That's so pathetic. So lame."

"Lavinia served as a false front. For a while, anyway."

"But you fell in *love* with her."

"Love? Hell, it wadn't love. It was much worse. I was *obsessed* with her."

"You just *had* to have her. One way or another. Is that it?"

"Liv had a face to launch a thousand ships. She was the second coming of Helen of Troy. And I discovered her *first*, Jack. Before you. Before anybody."

"So what?"

"I just needed her is all."

"She was your meal-ticket."

"Don't you dare insult me, Jack. She was *your* meal-ticket."

"Screw you, Pehcy!"

"I was just after her daddy's *money*."

"More than her?"

"No. Not more than her."

"But she and her fatheh's money came as a package."

"I fully realize how messed-up I am, Jack. In case you don't know."

"Now you have zippo."

"I have Evan."

"Lucky him."

"It was a real sweetheart deal, by the way. It was just about perfect."

"Andrew trusted Evan."

"Evan knew just which of Andrew's buttons to push. He knew how to lowball a business valuation. He knew Andrew's buying threshold. When Andrew would buy. And when he wouldn't."

"Evan is an inside tradeh, Pehcy."

"Can you just picture Andrew's face when he hears it? That Evan outfoxed Rex. Hailing the king's genius for business. His worthiness to reign. Evan may have stooped to conquer. But, beneath it all, so much ego made him sick."

"Evan stole Andrew's integrity. His dignity. His dream."

"No more than you stole from me, Jack. When you walked off with Lavinia. With *every damn body* in New Orleans watching. How do you think that made me feel? To have so many witnesses to my . . . shame. What choice did I have? Except to fight. To defeat you. I wanted you to know my disgrace. Maybe it makes no sense to you. But I had my honor to protect. My pride."

"It's beyond bizahhe. The big act. As a flambeaux man . . ."

"I've been a flambeaux man, Jack. For my father's krewe. Comus."

"But the jive. The knife. It's . . . *surreal*. Why did you do it?"

"Because people would think it was some poor crazy ex-con just out of Angola. Driven by the heat. Or hunger. Or homelessness. To commit a simple robbery. Who then decided to take her. Purely, out of lust. And everyone would think that it just got a little crazy. A little out of hand."

"Everyone would just assume it. Especially her."

"Of course. They'd think she had it coming. Because she's too sexy for her own good. And crimes like this occur all the time. On the streets of America. A sad fact of life in the big city. When I couldn't have her anymore, it made me . . . well. You can see . . . See what I brought upon myself?"

"I thought I was losing my mind."

"That was the idea, Jack."

"You're a mad bastahd, Tuhneh."

"Liv *drove* me to it."

"She's innocent."

"There's no other word for it — she's a siren, Jack. Who sold her hot looks. To the highest bidder. For cool cash. Remember how she sent us crashing onto the rocks? To drown in a cruel sea? And everybody just wanted her. So much. They'd pay any price."

"Look at the price you paid, Tuhneh."

"And what do I have to show for it?"

"It was a deviant dream, Pehcy."

"Every fantasy is deviant. Isn't it? That's why it exists. Because reality is so unbearable. Who knows better than you? The broke photographer of the rich."

"You unbelievable prick, Pehcy."

"Fantasy is your stock in trade. Now, your fantasy is to watch me die."

"You're already dead, Tuhneh."

"Not quite. Now, hand me what's left of my fishing knife. Like a good ole boy. So I can finish what I started. I control my own destiny. And I know how to die at the right time."

"I won't be a pahty to it, Pehcy."

"Come on, Jack. Just hand me my fishing knife. Consider it my last request."

"No way."

"After I ruined your life. Your wife. Your fiancée. Your buddy. And bidness. Help put me out of my own misery. Before I lose it completely. And phryg out. I want to die with dignity."

"No, Pehcy, you idiot."

Percy began to crawl toward the knife. And in his slithering the pain hissed out of him like Lavinia's flat tyre. He bled. As he fished for his fishing knife. Which Aeneas then kicked out of reach.

"Yankee prick!" Percy screamed.

"Go to hell, Pehcy!"

"I'm there."

"You'll live to see hell on earth. And wish you were dead."

Percy shrieked wildly with insane rage. Gripping the impaled blade with hands in sheik leather driving gloves, he withdrew the thin shaft from the sheath of his body. His face registered the shocking agony in wincing eyes and gaping mouth.

Nearly passing out, Percy stood. Gasping. Defiant. Mad from the adrenaline shock to his system. He attacked furiously.

Percy slashed the blade tip at the temple of Aeneas. Who parried the madman's flashing attack. But the lash of the blade grazed Aeneas just above the left eye. The lance launched a meager branch of blood into his eyes.

His vision partially blurred, Aeneas kicked at Percy's wrist. Hoping to send the silver, razor-sharp shaft in flight harmlessly from his adversary's grip. But it was no good and Aeneas missed.

"The cork's out of the bottle, Jack. I'm nearly out of juice. I may just bleed to death."

Sirens grew louder and ceased on Felicity Street. And outside the window on the street a truck parked beneath the streetlight and cut its diesel engine.

"Your ambulance, hotshot," Aeneas said. "And the police."

Percy hung his head, chin to chest. As if he were lynched.

"What a disgrace, Jack."

"You're alive."

While his own wound was manageable, Aeneas observed the bleeding worsen in Percy. Who refused to capitulate.

"So Lavinia is yours now?" Percy asked. "Is that it?"

"We were meant to be togetheh. From the staht."

"She was *mine*!"

"You've gone off the phrygging deep end. Lost it completely. I don't know what else to say, Pehcy."

"Just promise me you'll . . . Shit, I may black out . . . Use your Fortune well."

Gravely wounded by his own hand with his fishing knife. In the decadent mansion on Felicity Street. Percy remained on his feet.
They could hear the policemen conversing with the deputy fire chief who entered the first floor. Ascending the first flight of stairs with heavy footfalls.

The arrival of the police triggered Percy's furious surge into another wave of rage. Raising his silver blade tip. With a burst of velocity empowered by pure, final, adrenaline-rich desperation.

He bellowed. Like a great, bleeding, ebony bull confronting the sword concealed in the seam of the toreador's cape. And enraged by the darts of picadors.

He charged Aeneas.

Increscunt animi, virescit volnere virtus. The spirits increase, vigor grows through a wound.

Adeptly, Aeneas sidestepped this mad and clumsy assault.

Infuriated, self-destructive Percy stumbled. And crashed through an archaic Victorian, living room, picture window that overlooked Felicity Street plumb below.

Aeneas heard the rotten, wooden, window frame splinter. As panes of glass shattered into silver shards that rained upon Felicity. Time stood still, as Percy plummeted.

An inexperienced and lost driver of a delivery van, clutching a spread roadmap of Uptown New Orleans, besieged the fire chief for clear directions to Coliseum Street across St. Charles Avenue. Amid the Chaos of street closures. Which the sinuous Uptown labyrinth created virtually *ad hoc* by parades down the Avenue. The chief advised the frantic driver simply to chill amid the gridlock. And take-in the parade.

At the sound of smashing glass, both the driver and fire chief glanced up from Felicity Street to witness the Fall of Percy. As he landed upon the sheet metal roof of the panel truck from General Overnight Delivery Services parked on Felicity. Sparing him impalement upon a row of spears pointing to Kingdom Come. Of a black wrought-iron fence encompassing the ancient manse.

"Man alive!" the driver cried. "Did you see that?"

"God damn!" the fire chief whispered.

With one good eye, Aeneas peered at Percy from the windowless gap in the Victorian manse. Lifelessly sprawled upon the roof of the delivery truck parked on Felicity Street.

The bewildered uniformed driver was reduced to stuttering, stammering and nearly catatonic panic.

"Look what he did to my truck!" the driver screamed.

"Look what your truck did to him," the chief mumbled.

The panel truck's logo in oversized capital letters simply read:

G.O.D.S.

The New Orleans police and medics with a stretcher hastened to attend to Percy. Whom they retrieved from the collapsed roof of the van's cargo hold. Carting him off in the ambulance without his regaining consciousness.

Aeneas pressed and tightly tied a white handkerchief to dress his forehead wound. Guided by penlight, he searched briefly and then, under the circumstances, soon abandoned the search for Lavinia's belongings.

Deciding that evidence would be better left intact to the NOPD.

Hastily, he exited the decrepit manse.

When he returned to Lavinia, she was still trembling but calmer.

Withdrawn and wrapped with arms folded in his pinstripe suit jacket.

She had heard the clamor but did not witness Percy's misfortunate demise. Gratefully, Aeneas accepted from the fire chief a Band-Aid patch for a war wound that would add yet another battle scar.

After he formally identified Percy to the police as her assailant, Aeneas rejoined Lavinia in the fire chief's car. Pitiably, she sobbed. Dismayed by the disgrace of unsound Percy. And by the ghastly laceration to Aeneas.

The shaken couple embarked in the fire chief's car. To accept safe passage home. Riding down Felicity and turning left at Saratoga, just before Simon Bolivar.

They embraced and kissed like true lovers and held each other intensely, desperately close.

Tacitly, they were highly aware that her Fate might have taken a tragic downturn, too. Except for the deep devotion of Aeneas.

As a semblance of peace finally descended, Aeneas broke their huddled silence in the back seat of the fire chief's car: "I have a gift foh you."

Gently, he opened the blossom of her unsteady palm. And dropped into it the silver and diamond-studded *fleur de lis* necklace. Once before, his present to her.

The old fire chief's eyes smiled in the rearview mirror.

Whispering into her lover's ear. With her sweet, trembling lips. In a soft, rich, sincere voice, Liv declared:

"I
owe
you
my life,
Aeneas."
* * *

EPILOGUE:
The Parade of Future Romans in the Underworld

Silvius
Alban Kings
Romulus
Caesar
Augustus
Tullus
Ancus
Tarquins
Brutus
Decii
Drusi
Torquatis
Camillus
Pompey
Mummius
Paullus
Cato
Cossus
Gracchi
Scipios
Fabricus
Serranus
Fabbii
Marcellus
— *The Aeneid, Book VI*

Intimations of Immortality

Xenophobia deftly smitten by all parties, in spite of the odds presented for cancellation due to high winds, it was agreed to set firmly the date for the wedding at June 1: the first day of hurricane season.

Lavinia coveted a ceremony in the Chapel of Sophie Newcomb.

Followed by a reception on the mansion's lawn at Audubon Place under a vast pineapple yellow-and-white striped canvas tent.

An affair too outlandish and ostentatious, Aeneas thought, without meddling in family plans. Andrew declared that, by God, his only daughter would be wed lavishly. And it wouldn't dare rain without the consent of the next Rex.

Aeneas was wracked with mixed feeling upon scouting the chapel with Lavinia. Whose face glowed like an altar candle. He felt a touch of involuntary nausea as he contemplated marriage again. Afraid such an institution could ruin a perfectly happy relationship. By simple virtue of the eternal nature of the beast. A great Trojan Horse. Offered in worship of treacherous gods. An engine of siege.

Had he rushed into nuptials? A state he found previously devoid of its much-advertised bliss. Heralded by a church of dogged, dictatorial celibates.

On the other hand, he deeply loved Lavinia. His manifest love, rescuing her. Inadvertently turning Percy Turner into ruin.

Aeneas earned Andrew's gratitude. And somewhat evened the score for having run so seriously amuck in the recent past. Mutual vulnerabilities tightly bonding the engaged couple. The third engagement was the charm.

Charles agreed to be best man. Consenting to stand for Aeneas both in divorce court and at the altar. His good faith restored for the play of the gods and their agents entangling him with the ex of Aeneas.

True tests of friendship passed.

In his duties as best man, Charles tried heartily to dissuade Aeneas to wed. With persuasive arguments and highly charged quotes from his forthcoming essay in *Esquire*. Leaving Aeneas unconvinced the sacred act was folly. Even if half the women at Snobs were in mourning, as Charles reported. Since the wedding announcement appeared in *Vivant* of the *Sunday Times-Picayune*.

What did Charles know anyway? Considering his screwed up love life.

Lavinia heartily resolved to wed no later than the advent of hurricane season. She needed a "serious commitment" from Aeneas. As she was prepared to sacrifice assignments to model undergarb for June Wilhelm in New York after the ordeal on Felicity Street.

She intended to embrace the respectable mantle of a wife in the aristocracy of high society in New Orleans. And become a mother some day. Although she would fulfill her contractual obligations modeling more conservative lines of apparel.

If wedding her were beyond Aeneas, after all bans were posted, then he simply should be honest with her. She would cope as best she could. And move on. Fair enough.

If all bets were off, she was bound for New York. Many a man from both Uptown New Orleans and Manhattan were in hot pursuit.

But if Aeneas truly loved her, he would marry her despite his marred prior marriage. Because life was an epic struggle to stand straight and tall to failure and tragedy and heartbreak. And a man is the sum of his decisions.

A court date was imminent for his divorce. Earnings at Aeneas Studios experienced controlled growth. Despite the sharp, sudden downturn in oil and gas prices. His nose to the grindstone. Cheerfully, he accepted Percy's former clients.

Briefly, Aeneas seemed to sail along smoothly with a semblance of stability provided by his new life with his beloved Liv. He felt grounded in his surrender to ancient values that gave life new meaning. As he banished Chaos from the subterraenean realm of his existence.

Then, less than a fortnight before Mardi Gras, Andrew Jackson Palmer died. Never to ride as Rex. Nor to see his only daughter wed.

Andrew suffered a massive stroke.

Thus, God dropped Rex. In his big easy chair. Sipping Banker's Club Bourbon. Waterford goblet dropping and smashing upon the hardwood
floor. Staining the balance sheet of his Fortune. His net worth slipping from his grasp. In his Temple of Jupiter on Millionaires Row. As he gazed in devotion upon his beloved Arabella's debutante portrait. In whose divine image Lavinia was born to save him. Andrew's last words according to Raymond were:

"Jingo's crickets!"

Bravely, Lavinia accepted her father's death. As is often the case in life, tragedies lash one in cruel waves. And she was forced to contend with the emergence of Andrew's stunning financial demise, which followed his death.

Evan was indicted for material breach of fiduciary trust and conflict of interest. For double-dealing with both Percy Turner and Andrew, who was livyd when he learned about the twin betrayals.

Scandal cursed Andrew's chances for Rex. People assumed it was a legal maeneuver. As Evan's comfortable lifestyle and financial future were both in jeopardy. His attorneys were sharp and Evan was determined not to go down without a battle royal. Who could blame him? He was simply fighting for his financial existence.

Rumor had it that Evan's side had leaked details of Andrew Palmer's balance sheet. Which had been such a lethal shock to his system.

The balance sheet showed that the book value of Andrew's assets in oil and gas had been reduced by more than half nearly overnight. As the Great Oil & Gas Bust had deepened and took its toll. Savagely pillaging the entire industry in Louisiana, Texas and Alaska in 1985.

Sworn pre-trial testimony emerged recklessly in the press. A quote from Evan exposed that Andrew was "over-aggressively leveraged." Leading to a gag order by the trial judge.

A big sale of his tangible assets, including the mansion on St. Charles and the Rolls, would soon be necessary. To cover staggering debt and mounting losses from Andrew's leveraging strategy implemented at the height of the Boom. And held too long. Investment immoderation ensnaring him early in the Great Oil Bust.

Bankers from his krewe were compelled to issue liens to protect investment principals at risk of write-offs. Attracting the attention of vulture venture capitalists.

The press also had learned from the balance sheet that one of Andrew's few profitable businesses, in his attempt to diversify, was the portrait studio and gallery.

Aeneas was constantly at Lavinia's side throughout the ordeal. Together the couple sorted through the morass and turmoil of Chaos. It proved almost too overwhelming for her.

Lavinia was engulfed in the vortex, the eye of a hurricane feasting ravenously upon a roiling sea. Surviving storm surges of personal trauma by clinging to the devotion of her island fortress, her rock, her trusty Aeneas.

Sympathy never amounted to anything from Andrew's krewe, former college classmates, millionaire neighbors, clients, business associates, fellow club members, financiers and political figures. In his death, business demise and in the wake of Evan's indictment, Andrew became a social pariah.

Percy Turner survived his physical mishaps. Saved in falling one story onto the collapsing, sheet metal, roof bed of the delivery truck of the G.O.D.S. parked on Felicity. He escaped with lacerations, severe contusions, stitches in the abdomen, a sprained wrist, a separated shoulder, fractured ribs and a broken heart.

Percy agreed to testify against Evan in the trial that was scheduled a fortnight after Mardi Gras. In exchange for a lighter sentence. What did Percy have to lose? The defense would have a field day with his credibility and stability. Ultimately, the jury wouldn't place much stock in his testimony.

Percy's trial would follow Evan's. Convening the week before Easter. His testimonial gambits and political connections among New Orleans' elected judiciary would spare the handsome young financier a far harsher reality. Of hard time in Angola for attempted rape. Plus counts for assault and battery.

Non compos mentis. Nolo contendre. Nolle prosequi.

Percy's trial would conclude in May with a settlement in the judge's chambers. And the judge would commit Percy to a mental asylum near Alexandria. His sentence would happen to commence on the first day of June: Lavinia's scheduled wedding day. When Percy would begin to try to cope with uncontrollable desires and unbearable losses.

The turnout at Andrew's funeral ten days before Mardi Gras was *nil*.

Nobody attended the open and well-publicized memorial service at St. Louis Cathedral. Except immediate family and close friends. Like Charles and Sibyl Helene plus a few of Lavinia's best girlfriends.

The ritual motions of standing, kneeling and sitting echoed within the cavernous sanctuary of the vast cathedral like old bones in an empty twenty-gallon oil drum. After the warmth of Andrew's golden days had seemed to touch graciously upon so many lives.

"Nobody loved daddy like me, Jack. And he made enemies running his business, as he did. But why didn't anyone turn up at his wake?" she asked, weeping and bitterly disillusioned.

I had no answer. Except to say that, to me, he was truly a great man. And I loved him, too. Like a father. As he gave me more than one chance. At making a life. And at loving his Liv. His only daughter. The second truly divine debutante of Andrew's lifetime.

Without Liv, I would be hopelessly adrift in a grim universe. Without redemption. A life without Liv an unthinkable void. Bereft of real meaning.

Senseless nothingness.

Andrew's funeral turnout was a precursor of broader social sentiment.

In death, Andrew was cast from the august heights of New Orleans legend to an object of abject pity. A fallen archangel. Paradise lost.

Fellow giants in the troubled energy industry knew that his financial demise foreshadowed their own forthcoming, unavoidable plights. Their troubled financial Fates. Their destiny to fall of out favor with fickle Fortune.

Andrew was one of the first corporate chieftains to succumb in the bitter battle of the Great American Oil Bust. But peering down at his visage in the open casket wake at St. Louis Cathedral, it bore an uncanny likeness to their own ruins.

Lately, Charles had begun to drink heavily, again. Imbibing too much, too frequently. Because the great bust of the mid-eighties in the oil and gas business was just beginning to hit his business hard, too.

Crude oil prices toppled from Olympian heights and plummeted to Stygian abysses – to new twenty-year lows about half of recent all-time highs. Charles' clients in the largest industry of New Orleans pulled back on their advertising budgets with a vengeance. Taking his agency slowly down with them.

Aeneas wondered if Charles weren't a borderline alcoholic headed for the depressing, self-destructive life of the lotuseater. From which Lavinia was born to deliver her father and Aeneas. But Charles was alone. An exile.

In his will, read forthwith after his death, Andrew left his entire oil empire to Lavinia. Current financial reports revealed that the debt burden from leverage and the impact of the oil bust were financially catastrophic.

His life's work upon his death amounted to a sum of nearly zero. Except for the value of the studio.

Lavinia had forged her own career. And opportunities prevailed at her option. She was a rising sun to her father's moon waning into total eclipse.

Her photogenic beauty was her chief remaining asset. But after the trauma of the Felicity Street fiasco, she lost interest in the modeling assignment for *Virginia's Fantasies*.

Although she appeared in images shot before the Felicity Street incident, she refused other generous offers of this kind. And the catalogue produced a great financial windfall for the client, heightening demand for her.

Lavinia alienated herself from June Wilhelm, who rather cavalierly branded her as "unreliable." Effectively shutting down Lavinia's New York option. Leaving her, by default or design, only the love of her dear Aeneas as solace.

This Queen of the American Nile reluctantly and broken-heartedly was deposed from Andrew's once vast empire. Like the Queen of Egypt after Actium. And Aeneas was Lavinia's devoted, unvanquished Antony.

Aeneas Studios alone stood as a recession-proof fortress built on solid ground. As long as there was Mardi Gras in New Orleans, he would thrive. Because Aeneas crafted immortality like the artisans of the Underworld.

His work was timeless, indestructible and outfitted its warriors against unspeakable fear of their demise. Arming them with the grace to endure.

Lavinia honored Andrew Jackson Palmer's instruction for cremation.

Deep in mourning and dressed chic in black from the stern of the Riverboat Natchez. She read a passage from *Job 14, 1-2*:

> "Man that is born of woman is of few days, and full of trouble. He cometh forth like a flower, and is cut down: he fleeth also as a shadow, and continueth not."

Then Lavinia scattered her father's ashes. And in their wake she tearfully and tenderly cast adrift a simple bouquet of white daisies. Upon the vast River that he so loved.

> Deep sixed,
> the quintessence
> of dust
> tossed and turned
> in the bed

of that merry widow,
Mrs. Sip,
into the Gulf
where she
surrendered him
to Dixie winds
that transformed
poor Rex
into a
thunderhead.
* * *

THE SHIELD OF AENEAS

*"Most of the scenes on this imaginary shield are incidents from
Italian wars depicted with vivid evocation: the wolf suckling
Romulus and Remus; the rape of the Sabine women; the   punishment of
Mettus Fufetius, dictator of Alba Longa; the Etruscan attack on Rome; the attack
of the Gauls; and scenes in the underworld. In the centre of this shield, in a ring
of silver dolphins feathering with white foam the silver sea and its golden waves,
is depicted Augustus' victory over Antony and Cleopatra at Actium."*
— *David West, Translator* from *The Aeneid, Book VIII*

The Flight of Fantasy

Ill-fated, elfin zephyrs of his divorce from Frances had drifted inoffensively into the distant Gulf. *Enfin*, Aeneas was at liberty to marry   Lavinia.

On the evening of Mardi Gras, they drove West in her Cadillac in a journey to Houston. All of her clothes, including the bridal gown, were ordered from *The Golden Bow Boutique*. But the groom needed new attyre, too. Apt justification to shop at the Galleria for their June wedding.

Thus, they fled the finale of Mardi Gras. Without their beloved Rex. It too saddened them to act as aenesthetized players within the celebrated pageant.

Aeneas could not shake from his consciousness the vision of Charles in the French Quarter on the previous evening. False bearded, drunk from Petite Sirrah and dressed shaggily as Bacchus. Aeneas had seen him veritably hug the lamppost at Toulouse Street. Prior to the parade of the Phunny Phorty Phellows led by Sir Knight of the Tooters down Bourbon Street.

Charles had begun to drink straight Wild Turkey at Napoleon House on the Friday before Mardi Gras. Since then, he spent the last three days inebriated. Refusing offers of assistance from Aeneas. Rambling on about the ruinous state of his business affairs. And attorneys pillaging him with oppressive legal fees. Mourning his messy divorce and lost custody battle with Barb. But, at least, the divorce was final.

Thus, he chose his prolonged state of drunken delusion. A taste of the grape. A kiss of the lotus. Until the passage of Fat Tuesday.

Aeneas had compiled a modest Fortune. In collaboration with the recently deceased Rex. Whose job God wanted. And whose life he took with it. To out-Rex Rex.

Aeneas learned that money did not guarantee happiness. It did complicate one's existence. And the overzealous, single-minded pursuit of financial gain could lead one blindly into a quicksilver quagmire in which to drown. Although money may buy creature comforts, he was more concerned with living a full life than a comfortable one.

Upon his deathbed, he was determined to pass judgment that he had lived to the hilt. Defiant in the dust and blood and bitter bile of defeat. Humble on the sweet angels' wings of victory. And refreshed in spirit by every miracle of mercy from man or deity.

On the Friday before Mardi Gras, Aeneas and Lavinia signed an agreement of sale of their studio to rival venture capitalists of Percy's investment consortium. For a tidy round sum. Thus, Aeneas would cash out his cash cow. And the couple would become self-made millionaires by selling the portrait business that so vexed Aeneas. Enabling him to focus upon the art he loved. With the woman of his dreams.

In Andrew's name, they decided to establish and charitably fund a pension for venerable jazzmen who had given their lives to their music. To keep the wolf from their doors. And a scholarship fund at Tulane for young, gifted, art students who yearned to photograph the singular souls of Bourbon Street. Inspired by that winsome widow, Mrs. Sip.

Aeneas drove through the trash on St. Charles Avenue. Comus, the last parade of Mardi Gras, had left Uptown New Orleans to consume its street revelry. Many masqueraders still straggled to catch the last passing parade. The final vestiges of merrymaking.

He turned onto I-10 West focusing upon the Mississippi River Bridge. Past the pedestal of the vigilant General Robert E. Lee with his eyes ever fixed upon the North. Tiger of the American Tiber. The Confederacy's Antony. Of the Nile of Dixie.

The striking New Orleans skyline. The full moon on this cool, clear, Delta night out-domed the Superdome.

He rubbed the sleep from his eyes. And yawned. A cup of *Café du Monde* chicory coffee recently drunk before their departure to Texas. To keep away the sandman in the night drive ahead.

As he glanced toward the River, he glimpsed the lit spires of St. Louis Cathedral. Amid the shadowy outline of French Quarter rooftops.

He passed a road sign for the turnoff to the exit at Elysian Fields. And he wondered what it meant to be in flight of fantasy.

The bright lights of Canal Street. Where mighty Comus rolled downtown. Among the final cheering throngs. Became distant and dim.

The montage of New Orleans reminded him of his first flirting vistas of the city from the high-rise bridge. When he came to New Orleans from New England as an exile. Much of Big Muddy had passed under the bridge since then. This time the panorama from the freeway was reflected in his rearview mirror.

Amid the swirls and eddies of the past, currents of grief absurdly engulfed him.

Until in his mind the pictures formed again. Flashing quick and easy. As they had a hundred thousand times before. In the viewfinder of his imagination.

Pictures of his epic Dixie printed in brilliant, radiant pixels.

Springtime along the Gulf Coast of Texas. With seas of bluebonnets and Indian paintbrushes growing wild upon brilliant new green pastures. The flowering of the Southwest.

The clean, new, glistening, glass Oz of the Houston skyline.

The pure, sugar, sand beaches and coconut palms of South Padre Island. Where, offshore, pods of dolphins and silver kings flashed, gleaming in the lucid aqua sea.

Aeneas looked at Lavinia who snuggled close to him. On the verge of sleep and weary from her grief and the rigors of their flight from Fat Tuesday.

He knew that he wanted to grow old with her as his partner. He saw the pictures that expectant bridegrooms perceive of their brides.

And the images in the gallery of his mind comforted him.

"Let's get married in Texas," Aeneas said.

"You mean, elope?" she replied.

"Let's just go find a justice of the peace in Houston."

"We could just extend our stay at the Remington. For our honeymoon."

"And then drive to South Padre Island foh a week."

"I would just adore to, sweetheart."

"You're the best there eveh was."

"Did you know what a miracle it is?"

"What?"

"Us."

"It is a wondeh that, of all the people on God's green eth, we should eveh find each otheh."

"So you did know it, too. Tell me when."

"Somehow. While wandering. Along a pixilating street. Way down deep in Dixie. God knows. I sure did, Liv."

"All I ever wanted in this world was you, Jackie Jam."

"I love you, Dreamface. And I *always* will."

When they reached the dark, deathly marshes of the Sabine River and crossed over into Texas, the iron tongue of the big clock on St. Louis Cathedral tolled midnight. And in the Municipal Auditorium, Rex and Comus raised champagne toasts to each other. Without Andrew. Or his only daughter. A sublime ransomed Sabine.

The krewes' vacuous, battle-scarred floats unceremoniously were towed away by tractors. Feckless wrecks of Rex. As street cleaners descended in brigades with brooms effectively to sweep away the vestiges of the day.

Thus, with a toast Mardi Gras clasped its finale. The grandest dream of all. Of Bourbon Street.

"Mahdi Gras is oveh," Aeneas whispered softly to Lavinia.

But silently beside him she slept.

The dream is done. At least, this one is.

Our dreams drive us so. One after another. Jasmine sprung bravely from the fertile soil of our suffering.

And who can live without dreams? Who loves their brief, sweet passage?

Dum vivimus, vivimus.

While
we
live,
let
us
live.
* * *

ABOUT THE AUTHOR

Born in Woburn, Massachusetts, David B. Lentz graduated from Bates College and has written professionally for more than 40 years.

Lentz is a member of the Academy of American Poets, the Poetry Society of America (New York), Connecticut Authors and Publishers Association, Royal Society of Literature (London) and the Center for Fiction (New York).

He has published six literary novels – *For the Beauty of the Earth, AmericA, Inc., Bloomsday, Bourbon Street, The Day Trader* and *The Silver King*.

Lentz has published a pair of stage plays, entitled *AmericA, Inc.,* and *Bloomsday: A Tragicomedy*, as well as three books of poetry, *Sonnets from New England, Sonnets on the Common Man* and *Old Greenwich Odes*.

His collection of literary works is published as *Essential Lentz*.

He has served Bates College as an Alumnus-in-Admissions, Board Member of the New Orleans Ad Club, Philadelphia Mayor's Council for Literacy, Stamford-Greenwich Literacy Volunteers of America, Healing the Children (Board), Midnight Run for New York City Homeless, Hurricane Katrina JazzAid: New Orleans (Founder), Hope + Heroes Children's Cancer Foundation, St. Baldrick's Foundation for Children's Cancer Research and in St. Paul's Chapel as a Volunteer at Ground Zero.

He has lived in Boston's Back Bay, the Garden District of New Orleans, Houston and Philadelphia's Main Line. Currently, he resides with his family in Greenwich, CT.

+ + +

Made in the USA
Las Vegas, NV
26 January 2026